FEAR NO

THE STORY OF TOM CULLEN, AN IRISH REVOLUTIONARY

⁕

Tom Cullen led an extraordinary life, flirting with death and danger at every turn. He was a friend and colleague to some of Ireland's most celebrated personalities and legendary heroes, in particular Michael Collins. His rebellious story captures the imagination. From a lad growing up in rural Ireland at the turn of the twentieth century to freedom fighter, intelligence officer, counter-spy and finally, a major-general in Ireland's new Free State army, Tom Cullen was one of Ireland's most unheralded but truly remarkable revolutionaries of modern time.

Described as handsome, intelligent, athletic, likeable, loyal and powerfully built, he was portrayed by his friends and allies as being as 'brave as a lion.'

Born in Co. Wicklow, he possessed an immense spirit, took great pride in his work and was totally devoted to his comrades-in-arms. This poignant chronicle of Tom Cullen is infused with the story of Ireland and its twentieth-century struggle for freedom and independence from Britain's unwelcomed rule.

Praise for Previous Award-winning Books by Cathal Liam

"In every case, the scenarios created by [Cathal] Liam ring as true as if a cache of long-hidden partisan letters has been unearthed."
–Carole L. Philipps, *The Cincinnati Post*

"One does not have to read too far…to know that [Cathal] Liam understands how to capture an era filled with colorful and tragic men and women."
–Rob Stout, *The Patriot Ledger* (Boston)

"[Cathal Liam] is passionate about his beliefs, but he is gentle in presenting them."
–Frank West, *The Irish American News* (Chicago)

"With is deft prose and his deep knowledge of Ireland–then and now–Cathal Liam has captured the evolving face of 20th-century Irish politics, history and culture…."
–Peter F. Stevens, author of *The Voyage of The Catalpa*

"Unabashed support for the men and women who fought for Irish freedom in the early years of the 20th century is a rarity in these politically correct and revisionist times. Cathal Liam sets himself against the tide…."
–*The Irish Echo* (New York)

"[Cathal] Liam's novel successfully characterizes the motives and mood of the Irish independent movement. Irish nationalists were united in their opposition to the British. Once that enemy was defeated, the victors fell into a tragic dispute over the terms of the treaty…."
–Dr. Timothy J. White, Professor, Xavier University

"Writer Cathal Liam's years of scholarly rambles in Dublin have produced his hero who is at one with the cause of Pearse, Connolly and Collins."
–Kevin Donleavy, author of *Strings of Life: Conversations with Old-Time Musicians*…& The *Irish in Early Virginia 1600-1850*

FEAR NOT THE STORM

Also by Cathal Liam

Consumed In Freedom's Flame:
A Novel of Ireland's Struggle for Freedom 1916-1921

Forever Green: Ireland Now & Again

Blood On The Shamrock:
A Novel of Ireland's Civil War

FEAR NOT THE STORM

THE STORY OF TOM CULLEN, AN IRISH REVOLUTIONARY

CATHAL LIAM

For Bernard – Much thanks + may your 83rd be the best ever. God bless + many happy returns. Cathal Liam

St. Pádraic Press
Cincinnati, Ohio USA

Fear Not The Storm: The Story of Tom Cullen, An Irish Revolutionary depicts the life and times of Tom Cullen from 1890-1926. It's both a true-life novel and a gently-fictionalised biography.

Please note: A mea culpa for any missing síneadh fada notations inadvertently omitted during manuscript preparation. As for typographical errors, the author regrets their appearance despite every effort to achieve perfection.

Set in Adobe Garamond

Printed in the United States of America

Cover and interior design by Mayapriya Long, Bookwrights Design, www.bookwrights.com/gallery

Front and back cover photo: GHQ Commandant-General Tom Cullen, 28 August, 1922, the day of Michael Collins's funeral, with the kind permission of Niall Bergin, Supervisor of Kilmainham Gaol Museum & Archives, Dublin, Ireland

First Edition, January, 2011

10 9 8 7 6 5 4 3 2 1

International Standard Book Number: 978-0970415530

Library of Congress Number: 2010926138

Published by
St. Pádraic Press
P.O. Box 43351
Cincinnati, Ohio 45243-0351

For further inquiries: www.cathalliam.com

For Ronnie & Mary Ann

CONTENTS

A Word To The Reader

Fear Not The Storm has been a labour of love filled with many highs and lows. Often confronted with "Who?" or "Why him?" when mentioning the subject of my latest book, I had my doubts too. But after all was said and done, I know in my heart Tom Cullen was the right choice. I've learned much about Ireland's history, met many wonderful, interesting people and experienced a wealth of adventures never envisioned when I began this project over three years ago.

As you can imagine, my years of studying Ireland's storied past introduced me to many noble people. A short list would include the likes of Patrick Henry Pearse, Michael Collins, Liam Mellowes, Tom Barry, Robert Emmet among others. Unfortunately, the lives of the most prominent are already well documented. No, I was hoping to find someone relatively unknown, a second or third level person, but one who'd made a special contribution worthy of note. Someone who'd stood up for Ireland's dream of freedom and national independence, yet had, to date, escaped the light of public scrutiny or acclaim.

Years ago after much consideration, I chose Seán Moylan, a North Corkman, who played an important role in Ireland's early twentieth-century thrust for independence. Then lo and behold in 2003, the Aubane Historical Society [Millstreet, Co. Cork] published *Seán Moylan: In His Own Words*.

Born in Kilmallock in 1889, Seán was 'out' in '16 and later elected O/C of Cork No. 2 Brigade during the War for Independence. He took the anti-Treaty side, favouring Éamon de Valera's political and military stance during the Irish Civil War. Interested in politics, Seán was elected a Sinn Féin TD for North Cork in 1921. He then joined Fianna Fáil at its inception in 1926. After organising his own business as a building contractor in Co. Cork, Moylan began a second career as a government minister during a twenty-year period from 1937 until his death in 1957. The great Irish artist Seán Keating featured this Cork officer, grouped with some fellow IRA men, as the central figure in his famous painting *Men of the West* which, incidentally, decorated the cover of my book *Blood On The Shamrock*. Clearly, Seán would have been a fascinating subject to explore had it not been for Aubane's pre-emption. [**Author's note**: In 2010, Mercier Press (Co. Cork) published a new biography of Seán's life entitled *Seán Moylan: Rebel Leader* by Aideen Carroll, his granddaughter.]

With disappointment put aside, I began casting about for another subject. Sure I did not have long to wait. Out of the blue Tom Cullen caught my fancy thanks to Tim Pat Coogan. In rereading his book *Michael Collins* [Arrow edition, 1991], the famed historian commented: "One of Collins's worst faults was his habit of baiting people, most notably [Joe] O'Reilly and Tom Cullen." [p. 135]

In the same vein, Tim Pat quoted an observation Ernie O'Malley, a Co. Tipperary IRA leader, made while visiting Dublin during the early stages of the War for Independence. On this surreptitious visit, O'Malley had the opportunity to study Collins's 'management style' and, in specific, to observe his treatment of Tom Cullen.

> Collins seemed to establish his personality quickly in the mind of his visitor; he was hearty, boisterous or quiet by turn; he was uncouth, as judged by my early standards. He had a habit of baiting Tom Cullen, the assistant quartermaster, and a few of the Dublin men. That I hated. I could understand, take or make use of a tell-off, but the prodding got on my nerves. One day I told Collins I could not stand it and I left the room in a rage. He never baited anyone in my presence afterwards. [1]

Another writer, Peter Hart in his largely unflattering 2006 book about Collins entitled *Mick: The Real Michael Collins*, also noted that Tom Cullen was "a much-berated (sic) assistant Quartermaster General." [p. 204]

As noted, Cullen was not Collins's only 'whipping boy.' Joe O'Reilly, another of Michael's devoted friends who acted as his aide-de-camp and loyal messenger, frequently was subjected to the same taunting and tormenting that Cullen faced. Like Tom, Collins and O'Reilly, both Co. Corkmen, had spent seven months in Frongoch Internment Camp in North Wales after the 1916 Easter Uprising. This experience helped copper-fasten their growing friendships. Frank O'Connor, resolute Republican, famed writer and astute Collins biographer, noted that Michael earned his nickname 'the Big Fella' in Frongoch for his often abrasive personality and annoying behaviours. O'Connor goes on to describe the nascent relationship of Collins and O'Reilly, adding credibility to the torment Joe occasionally endured at Collins's hand.

Both men were released from internment at Christmastime, 1916 and immediately returned to Dublin. O'Connor described their reunion.

> He [Collins] arrived back in Dublin on Christmas morning 1916. He and [Gearóid] O'Sullivan burst in the locked door of the room which Joe O'Reilly was sharing with a friend, looking for 'a bit of ear'. 'A bit of ear' was the goal of all Collins' wrestling matches. Having bitten O'Reilly's ears till they bled, pinched and savaged him and emptied part of a bottle of port down his [Michael's] throat, they left him [Joe] to explain to his terrified room-mate (sic) that this was merely Collins' idea of fun. [2]

Needless to say, the idea that Tom Cullen, despite the tormenting, chose to become a close friend and valued colleague of Ireland's most charismatic and dynamic leader endeared him to me. [I have always been one to cheer for the underdog. Sure being Irish gives one lots of practice.]

So the more I studied and probed into the events of Tom's life, the more I admired and respected him. I felt a bond growing between us. Unfortunately, the details of his life were few and far between. Little had been written about him, but I became convinced that was necessary given the tenor of the time, so I pressed on.

Being an undercover operative for Collins, an intelligence officer attached to Dublin's IRA Brigade GHQ staff, Tom's life often hung in the balance during those British, spy-ridden days of Ireland's War for Independence. Sure his welfare depended on *not* having his photograph gracing the front pages of the evening newspapers or *not* having his name on the tip of every tout's, quisling's or policeman's tongue. It was a deadly game of chance and Cullen, to his credit, became a skilled player, mastering its intricacies. One mistake could mean forfeiting his life, but full of idealism and possessing a quick wit, he soldiered on, risking all.

Yes, Cullen, like so many others, unassumingly accepted the charge and played his part, courageously adding his name to the litany of Irish who willingly stood up for the cause of freedom down through the ages. Indeed, many Irishmen and women, filled with an inheritance of inspiring heroes, and cursed by a brave but bloodied past, resolutely marched forward into the 'bhearna baoil' [gap of danger] during the early years of the twentieth century, each determined to affirm their nation's identity.

Heartened by those who'd gone before and testing the metal of those now in its midst, Ireland counted on anonymous individuals, such as Tom Cullen, to help achieve its independence from Great Britain.

Much in keeping with the persona of my imaginary hero Aran Roe O'Neill, whose adventures fill the pages of two earlier historical novels, I sought to bring the true story of Tom Cullen to life. But the more I delved into the project, the more frustrated I became. There were just too many unanswered questions and my hope of writing a factual, comprehensive biography began to fade. Determination, however, overcame doubt.

I sought the counsel of many, including the fine historian Sean O Mahony. With the help of Tim Pat Coogan, I arranged to meet Sean at his home in a southern suburb of Dublin. We talked of Tom Cullen, his possible role in the Easter Uprising, his relationship with Michael Collins and his involvement in the 1924 Irish army mutiny. Though encouraging, Sean could add little to what I'd already discovered.

Expressing frustration over my disappointment, I mentioned I might be forced to fictionalise Tom's life and write another historical novel with Cullen as the main character. Sure, hadn't I successfully employed that medium in the past, and wasn't my readership interested in more of the same? But Sean's reply to this possibility shook me to the core. As I stood up from his kitchen table, preparing to leave, he simply said, "I hope not!"

Crushed and disheartened, I stewed about what to do as I continued my research. Then, as if by some little miracle, my wife brought home a book by Jeannette Walls entitled *Half Broke Horses*. There on the cover was the answer to my quandary. Walls called her book about her grandmother a true-life novel. Sure hadn't she faced a similar problem, much like the dilemma confounding me?

In her author's note Walls explained:

> My grandmother was – and I say this with all due respect – quite a character. However, at first I resisted writing about her. While I had been close to her as a child, she died when I was eight, and most of what I knew about her came secondhand. [3]

Later, she added:

> At the time I didn't think of the book as fiction. Lily Casey Smith was a very real woman, and to say that I created her or the events of her life is giving me more credit than I'm due. However, since I don't have the words from Lily herself, and since I have also drawn on my imagination to fill in details that are hazy or missing…the only honest thing to do is call the book a novel. [4]

Another breakthrough came in the autumn of 2009. Of all the bothersome voids in Tom's life for which I could find no answer, the central one concerned his participation, or lack of it, in the 1916 Easter Uprising. Was he 'out' in '16 or not?

I found it hard to believe that such an Irish revolutionary, who'd won the admiration and friendship of so many and who later often risked his life for Ireland's independence, would have missed the chance to strike a blow for the Holy Ground. Surely, he must have turned out with his fellow Volunteers during Easter Week, 1916, but try as I might, I could uncover no credible evidence to support this assumption.

Had Eoin MacNeill's [titular head of the Irish Volunteers] last-minute countermanding of orders for the planned Easter-Sunday manoeuvres, marking the IRB's initiation of its carefully planned yet surreptitious revolt, caused Tom to stay home? But where was he? At his family's home in Blessington? In Wicklow Town with his brother, Andy? Somewhere in Dublin? Or was he ill and unable to march? Surely, if he was able, this West Wicklow man was just the one for seizing the moment and turning out to fight the Sassenach...the greatest premeditated national Anglo-Irish confrontation since the spring of 1798.

Thanks, however, to the Sunday, 2 April 1911 census, the date of the most recently published [2010] national survey, I knew Tom was living in Dublin, at #58 [South] Circular Road, not far from Portobello Barracks. [Portobello British Barracks, 1815-1922, was renamed Cathal Brugha Barracks, 9 May 1952.] Furthermore, five years on, the *1916 Easter Rebellion Handbook* lists *a* Thomas Cullen residing at #26 Landerdale Terrace, New Row South, Dublin. Was this Tom's new Dublin address or simply a convenient postal drop? [5]

This 1916 address only created more uncertainty until, happily, I finally confirmed Tom's Easter Week participation. Documented evidence revealed that four Thomas Cullens were involved in the fighting during that historic confrontation. [Unfortunately for my research, Cullen, an Irish name of likely Gaelic or Norman origins, is a common one in Ireland.]

There was a Thomas Cullen from Duncormick, Co. Wexford; [6] a Captain Tom Cullen, later a noted architect, international rugby player and O/C of Dublin's K Coy, 3rd Battalion IRA; [7] a Thomas Cullen, 1st Battalion IRA, who saw action in the Four Courts area during the revolt; [8] and finally *my* Thomas J. Cullen, Irish Volunteer, assigned to the 4th Battalion, B Coy, stationed at South Dublin Union under the leadership of Commandant Éamonn Ceannt. [9]

[**Author's note**: Sadly, I've never been able to decipher the 'J' in Tom's name. Was it simply Thomas J. Cullen or did the 'J' stand for James, Joseph or maybe John? I just don't know.]

Much of the credit for uncovering Tom's Easter Week involvement with the 4th Battalion belongs to James Langton and Ronnie Daly. James, whose family is from Inchicore, Kilmainham, had several relatives who also fought with Ceannt. In combing through records he discovered Tom's name and signature on several documents.

Today, though, despite more than three years of researching, interviewing and reading, much of Tom Cullen's life still remains a mystery. The fact that he and his wife Delia 'apparently' had no children, and that I was unable to locate anyone who knew Tom personally were major disappointments. That aside, the events of his life which I did uncover paint a picture of a man who daringly fought for his country and valiantly supported its quest for achieving the freedom and independence it had sought for so long. It was individuals like Tom Cullen to whom Ireland today owes a great vote of thanks. For without his gift of loyal dedication and resolute bravery, Ireland's dream of a united, thirty-two county nation might never be obtained.

Finally, I would hope, after reading Tom's story, you may come to realise you have some details of Tom's life that are missing from the story I've portrayed. If so, please contact me. It's my hope a future edition will contain updated particulars thanks to my readership.

Now, as a personal aside, I'd like to share a fond memory. Early one Sunday morning last November, as Ronnie Daly drove me to the airport for a flight back to the States, he turned, looked over at me and said, – Cathal, yesterday when James, you and I were walking around the grounds of the Union, we stopped for a long moment just there in front of the Nurses' Home...remember?

A sudden chill ran down my spine. A lump rose in my throat for I knew exactly what Ronnie was going to say.

– Staring at the windows of that building in the gathering twilight, Cathal, I thought I saw Tom looking down at us.

– Yes, I said slowly, – I believe I saw him in the window too.

Cathal Liam
Cincinnati, Ohio
Summer, 2010

ACKNOWLEDGMENTS

I gratefully accepted and now wish to acknowledge the generous kindness of many individuals whose help made this book possible. Sure some say writing is a lonely pursuit and in a sense, it's true, but looking back on all that has gone into the telling of Tom Cullen's story, it was far from an isolated activity. Many eagerly stepped forward, offering their wholehearted assistance. Others, uncertain of who I was or what I was about, guardedly volunteered bits and pieces of information or simply declined. This cautiousness always left me wondering, what if….

My heartfelt thanks to…

…Rosie & Tommy Allen, whose Wicklow B&B hospitality sustained me for a month in 2007;

…Niall Bergin, Supervisor, Kilmainham Gaol Museum, Dublin, who gave so generously of his time & resources;

…Robert Butler, Librarian, Bray [Co. Wicklow] library, who unselfishly helped me access old Wicklow newspapers;

…Orla Coleman, née Fallon, who kindly shared her Cullen-Considine family history with me;

…Tim Pat Coogan, Irish historian & author, for his time, reflections, encouragement & wealth of writings;

…Shay Courtney, for his insightful introduction to 1916 Dublin, his astute e-mails & his urging to include 'lots of photographs';

…Brian Cunningham, for his kindness, generosity and willingness to tell me the story of his father Eamonn Cunningham;

…Noeleen Daly, for her interest, amity & her fabulous Dublin coddle and Irish stew;

…Ron 'Ronnie' Daly, for his tireless, unwavering help, his friendship & for his constant support to see this project through even when I felt frustrated & discouraged…this book could not have been written without him;

...Chris Duffy, who shared information about his great-great-grandfather Irish Volunteer Thomas Cullen [no relation to Thomas J. Cullen];

...T. Ryle Dwyer, historian & author, for his tireless research & abundant writings;

...Pat Fallon, Irishman, entrepreneur & a kind, generous friend;

...John Finley, Wicklow historian, for his wonderful walking tour of Wicklow Town plus his thoughtful assistance & generous sharing of information;

...John Fitzgerald, friend, Irish entrepreneur & long-time supporter of my writing;

...Maeve Flannery, Wicklow Town historian, whose willing recollections were only a telephone call away;

...Joe Kavanagh, writer, musician & Wicklow acquaintance, who opened important doors;

...James Langton, for his friendship, interest, encouragement, helpfulness & photographic expertise;

...The staff of the National Archives Reading Room, Bishop Street, Dublin, especially John Delaney, David O'Neill & Mary Carney for their tireless help with finding & copying materials;

...Sean O Mahony, historian & author, for his sharing of materials, personal insights & a lovely cup of tea;

...John O'Brien, Jr., friend, writer, Irish festival director & co-publisher/editor of the *Irish American News Ohio*;

...Paul O'Brien, historian & author, for his astute writings, detailed knowledge of Easter Week & his determination to keep the spirit of 1916 alive in the hearts and minds of so many;

...Bonnie Jean O'Grady, for her family information regarding William O'Grady;

...Chrissy Osborne, for her kind assistance in obtaining an important photograph of Tom Cullen, Michael Collins & Liam Tobin;

...Anne-Marie Ryan, Kilmainham Gaol Museum, for her thoughtful research assistance;

...Ronan O'Sullivan, for his brilliant photography & his resolute commitment to come to my assistance;

...John O'Toole, who shared information about his relative Liam Tobin & his interest in this project;

...Irene Parsons, who sent photographs & personal remembrances of Tom & Delia Cullen;

...Major-General (Ret.) John Vize, for reminiscences about his father, Major-General Joe Vize (1882-1959) & John's forty-year career in the Irish Defence Forces including his tour as O/C of UN forces on the Kuwait/Iraq border during the 1ˢᵗ Gulf War;

...Tommy Webster, a Roundwood, Co. Wicklow farmer, who kindly took me on a wonderful tour of Lough Dan;

...Monica White, St. James Parish secretary, Dublin, who helped uncover important information about Father Eugene McCarthy's role as parish priest for Kilmainham Gaol during spring, 1916.

Also special acknowledgement and my debt of thanks to...

...Marcia Fairbanks, for her willingness to come out of 'retirement' and read the manuscript, for her insightful comments and attention to detail, for giving me hope & for helping make this book a better one;

...Mayapriya Long, Bookwrights Design owner & master artist, for her patience & expertise in designing the cover & organising the manuscript as well as for her long-time friendship & unflagging wisdom which continually sustains me;

...Mary Ann, my wife, who lovingly supports all my writing 'hobbies' & offers invaluable insights into my written words while lovingly standing by my side through the good times and bad;

...and always lurking there in the recesses of my mind, almost as if they were standing over my shoulder as I type away, are my dearly departed parents, my Rathfarnham & Pearsian friend Turlough Breathnach and my friend & devoted man of God Fr. Francis Miller...and to Gay Cooley, Jim Cooney, Niamh O'Sullivan, May & Tom Richardson & Jim 'Lamar' Wendell... God bless and keep them all.

Finally, I would like to thank the many others who helped provide research materials, who answered my endless stream of queries & who offered their encouragement.

LIST OF PHOTOGRAPHS

Front Cover: GHQ Commandant-General Thomas J. Cullen, Dublin, 28 August 1922, the day of Michael Collins's funeral (Courtesy of Niall Bergin, Kilmainham Gaol Museum & Archives, Dublin)

Pg 61: Back of Dublin Castle, as seen in c. 1994 (Author's collection)

Pg 61: #58 South Circular Road, Dublin; residence of Patrick Dowling & home of Tom Cullen in 1911 as seen in June, 2010 (Photograph courtesy of James Langton)

Pg 62: East Pier, Howth, Dublin; the site of the *Asgard* landing & the unloading of German rifles by Irish Volunteers on 26 July 1914 as seen in September, 2010 (Author's collection)

Pg 62: #26 Landerdale Terrace, New Row South, Dublin; possible 1916 residence of Tom Cullen as seen in May, 2009 (Photograph courtesy of James Langton)

Pg 63: Emerald Square, the site where Tom Cullen & others of B Coy, 4th Battalion, mobilised on Easter Monday, 24 April 1916 as seen in November, 2009 (Author's collection)

Pg 63: Lt. William T. Cosgrave, B Coy, 4th Bn, Irish Volunteers, c. 1916 (Courtesy of Kilmainham Gaol Museum Archives)

Pg 64: The Nurses' Home, SDU, 4th Bn HQ during Easter Week, 1916 as seen in February, 2010 (Photograph by Ronan O'Sullivan)

Pg 64: Mount Brown & north wall of South Dublin Union [facing east] as seen in November, 2009 (Author's collection)

Pg 65: Back of St. Patrick's Park along Bride Street where members of the 2nd & 4th Battalions surrendered to the British on 30 April 1916 as seen in November, 2009 (Author's collection)

Pg 148: Wicklow Town courtroom where Tom Cullen was tried, convicted & sentenced to six-months imprisonment, 8 April 1918, as seen in May, 2007 (Author's collection)

Pg 148: RIC barracks, Wicklow Town; the building where Tom Cullen was held after his trial & site of town 'riot' over his pending removal to Dublin, 8 April 1918, as seen in May, 2007 (Author's collection)

Pg 149: Church Hill, site of Wicklow Town 'riot' over Tom Cullen's pending removal to Dublin, 8 April 1918, as seen in May, 2007 (Author's collection)

Pg 149: Brickfield Lane, site of Wicklow Town 'riot' over Tom Cullen's pending removal to Dublin, 8 April 1918, as seen in May, 2007 (Author's collection)

Pg 150: Wicklow Town rail station; site of town 'riot' over Tom Cullen's pending removal to Dublin, 8 April 1918, as seen in May, 2007 (Author's collection)

Pg 150: The Wooden Bridge [1860-1946] over the River Vartry, Wicklow Town; the bridge over which Tom Cullen was escorted by British soldiers from the RIC barracks to the Goods Yard beside The Murrough, 8 April 1918, as seen in May, 2007 [Today's concrete bridge, renamed the Parnell Bridge in 1946, is a replica of its wooden predecessor.] (Author's collection)

Pg 210: #12 Main Street, Wicklow Town, residence of William O'Grady and family in 1918 & beyond as seen in May, 2007 (Author's collection)

Pg 211: William O'Grady on his Douglas motorcycle c. 1920; man with hat in doorway is a friend, Ned Kennedy (Photograph courtesy of Bonnie Jean O'Grady)

Pg 211: Wicklow Town Gaol [c. 1705-1924] in which William O'Grady was imprisoned several times during Ireland's War for Independence, as seen in September, 2010 (Author's collection)

Pg 316: Tom Cullen, Michael Collins & Liam Tobin, Grisham Hotel, Dublin, January, 1922 (Photograph courtesy of Chrissy Osborne)

Pg 317: Front door, 15 Cadogan Gardens, London; rented lodging for Michael Collins & associates, including Tom Cullen, during the Treaty Talks, autumn, 1921 as seen in c.1996 (Author's collection)

Pg 317: Company Quartermaster Sergeant Eamonn 'Ned' Cunningham, likely photographed at Wellington Barracks, Dublin, spring, 1922 (Photograph courtesy of Brian Cunningham)

Pg 318: Officer's sword with inscription on the blade: 'General Michael Collins' & 'Presented by Major General Cullen,' c. July, 1922 as seen in December, 2009 (Photograph courtesy of Ronnie Daly)

Pg 318: Comdt.-Gen. Tom Cullen marching directly behind Commander-in-Chief Michael Collins at Arthur Griffith's funeral procession, 16 August 1922; Gen. Richard Mulcahy is beside MC; 2nd row from left: Maj.-Gen. Gearóid O'Sullivan & Maj.-Gen. Emmet Dalton; Minister Kevin O'Higgins is seen over Tom Cullen's left shoulder; Maj.-Gen. John Prout [with moustache] is at back on right (Unknown)

Pg 319: Site of Michael Collins & party's ambush, Béalnabláth, West Cork as seen in c. 1997 (Author's collection)

Pg 319: Ratra House or the 'Little Lodge,' Phoenix Park, Dublin as seen in June, 2008; the home to a young Winston Churchill c. 1876-1881; the home of Tom & Delia Cullen, 1922-1924 while he served as ADC to Timothy Michael Healy, 1st Governor General of Soarstát na hÉireann (Author's collection)

Pg 320: Michael Collins's remains being carried down the steps of St. Vincent's Hospital, St. Stephen's Green, Dublin. c. 25 August 1922; Tom Cullen, in uniform [with troubled, tearful face] is second man on left carrying coffin; Kevin

O'Higgins, in uniform [with a high dome] is directly behind Tom; Joe O'Reilly, in uniform is directly in front of Tom; Liam Tobin, in uniform [facing coffin] is first man on right supporting the coffin with side view of his face; on Tobin's right is Tom Ennis & to his right is Diarmuid O'Hegarty, both in uniform; nurses form a guard of honour as Collins's coffin is removed to Dublin City Hall for three days of public viewing [**Author's note**: In the doorway at the very back, barely in camera view, are the heads of Joe Leonard & behind him W. T. 'Willie' Cosgrave] (Photograph courtesy of Glenn Dunne & the National Library of Ireland Collection, Dublin)

ABBREVIATIONS

The following abbreviations are used throughout *Fear Not The Storm*.

ADC: Aide-de-Camp

ASU: Active Service Unit (IRA)

BA: British Army

Bn: Battalion

Br.: Brother

c.: circa (about)

C-in-C: Commander-in-Chief

CID: Criminal Investigation Department

C/S: Chief of Staff

CnmB: Cumann na mBan

Co.: County (Ireland)

Coy: Company (a military unit)

D/I: Director of Intelligence

DMP: Dublin Metropolitan Police

FÉ: Na Fianna Éireann

FS: Irish Free State

Fr.: Father (priest)

GAA: Gaelic Athletic Association

GHQ: General Headquarters, Dublin

GPO: General Post Office, Dublin

HQ: Headquarters

ICA: Irish Citizen Army, Dublin

I/O: Intelligence Officer

IPP: Irish Parliamentary Party

IRA: Irish Republican Army

IRB: Irish Republican Brotherhood

ITGWU: Irish Transport & General Workers' Union

IV: Irish Volunteer

Lt.: Lieutenant

O/C: Officer Commanding

PG: Provisional Government

PM: Prime Minister

MC: Michael Collins

M/D: Minister for Defence

MP: Member of British Parliament

NCO: Non-commissioned Officer

NI: Northern Ireland

PM: Prime Minister

Ret.: Retired (military)

RIC: Royal Irish Constabulary, 1867-1922

RUC: Royal Ulster Constabulary, 1922-2001

s: Shilling (a monetary unit)

SDU: South Dublin Union

SF: Sinn Féin, an Irish political party

TC: Tom Cullen

TD: Teachta Dála (member of Irish Dáil)

UCD: University College Dublin

UVF: Ulster Volunteer Force

WS: Witness Statement, Bureau of Military History, 1913-1921; collected 1947-1957

IMMEDIATE FAMILIES

MARY BEDILIA [Brigid] 'DELIA' CONSIDINE

MOTHER	FATHER
Maria Anna 'Marianne' Bergin	Jacobus Considine
(born c. 1861)	(born c. 1864)

CHILDREN
Mary Bedilia 'Delia,' born 3 April 1890
Donald Jacobus, 8 January 1892
Cecilia Maria, 26 February 1894
Maria, 24 April 1897

From a previous marriage to Joseph Fallon

Edith M. Fallon, born c. 1880
James Joseph 'J. J.' Fallon, c. 1885

THOMAS J. CULLEN

MOTHER	FATHER
Anne McGrath	Andrew Cullen
(born c. 1858)	(born c. April 1860)

CHILDREN
Maria Anna, born 13 November 1880
Patritius (Patrick), 18 December 1882
Margaret, 30 April 1884
Andrew, 1 April 1887
Thomas J. (Tom), 20 December 1890
James, August c. 1891
James, c. 1898-1899
Annie, c. 1902

CHILDREN OF TOM & DELIA CULLEN
No issue

A Chronology:
Thomas J. Cullen

1890

20 December: Tom Cullen [TC] born, Blessington, Co. Wicklow

21 December: TC baptised, Blessington

C.1895

TC attends St. Mary's Catholic National School, Blessington

C.1898

TC & family move to Grantstown, Queen's County [Co. Laois]

1905

5 May: Arthur Griffith launches Sinn Féin political party, Dublin

1909

16 August: Irish nationalists establish Na Fianna Éireann, a youth organisation intended to inspire nationalists' ideals & Irish independence, Dublin

1911

2 April: TC resides & is employed as a grocer's assistant, #58 & #59 South Circular Road, Dublin

11 April: 3rd Irish Home Rule Bill introduced in the House of Commons, London

1913

13 January: Ulster Volunteer Force established by Ulster Unionist Council, Belfast

26 August: Dublin's five-month 'Lock-Out' begins as c. 20,000 workers strike for labour reform & the right to unionise against c. 300 employers who, in turn, lock-out their employees

11 November: Irish Volunteer initial planning meeting, Wynn's Hotel, Dublin

19 November: The Irish Citizen Army founded by labour leaders James Larkin & James Connolly

25 November: TC joins the Irish Volunteers at initial membership meeting, Rotunda Rink, Dublin

1914

20 March: 'The Curragh Incident' occurs as British army officers choose to resign their commissions rather than enforce any pending Home Rule Bill legislation in Ulster, The Curragh, Co. Kildare

5 April: Cumann na mBan formed as part of the Irish Volunteer movement, Dublin

24 April: Loyalists in NI, opposed to Irish Home Rule, land a large cache of German rifles & ammunition at Larne, Co. Antrim and at Bangor & Donaghadee, Co. Down

28 June: Archduke Franz Ferdinand of Austria & his wife Sophie, Duchess of Hohenberg assassinated by Yugoslav nationalist Gavrilo Princip, Sarajevo, Yugoslavia

21-24 July: Buckingham Palace Conference; King George V calls representatives of Irish nationalists' & unionists' factions together to discuss pending Home Rule legislation in the hopes of avoiding a possible Irish Civil War

26 July: TC on hand as Asgard lands & supplies Irish nationalists with a cache of German rifles & ammunition, East Pier, Howth, Dublin

28 July: World War I begins as Austria-Hungary declares war on Serbia, Sarajevo, Yugoslavia

1 August: Kelpie lands & supplies Irish nationalists with a small cache of German rifles & ammunition, Kilcoole, Co. Wicklow

4 August: Great Britain declares war on the German Empire in response to Germany's invasion of Belgium

5 or 9 September: Supreme Council of the IRB meets to plan an 'Irish revolt,' Gaelic League Office, #25 Rutland Square, Dublin

18 September: 3rd Irish Home Rule Bill placed on Statute Book but suspended until WWI ends, London

20 September: Irish Volunteer movement splits: c. 180,000 men, supporters of John Redmond & his IPP, are renamed National Volunteers; c. 12,000 men retain title of Irish Volunteers under the titular leadership of Eoin MacNeill

1915

7 May: RMS Lusitania is torpedoed by German submarine eight miles off Kinsale, Co. Cork; it sinks in eighteen minutes with 1,198 lives lost

29 July: Irish nationalists/republicans, led by Patrick Henry Pearse, assume control of the Gaelic League; this precipitated its co-founder & President Douglas Hyde's resignation as he felt Irish culture/language should trump Irish politics

1 August: Jeremiah O'Donovan Rossa's funeral, Glasnevin Cemetery, Dublin; Patrick Henry Pearse delivers his famous "The Fools..." oration over Rossa's grave

1916

c. January-February: TC first meets Michael Collins, Larkfield estate, Kimmage, Dublin

24-30 April: TC takes part in 1916 Easter Uprising as member of B Coy, 4th Bn, Dublin Brigade, positioned at South Dublin Union

25 April: Martial Law proclaimed throughout Dublin Town & Co. Dublin by British authorities

28 April: General Sir John Grenfell Maxwell arrives in Dublin; appointed by British PM Herbert Asquith as military governor, he has plenary authority under martial law; he also holds the title of Commander-in-Chief of all British forces in Ireland

29 April (noon): Patrick Henry Pearse, Commandant-General, Commander-in-Chief of the Army of the Irish Republic & President-elect of the Irish Provisional Government contacts Brigadier-General William Lowe, OC of all British forces in Dublin, to discuss surrender terms, Great Britain Street, Dublin

29 April (afternoon): Patrick Henry Pearse unconditionally surrenders his command to Brigadier-General Lowe, Great Britain Street, Dublin

29 April (4.00 pm): Official announcement of a 'cease fire' given to British troops in Dublin Town centre

29 April (evening): James Connolly, Commandant-General of Dublin's military forces including the Irish Citizen Army, adds his coda to Pearse's unconditional surrender order, Dublin Castle

30 April (afternoon): Thomas MacDonagh, Commandant, 2nd Battalion, & Éamonn Ceannt, Commandant, 4th Battalion, agree to honour the terms of Pearse & Connolly's unconditional surrender orders

30 April (afternoon): TC & all 2nd & 4th Battalion Volunteers of the Dublin Brigade surrender to the British, St. Patrick's Park, Dublin

30 April (evening): TC & all 2nd & 4th Battalion Volunteers of the Dublin Brigade interned by British authorities, Richmond Barracks, Inchicore, Dublin

3 May: Thomas Clarke, Thomas MacDonagh & Patrick Henry Pearse, executed, Kilmainham Gaol, Dublin

3 May: Commandant Éamonn Ceannt tried by field general court-martial, Richmond Barracks

4 May: Joseph Mary Plunkett, Edward Daly, Michael O'Hanrahan & William Pearse executed, Kilmainham Gaol

c. 4 May: TC transferred from Richmond Barracks to Kilmainham Gaol, Dublin

5 May: John MacBride executed, Kilmainham Gaol

5 May: Éamonn Ceannt's military court-martial concludes, Richmond Barracks

6 May: TC removed from Kilmainham Gaol & deported to Wakefield Detention Barracks, West Yorkshire, England

7 May: Éamonn Ceannt found guilty of taking part in an armed rebellion & waging war against His Majesty the King & sentenced to death, Richmond Barracks

8 May: Éamonn Ceannt, Michael Mallin, Seán Heuston & Cornelius Colbert executed, Kilmainham Gaol

9 May: Thomas Kent executed, Cork British Detention Barracks, Cork City, Co. Cork

12 May: Seán MacDiarmada & James Connolly executed, Kilmainham Gaol

c. 9 June: TC transferred from Wakefield to Frongoch Internment Camp, Bala, North Wales

3 August: Sir Roger Casement executed, Pentonville Prison, London, England

23 December: TC released from internment & returns to Ireland [This is the first significant 'mass' release of 1916 Irish Volunteers from internment.]

1917

Early 1917: TC appointed captain & commandant, East Wicklow Irish Volunteers, Wicklow Town

5 February: Count Plunkett elected SF MP for North Roscommon

6 April: United States enters WWI on the side of the Allied Powers

[Great Britain, France & Russia] by declaring war against the Central Powers [Germany & Austria-Hungary]

9 May: Joe McGuinness elected SF MP for South Longford

15 June: The British government announces that all remaining Easter, 1916 prisoners [c. 122] are to receive their immediate & unconditional release

18 June: Easter, 1916 prisoners return to Dublin before huge crowds of cheering onlookers

11 July: Éamon de Valera elected SF MP for East Clare

11 August: William T. Cosgrave elected SF MP for Kilkenny

18 August: Thomas Ashe arrested at Nelson Pillar, Sackville Street, Dublin & charged with "causing disaffection among the civilian population" for a seditious speech given days earlier in Ballinalee, Co. Longford; he was eventually imprisoned in Mountjoy Jail, Dublin

25 September: Thomas Ashe dies on hunger strike after 'forced feeding' in the Mater Hospital, Dublin

30 September: Thomas Ashe's funeral & burial in Republican Plot, Glasnevin Cemetery, Dublin

25-26 October: Sinn Féin Ard Fheis, Dublin; Éamon de Valera elected president of Dáil Éireann: Michael Collins elected to SF Executive Council

27 October: Irish Volunteer Convention, Dublin; Éamon de Valera elected president; Michael Collins chosen Director of Organisation, IV

1918

April: Michael Collins assumes the 'unofficial' duties of Adjutant-General of the Irish Volunteers [IRA]

8 April: TC arrested & charged by British authorities for the illegal drilling of Irish Volunteers, Wicklow Town; TC refuses to post bail; sentenced to six months imprisonment & transported to

Dublin by train after day-long 'rioting' in Wicklow; imprisoned, Mountjoy Jail, Dublin

c. 9 April: TC transferred from Mountjoy Jail, to Belfast Jail, Co. Antrim

c. 10 April: TC receives written order from Michael Collins to post bail

c. 12 April: TC returns [briefly?] to Wicklow Town after Larry Byrne posts his bail

18 April: British Military Service Bill becomes law, London; it authorises imposition of conscription in Ireland; Irish Anti-Conscription Committee meets, Dublin

21 April: Anti-conscription pledge signed throughout Ireland

c. late-April: TC reports to Dublin & begins working for Michael Collins as an Honourable Secretary to the National Aid Association, #10 Exchequer Street & #32 Bachelor's Walk

10 May: William O'Grady arrested, tried, convicted [Wicklow Town] & imprisoned [Mountjoy Jail, Dublin] for his part in the 8 April 'riot' surrounding TC's arrest & trial

17 May: "German Plot" mass arrest of Irish nationalists throughout Dublin & their internment in English prisons by British authorities

24 May: Henrietta O'Grady arrested, tried & found guilty of 'spitting' on members of the RIC, Wicklow Town

Summer: Michael Collins resigns as secretary to the National Aid Association, Dublin

Summer: TC appointed Acting Quartermaster General with offices at #32 Bachelor's Walk, Dublin

Summer: TC initiated into the ranks of the Irish Republican Brotherhood, a secret oath-bound society at #46 Rutland Square [HQ of the Keating Branch of the Gaelic League], Dublin

3 June: Dublin Castle issues an 'Enlistment Proclamation' seeking 50,000 Irish recruits for the British army

21 June: Arthur Griffith elected SF MP for East Cavan

3 July: British government suppresses SF, IV, CnmB & Gaelic League

15 August: TC assumes responsibility for the distribution of *An Óglách* [*The Volunteer*], a bi-monthly, Irish republican [IRA] journal edited by Piaras Béaslaí at Michael Collins's behest, Dublin

11 November: Armistice declared; World War I ends

December: Michael Collins sets up an office in the basement of Cullenswood House, #21 Oakley Road, Ranelagh, Dublin; it's nicknamed the 'Republican Hut'

14 December: General election in Britain & Ireland

30 December: General election results announced; Sinn Féin candidates score a resounding victory over IPP candidates, but refuse to take their seats in London's House of Commons

1919

January: MC appoints Liam Tobin, Tom Cullen & Frank Thornton as his three key intelligence operatives with offices at #3 Crow Street, Dublin; TC becomes Assistant Director of Intelligence

7 January: Twenty-four recently elected Sinn Féin MPs take an oath in support of establishing an independent Irish Republic, Dublin

21 January: Soloheadbeg ambush, Co. Tipperary; two RIC policemen are killed; Ireland's War for Independence 'unofficially' begins

21 January: 1st Dáil Éireann convened, Mansion House, Dublin; Michael Collins appointed Minister for Home Affairs

3 February: MC & Harry Boland free Éamon de Valera, Seán Milroy & Seán McGarry from Lincoln Jail, Lincoln, England

April: Éamon de Valera elected President of Dáil Éireann or Príomh Aire [First Minister]; Michael Collins appointed Minister for

Finance & surrenders Home Affairs portfolio to Arthur Griffith

10 April: Éamon de Valera declares public campaign of passive resistance against the RIC rather than engaging in armed confrontation

1 June: Éamon de Valera leaves Ireland for America; he spends the next eighteen months lobbying for official recognition & public support for the newly declared Irish Republic; he begins raising funds, through the sale of bonds, to help finance Dáil Éireann

28 June: Treaty of Versailles signed [Paris], officially ending World War I; Ireland's petition for recognition is ignored

Early-July: Joe Dolan, Frank Saurin, Joe Guilfoyle, Charlie Dalton & Paddy Caldwell added to Michael Collins's Crow Street intelligence staff, Dublin

Mid-July: TC continues intelligence work while carrying on duties as Assistant Quartermaster, #32 Bachelor's Walk, Dublin

Mid-July: Michael Collins uses multiple offices for conducting intelligence, finance & military duties in order to avoid arrest: Cullenswood House, #21 Oakland Road; #32 Bachelor's Walk; #6 & #76 Harcourt Street; #22 Henry Street; #29 Mary Street; #5 Mespil Road, Dublin

Mid-July: Michael Collins's 'Squad' first formed with Mick McDonnell as the ASU's O/C, Dublin

30 July: Police Detective Captain Patrick Smyth, aka 'Dog Smyth,' shot by the Squad, Drumcondra, Dublin [Smyth was first 'G-man' to be killed in the Irish War for Independence]

20 August: The Irish Volunteers officially swear allegiance to Dáil Éireann

Autumn: TC meets Lily Mernin, shorthand-typist, Dublin Castle

7 September: British soldier killed by a unit of Irish Volunteers [IRA], Fermoy, Co. Cork; [This is the first British military combatant's death in Ireland since Easter Week, 1916.]

12 September: British government suppresses Dáil Éireann, Sinn

Féin, the Gaelic League & Cumann na mBan; Ireland's leaders view this action as tantamount to a declaration of war

12 September: DMP raids Sinn Féin HQ, #6 Harcourt Street, Dublin; MC narrowly escapes arrest

12 September: Detective Constable Daniel Hoey shot by the Squad, Brunswick Street, Dublin

19 September: 'Official' founding of the Squad, #46 Rutland Square, Dublin

8 November: DMP raid a second Sinn Féin office, #46 Harcourt Street, Dublin; MC successfully escapes over building rooftops

10 November: Detective Officer Thomas Wharton shot & wounded by the Squad; Cuffe Street, Dublin

30 November: Detective Sergeant Johnny Barton shot by the Squad, College Street, Dublin

19 December: Field Marshall John Denton Pinkstone French, British Viceroy & Lord Lieutenant of Ireland narrowly escapes ambush, Ashtown, Dublin

1920

c. 15 January: TC begins shadowing Forbes Redmond, Standard Hotel, #74 Harcourt Street, Dublin

20 January: TC successfully warns MC & Richard Mulcahy of DMP raid, Cullenswood House, #21 Oakley Road, Dublin

21 January: Forbes Redmond, head of G Division, DMP, shot by the Squad, Harcourt Street, Dublin

24 January: TC likely involved as Constable James Malynn is shot & badly wounded in RIC barracks attack, Baltinglass, Co. Wicklow

18 February: Henry Timothy Quinlisk, a former Irish corporal, Royal Irish Regiment, shot by Cork #1 Brigade in outskirts of Cork City

25 February: Government of Ireland Bill (the 4th Irish Home Rule Bill) introduced in the House of Commons, London

Spring: TC, Liam Tobin & Frank Thornton share a bachelor flat in Grosvenor Road, Rathmines, Dublin

Spring: Igoe Gang, aka 'The Murder Gang,' surfaces in Dublin led by former Co. Galway Head Constable Eugene Igoe [The Igoe Gang was composed of RIC plain-clothes men from various counties; they patrolled Dublin streets seeking to identify & arrest IRA men from Dublin & down the country.]

Early March: General Sir Nevil Macready appointed new British Commander-in-Chief in Ireland & General Henry Hugh Tudor appointed new Chief of Police, Dublin

Early March: MC establishes the Squad as a paid, full-time ASU, Dublin; now composed of twelve [Squad] members, they are nicknamed 'the Twelve Apostles'

2 March: John Charles Byrnes, aka 'Jameson,' shot by the Squad, Phibsborough, Dublin

20 March: Tomás MacCurtain, the Lord Mayor of Cork City, is shot to death in his home by some newly arrived Black & Tans, likely the Tans' first act of spiteful violence

25 March: Sergeant Fergus Brian Mulloy, BA, shot by the Squad at the corner of William Street South & Wicklow Street, Dublin

c. 25 March: Under General Hugh Tudor's command, RIC Black & Tan reinforcements begin arriving into Ireland

26 March: TC, Liam Tobin & members of the Squad team up to shoot Resident Magistrate Alan Bell, Blackrock, Dublin

3-4 April: The 'Night of the Burnings'; IRA Volunteers throughout Ireland attack Income Tax Offices & homes of tax officials, burning important records; 315 evacuated RIC barracks also are torched

5 April: TC & Piaras Béaslaí, among others, flee Vaughan's Hotel to avoid arrest as British military occupy Rutland Square, Dublin

c. 12 April: IRA Volunteers again attack more Income Tax Offices & burn an additional c. 100 evacuated RIC barracks

c. 14 April: TC loses a bag of IRA documents during police raid, #32 Bachelor's Walk, Dublin

20 April: Detective Constable Laurence 'Larry' Dalton shot by the Squad, Broadstone Station, Dublin

c. 25 April: Detective Sergeant Richard Revell shot & wounded by the Squad, Phibsborough, Dublin

c. 30 April: Additional British military personnel arrive in Ireland with 2,000 troops landing in Co. Cork

11 May: Colonel Ormonde de l'Épée Winter, nicknamed 'O' or 'the Holy Terror,' appointed Chief, British Army Intelligence & Deputy Chief of Police, Dublin & plays a key role in deploying the Cairo Gang, Dublin

20 May: Irish dockers & railway workers initiate an industrial action, embargoing British troops & munitions

Spring-Summer: TC, Liam Tobin, Frank Thornton & others, become regulars at Rabbiatti's Saloon [Marlborough Street] & Kidd's Back Restaurant & Bar [Lower Grafton Street], two haunts of British intelligence & their secret service agents, Dublin

Summer: TC intercedes with Michael Collins on behalf of Mick McDonnell

June: MC is befriended by Liam Devlin & wife, who place private rooms in their public house [#68-69 Parnell Street] at Collins's disposal; Devlin's pub soon becomes known as 'Joint #2', Dublin

22 June: RIC Assistant Inspector-General Albert Roberts shot & wounded by the Squad, Beresford Place, Dublin

30 July: MC declares British non-combatants legitimate IRA targets if they actively support the new British hardline policies

30 July: Frank Brooke, chairman of the Dublin and South Eastern

Railway Co., shot by the Squad in his Westland Row Rail Station office, Dublin

July-August: Later additions to 'the Squad' include Peter Magee, Ned Kelleher, Dan MacDonnell, Charlie Byrne, Paddy Kennedy, James Hughes, Con O'Neill, Bob O'Neill & Jack Walsh, Dublin

August: Under General Hugh Tudor's command, Auxiliary Cadets, new RIC reinforcements, begin arriving in Dublin

2 August: "The Restoration of Order in Ireland" legislation introduced in the British House of Commons, London

12 August: Terence MacSwiney, the Lord Mayor of Cork City & commandant of the 1st Cork Brigade, along with others, are arrested for possessing 'incriminating' documents, Cork City

13 August: Restoration of Order in Ireland receives the Royal Assent & becomes law

15 August: TC & others shoot & kill District Inspector Percival Lea Wilson, Gorey, Co. Wexford

20 September: BA ration party attacked by IRA outside Monk's Bakery, Upper Church & North King Streets, Dublin; three British soldiers killed & Kevin Barry, an eighteen-year-old medical student & IRA Volunteer, is arrested

26 September: TC & Mick McDonnell lead an aborted plot to assassinate a group of senior DMP officers, Dublin Castle

11-12 October: At 'Fernside,' home of Professor Carolan, Dan Breen & Seán Treacy are ambushed by the Cairo Gang, Drumcondra Road, Dublin; British army Major George O. S. Smyth & British Captain A. L. White are killed as is Professor Carolan, who is put up against a wall of his house and shot; Breen badly wounded while Treacy escapes almost unscathed

14 October: TC and others escape The Republican Outfitters [a retail clothing shop], but Seán Treacy is killed in the British army raid, Talbot Street, Dublin

17 October: Sergeant Roche & Constable Fitzmaurice, two Tipperary RIC men, are attacked by the Squad along the Quays, Dublin; Roche is killed & Fitzmaurice is wounded

25 October: Terence MacSwiney dies on the 74th day of his hunger strike, Brixton Prison, London

1 November: Kevin Barry hanged by British authorities, Mountjoy Jail, Dublin

Early November: Frank Thornton 'lifted' by Cairo Gang & held for ten days then released, Dublin

9 November: David Lloyd George, British PM, declares England has 'murder by the throat' in Ireland

10 November: General Richard Mulcahy fortuitously escapes arrest from home of Professor Michael Hayes, South Circular Road, Dublin but leaves incriminating documents behind

c. 16 November: TC & Liam Tobin bluff their way from arrest by Cairo Gang, Vaughan's hotel, Dublin

c. 19 November: TC & Liam Tobin again escape arrest at Vaughan's Hotel, Dublin

20 November: TC & Liam Tobin met James McNamara & David Neligan, 'G-men' & IRA undercover detectives, at the Gaiety Theatre, Dublin; Neligan warns TC not to attend Croke Park's Gaelic football match the next day

21 November (early AM): Dick McKee, Peadar Clancy & Conor Clune arrested by Auxiliaries, Dublin

21 November (morning): 'Bloody Sunday' as twelve British intelligence agents & two Auxiliary Cadets are shot by the Squad & others, Dublin

21 November (afternoon): TC attends Gaelic football match, Croke Park, Dublin at which RIC, Tans & Auxiliaries open fire killing seven civilians plus fatally wounding five others; an additional two more are trampled to death by the panicked crowd; hundreds also are injured in the resulting mêlée

21 November (evening): McKee, Clancy & Clune tortured & 'shot while attempting to escape' by Auxiliary police, Dublin Castle

25 November: TC, MC, Frank Thornton & Gearóid O'Sullivan carry the coffins of Dick McKee & Peadar Clancy during their funerals & burials in Glasnevin Cemetery, Dublin; Clune's body is transported to Co. Clare for his funeral & burial

26 November: Arthur Griffith arrested & jailed for a month; MC becomes acting Irish president of Dáil Éireann

27-28 November: IRA burns 17 warehouses in Liverpool, England

28 November: Tom Barry leads IRA flying column in a successful Auxiliary ambush, Kilmichael, Co. Cork

30 November: Constable James Malynn dies in Moate, Co. Westmeath of wounds sustained during the 24 January 1920 RIC barracks' attack

c. end of November: Cathal Brugha's 'madcap schemes' to kill British MPs thwarted as House of Commons closes its public gallery & barricades Downing Street

1 December: British PM David Lloyd George indicates an interest in initiating peace talks with the Irish

9 December: British PM David Lloyd George declares martial law in parts of Leinster & Munster

11 December: Black & Tans run amuck & burn much of Cork City

17 December: DI Philip J. O'Sullivan shot by the Squad, Henry Street, Dublin

23 December: TC & Batt O'Connor greet Éamon de Valera upon his return from his eighteen-month tour of America, Custom House Quay, Dublin

23 December: The Act to Provide for the Better Government of Ireland or more simply the Government of Ireland Act, 1920 is approved by British Parliament; it provides for Irish Home Rule, which later leads to the partitioning of Ireland, London

24 December: TC, Rory O'Connor, Gearóid O'Sullivan & Liam Tobin enjoy a Christmas Eve dinner hosted for them by MC; they barely escape arrest by Auxiliaries who unexpectedly disturb their revelry, Gresham Hotel, Dublin

31 December: TC's intelligence files discovered in Auxiliary raid of Eileen McGrane flat, #21 Dawson Street, Dublin

1921

3 January: TC's stag party at Devlin's public house, Dublin

4 January: TC marries Mary Brigid 'Delia' Considine, St. Nicholas of Myra Church, Francis Street, Dublin

29 January: William 'Willie' Doran, hall porter at the Wicklow Hotel, shot by the Squad in hotel's lobby, #4 Wicklow Street, Dublin

Early February: TC & Frank Thornton unsuccessfully attempt to lure British military into an IRA trap, Seville Place, Dublin

5 February: Corporal John Ryan shot by the Squad, Hynes's pub, Old Gloucester & Corporation Street, Dublin

29 March: Captain Cecil Lees shot by the Squad in front of St. Andrew's Hotel, Wicklow Street, Dublin

Spring: Brigadier General Frank Percy Crozier, O/C of Auxiliary Cadet Division, resigns his command, Dublin

1 April: Auxies raid one of MC's offices, #5 Mespil Road, Dublin; MC saved by Miss Hoey, Joe O'Reilly & TC's heroics

Mid-April: TC, Liam Tobin & Joe Hyland accompany Lord Derby on a British peace initiative, Dublin

Early May: TC, Liam Tobin, Dan McDonnell fortuitously escape capture by Auxiliaries, La Scala Restaurant, Dublin

3 May: Northern Ireland, a six-county political unit, is formed as Ulster opts out of a united Home Ruled Ireland; the island of Ireland is legally partitioned, re: the Better Government of Ireland Act of December, 1920, London

24 May: Irish general election establishes a Northern & Southern House of Commons; in the partitioned 'Northern Ireland' 52 British House of Commons seats are filled by unionists while in 'Southern Ireland' no polling takes place as all 124 'sitting' Sinn Féin TDs are returned unopposed; southern unionists, representing Trinity College, claim the remaining 4 seats; these 128 legislators form the 2nd Dáil Éireann

25 May: IRA attack & burn the Custom House, Dublin; 5 IRA men are killed, 12 are wounded & c. 80 IRA men are captured by the British military

Early June: The Dublin Guard is created from an amalgamation of the Dublin Brigade's ASU, the Squad & the Crow Street intelligence corps; MC retains his position as Director of Intelligence but his IRA influence begins to wane

26 June: The newly formed Dublin Guard kill an Auxiliary Cadet officer & wound another, Mayfair Hotel, Dublin

11 July (12 noon): Truce declared ending Irish War for Independence, Dublin & London

16 August: Éamon de Valera is formally elected President of the Irish Republic by Dáil Éireann

22 August: TC & Delia attend Leslie Mary Price & Tom Barry's wedding at St. Joseph's Church, Berkeley Road; a reception at Vaughan's Hotel, Dublin follows the ceremony

9-10 October: TC, Liam Tobin, Emmet Dalton, Ned Broy, Joe Guilfoyle, Joe Dolan & Seán MacBride join Michael Collins as part of his exclusive intelligence team & cadre of personal bodyguards, 15 Cadogan Gardens, London

11 October: Anglo-Irish Treaty talks begin, London

6 December: Anglo-Irish Treaty signed, London

8 December: TC greets a London-returning MC & Arthur Griffith at the North Wall Quay, Dublin & reports, "What's good enough for you [MC] is good enough for them [their IRB colleagues]."

8 December: Irish cabinet votes 4-3 to endorse the Anglo-Irish Treaty & forwards it to Dáil Éireann for possible ratification, Dublin

10 December: IRB Supreme Council, with MC as its president, votes to endorse the Anglo-Irish Treaty 11-4, Dublin

14 December: Dáil Éireann begins thirteen days of Anglo-Irish Treaty debates, Dublin

16 December: British House of Commons ratifies Anglo-Irish Treaty 401-58; House of Lords ratifies Treaty 166-47, London

1922

7 January: Dáil Éireann ratifies Anglo-Irish Treaty by a 64-57 vote, Dublin

10 January: Arthur Griffith elected President of Dáil Éireann; Éamon de Valera & his followers walk out of Dáil Éireann in protest

14 January: MC is chosen President of the newly created Provisional Government, a year-long, coalition, caretaker administrative unit, as per terms of the 1921 Anglo-Irish Treaty, Dublin

16 January: The Lord-Lieutenant, Britain's official representative in Ireland, hands over the power of government to MC, Dublin Castle

31 January: Irish National army takes over Beggar's Bush Barracks from the British army & establishes it as their 'temporary' GHQ

14 April: Anti-Treaty forces take over the Four Courts & other city-centre buildings, Dublin

17 May: Irish National army occupies Portobello Barracks & it becomes army GHQ

c. Summer: MC initially organises CID in Oriel House with Liam Tobin as head & TC as a member of its corps

16 June: 3rd Dáil general election; the Irish people vote, ratifying the Anglo-Irish Treaty with a 72% approval vote

22 June: Field Marshal General Sir Henry Wilson assassinated, London

c. end of June: TC sent to London by MC to try & arrange the escape of Reginald Dunne & Joseph O'Sullivan, who'd been arrested for the murder of Sir Henry Wilson

28 June: MC orders the Four Courts attacked by National army forces; the Irish Civil War begins, Dublin

2 July: Dunne & O'Sullivan tried & found guilty of Wilson's assassination, The Old Bailey, London

5 July: Civil War fighting ends in Dublin Town as IRA Republicans retreat down the country

12 July: MC assumes the role of Commander-in-Chief of the National army & effectively hands over the responsibility of heading the nascent Provisional Government to William T. Cosgrave, Dublin

c. 15 July: TC (most probably) appointed a Commandant-General, National army by order of MC

c. 15 July: TC (most probably) presents General Michael Collins with an engraved officer's sword, Portobello Barracks, Dublin

31 July: TC likely ends Oriel House association as its O/C Liam Tobin is replaced by Captain Pat Moynihan

10 August: Dunne & O'Sullivan hanged for Wilson's assassination, Wandsworth Gaol, London

11 August: Cork City captured; led by General Emmet Dalton, IRA Republicans retreat westward

12 August: Arthur Griffith dies of 'heart failure,' St. Vincent's Nursing Home, Dublin

16 August: Funeral of Arthur Griffith, Dublin; burial, Glasnevin Cemetery, Dublin

17 August: TC (most probably) & other bodyguards kill an assassin named Dixon threatening MC, Furry Park, Dublin

19 August: TC's (most probably) last meeting with MC

20 August: MC leaves Dublin for military inspection tour of southwest Ireland

22 August: MC killed in an IRA ambush, Béalnabláth, Co. Cork

23 August: TC & Joe O'Reilly learn of MC's death from Gearóid O' Sullivan, Portobello Barracks, Dublin

c. 25 August: TC & other close comrades carry MC's remains from St. Vincent's Hospital, Dublin

28 August: MC's funeral, Dublin; burial, Glasnevin Cemetery, Dublin; TC marches along side of MC's coffin in funeral procession

6 December: TC & Liam Tobin, both major-generals, & Commandant Seán O'Connell appointed ADCs to Timothy Michael Healy, 1st Governor-General of the Irish Free State, Áras an Uachtaráin, Phoenix Park, Dublin

6 December: An independent thirty-two county Ireland formally secedes from the United Kingdom & becomes a dominion of the British Commonwealth; it is entitled the Irish Free State or Soarstát na hÉireann as per terms of the 1921 Anglo-Irish Treaty

8 December: The six-county Northern Ireland entity opts out of Soarstát na hÉireann, rejoining the United Kingdom, according to the terms of article twelve of the 1921 Anglo-Irish Treaty, thus copper-fastening Ireland's partition

c. 15 December: TC & Delia move into Ratra House following his appointment as ADC, Phoenix Park, Dublin

1923

January: TC, Liam Tobin & others establish the Irish Republican Army Organisation that becomes known as the Old IRA as part of their protest against the nascent Irish government's demobilisation policy

24 May: Irish Civil War fighting 'officially' ends as Anti-Treaty forces declare a ceasefire & dump arms

1924

3 March: Liam Tobin & Seán O'Connell terminated as ADCs, Dublin

11 March: TC terminated as ADC, Dublin

19 March: TC, Liam Tobin, Frank Thornton and others participate in a 'bloodless' Free State army mutiny, Devlin's pub, Dublin

c. 20 March: TC resigns his military commission & retires from the Irish army as a major-general

April: TC & Delia reside at 27 Herbert Place, Dublin

1926

20 June: TC drowns, Lough Dan, Co. Wicklow

21 June: TC's medical inquest, Roundwood, Co. Wicklow

22 June: TC's funeral, Wicklow Town; burial, New Cemetery, Rathnew, Co. Wicklow

17 July: Delia writes to President William T. Cosgrave asking for personal assistance

1933

27 August: Death of Delia Cullen, Wicklow Town

29 August : Funeral of Delia Cullen, Wicklow Town; burial, New Cemetery, Rathnew

"For the great Gaels of Ireland
Are the men God made mad,
For all their wars are merry
And all their songs are sad."

–G. K. Chesterton

"No man shall have the right to fix the boundary to the march of a
Nation. No man has a right to say to his country thus far shalt thou
go and no further."

–Charles Stewart Parnell

"Come all ye young rebels, and enlist while I sing,
For the love of one's country is a terrible thing.
It banishes fear with the speed of a flame,
And it makes us all part of the patriot game."

–Dominic Behan

"The President's [Éamon de Valera] *attitude is very simple and*
plain – and whether in public or in private, the same. It expresses
the attitude of the Nation. England is the aggressor. Once the aggres-
sion is removed there can be peace. If the aggression and interference
is maintained it will be resisted."

–Éamon de Valera, 24 April 1921

"If you strike us down now, we shall rise again and renew the fight.
You cannot conquer Ireland. You cannot extinguish the Irish passion
for freedom. If our deed has not been sufficient to win freedom, then
our children will win it by a better deed."

–Patrick Henry Pearse

FEAR NOT THE STORM

I

AN INTRODUCTION

"WHEN FACTS BECOME LEGEND, PRINT THE LEGEND."
—TIM PAT COOGAN

Tom Cullen was the fifth child born to Andrew and Anne Cullen. With great anticipation, his mother thought the birth would take place after the New Year of 1891, but by early December, she knew her days of carrying were growing short. During her previous pregnancies, Anne never experienced such stirrings inside her. All the movement and kicking told her the child she carried must be a boy.

Sure he'll be a fighter this one, she thought.

Anne even began calling her unborn 'Thomas,' the name her husband favoured if the baby were not a girl.

Despite the feeling of impending joy, this had been a particularly difficult time for Anne. Her husband Andrew was away in Dublin. He'd left in late summer and wasn't expected home until Christmas Eve. Finding work in Blessington [Co. Wicklow] wasn't easy, so he'd gone north to work on a building construction project. The money was good, but his absence put an extra burden on her.

Besides all the encumbrances of pregnancy, Anne had four small children to take care of plus she took in people's sewing to earn the extra bob or two. Then there was always the cottage to mind and lately, thoughts about the upcoming holidays crept into her head. Christmases in the Cullen home were simple affairs, but with the children growing older, there were more things to look after for their sake.

The two girls seemed to understand their mother's disquiet more than their brothers did. Maria Anna was the oldest at ten. She helped a great deal with the chores and had begun learning a thing or two about mending clothes. Margaret, aged six and a half, tagged along behind her sister, trying her best to help. She enjoyed acting older than her years much to the annoyance of her brothers.

As for the two lads, well, they were another story. All Patrick, soon to be eight on the eighteenth, wanted to do was count the days to his birthday, read his books, pal around with the neighbouring children and stay out of his sisters' way. Andy, three and a half, still hadn't grasped the fact his status as the youngest in the family would soon be eclipsed by the birth of the new baby. Mostly oblivious to the mounting excitement around him, he went about his chores of feeding the hens, collecting their eggs and minding the dog.

Despite the mounting expectation of another addition to the family, Andrew Cullen's return still two weeks away and the coming of Christmas, the family carried on as best they could.

Early on Saturday morning, the 20th, Anne woke the children. Her water had broken. The baby would be born soon. She ordered the girls to build up the fire and boil water.

Clean sheets and a stack of cloths had been set aside for days. Just as she'd been instructed, Margaret excitedly busied herself with organising them, while Maria hovered over her mother, comforting her as best she could.

Patrick dressed quickly and was out the door within minutes of his mother's cry. The midwife lived well over two miles away. Understanding the urgency of the moment, he ran most of the way.

The morning was cold. The air burned the back of his throat, and despite the December darkness, he still could see the whiteness of his breath. The cobblestones beneath his feet were slippery and he fell twice. There'd been a heavy frost overnight, but when his feet finally reached the dirt path, he knew he was more than halfway there. Now he could accelerate safely and the lad fairly flew over the hard-packed ground.

As the rays of the winter's sun finally broke through the morning overcast, the cries of a new born echoed through the three-room cottage. On the eve of the winter's solstice, Thomas J. Cullen took his first breath. Happy and surprised faces were there to greet him.

Holding her baby son in her arms, Anne knew there would be many curious questions to answer once the excitement died down. Childbirth was a remarkable but mysterious happening.

The following morning, the family attended Mass at St. Mary's Church in Blessington. Afterwards, under the guidance of Father Edward Rowan, P.P., the family with Godparents Patrick Lawler and Mary Doyle, gathered around the carved granite baptismal font.

With prayers, promises and the sprinkling of Holy Water, Thomas received the Sacrament of Baptism. His skull still red from yesterday's birth, and in the presence of his loving family, Tom, as he soon would be called by most, was welcomed into God's Church and became one with the Lord.

Looking down at the child, Anne silently said her own prayer:

– My dearest Lord, please bless this child in my arms. May he grow up to be strong and good and true. With your loving help, may he lead a long and happy life. I pray this in the name of the Father and the Son and the Holy Ghost. Amen.

❧

Late on Christmas Eve morning, Andrew Cullen returned home from Dublin via the newly inaugurated Dublin and Blessington Steam Tramway [1888]. This rail service greatly facilitated travel to and from Ireland's capital. It originated each morning in Terenure, a village on the southern outskirts of Dublin. The fifteen-mile distance took one-and-a-half hours to complete instead of the usual four-hour bicycle journey.

Waiting to greet his father at the rail terminus was Patrick. He was delighted to see him and could hardly talk fast enough.

He first reminded his Da that his birthday was just Thursday last, hoping in his heart he'd remembered.

His father's nod and smile told him he had.

Taking the smaller of his Da's two cases, Patrick told his father about Thomas's birth and his baptism. Almost without pausing, he went on to describe how Andy and he had cut evergreen boughs to decorate their cottage. Then he blurted out about the surprise welcome Mama had planned and how his sisters had on their Sunday dresses just for his return.

Twenty minutes later, Patrick burst through the cottage's door, announcing his father's arrival, but his coming was hardly a surprise. Margaret had spied them walking up the lane and shouted with joy upon seeing them.

After greetings had been wholeheartedly exchanged, Andrew walked over to the cot near the turf fire. He scooped up the wee infant in his large, calloused hands.

– Oh Anne, what a fine young lad ye've given us. Sure this will be a Happy Christmas indeed, he said.

✻

Blessington, historically called Ballycomeen or Baile Coimín [Coimín's townland] was a town in west Co. Wicklow. By the end of the nineteenth century, most of the surrounding arable land was under tillage and pasturage. The Wicklow Mountains, to the east, were partly covered with blanket bog and contained large deposits of granite. The stone was quarried and much of it transported to Dublin for use in building construction.

Back in 1667, Archbishop Michael Boyle, a leading cleric of the day and the Archbishop of Dublin and Armagh, Primate of all Ireland, received a Royal Charter to establish the town of Blessington. It was situated hard by the River Liffey and on the high road to Dublin. Original town documents state it had one street, a church and fifty houses. Classified as a market and post town, Blessington had the legal right to hold markets and have its name on postal addresses.

During the Rebellion of 1798, much of the town was destroyed. Rebuilt by 1837, Blessington and its surrounding parish had one-and-a-half thousand residents with over four hundred living within the town boundaries.

The nineteenth century saw many changes in Blessington. With the passage of the Stanley Education Act in 1831, a national school system in Ireland was established. A free, non-denominational education [no religious instruction or display of religious objects] was available to all youngsters. By the 1850s, there was a national school in every parish in Ireland. All children, regardless of religion or economic standing, could, in theory, attend. Alas, English was the language of instruction as Irish was outlawed, even in Gaelic speaking parts of the country. The core subjects of reading, writing and arithmetic formed the basis of the curriculum, but only 'English' history was taught with no mention of Ireland's storied past permitted.

Primary education was made compulsory in 1891 and children were legally required to attend school until age fourteen. Further secondary educational instruction was available, but only a few wealthy students opted to attend. Most left school to take up work or learn a trade. This was the case with the Cullen children.

Blessington underwent a form of an 'educational revolution' in 1882. According to *A History of St. Mary's National School*:

> On Sunday the 30th of April 1882 a public meeting was held in Blessington with the object of raising funds for the erection of a Catholic school in the village, entirely under Catholic patronage. The Rev. Edward Rowan P.P. Blackditches [parish] was the main speaker. In a forthright and trenchant address to the meeting he objected to the existing National school in the village 'because Protestant teachers were employed to teach Catholic children.' He also stated, that 'it is monstrous in this age of religious liberty and enlightenment to have a school in a Catholic town, where the Catholic children outnumbered the Protestants by 7 to 1, conducted by a Protestant teacher, without the pastor of the Catholics having the smallest share in the management.' [1]

In actuality, Larry McCorristine, a present-day teacher at St. Mary's Senior National School, stated:

> Almost immediately, however, the new national schools were opposed by clergy of all the main churches: Catholic, Protestant and Presbyterian. This was because of their non-denominational status, permitting no religious instruction or display of religious objects. Some Catholic bishops regarded the new school as Colonialist on the basis that neither Irish history nor the Irish language was taught.
>
> Effectively, by the 1850s National Schools, throughout Ireland, had in fact become denominational schools, with their own clerical managers. [2]

Regarding this Blessington 'educational revolution,' a regional newspaper of the day, the *Leinster Leader*, of 8 July 1882 noted:

> On Friday a demonstration came off in Blessington. It having become known that the new school wanted materials for the building, one hundred and sixty farmers of the parish of Blackditches turned out their horses almost at a moments notice and each brought a load of stones from the magnificent granite quarries at Ballyknockan. The imposing cortege far extended beyond the whole length of the town and was accompanied from Ballyknockan by Rev. E. Rowan P.P. and Rev. Mr. Hickey C.C. who where (sic) enthusiastically cheered. [3]

Such were the circumstances the Cullen children encountered during their early years. The 'new' St. Mary's Catholic School opened in January, 1883. By month's end there were thirty-four boys and thirty-six girls attending. In June, school attendance rose to seventy-four and by July eighty-seven students were enrolled.

Tom Cullen's first school days were spent at St. Mary's as were those of his four older siblings. [**Author's note:** In 1891, James, a sixth child was born, but likely died at or soon after birth.]

As mentioned above, Tom's studies centred on the 3Rs. But his parents, especially his father, were well aware of the school's curriculum discrepancies. Over the years, many hours were spent around the kitchen table reliving and discussing Ireland's celebrated past. Important dates, heroic figures and England's unwelcomed incursion into Irish life were the main topics of these 'home lessons.' Both Tom and Andy took a keen interest in their Da's teachings. It was thus, within the confines of home and surrounded by family that a love for and appreciation of Ireland's plight took seed and sprouted in Tom's mind.

In addition to Ireland's illustrious but troubled past, Andrew Cullen made a point of instilling in his offspring an appreciation of their family's proud name.

[**Author's note:** the name Cullen may be of Gaelic or Norman origin. In Gaelic, Ó Cuillin comes from the word "Cuileann" meaning 'holly-tree.' The name originated in southeast Leinster, and remains strong there until this day. The Norman name can be derived either from the city of Colwyn (Conwy, Co.) in Wales, or the city of Cologne in Germany. The Norman clan's territories were based around Cullenstown in Co. Wexford. Today, Cullen is the 84th most numerous surname in Ireland.] [4]

As a youth, Tom's athletic reputation grew. Both Andy and he had ample opportunities to test their budding talents during uninvited visits to the nearby eighteenth-century Russborough House's walled demense and manicured gardens. Their daring raids were discouraged by their mother.

– Sure what have I told you boys before about going up there?

But being a practical woman, Anne Cullen reluctantly accepted the occasional sack of apples and the odd cabbage or two.

On warm days, after their chores and lessons were finished, the three brothers spent time together fishing or swimming in the Liffey. They developed a familial closeness and brotherly camaraderie growing up in Blessington.

The Cullen home was a happy one as well. The children were raised in an atmosphere of kind respectfulness which was unusual for the day. More typically, families were dominated by authoritarian fathers. Children were taught to obey their elders and speak only when spoken to. Spare the rod and spoil the child was the rule heard in many homes.

Beside a nurturing childhood, the Cullen household was more fortunate than most. Both Andrew and Anne were hardworking parents. The children seldom went without shoes which was often the case with neighbouring families. There was always a dry roof overhead, a warm fire to sit by and a nourishing meal on the table, at least for the noontime meal.

※

Sometime prior to the 31 March 1901 census taking, several important family events occurred. Likely because of a new employment opportunity for Andrew, the family moved to #4 Shanavanghey, Grantstown, Queen's County.

[**Author's note**: Queen's Co. was named in honour of England's Queen Mary I, who first shired or 'planted' Ireland in the sixteenth century. England had confiscated/annexed land from the O'Mores and Fitzpatricks, colonising it with settlers. After independence in 1922, the county's name was changed to its present-day designation of Laois or Leix.]

On Tom's 1890 birth cert, Andrew was listed as a 'labourer.' In 1901, his occupation was designated as 'herder.' But even with the move and new work, the family's economic status didn't improve greatly. They were still living in a three-room, stone cottage with, most probably, a thatched or possibly a corrugated metal roof. It was labelled a third-class house with two front-facing windows. The property, rented/leased from Mr. Arthur Owen, had two out buildings *in situ*: a piggery and hen house. [The owner of the aforementioned farm stock is unknown.]

Maria Anna Cullen, the eldest daughter, who would have been twenty, was no longer residing with the family. She likely died, moved away or was now married and had left home.

Sadly, James, born in 1891, was not listed either. In his place was another child christened James, doubtlessly named in honour of his dead brother. James, now two years old in 1901, was born in Queen's Co. Thus, it can be assumed the family moved from Blessington around the turn of the century as Tom would've been about ten years old.

[**Author's note:** As of the 31 March 1901 census, the family ages were listed as Andrew, 42; Anne or Annie, 43; Patrick, 18; Margaret, 16; Andrew or Andy, 14; Thomas or Tom, 10; James, 2.]

By 1901, it should be noted that Patrick was following in his father's footsteps. His occupation was also listed as 'herder' while the other four children were categorised as 'scholars.'

Ten years later, based on information gleaned from the 2 April 1911 census, the Cullen family details have undergone further changes. Once again, they had relocated. This time it was to #1 Ravensdale, Maynooth, Co. Kildare. Economically, the family's lot in life had improved. Andrew was now part of a 'management team.' His occupation was listed as 'steward.'

The Cullens' living accommodation was upgraded too. Their domicile consisted of five rooms, not just three as before. It had six front-of-house windows and met the requirements for being a second-class abode, but there were only four family members residing in the house on that census day. With fewer mouths to feed and a better paying job, Andrew appeared more successful.

The very sad news, however, was that Tom's mother, Anne, had died. [**Author's note:** Divorce or women leaving their families in the early part of the twentieth century was virtually unknown in Ireland.]

Sometime in early 1902, Anne died, possibly during complications encountered while giving birth to her third daughter. The 1911 census indicated a new child, born in Queen's Co., was nine years old and named Annie, most likely after her mother.

A while after this tragedy, Andrew remarried. His new wife, Mannie, aged fifty-two in 1911, had become part of the family. Gone, however, from the 1911 Cullen family registry are Patrick, Margaret, Andrew and Tom.

Again, thanks to the recently published 1911 census, the three brothers can be accounted for, not so for Margaret, who by now had died or was more likely married.

Patrick, still living in Queen's County, was listed as a 'boarder,' residing with a family named Connolly. Matthew Connolly, aged thirty-eight, and Mary, his thirty-year-old wife, were living with their two-year-old son, Matthew, at #8 Rahanavannagh, Blandsfort. Matthew's occupation was listed as 'carpenter' while Patrick Cullen continued his work as a 'herder.'

The Connolly home seemed a comfortable one with its three rooms and six front windows. The cottage ranked as a second-class residence rented or leased from Mr. Hume Bland, who owned several other nearby houses.

The census also indicated that Andy Cullen was living in Wicklow Town, working as a 'foreman butcher' while Tom Cullen was now in Dublin, employed as a 'grocer's shop assistant.'

❧

As an interesting aside, the roots of Tom's attraction to and fondness for horse racing can be traced to his boyhood days growing up in West Wicklow and southeast Queen's Co.

Ireland's long tradition of horse breeding, training and racing captured Tom's interest. He took delight in the 'Sport of Kings.' When not in school, he spent the lion's share of his time grooming, training and exercising thoroughbred race horses. Later in life, living in Dublin, he'd often be seen roaming the paddock or standing along the rail at The Curragh, Fairyhouse or Leopardstown racetracks. One of the only two known photographs of Tom and his wife Delia was taken at The Curragh, most likely during the summer of 1924 or 1925. Their fashionable attire and relaxed manner reflect the ease the couple felt in their racetrack surroundings.

❧

It is uncertain when Tom moved to Dublin, but based on the 1911 census, he was living in the city at #58 [South] Circular Road in April of that year. Employed as a grocer's assistant, he worked nearby at #59 for a family acquaintance, Patrick Dowling. Sharing the work in what was a busy enterprise were William King, aged twenty-nine, and Nicholas Pollards, just sixteen. Dowling, the grocery's owner, was single, thirty-four and a successful shopkeeper. He'd taken over the business from his father, building it up gradually year after year.

The four lived together in a comfortable, eight-room, two-story house. Classified as a second-class dwelling, it had four large windows facing out onto the main road. Living in the same building was a fifty-year-old widow named Ellen Curtis. She was employed by Dowling as a 'general domestic servant' and looked after the cleaning of #58 and #59 as well as preparing meals for the men.

South Circular Road was a prosperous, middle-class neighbourhood south of Dublin which ran more or less parallel to the Grand Canal.

The imposing St. Kevin's Catholic Church, consecrated in 1872, was just a short walk from Tom's residence. Situated near the point where the South Circular Road becomes Harrington Street, the building was usually referred to as the Harrington Street Church by the local residents. Patrick, Billy King and Tom often attended weekday Masses there prior to beginning their workday at the grocery.

Portobello [Spanish for beautiful harbour] Barracks, a British military installation, opened in 1815, was also close at hand. Most of the neighbouring dwellings along this main road were two-story, private residences but several of the buildings to the west of #59, Dowling's grocery, were commercial businesses with residences situated above them. Just beyond Dowling's was a chemist shop, followed by a green grocer, two butcher shops, a tobacconist, a dairy merchant and a bank.

❧

What was life like living in Dublin at the beginning of the 1900s? Ireland's 1911 census website provided some interesting detail. Needless to say, Dublin Town was in rich contrast to the life Tom knew growing up in rural Ireland.

> Dublin, in 1911, was a mass of contradictions. A second city of the British Empire, Dublin was also the first city of nationalist Ireland.... This was a city of genuine diversity...rich and poor, immigrant and native,

nationalist and unionist, Catholic, Protestant, Jew and Quaker…all bound together in the life of the city. [5]

The second decade of the new century brought great changes to Dublin and Ireland. Labour unrest, a renewed effort by Westminster to see Home Rule implemented, a devastating World War, the 1916 Dublin Uprising, the establishment of a new Irish parliament [Dáil Éireann] and finally, the initiation of a brutal War for Independence all combined to mark the ten years between 1911 and 1920 as momentous ones.

> And yet, in 1911, the notion of national independence seemed a distant illusion beside the reality of British rule. At the heart of the city stood the huge stone fort of Dublin Castle [1204]…the focal point of British rule in Ireland.
>
> The iconic streets of Bloomsday [16 June 1904] were already being lost. The city was changing as the suburbs grew in scale and importance. Nothing transformed the physical appearance of Dublin as profoundly as the evolution in transportation. Trams, horses and bicycles still dominated transport in Dublin but the private motor car was growing in importance. [6]

Though Dublin was Ireland's first city, a port city with almost half-a-million residents, it stood a distant second in manufacturing to the other British port cities of Belfast, Liverpool or Glasgow. Jobs were scarce. Working conditions were often poor. Labour unrest was rife. Dublin had the worst slums in the United Kingdom…overcrowded, ill-fed, disease-infested, a ghastly haven for the unemployed and almost totally ignored by Dublin's more successful residents.

> Of interesting political importance were the expanding Catholic middle classes, gaining steady prominence in the city's professional and administrative ranks. Throughout the nineteenth century, power in Dublin slowly shifted from the Protestant ascendency to an

emerging Catholic elite, who were apparently nationalist in aspect.

As the centre for British rule in Ireland for eight centuries, Dublin was the focal point of the substance and
symbols of British culture. This culture   its literature,
its newspapers, its sport, its music, its entertainment
was adopted with little modification by many amongst
the middle classes, eager for advancement, unashamed
by the pursuit of prosperity. [7]

The feeling of 'Britishness,' the image of the Crown and the
visible might of the Empire were dominating influences affecting
the lives of the Dubliners as Tom began his new life in the city
by the Liffey.

With the Union Jack flying overhead, with every postage stamp
purchased, with each bank note or coin in your pocket…they were
a collective and constant reminder of England's domination of
Ireland. But despite the willingness of the majority to seemingly
adopt the trappings of its colonial overlords, a strong undercurrent
of Irish nationalism was gaining a foothold in Dublin.

Reflective of nationalist movements that had redrawn national
boundaries and sparked both political and cultural reforms in
nineteenth-century Europe, Ireland was experiencing its own
stirrings. Begun in the last quarter of the 1800s, an Irish-Ireland
resurgence was under way, much of it centred in Dublin. Inspired
by a romantic view of rural Irish life and steeped in a renewed
interest of its Gaelic past, an Irish cultural revival was taking hold.

The Gaelic Athletic Association [GAA], founded in 1884,
sought to reacquaint Ireland with its ancient sports, particularly
hurling and Gaelic football, as well as its traditional music, dance
and now seldom spoken national language. In the 1890s, literary
groups sprang up in London and Dublin, emphasising Ireland's
rich legacy of ancient folklore and its resurgence of burgeoning
Irish writers.

The Gaelic League's emergence in 1893 launched a national
effort to preserve and extend the use of the Irish language and a
unique but often ignored national culture.

At the turn of the century, Arthur Griffith, a newspaper man and diehard Irish nationalist, founded the Sinn Féin political party [1905]. It emphasised Ireland's capability for economic self-sufficiency and its need for political separation from Great Britain. It also succeeded in arousing Irish national consciousness, attracting not only the young, but mature men and women of all ages.

Finally, another emergent figure in the early twentieth century was educator and Gaelic scholar Patrick Henry Pearse. In 1908, this charismatic Irishman founded a bilingual [Irish/English] boys' school in Ranelagh. Two years later, this budding concern, in need of additional space for its growing student body and expanding educational offerings moved further south to the village of Rathfarnham. Pearse sought educational reform as opposed to the rigid constraints of traditional British education which he labelled 'a murder machine.'

The 1911 census website further noted:

> …this was a resurgence which did not play easily with urban life. Dublin could not be easily accommodated in any vision which idealised rural life. And yet, Dublin lay at the heart of this Gaelic revival, home of Patrick Pearse and many of the writers, educationalists and intellectuals who recast the idea of Ireland as a sovereign Gaelic nation, free from the control of it imperial master. [8]

Sean O Mahony in his book, *Frongoch: University of Revolution*, concluded his edifying narrative about the prison camp in which almost two thousand 1916 Easter Uprising veterans were interned from June to December, 1916 with some sage observations about life in Ireland after the Rising.

> The men returned to a country that had changed utterly since they had left a short time before. The Home Rule Party [IPP] was doomed to extinction; the middle classes were nervous and insecure; the government was watchful and suspicious and the church, as always, was determined to be on the winning side. But the most important transformation had taken place among the ordinary people. For a while at least they were deter-

mined to have done with an empire that had trodden on them for centuries. The spirit of freedom was blowing across the land. The men of Frongoch had indeed returned home for Christmas, but soon they would be ready to strike another blow against the ancient enemy. The next time they would not be beaten. [9]

※

Firsthand descriptions of Tom Cullen are almost non-existent. But after careful examination of photographs, I imagine this West Wicklow man stood about five feet, ten or eleven inches tall and weighed approximately twelve stone. He had a fit, athletic build and likely walked with a confident, purposeful gait. Wearing his hair short, as he did, accentuated his slightly protruding ears. He had a bit of a 'boxer's' nose, possibly resulting from some boisterous, youthful rough housing or perhaps from a serious bout of fisticuffs. Upon smiling, Tom's right lateral incisor appeared discoloured, indicative of past dental difficulties or the end result of a pugilistic encounter.

Tom's eyes had a sparkle to them and he had, as some would say, an infectious smile, reflective of a cheerful disposition. His face was boyishly handsome, even impish at times. It was easy to see he possessed a sense of humour, a positive self-image and an optimistic outlook on life. I further believe he made friends easily and was a good friend to others close to him. Many of these traits were certainly assets when engaging in a disarming battle of wits with British secret service agents, Dublin's undercover spies and RIC detectives.

From his occupational pursuits, it's clear he was intelligent, could think quickly on his feet and wasn't afraid to step into the 'bhearna bhaoil' [gap of danger]. His loyalty to his comrades was unquestioned. Proof of these qualities is a testament to the enduring relationship he developed with his closest friends, especially Michael Collins, Liam Tobin, Frank Thornton and Piaras Béaslaí among others. Michael, for one, was noted for seeing through the veil of deceit and dishonesty often perpetrated by those wishing to curry favour with him. If Tom wasn't all that he appeared to be and constantly chose to test the limits of their friendship, the big Fella would've immediately terminated his association with this West Wicklow man.

Despite the fact that Tom Cullen and Michael Collins's lives paralleled each other in many surprisingly similar ways, there was one big difference between the two men. Tom was not politically ambitious. Yes, they were both brave warriors, but Tom wasn't the skilled politician Michael and others later proved to be. Certainly, Tom was no Éamon de Valera, Arthur Griffith, William T. Cosgrave or Kevin O'Higgins. He wasn't a philosopher or scholar like Patrick Pearse, Eoin MacNeill or Douglas Hyde. He was, however, a dreamer as most of those around him were. He envisioned an Ireland free of the entanglements, the deceptions and the conniving manipulations characterised by its colonial overlords. Undoubtedly, he did believe in the political process, but when a higher authority continually deprived its people of their democratic rights, Tom willingly, without hesitation, took up the banner of 'freedom from tyranny' and marched forward regardless of the cost to himself.

Tom was a revolutionary not a pacifist. He was a 'democrat' who, when forced to, advocated and voluntarily participated in 'revolution.' He wasn't afraid to place his life on the line for Ireland's freedom. He often risked it all, knowing the opposition could kill the revolutionary, but they couldn't defeat the coming revolution.

Proudly, Tom Cullen participated in Ireland's early twentieth-century drive for independence in 1916, and later, his actions helped bring to partial fruition the dream of full Irish self-determination and self-governance. In reality, he was just one of many who were in the right place at the right time. He stood up for whom and in what he believed. As history noted, he freely faced off with agents of Britain's Empire; he gave them blow for blow; he answered the use of violence with the use of violence; he connived and schemed as the enemy facing him had; and he did his damnedest to break the hated connection with England. But happily, with the brutality and bloodshed behind him, Tom Cullen stepped back and became a 'citizen' of Soarstát na hÉireann.

❧

If Tom possessed an unfavourable trait, it was his affinity for drink. Alcoholic overindulgence was a dangerous addiction, especially in his line of work: espionage and counter-intelligence. To his credit, Tom successfully managed his enjoyment of 'having a good time' during those traitorous, tout-ridden days in the run up to and during the War for Independence. Later, he still needed his wits about him during the epoch Treaty negotiations and its ensuing debate, the Treaty split and Ireland's Civil War days when his friendship with Michael Collins reached its zenith.

Because of Collins's critically important role in both Ireland's military and political evolution of the day, the Big Fella often came under close scrutiny and public criticism. To a lesser extent, Cullen suffered the same slings and arrows of public condemnation as Collins. Stories of their drinking bouts became the fodder of popular folklore. The famous 1920 Christmas dinner at the Gresham Hotel stood as one example. Another was the revelry surrounding Tom's bachelor party in early January, 1921. Collins and his comrades, which included Tom, were publically vilified for their so-called 'drinking carryings-on' staged at #15 Cadogan Gardens during the London Treaty talks in autumn, 1921.

There's no doubt drink was very much a part of Tom Cullen's lifestyle in Dublin. In fact, it well may have played an important role in the tragic events of June, 1926. But I attribute all the excessive alcoholic influence to the horrific pressures of living and surviving in Dublin during those deadly days of 1918-1924 rather than to some 'Irish' character fault.

Most of the men living in Dublin who opposed the British provocateurs were single and called rural Ireland home. As a group, many were unaccustomed to the vagaries of 'big city' life. Vulnerable to emotional frustration, they knew loneliness, disillusionment and violence while forced to endure living life 'on the run.' Drink was one of their few pleasures. It also should be remembered that many of their 'safe houses' were actually public houses where alcohol was readily available.

There is no doubt that being an intelligence officer during Ireland's early twentieth-century 'troubles' was enough to drive a healthy person off the rails. Fear remained Tom's constant companion. Violence and death waited around every corner. He never knew if the next bullet was marked for him.

❈

The only critical remark I ever read about Tom was made by Dan Breen, the indomitable Irish Republican and great friend of Seán Treacy. In his Witness Statement, the Tipperary man said, "We took [Tom] Cullen out a few times and he was a very bad shot."

I'm unsure if Breen wasn't poking fun at the expense of Tom's memory or was, in some way, having the reader on because in his next sentence Dan pays Tom a compliment, "He [Tom Cullen] was a very fine character." [10]

❈

The fine Irish historian Tim Pat Coogan added important detail to life in Dublin during those 'troubled' years. He told the story of how Liam Devlin and his wife returned to Dublin from Glasgow, Scotland in the summer of 1920. It was there they purchased/leased a public house at #68-69 Great Britain Street, just at the bottom of Rutland Square [later renamed Parnell Square] and opposite the Rotunda Hospital. Devlin, as an active Sinn Féiner in Scotland, gained the friendship of Michael Collins through some mutual IRB contacts. The Devlins offered the Big Fella the use of their pub as a meeting place and office. It was centrally located with lots of foot traffic. Mick gladly accepted the invitation, as his people could come and go virtually unnoticed. [**Author's note:** Devlin's pub was nicknamed 'Joint #2.' Only a block away, also facing Rutland Square, was 'Joint #1,' #29-30 Vaughan's Hotel.]

Coogan goes on and quotes Frank Thornton's memoirs:

> We used Devlin's extensively and every night Mick, Gearóid O'Sullivan, Liam Tobin, Dermot O'Hegarty, Piaras Béaslaí, Frank Thornton, Tom Cullen and Joe

O'Reilly met there, the events of the day were discussed and plans were made for the following day.... Mrs. Devlin acted in the capacity of a very generous hostess. Visitors from the country never left without getting a meal and in quite a large number of instances a bed for the night. [11]

Tim Pat also described the wrestling matches, called 'exercise' by Collins, that Mick and his comrades often engaged in at Devlin's. Again, it was something, anything, to help break the fear and tension so dominating their young lives at the time.

The rollings on the floor with Liam Tobin, Gearóid O'Sullivan and Tom Cullen were roisterings between men who were taking life and knew that at any second their own could be snuffed out. The heaving mass on the floor striving for 'a bit of ear' was after all the hunted Leadership of the Irish Republican Army. [12]

It wasn't blood and guts all the time. Bodies weren't being slopped out by the twos or threes. Collins enjoyed a good laugh. So did Cullen and his other comrades with Liam Tobin being the possible exception. Liam often seemed overly serious.

Frank O'Connor, a contemporary of the Collins crowd and one of Mick's biographers, told two short stories.

Once in a public house he [Collins] saw an argumentative soul whose elbow, as he grew more impassioned, edged closer to his [Collins's] glass. Collins watched it in fascination. Then he gently pushed the argumentative soul away.

'Excuse me,' he said, 'I'd rather see a church fall.' [13]

And...

Cullen, who was a champion runner, came in for a lot of it. A press photographer once succeeded in photographing him [Collins] with his head over his [Cullen's] shoulder. Collins, a runner himself knew what that meant. Next day Collins, finding him [Cullen] in a pub, professed to be shocked.

'Honest to God, Mick, I'm sober.' He [Cullen] declared. 'Look, I can walk straight!'

You can't run straight though,' said Collins with a grin. [14]

※

Piaras Béaslaí was another close friend and colleague of Michael and Tom's. Considered by many to be the definitive Collins biographer, Piaras was a writer, playwright and revolutionary born in Liverpool of Irish parents. He offered a rare, first-hand glimpse into Cullen's life.

> Tom Cullen at this time [May-June, 1918] was doing the work which in a later period devolved on a Quartermaster General superintending the import and distribution of arms, ammunition and military equipment, and the circulation of *"An tÓglách" [The Volunteer]*, the official organ of the Volunteers. Of course all this work had to be done secretly. Cullen was a powerfully built, athletic young man, with a cheery open manner that disarmed suspicion, and later proved a valuable asset in his work as Intelligence Officer. [15]

Another contemporary of Tom Cullen was David Neligan, born in Co. Limerick in 1899. With little future at home in rural Ireland and on the urgings of some school friends, he applied for a position with the Dublin Metropolitan Police [DMP] whose duty it was to keep the peace in Dublin and its surrounding county. In the spring of 1918, he was called to Dublin.

In his autobiography, *The Spy In The Castle*, David wrote there were two police forces in Ireland at the time. The unarmed Dublin Metropolitan Police patrolled the capital's urban environs while the armed Royal Irish Constabulary [RIC] was a countrywide, semi-military police authority. They had responsibility for maintaining law and order outside of Dublin. Often stationed in remote areas, life in the RIC could be dull and lonely. Neligan was looking for something more.

As an alternative, one of his friends suggested he consider a position with the DMP.

> It appeared that it was money for jam: the duty was so easy that one got paid for strolling around. Those fellows [the DMP] cut a dash when on leave; they wore fine suits, good hats and shoes and cycled about on bicycles with strengthened frames. Money jingled in their pockets. [16]

Needless to say, such an opportunity appealed to Neligan. Additionally, being a Catholic was not a handicap, at least for advancement in the junior ranks. All he had to do was score well on the examinations, which he did.

In the autumn of 1919, tired of walking a beat, Neligan applied and was accepted into the DMP's 'G' or detective division. With a few more shillings a week in his pay packet, he no longer had to wear a uniform, pull night duty or patrol the streets. As a 'G-man' with offices in Dublin Castle, he carried a .38 automatic pistol and was soon immersed in 'political' work. Possessing strong pro-Irish/anti-British sentiments, he eventually met Collins and soon after Cullen. In short order, Neligan became one of Mick's important undercover operatives inside Dublin Castle and a key cog in Michael's expanding intelligence network.

> Tom Cullen, Collins' intelligence officer…used to come along to our meetings with [Liam] Tobin [Deputy Director of Intelligence]. He was a handsome man with fresh complexion and sparkling eyes. A poor shop assistant, he was brave as a lion. A very likeable fellow in every way, he was a native of Wicklow. [17]

Neligan went on to describe an incident involving Tom.

> One day a prominent Sinn Féiner named R. [Robert] C. Barton, also from Wicklow, was, while a prisoner having been sentenced by court martial being moved

from the castle to Mountjoy Prison. It was proposed to rescue him *en route*. It was known that he would be in a covered lorry. Cullen waited at the castle. When this vehicle emerged, he ran as fast as his legs could carry him to Berkeley Road, a distance of two or three miles, getting there in time to alert the rescuers. They immediately held up the lorry, only to find that it contained a lot of poor devils of Tommies on their way to the glasshouse. They allowed them to continue on their dolorous journey. [18]

David Neligan also provided another titbit about Tom's interests.

Cullen was fond of horse-racing and often saw British secret-service men at the meetings. He [Cullen] used to call them tick-tack men those nimble signallers of the track. [Tick-tack: a traditional method of hand signs used by bookmakers to communicate odds on horses running in the next race.] [19]

How did Tom Cullen and Michael Collins's lives become so intertwined? What forces drove both men to risk all for the cause of Irish freedom? Indeed, it's a fascinating story, the details of which follow in subsequent pages, but first some brief introductions.

Tom Cullen first bumped into Michael Collins in Dublin during the spring of 1916, several months prior to the Easter Uprising. They most likely met at Larkfield, Count Plunkett's home in Kimmage, just south of town. As their friendship grew, they discovered they'd much in common.

Then in the spring of 1919, because of a blossoming sense of mutual admiration and shared respect, Collins picked Cullen as an important cog in the intelligence network he was setting up.

Irish historian and writer T. Ryle Dwyer painted a word description of those early beginnings in his book, *The Squad and the Intelligence Operations of Michael Collins*:

In January 1919 he [Collins] took over as director of intelligence from Eamonn Duggan, who had merely run intelligence as an adjunct of his legal practice and had only one man working for him.

Collins set up a far-reaching network, incorporating intelligence gathering, counter intelligence and matters relating to prison escapes and smuggling (both arms and people). He was the brains behind the whole network and his industry was phenomenal. He retained personal control over work similar to that done by three different intelligence agencies in Britain: MI5 [domestic], MI6 [foreign] and MI9 [military]. [20]

The Big Fella, also referred to as the Director of Information, arranged to have his central intelligence office housed on the first floor of #3 Crow Street, just above J. F. Fowler's print shop. The narrow alley was but a few steps from Dame Street and five short blocks from the lower entrance of Dublin Castle. With four-story buildings lining both sides of Crow Street, the laneway appeared dark even on sunny days. At the bottom of the alley, Crow Street forked both left and right, leading out to Essex Street and onto the Quays. If necessary, avenues for a quick retreat were readily at hand.

Some say Collins never once stepped foot inside #3, his own intelligence HQ. Instead, he relied on his loyal batman and aide-de-camp Joe O'Reilly to be his Crow Street courier.

Michael put a fellow Corkman, Liam Tobin in charge of day-to-day activities and empowered him with the title of Deputy Director of Intelligence. Ryle Dwyer said this about Liam:

> He was an inconspicuous individual, tall and gaunt, with a tragic expression. He walked without moving his arms, which made him seem quite listless, in marked contrast with Collins who bounded from place to place. [21]

Dwyer briefly described Cullen and Frank Thornton, the next two men in Collins's line of command.

Tobin's deputy was Tom Cullen [Assistant Director of

Intelligence], an affable, quick-witted individual from Wicklow who had fought in the Easter Rebellion [as Tobin had]. He was not only intelligent but also a good athlete and a handsome young man with a fresh complexion and sparkling eyes. Frank Thornton [Deputy Assistant Director of Intelligence and another veteran of Easter, 1916] was next in the chain of command at the headquarters, along with Frank Saurin, who stood out as one of the best-dressed men in the movement. [22]

Béaslaí, in his Collins biography, added more detail to the Tobin-Cullen partnership:

He [Collins] had already become intimate with Liam Tobin, who was at the time Intelligence Officer to the Dublin Brigade, and he selected him as his Chief Intelligence Officer. Tom Cullen was afterwards drafted into Intelligence, while still carrying on his work as Assistant Q.M.G., and, in his office at [#32] Bachelor's Walk, combined the business of the two departments. Collins had now three offices, Cullenswood House [Ranelagh], Bachelor's Walk [on the Quays], and a Finance Department office at 6 Harcourt Street [just off Stephen's Green]. [23]

Collins's intelligence/counter-intelligence operation focused on three critical areas: compiling information on people and places of interest; detailing all British troop movements; and gathering information about members of the British secret service, British intelligence service and police intelligence officers centred in and around Dublin.

As a pro-Irish intelligence agent, some of Tom Cullen's early responsibilities included screening individuals wishing to contact Michael and identifying specific undercover agents for possible elimination by members of the Big Fella's political assassination team, the Squad.

Tim Pat said to me when I talked with him about Tom and Michael several years ago, "When facts become legend, print the legend."

He also related a story regarding Tom's intelligence work during the early stages of the War for Independence. The celebrated historian mentioned Piaras Béaslaí's cousin, Lily Mernin, who worked for Britain's administration in Dublin Castle as a copy-typist. Privy to classified information that required typing, Lily, secretly working for Collins, simply inserted an additional piece of carbon paper into her machine, thereby producing an extra copy exclusively for Irish intelligence eyes.

Additionally, Coogan wrote of Lily:

> As the war intensified Dame St and Grafton St swarmed with British agents of all sorts, many of them Army Intelligence Officers dressed in mufti. Mernin used to walk up and down the streets, ostensibly window-shopping on the arm of either Frank Saurin or Tom Cullen, identifying these agents for the Squad. [24]

Needless to say Michael Collins, Tom Cullen, Liam Tobin and their associates soon were wanted men by the Dublin [British] authorities. As men on the run, they seldom slept in the same bed two nights in a row.

Piaras Béaslaí offered a good description of those times:

> At the time these English Secret Service men, and their "touts," caused us no great perturbation. Borrowing the slang of the racecourse, Collins and his associates nicknamed the latter "tick-tack men." At this time Vaughan's Hotel [Joint #1] was largely used by Collins and his colleagues. He usually had his evening meal there. A large bedroom in the hotel, containing four large beds, was practically set aside for "men on the run." Collins, Tobin, Cullen, Gearóid O'Súilliováin [O'Sullivan], Seán Ó Murthuile [O'Hurley] and I frequently shared this room. It was at this period [June-July, 1920] that an English Secret Service officer came to stay at Vaughan's Hotel, accompanied by his wife. [25]

Vaughan's Hotel soon became a magnet for both the IRA, British secret service and the Auxiliaries [British military police].

Again, Béaslaí recalled another nearly fatal incident. On Holy Saturday evening, 3 April 1920, the IRA, as per Collins's order, had torched three hundred evacuated RIC barracks and almost one hundred tax offices throughout Ireland. The event quickly became known as 'the Night of the Burnings.'

Béaslaí, writing in his two-volume biography of Collins, noted that a group of Dublin's IRA leadership had assembled in Vaughan's, waiting for reports of the evening's successes down the country.

Finally, about midnight and chuffed at the news concerning the night's accomplishments, the men prepared to leave for other lodging when Christy, the night porter, rushed in to say that a large body of soldiers had surrounded Rutland Square. Collins and three others headed out the back door, climbed over the garden wall and eventually hid under the cover of the wall bordering Dominick Street Chapel.

Piaras then picked up the threads of the story.

> Tobin, Cullen and I left the hotel by the back a few moments later, but fared a little better [than Collins and the others]. Not knowing where the others had gone, we proceeded to work our way down the [Rutland] Square, climbing over walls and roofs; doing some climbing and jumping feats which only the danger of death could teach us. [26]

At long last, seeking the safety of an abandoned building, the three men made beds for themselves from some discarded matting and enjoyed a satisfying night of sleep.

In the morning, the trio returned to Vaughan's feeling refreshed only to encounter Collins and his party looking red eyed and bedraggled. They'd been forced to spend the night freezing in the cold. As the three men were having a good laugh at Collins's expense, it was learned that though the hotel had been surrounded it hadn't been raided. They'd become the victims of their own justified fears. As it turned out, they all could have slept at the hotel without worry.

In an assemblage of personal accounts, first compiled in 1948 by the *Kerryman* newspaper, Ernie O'Malley described another harrowing escape from Vaughan's as British intelligence agents again swooped down on Cullen and Tobin. It happened just prior to 'Bloody Sunday,' 21 November 1920.

> A week before the date fixed, Tobin and Cullen, who were sleeping in Vaughan's Hotel, were awakened by a gang of men at night. Some of the men they knew, amongst them Bennet and Aimes, who were on their list [to be shot]. Both Tobin and Cullen were able to persuade the raiding officers of their assumed identity after a long interrogation. In the end Cullen was talking freely about racehorses to some of them and giving them 'certain' winners, but the raiders were hard to convince and reluctant to leave. Some nights later on the raiders returned asking for Tobin and Cullen by name, having made sure of their identity in the meantime. There would have been only one end to the two men if there had been any doubt in the minds of their visitors.[27]

Whether Neligan was retelling this same story, while adding his own personal twist, or simply describing a different harrowing event, his following account reiterates the fearsome dangers Tom Cullen and others faced, almost daily, over a two-year-plus period. In his own words, Dave wrote:

> The British secret service made many efforts to trap them [Tobin and Cullen], though all failed. One of their closest escapes was in Vaughan's Hotel which was then a favourite roosting place for such as they. The British undoubtedly watched the place [in fact a resident spy lodged there according to Beasley (Béaslaí)]. One night they sent a military raiding party to arrest them. Both men slept in a room on the top floor, and were awakened about 3 a.m. by a knocking at their door. They opened it to be confronted by a British captain and his men, who invited them to dress and come on. They spun some yarn covering up, and partly convinced the officer that this was a case of mistaken identity. Innocently enough,

he told them to stay there until he went downstairs to phone. Getting speech with his superiors he was sharply told not to be a damned fool, but go back and arrest them. On his return, the birds had flown. Admittedly, they had not flown far. They were crouched on the window-sill outside, high above the street. The Captain never thought of raising the blind. They [Tobin and Cullen] avoided Vaughan's after that. [28]

The same story was repeated to me on several occasions with a slightly more dramatic flair. Instead of 'crouching on the window sill,' it's been said that Tobin and Cullen were, in fact, 'hanging by their finger nails' with just the tips of their toes resting on the protruding window frame of the room below.

[**Author's note:** Two definitive books on the life of Michael Collins include Piaras Béaslaí's two-volume set entitled Michael Collins and the Making of a New Ireland, (reprinted, 2008) & Tim Pat Coogan's Michael Collins, (reprinted, 2002).]

2

"I WILL COUNT TO FIVE. EITHER
SURRENDER OR WE ARE COMING IN."

–AN EDUCATED ENGLISH VOICE DEMANDED. [1]

Tom Cullen's arrival into Dublin Town was no different from that of hundreds of other Irish men and women who'd also left their rural homes in search of work and the chance for a new life. Each month, the young and not so young flooded into Dublin. Some were lucky. They found employment and a reason to stay. Others used the 'big city' as a stepping stone. Unable to find a decent job and with limited resources, they pressed on, sailing for England…London, Manchester, Liverpool and points beyond. They found in all of those 'foreign' cities 'Irish communities' crowded with immigrants hoping to make a go of it. Some had needy families back home who counted on the extra money posted to them each month. But Tom Cullen considered himself lucky… on two counts. He had a job and there were no hungry mouths depending on him for financial support.

Pat Dowling, his new employer and family friend, was generous. Besides the job as a grocer's assistant which paid him £1 10s [one pound, ten shillings] a week, he received his room and board gratis.

Tom shared a room with William King, nine years his senior, in the back of the house at #58 South Circular Road. Coming from King's County, Billy, as he preferred to be called, had worked in Dublin for three years. After labouring as a navvy on the Quays for the first two, the job as grocer's assistant seemed a welcome change. With a steady income and few back-breaking tasks, he joked that working for Pat was almost as pleasing as taking a holiday.

31

Nicholas Pollards, four years younger than Tom, disliked living in Dublin. He was homesick for his family and life back on the farm in Co. Carlow. It was his intention to leave Dowling's employment at the end of the summer and return home. He spent most of his days in the grocery complaining about one thing or another, and speaking for himself, Billy was glad to see him go.

Tom didn't involve himself much with the interpersonal dynamics of their little group. He liked Pat and Billy well enough, and as long as Nick did his job, all was right with the world as far as Tom was concerned.

Nicholas's leaving was one of the reasons Pat had offered Tom the job. His business was thriving. In addition to supplying fruit and vegetables to the neighbouring residents, Pat had recently signed a contract to supply the local British barracks with some of their commissary needs.

Besides family and the beauty of the green, rolling country of home, Tom also missed being around horses. Their care and exercising had filled many a happy hour for him. He missed the thrill of galloping across open fields with only the sun and a good breeze in his face. Sometimes, he closed his eyes and imagined he was actually 'riding the wind.' A knight of old rushing to save a damsel in distress or winning the Irish Derby at The Curragh.

He had indulged in such moments of fanciful delight during his school days and beyond when he ran foot races. In those youthful moments, his legs became the legs of a race horse flying across a playing pitch or down a grassy hill toward the finish line. With his feet scarcely touching the ground and his breath coming in gasps, the thrill of leading the pack was its own reward.

Now in Dublin, the only substitute for those past pleasures was a Sunday afternoon at the races. At first he ventured off on his own. Heading to nearby Leopardstown or maybe Fairyhouse after Mass, an air of excitement filled him as he drew nearer the racecourse. He revelled in crowds of people, the ladies in their fine hats, the tick-tack men with their binoculars, tote boards and semaphore signals and of course the jockeys and the horses.

Standing along the rail or watching the thoroughbreds parading around the paddock, Tom felt in his element. He carefully scrutinised both riders and mounts. With analytical wisdom born of experience, the Wicklow man calculated the odds and placed his wagers. Though he had precious little to bet, he combined luck with knowledge and most often left with more pounds in his pocket than he had that morning.

Back at the shop, Billy often watched him reading the racing results in the *Independent*. After a few probing queries, Tom invited him to come along on his next Sunday outing and see what it was all about first hand.

One excursion to Leopardstown and Billy was hooked. With Tom's careful tutelage, Billy tripled his wagers. But that was just icing on the cake. The two young men became friends outside of the racing. Together, they'd head off for Saturday evening dances organised by local Gaelic Leaguers or linger over pints of beer at Leonard's Corner along Clanbrassil Street, discussing the news of the day. Much of their conversations centred on the political developments coming out of Belfast.

After work on Wednesday evening, August 9th [1911], they took a tram to the city centre to see the new monument installed earlier that day in honour of Charles Stewart Parnell. The statue, still draped and waiting its unveiling in a few weeks' time, stood at the top of Sackville Street, just beside the Rotunda Hospital. It made a fitting bookend for the monument at the opposite end of Dublin's grand boulevard, the one honouring Daniel O'Connell. 'The Liberator' would soon have a worthy companion, both dramatic reminders of Ireland's two great, recent political leaders.

Up and back, Tom and Billy debated the merits of the Uncrowned King's political accomplishments and his rise and fall in the eyes of the Irish people and the Catholic Church.

As if by some strange coincidence, the following day's headlines blared out the news that The Parliament Act of 1911 had passed the House of Commons in London. It removed the House of Lords' control on budgetary matters and limited its veto power over other legislation to a two-year suspensive vote. It was the Lords' veto that had killed Ireland's 2nd Home Rule bill in 1893.

Tucked away at the bottom of page two of the newspaper was a short piece speculating what the impact of the new act would have on Ireland. The author concluded that the passage of The Parliament Act, depriving the Lords of absolute power to veto legislation, would pave the way for another bid at Irish Home Rule, which could eventually lead to civil war in Ireland. Would Parnell turn over in his grave knowing that Irish Protestant unionists would stoutly refuse to grant Irish Catholic nationalists any freedom of self-governance impinging on their own political and economic powers of control? It cautioned that British Prime Minister Herbert Asquith would be biting off more than he expected. Would the 'Uncrowned King's long-dreamt wish die yet another death?

Tom knew the House of Commons and the House of Lords had been jousting for legislative control for several years. In 1910, the British Liberals lost control of the Commons. They now depended on John Redmond's Irish Parliament Party's vote of support to pass any of their legislative agenda. The quid pro quo for such cooperation would be Irish Home Rule. By breaking the House of Lords' power to defeat pending budgetary proposals, something Asquith desired, he was obligated to initiate a third try at Irish devolution.

The first steps toward inciting clashes between the two bickering Irish elements occurred just a month later. On 23 September, over seventy thousand unionists and Orangemen marched in Belfast to protest possible Home Rule in Ireland.

The following April, on the eve of Asquith's introducing Ireland's new Home Rule bill, a quarter-million Orangemen congregated at Balmoral Showground in Belfast to protest Home Rule and to state for the record they would do all in their power to see such a measure fail.

Just as the papers were filled with news of a possible unionist and nationalist clash, the tragedy of the RMS *Titanic*'s sinking blotted out all possible political upheaval. Life in Dublin suddenly came to a standstill as many in Ireland mourned those lost at sea.

Soon, however, threats and countercharges re-emerged in the press and at political gatherings. The idea of a partitioned Ireland attracted the fancy of some unionists. Home Rule would mean a divided Ireland. Ulster's nine counties would be set aside for the majority Protestant unionists and Ireland's other twenty-three counties to the south would be left to Catholic nationalists. There would be no 'popish rule' in Belfast, not if Ulster could help it.

The idea of granting all of Ireland some measure of Home Rule grated against the thinking of many northern unionists. It was their hard work and initiative that had seen Belfast and Ulster prosper with the rise of industrial progress. Wasn't Belfast Ireland's largest and most progressive city? Weren't its trade links with Great Britain the grist that fed the mill of economic advancement in Ireland? There was no way Ulster was going to take a backseat to a rurally-dominated Dublin who'd likely have different economic and political priorities. No, southern farmers would have to bow to northern industrialists, not the other way around. Ulster was different. They would have to be treated with deference and respect...they'd demand it.

Unionist leaders divided over this idea of partition. James Craig, a northern unionist, favoured it, but Edward Carson, a southern unionist, was opposed. He had no appetite for leaving the fate of a quarter-million of his 'Protestant' followers in the south to the fancy of dominant southern 'Catholic' nationalists.

Arthur Griffith, the founder of Sinn Féin, spoke for many when he vehemently objected to any Home Rule proposal that would grant Ulster special consideration or an exemption. He maintained Ireland was 'one nation' indivisible. He viewed any Home Rule proposal which divided Ireland as unacceptable.

Tom Cullen was clearly on Griffith's side. There was no way he'd ever support a partitioned land. It struck at the heart of what he'd always believed...what Irishmen and women had so long wanted and fought for down through the centuries. Sure it was the idea of Irish national unity that was at the core of his father's teachings as Patrick, Andy and he sat around the kitchen table years ago. It was why the famous Wicklow hero Fiach McHugh O'Byrne had stood up against the forces of Elizabeth in the sixteenth century. It was why Irishmen and women had risen in 1641 and why they fought the soldiers of the Crown in 1798. It was what inspired the bold Irish leader William 'Billy' Byrne of Ballymanus at the Battle of Arklow and drove the United Irishman

Michael Dwyer to stand up against the English in the Glen of Imaal, nestled peacefully among 'his' Wicklow Mountains. And who could forget Wolfe Tone and Robert Emmet and the Men of '48 and '67? No, Tom would have none of it. Ireland would not be divided if he had any say in the matter.

※

Throughout 1912 the Home Rule-Irish partition pot simmered, sometimes boiling over.

In May, the second reading of the Home Rule bill was approved. Andrew Bonar Law, British Conservative party leader, opposed the bill as did outspoken Edward Carson.

In September things hotted up. On the 28th, 'Ulster Day,' nearly half-a-million unionists throughout Ulster signed an 'Ulster Covenant,' some with their own blood, in opposition to Irish Home Rule. The extraordinary event, organised by Carson, dramatised to the British and Irish world that the vast majority of unionists wanted Ulster excluded from any 'all-Ireland' bill.

Early in the following year, the Ulster Unionist party, backed by the Orange Order, voiced their views, not in words or signatures, but in actions. They organised an Ulster militia, the Ulster Volunteer Force [UVF]. Over a hundred-thousand men enlisted to oppose, by force if necessary, any British attempt to re-establish an all-Ireland Dublin government via Home Rule legislation.

※

The year 1913 proved eventful. Rather than Belfast, the spotlight shifted to Dublin. Instead of Home Rule and partition, the topic demanding Irish attention centred on labour unrest. An unusually warm Irish summer grew only hotter as members of James Larkin's Irish Transport and General Workers' Union [ITGWU] faced off against Irish businessman, journalist and politician William Martin Murphy.

Concerned that Larkin's trade union would dilute his monopolistic control over Dublin's tramway system, Murphy led other local businessmen in opposition to workers' union membership.

Larkin, born in Liverpool, England of Irish parents, spent his life as a labour organiser. Living in Belfast in 1907, he founded the ITGWU there. A year later he headed south and began organising workers in Dublin, Cork and Waterford. In 1909, he moved to Dublin which then became his centre for union operations. With the help of James Connolly, an Irish socialist and union man who'd been born in Edinburgh, Scotland of Irish immigrant parents, they soon experienced some successes representing Dublin workers who wished for better wages and improved working conditions. Using strikes and boycotts as their weapons, the lot of the working class improved.

The Guinness Brewery and Dublin's United Tramway Company were two of the city's largest employers of both skilled and unskilled employees. Larkin and Connolly concentrated their organising efforts on the plight of the less accomplished and the most abused workers.

The Guinness workers, better treated by the brewery's management than most Dublin industries, refused to side with Larkin, but not so with the vastly underpaid tramway employees. Murphy, feeling threatened by the prospects of his men joining a union and fearing a strike, began flexing his muscles and dismissed several hundred workers. Larkin retaliated on 26 August, calling for a tramway strike.

Murphy, not accustomed to being challenged, called together some three hundred local employers. Convinced they could defeat Larkin and Connolly's unionising efforts, the labour bosses agreed not to employ any man unless he pledged not to join a union or go out on strike. An impasse resulted.

The ensuing labour 'Lock-Out' led to street rioting, looting and attempted tramway-rail destruction. Employers, supported by the DMP, answered employees' actions with strikebreakers and 'scabs' from England. On Sunday, 31 August, a labour rally was broken up by baton-wielding policemen. Two workers were killed and several hundred were injured in the mêlée. The day became known throughout Dublin as 'Bloody Sunday.'

Dublin workers, some of the poorest paid and often living in horrendous conditions, stuck it out for six months, surviving on meagre donations from various Irish charities and sympathetic

British labour unions. Tragically, the Irish Catholic Church opposed the British help fearing Irish children would be subjected to undue 'Protestant influences.'

The strike ended in January, 1914. Irish workers, with their heads bowed, returned to work after agreeing not to join a union. Murphy, now nicknamed William 'Murder' Murphy had won. Murphy's three Dublin newspapers portrayed Larkin and Connolly as the villains while publicly admired figures such as Patrick Henry Pearse, Countess Markiewicz and William Butler Yeats continued speaking out and supporting the workers' plight.

One seemingly overlooked product of this labour dispute was James Connolly's organising of a workers' militia, the Irish Citizen Army [ICA], on 19 November. Inspired by 'Big Jim' Larkin and led by Connolly, an ex-British army captain named Jack White headed up the training of the three hundred or so quasi-military force formed to protect workers against the police and their employers' brutalities.

❧

Though Tom Cullen was not directly involved in the 1913 labour disputes and resultant conflict, he followed the developments closely. Through Pat Dowling's generous contributions, both Billy and he often delivered unsold veg and fruit to Liberty Hall, the headquarters of the ITGWU. From there the food was distributed to needy families. Tom often lingered at labour headquarters, hoping to catch a glimpse of either leader or of White drilling members of the ICA in Beresford Place, but his direct involvement in Ireland's budding social and military evolution began on Tuesday, 25 November 1913.

Relying on testimony given to the Bureau of Military History 1913-1921 by Larry Nugent of Athy, Co. Kildare, it is possible to imagine Tom reading the same announcements Nugent did:

> On Saturday, 8th November, 1913, an article appeared in *An Claidheamh Solus* [*The Sword of Light*, the Gaelic League newspaper] and *The Leader*, advocating the formation of a Volunteer Corps. On Saturday, November

15th, 1913, *The Evening Telegraph* published a news item that a movement was on foot for the formation of a Volunteer Corps. On November 19th, 1913, an advertisement appeared, announcing a meeting to be held in the Round Room, Rotunda, on Tuesday, 25th November, 1913, for the purpose of forming a Volunteer Corps. "All citizens are invited to attend. Further Announcements later." [2]

Nugent goes on to describe the atmosphere in Dublin that November, a mood Tom certainly would have experienced too.

> The feeling aroused among the Nationalist population of the City and County of Dublin by the above publications were indescribable. In business houses, workshops, offices and various professions, a feeling of comradeship which never previously existed sprung up. Men who had only a nodding acquaintance shook hands when they met in the street. The young men clicked their heels when they met their pals and actually hugged and pulled each other around: all were joining up. Would Tuesday ever come? [3]

❧

With Pat Dowling's approval, Tom Cullen left work early on Tuesday, the 25th for the Rotunda. If possible, he'd be a Volunteer by nightfall.

Billy desperately wanted to join him, but labour unrest was rife in Dublin and Pat needed him in the grocery to serve customers and mind the shop. Besides, Billy had lost the coin flip with Tom to see who would go to the meeting...so the matter was settled.

With his white grocer's coat on the hook in the corner, Tom headed on foot, passed the Harrington Street Church, toward Camden Road. Few trams were running and even if they were, he'd refuse to take one in support of Larkin's boycott.

Talk in the grocer's shop of Home Rule and partition had been replaced two months ago with news of the Lock-Out. He'd overheard James Connolly's name mentioned a good few times in passing and one woman proudly told him her son had joined the ICA.

Thirty minutes later, Tom passed through College Green and headed up toward Sackville Street. Beyond the GPO and Nelson's Pillar, he could see the sunlight glinting off the gold lettering on Parnell's new monument. The 'Uncrowned King's' words boldly stated beliefs the Wicklow man held dear: *No man has a right to fix the boundary to the march of a nation. No man has a right to say to his country thus far shalt thou go and no further.*

The round Rotunda Rink was just beyond the statue to its left. Even though he was an hour early, there was a large crowd of men milling about in front of the handsome building. They spilled out blocking much of the Rutland Street East to passing traffic. The Rink itself was another one of Dublin's granite-block buildings. Tom imagined its stones were likely quarried back home in Blessington.

When the doors finally opened, he was able to gain entrance, taking a seat near the back. After the usual delays, the meeting began. A number of prominent nationalists spoke, among them Michael O'Rahilly, a member of the Gaelic League's governing body, Eoin Mac Neill, Professor of Early and Medieval Irish History at University College Dublin and Patrick Henry Pearse, headmaster of St. Enda's School and another well-known member of the Gaelic League.

Inspired by and responding to the founding of the UVF a year earlier, the Dublin men signing up at the Rotunda Rink came together against the backdrop of the fervour of rising militancy now gripping Ireland.

> The Ulster Volunteers had been called into being by a Dublin unionist, Edward Carson, and the Ulster Unionist council to prevent the Protestants of Ulster being ruled by an all-Ireland home rule government located in Dublin. Aided and abetted by a powerful and unscrupulous section of the [British] Conservative Party, they threatened rebellion and civil war to thwart the rule of law.

If granting home rule was going to cause a civil war, not granting it was also going to cause a civil war. Nevertheless, they forebore to openly criticise the Ulster Volunteers. In his Ulster speech in the Rotunda Rink on 25 November 1913 [Patrick] Pearse stressed the point that the movement they were inaugurating was not one in antagonism to the Volunteers companies which had been raised by the unionists in the north east of Ulster. He recognised that they might differ as to the degree of autonomy which was desirable for Ireland but emphasised that it was for Ireland herself and not for any external power to determine that degree. [4]

❈

After the speeches concluded, Tom managed to secure himself a place in line at one of the enlistment tables set up outside. After a patient wait he had his name and address added to the enrolment register. He was now officially an inaugural member of the Irish Volunteers.

Larry Nugent, who was also among the throng of men at the Rink that day, stated:

> The meeting in the Rotunda was a great success — a large number of men were unable to gain admission. The principal business was a resolution proposing to found a Volunteer Corps for Ireland. Aims and objectives were explained by a number of well known men in the Gaelic League and G.A.A. and other supporting organisations, but the politicians were absent. We were informed as to the best way to form Companies and that further instructions would be issued later. I succeeded in having my name registered that night. [5]

Elated he'd managed to sort his way through the crowd of eager men and enlist, Tom walked back home to his residence with a great feeling of pride and eager anticipation for the training and camaraderie that lay ahead.

The following day, the papers were full of the success of the Volunteer meeting the evening before. In analysing the recent developments and reflecting upon what had transpired lately in Belfast, one commentator reported:

> Both [John] Redmond and [Edward] Carson believed in the benefits of belonging to the British empire. But Carson believed that Irish home rule would be disastrous for the imperial connection whereas Redmond, in common with [William] Gladstone [British PM in the late 19th-century] before him, believed that home rule would copperfasten the union and enhance the empire. Redmond simply wanted Irishmen to get the credit which was rightfully theirs for their significant contribution to building up that empire. He recognised the imperial commonwealth of states as a reality and felt that within one commonwealth there could not be two standards of justice. [6]

❧

Billy joined the Volunteers at week's end. Both Tom and he were assigned to B Coy, 4th Battalion, as were many who lived in the surrounding south Dublin suburbs.

A local man Éamonn Ceannt, originally from Co. Galway, who worked in the financial offices of the Dublin Corporation, was appointed battalion commandant.

[**Author's note**: Living less than a mile from Dowling's grocery at #2 Dolphin's Terrace, Áine Ceannt, Éamonn's wife, likely would have shopped at Pat Dowling's grocery and, thus, would have met Tom. Today, the Ceannt street address has been renamed & renumbered as 283 South Circular Road.]

Ceannt's biographer William Henry added greater understanding to the events surrounding the Volunteers' formation:

> On 10 November 1913, The O'Rahilly invited Ceannt to attend a meeting which was to be held in Wynn's

Hotel, Dublin the following day. The purpose of the meeting was to decide on the formation of the Irish Volunteer Force, which was welcomed by all who attended.

...once the decision was taken to form the Irish volunteers, Ceannt and the others lost no time in getting the movement off the ground with a public meeting being arranged for 25 November at Rotunda Rink, Dublin.

The venue [the Rink] could cater for 4,000 people, but about 7,000 attended and a number of speakers, including Pearse and MacNeill, addressed the large gathering. Overall the meeting was a huge success, with 3,000 recruits signing up immediately for the new Volunteer force. According to Áine [Ceannt's wife], it was agreed prior to the meeting that Ceannt and a number of other extreme nationalists would not speak at the meeting to avoid attracting any attention, as the British authorities were keeping a careful eye on the situation. [7]

Another man, James Kenny of Rathfarnham, Dublin, also assigned to the 4th Battalion [E Coy rather than B Coy], would have shared many similar experiences with Tom and Billy.

I was issued with a membership card and paid a weekly subscription of 2d (cents) or 3d which was entered on the card. I also subscribed 1/- (one shilling) each week towards the purchase of a rifle and equipment. In addition I bought my own uniform.

We had a parade one night each week at which we were drilled and instructed in the use of the rifle and bayonet by an ex-N.C.O. of the British Army. His name was Thompson. He was not a member of the Coy as he was paid for his services. [8]

Like Tom and Billy, Liam Ó Flaithbheartaigh of Kimmage, Dublin was a member of B Coy, 4th Battalion. The three would have known each other and trained together. Liam noted in his Witness Statement:

> I joined the Irish Volunteers at the inaugural meeting in
> the Rotunda in 1913. I was allotted to "B" Company,
> 4th Battalion, and notified to attend at the Fianna Hall,
> [#34] Camden street (sic), for drills. Drilling transferred
> afterwards to Larkfield Green Lanes. [9]

Tom and Billy would have attended training sessions on
Camden Street during December, 1913 and on into the beginning of 1914. The precise date of the change of sites to Larkfield,
Kimmage is uncertain, but certainly it was completed by the end
of January, 1916.

Tim Pat Coogan filled in detail about one important Larkfield
resident, Michael Collins, who left England for Dublin on 15
January 1916:

> His [Collins] first job in Dublin was, as he described
> it, 'financial advisor' to Count Plunkett for three days
> a week. The job brought him £1 a week and his lunch
> at the Plunkett home at Larkfield, Kimmage. It also
> brought him into touch with 'the refugees', the group
> of Irish camping at Larkfield, who like himself had
> come over to Dublin to get away from conscription
> and to take part in the rumoured uprising. At least one
> member of the Plunkett family obviously had more in
> mind for Collins than the family bookkeeping. This
> was Joseph Plunkett [Count Plunkett's oldest son], the
> tubercular poet and an organiser of the 1916 Rising,
> who was literally to lean on Collins' shoulder when the
> fighting started. [During the Uprising, Captain Collins
> served as aide-de-camp to Joe Plunkett.] [10]

The *Dublin Brigade Review* (undated) provided another
insightful look at 'the goings on' at Larkfield for the Volunteers
of the 4th Battalion:

> Situated in the Kimmage district, at that time open and
> largely country, Larkfield was garrisoned up to the date
> of the Rising. In addition to its use as Headquarters of
> the battalion, it was garrisoned as a General Headquar-

ters by a company of volunteers consisting of Irishmen who had returned from England to take part in the fight.

Weekly collections for the purchase of arms were made in the ranks. Instruction in the use of rifles and other training was given for the momentous days ahead. A ballot used to be held in the units for the rifles purchased as they became available. The source of supply, however, could not fulfil the demand, and the now well-known decision to import arms on a large scale was taken. This would provide an opportunity to test the volunteers, and the success of the training could be judged. The decision to import arms was destined to be the first of the most notable events that preceded 1916, and is known to-day as the Howth Gun Running. [11]

[**Author's note**: On 5 April 1914, Cumann na mBan was launched as a women's auxiliary to the Irish Volunteers. Its first meeting was held in Wynn's Hotel, Abbey Street Lower. This paramilitary Irish republican organisation was first led by Kathleen Lane-O'Kelley and though independent of the Volunteers, their governing body was subordinate to the IV executive. In May, 1914, Inghinidhe na h-Éireann (Daughters of Ireland), established Easter Sunday, 1900 by Maud Gonne to counter Queen Victoria's April visit to Ireland, merged with Cumann na mBan making it the largest nationalist women's organisation in Ireland. Several of its prominent members included Countess Constance Markiewicz, Helena Moloney, Mary MacSwiney, Kathleen Clarke, Elizabeth O'Farrell, Áine Ceannt, Ada English, Máire Comerford, Sheila Humphreys and Jenny Wyse Power. When the Volunteer movement split in the autumn of 1914, most of the Cumann na mBan membership elected to follow the minority Irish Volunteers instead of the siding with the National Volunteers.]

❧

Tom Cullen and Billy King, as members of the 4th Battalion, would have most certainly taken part in the Howth gunrunning affair. Again, the determined nationalist leadership in Dublin, the men who were the organising force behind the Irish Volunteer movement, were reacting to their northern countrymen's actions.

The Ulster Unionist Council, in an effort to arm the men of their Ulster Volunteers, arranged for the importation [smuggling] of a large quantity of rifles and ammunition into the ports of Larne, Co. Armagh and Donaghadee and Bangor, both in Co. Down. So under cover of darkness and with the local police force looking the other way, the weaponry, purchased from an arms dealer in Hamburg, Germany, arrived in the early hours of 25 April 1914. Hundreds of privately owned motor cars lined up at the three quaysides to safely transport 'the goods' away. History notes that this may have been the first time motor vehicles were used on a large scale for a military purpose.

Once more, Ceannt's biographer William Henry helped fill in the details:

> The tense situation in Ulster led to the illegal importation of arms at Larne, County Antrim in April 1914, with the Ulster Volunteer Force landing a consignment of arms consisting of 20,000 rifles and almost three million rounds of ammunition. The Irish Volunteers were well aware of the situation developing in Ulster and were also preparing to arm themselves. On 26 July 1914, the Irish volunteers landed a shipment of over 900 Mauser rifles and 26,000 rounds of ammunition at Howth, County Dublin. The yacht *Asgard*, owned by an English-born sympathiser, Erskine Childers, was used for the transportation of the arms. Ceannt [accompanied by the men of the 4th Battalion] was in command of one of the sections responsible for the distribution of the arms. As the volunteers returned to Dublin the military [the King's Own Scottish Borderers and about eighty RIC policemen] intercepted them [at Clontarf]. During the confrontation Ceannt drew his pistol and fired on the British soldiers. Most sources maintain that a catastrophe was avoided because the soldiers thought that the shots had come from the onlooking crowd. [12]

Several of the IV leaders, Thomas MacDonagh, Darrell Figgis and Bulmer Hobson in particular, engaged the military and police officials in conversation while the Volunteers, each with a rifle but no ammunition in hand, quickly melted into the surrounding locale.

Lt. W. T. Cosgrave, who like Tom joined the Volunteers at their inauguration in November, 1913 and was appointed lieutenant of B Coy, 4th Battalion soon after, gave a personal accounting of the Howth gunrunning incident in his Witness Statement to the bureau of Military History 1913-1921. As Tom and Billy's immediate commanding officer, Cosgrave's description of the day was particularly informative.

> On the 26th July, 1914, the 4th Battalion marched with the Dublin Brigade to Howth, arriving there about midday. We halted at the harbour for some little time awaiting the arrival of a yacht which was rounding the bar. Then, although we were tired after a march of some 8 or 9 miles, we went at the double down the pier where [Eoin] MacNeill, Laurence J. Kettle and some others were distributing rifles. MacNeill said to me: "You are a Volunteer, take that", handing me a rifle. We reformed our ranks when we had been supplied with the rifles, and marched back toward the city, deflecting from the Howth road to the Malahide road when we perceived that some battalions in front had been halted by military and police. I saw volunteer J. J. Burke wounded there. There was a scuffle followed by negotiations, but as far as I could see, no attempt was made to disarm the Volunteers at this stage. [13]

❧

Hiding his antique, nineteenth-century Mauser rifle under his trench coat, Tom hurried along the Malahide Road. A few blocks from Marino Park he hopped aboard a tram going into the city centre. Billy was nowhere in sight. Tom guessed he'd taken another avenue into town.

Ignoring the curious stares of the passengers at his rifle's barrel protruding from the bottom of his coat, he settled back on a bench to consider his next move.

He exited the tram at the Rotunda Hospital. Taking to the back streets where he'd attract the least attention, Tom made his way south toward the Quays. Crossing the Capel Street Bridge over the Liffey, he caught a second tram by Christ Church that was heading for Leonard's Corner on the South Circular Road.

The six o'clock Angelus was ringing as he slipped in through the back garden of #58 and up the stairs to his room. First saying a prayer for his safe deliverance, Tom then spent the next thirty minutes admiring his new acquisition. It was heavy to lift and hold at shoulder level, but its wooden stock and shining black barrel gave him a new sense of self-confidence. With talk of a rebellion in the wind, the Wicklow man longed for the day when his rifle would speak for Ireland.

❧

An hour later, as Tom was preparing to head down to Leonard's Corner for a pint, he heard Billy on the stairs.

Arriving into their room, the King's Co. man, still energized by the day's adventure, explained he too had safely avoided the long arm of John Bull by taking refuge in the Clontarf house of a friend. Rather than transporting his new weapon across town, he'd decided to leave it there, collecting it later after all the excitement died down.

Exchanging details of their day's adventures, the two young men headed up the road to the corner. Both were intent on quenching their well-earned thirsts.

❧

Later that same day, unbeknownst to Tom and Billy, the British soldiers who'd tried to block entry of the German Mausers into Dublin were assaulted with stones, bottles and rotten fruit by a seething crowd of angry Dubliners.

The troopers had returned from Clontarf via streets that led them through a 'rough' part of Dublin. As they neared the Liffey, heading for their quarters in Royal Barracks [later renamed Collins's Barracks], the following mob grew more hostile. Many of those in the throng had no great love for the occupying soldiers and some, no doubt, had personal grudges they wished to settle.

As the two elements spilled out onto the Quays at Bachelor's Walk, another group of rioting Irish came down Liffey Street and confronted the military, armed with a fresh supply of stones and fruit.

Embarrassed by their earlier failure to stop the Volunteers and now attacked by a raging mob, the soldiers lost control. Major Alfred Haig, bleeding from open facial wounds received when he was struck by three separate stones, ordered twenty men at the rear of his column to reverse. Ten men knelt down while the other ten closed ranks behind them.

Haig again shouted to the stone-throwers to back off. They didn't. Suddenly, a shot rang out. Then without an order to fire, the besieged line of soldiers open fire, sending a deadly volley of bullets into the irate crowd.

Three were killed and thirty-two lay wounded. One of the wounded died several days later of bayonet wounds he'd received in the mêlée.

Patrick Henry Pearse called it an iconic moment in Ireland's struggle for independence. The incident, sadly but dramatically, focused world attention on the Irish Volunteers, and exposed a glaring British double standard: British authorities looked the other way when the UVF armed themselves versus killing and wounding civilians when the IV attempted the same.

❧

Two other developments, more Irish Volunteer arming and an extravagant offer by Redmond, occurred during the summer of 1914. Both directly affected Éamonn Ceannt and Tom Cullen. William Henry described them with clarity.

Ceannt was also present on 1 August 1914 when 600 rifles and 11,500 rounds of ammunition were successfully landed at Kilcoole, County Wicklow. He had been acting as adjudicator at an oireachtas piping [musical] competition when he was advised of the situation and he left immediately for Kilcoole. [14]

And…

On 4 August 1914, Britain declared war on Germany. In his speech to the House of Commons the previous day, John Redmond suggested that Britain could safely withdraw her forces from Ireland and leave the defence of the country to the Irish Volunteers. However, this declaration was misinterpreted as a pledge of total Irish support for England's war effort and was met with great enthusiasm by an emotionally charged House of Commons. After the meeting, Redmond wrote to MacNeill explaining the situation and requesting his support; he ended by writing: 'Do not let us by our folly or temper destroy the situation.' [15]

But Redmond *had* destroyed the situation. Earlier in June, the IPP leader wrestled control of the Volunteer executive away from its hard-line, IRB republican founders; men like Patrick Pearse, Éamonn Ceannt, Thomas MacDonagh, Seán Mac Diarmada, Bulmer Hobson, Liam Mellowes, Piaras Béaslaí, Joseph Plunkett and The O'Rahilly among others. With Eoin MacNeill as the benign, titular head of the Volunteers, the revolutionaries surreptitiously began planning to use the IV not as a defence bulwark against a foreign invader as publicly stated, but as an offence corps designed to militarily engage its reviled colonial occupier.

With Redmond's men now holding majority control of the executive council, the militants were effectively stymied, but not for long.

As the war in Europe entered its second month, Redmond made another grand gesture. On 20 September at Woodenbridge, Co. Wicklow, he, in effect, offered the aid of the IV to King

George V and Great Britain by urging the Volunteers to enlist in the British army.

Besides supporting England's war effort, Redmond was hoping his grandiose offer would guarantee the enactment of the Irish Home Rule legislation just signed into law on 18 September but with one stupefying caveat. Because of the European conflict, a last minute amendment had been added. The Home Rule Act of 1914 would be suspended, put on hold, until the war's end.

This infuriated the Irish nationalists and, of course, the hard-line republicans. Outraged by Britain's postponement of Home Rule and by Redmond's encouragement of Irishmen to fight in the Sassenach's war, the Volunteer movement split.

Approximately 180,000 Irishmen, many unemployed and fancying a pay-packet, decided to 'take the King's shilling' and enlist. Besides, the prevailing thought at the time believed the war would be over by Christmas, the men would be coming home and Ireland would have its devolved privileges. This left the original Irish Volunteers, under MacNeill's token leadership, with a skeleton force of 12,000-14,000 men.

But Pearse and the others were not to be denied. Influenced more by the outbreak of the war than with Redmond's British bullishness, the IRB leadership lost no time and pressed forward. Spurred on by the old Fenian motto, "England's difficulty is Ireland's opportunity," they began reorganising.

> On 5 September 1914 it was agreed at a meeting of the IRB supreme council that a rebellion would take place and that they should accept any assistance that Germany would offer. Although no definite date was set for the rebellion, it was decided that any of the following reasons would prompt immediate actions: if Germany invaded Ireland; if England tried to force conscription in Ireland; or if the war looked like it was coming to an end. It was also agreed that a declaration of war on Britain would accompany the insurrection. [16]

James Kenny, a member of C Coy, 4th Battalion, described the impact of the Volunteer 'split' in his Witness Statement. Tom

Cullen, Billy King and the men of B Coy would have experienced a similar result.

> The Coy was about 100 strong when Redmond deliv-
> ered the speech at Woodenbridge which caused a split
> in the Volunteers. We did not hold a meeting to decide
> which side to take, nor was it discussed at any parade.
> Those who followed Redmond just drifted away. About
> 50 remained with the Irish Volunteers. Recruiting after
> the split was very bad, in fact I don't think we got any
> recruits except a few senior boys from [Pearse's] St.
> Enda's College. After the gun-running at Howth and
> Kilcoole rifles were brought to the Company in small
> quantities at short intervals. They were drawn for by
> lot as they arrived. I got one of the first batch to arrive
> a Martini Henry. We were allowed to bring our rifles
> home. Later we were issued ammunition which we also
> kept at home. [17]

❧

Needless to say, the planning for the Uprising took place behind Tom Cullen's back. As a Volunteer, he wasn't privy to any of its schemes or carefully conceived details.

He continued living life much as before the split. Sure there was talk and speculation about what the future had in store for the Volunteers, but most of the time it was simply 'getting on with it.'

❧

Naturally, the war in Europe occupied much of everyone's attention. Its progress, or lack of it, dominated the news media and family kitchen-table discussions. Many of the men in the UVF enlisted in Britain's war effort. Talk of Home Rule and an Irish Civil War subsided.

But with the arrival of the Irishmen from England at Larkfield in early 1916, talk of a rebellion resurfaced among the Volunteers.

'The refugees' presence testified to the fact that 'something' was up...something big.

Drilling and military training intensified. A 'bomb' making factory was organised at Larkfield. An added effort was made to procure weapons. British soldiers were offered as much as £5 for a rifle. If that wasn't enough, many were plied with liquor or simply physically relieved of their weapons.

> On St. Patrick's Day 1916, the Dublin battalions of the Irish Volunteers assembled at College Green. They planned to attend a special military mass which was to be held in St Michael and John's Church at 9 a.m. Ceannt's fourth battalion served the mass and provided the guard of honour. After the mass the Volunteers, complete with rifles and fixed bayonets, marched to College Green where Eoin MacNeill inspected them. Martin Daly later recalled that Ceannt was in full Volunteer uniform marching at the head of his men. They spoke a few words in Irish. Martin said: 'A great day for Ireland', and Ceannt replied: 'Let us hope so'. [18]

❧

The Uprising was carefully planned and, with any good measure of luck, it might have succeeded, at least in large part, but it didn't.

As the final days ticked off before the planned Easter-Sunday mobilisation, nothing seemed to go right. A ship carrying additional German arms, scheduled to arrive in Co. Kerry, was intercepted by the British navy. Rather than face surrendering his ship, the captain scuttled his vessel at the mouth of Queenstown harbour with all weapons still onboard.

Sir Roger Casement, returning from Germany where he'd tried unsuccessfully to recruit a force of captured Irish prisoners-of-war to return home and fight for Ireland against the English, was himself captured by the RIC at Banna Strand, near Tralee, Co. Kerry.

In an effort to further insulate MacNeill from discovering the plans for the rebellion, Bulmer Hobson, a close associate of his and someone who'd learned of the scheduled insurrection, was kidnapped and held at a safe house.

Finally, a purported 'authentic' Dublin Castle document was discovered, stating that the local authorities were planning a big round-up of Sinn Féin, Volunteer and Irish nationalist activists.

Eoin MacNeill, confused by the last-minute happenings and outraged that Pearse and others had deceived him over the use of the Irish Volunteers, rebelled himself. On Holy Saturday, MacNeill, acting alone and without informing any of those who'd so carefully planned the Uprising, dictated an order countermanding the scheduled 4 PM Easter-Sunday parade.

MacNeill's statement, published in the *Sunday Independent*, read:

> Owing to the very critical position, all orders given to Irish Volunteers for to-morrow, Easter Sunday, are hereby rescinded, and no parades, marches or other movements of Irish Volunteers will take place. Each individual Volunteer will obey this order strictly in every particular. (Signed by himself as Chief of Staff) [19]

Tom and Billy were confused when they read the announcement on Easter Sunday morning. After Mass, the Wicklow man walked over to Ceannt's house. Áine, his wife, answered the door. Recognising Tom, she invited him to come through.

> As the morning wore on, Volunteers of the fourth battalion besieged the house, all seeking an explanation of the countermanding orders they had just read in the morning newspaper. Áine could give them no information, merely saying that the commandant had been called out early and suggested that they should await his return. Soon the drawing-room was uncomfortably filled and the bicycles were stacked four deep in the front garden.
>
> At about 1p.m. Ceannt returned and had a meeting with the men. He instructed them not to leave the

city and that if they left home, even to go for a walk, they were to state where they could be located at short notice. [20]

Later that evening, the two grocery assistants received a message from Ceannt. In his own handwriting, the Galway man simply stated: Tomorrow. 11 am. Emerald Square. Full kit as previously ordered. E. C., Commandant.

❧

Emerald Square was a hundred-yard-long or so cul-de-sac with a right-hand bend partway along its stubby length. The secluded street was just north of the South Circular Road, off Cork Street. A row of compact Victorian brick houses lined both sides of the little square. Most of it was hidden from the view of passersby along the main road. Several hundred men could be easily sequestered in its secure confines. Ceannt had chosen it as his mustering site after careful consideration.

All weekend, loads of rifles and various pieces of military paraphernalia arrived in motor cars and wagons under the safety of darkness and were stored in two of the houses at the back of the square.

❧

Desmond Ryan was a pupil of Patrick Henry Pearse prior to 1916. After graduating, he continued living at St. Enda's while taking classes at University College Dublin. While there, he acted as Pearse's secretary and during the Easter Week Uprising he served in the GPO beside his beloved headmaster. In Ryan's 1949 book, *The Rising*, he offered great insight and personal reflection about the events leading up to and during the fighting.

When Éamonn Ceannt had issued his sudden mobilisation call to the Fourth Battalion at Emerald Square near Dolphin's Barn for an hour before noon, on Easter Monday, he discovered in due course that Sunday's countermand had indeed dispersed his men: of the battalion roll of 1,000 Volunteers less that 200 took part in the Rising in various positions, and of these less than 100 appeared at Emerald Square while Ceannt had little more than sixty Volunteers under him in the South Dublin Union [SDU].

The task set Ceannt and his Vice-Commandant, Cathal Brugha, required, in fact, for its success something more than the skeleton strength they succeeded in mustering. His lieutenants had done their best. As one of them, who received his orders at 10 o'clock, gathered a handful by a wild three-quarter hour dash over a wide and scattered area in South County, Dublin, arrived at Emerald Square just before noon, he found the battalion preparing to march off. Near Harold's Cross Bridge he had passed the men of the Kimmage garrison, exiles all, swinging along with a determined tread, headed by their commanding officer, George Plunkett, armed with an extraordinary variety of weapons, pikes, shotguns and rifles, some wearing gaily-coloured scarfs and wide hats, all tramping resolutely and briskly with an anticipation of adventure in their eyes, if not that day, some day anyway. [21]

Ryan's chapter, detailing the 4th Battalion's role in the Easter-Week fighting, continued:

[Tom Cullen and the other men mustering in]... Emerald Square little suspected that bullets would be whistling round their ears before the hour had passed, and some of them lying dead or wounded in the open fields at Mount Brown, and British soldiers advancing on them to a din of rifles and machine-gun. Yet Ceannt's first words were a very plain statement of what faced them.

Ceannt told his men tersely: "You are in action to-day!" and...that their objective was the South Dublin Union, which lay between Rialto Bridge and James's

Street. It was one of the most important links in the Volunteer chain of positions, a great fifty-two acre cluster of buildings, a position of high strategic value, near at once to Richmond and Islandbridge Barracks, to Kingsbridge Railway Station and, above all, to the British military headquarters in Ireland, the Royal Hospital. [22]

On Easter Monday morning, after enjoying a large breakfast prepared by Mrs. Curtis, Tom and Billy shook hands with Pat Dowling and headed off west along the tree-lined South Circular Road toward Leonard's Corner and beyond to Emerald Square.

Both were dressed in their Volunteer uniforms. As directed, the two carried a day's worth of rations, full arms and equipment. They held their antiquated, German Mauser 'Howth' rifles in a non-military fashion, clutched in their right hands, thigh high. They thought to display them in the military-like slope position might draw unwanted attention or even arrest if stopped by some inquisitive British military personnel.

But due to the nature of the holiday, there were few people and almost no motor vehicles on the road at that mid-morning hour.

Michael McNally added interesting detail to Ryan's words above:

> The 4th City Battalion had arguably been given the hardest task of all to defend against the inevitable British counterattack that was expected to come from the base at the Curragh in Co. Kildare, some 30 miles southwest of Dublin. Commanded by Éamonn Ceannt, probably the most aggressively minded of the four battalion commanders, the unit mustered in the south-western suburb of Dolphin's Barn and was probably the hardest hit by the reduced turn-out of Volunteers, mustering a mere 100 men to occupy the largest of the four battalion areas which, centred on the South Dublin Union, covered the area to the south of Kilmainham.
>
> At about 1000 hrs those Volunteers who had received their changes of orders began to congregate at their various muster points. These ranged from men in

full uniform to those whose sole acquiescence to such regulations lay in the ammunition bandoliers they wore draped over their shoulders or a yellow armband denoting their volunteer membership; from those who carried modern rifles and shotguns to those who bore antique firearms or even home-made pikes, which would have seemed more in place in 1798 than in 1916. [23]

✻

An unidentified 4th Battalion Volunteer's description of the initial events of Easter Monday appeared in a 1966 edition of *The Capuchin Annual.*

The battalion, fully equipped, mobilised at Emerald Square, Dolphin's Barn, on Easter Monday about 11 a.m., and about 11.30 a.m. left in four or five parties. Commandant Kent [Ceannt] with about a dozen cyclists, and followed by about thirty men on foot, proceeded through the "Back-of-the-Pipes" [back of the Guinness Brewery complex] along the canal bank to Rialto bridge. Another group proceeded to the Union by Grand Canal harbour and Ewingstown Lane, and passed in by the front entrance in James's Street. The other parties proceeded respectively to Jameson's distillery in Marrowbone Lane, Watkin's brewery in Ardee Street, and Roe's malt house, Mount Brown.

Commandant Kent's party entered [SDU] at Rialto by the small door at the corner of Brookfield Road, and took possession of the keys despite the expostulations of the amazed gate porter. The telephone wires were also cut. At first the [SDU] officials supposed their visitors were merely engaged in field manoeuvres, but they began to realise the seriousness of the situation when they took up positions and the firing commenced. [24]

✻

Feeling the pressure of having an undermanned force, Ceannt was forced to leave only Captain George Irvine and nine other men to secure the Rialto opening, certainly an inadequate number to hold such a key position.

> The Volunteers occupied a nearby corrugated iron shed. This building was used to house the male mental patients of the Union. It was 300 feet long, twenty-six feet wide and divided into six dormitories by wooden partitions that were connected by narrow corridors. Captain Irvine instructed his men to fortify their position, which they proceeded to do, using mattresses, chairs, tables and bed ends to reinforce walls of the corrugated building. One Volunteer proceeded to dig a slit trench in front of the gate. [25]

Under the leadership of Lieutenant-Colonel R. L. Owens, officers and troopers of the 3rd Battalion of the Royal Irish Regiment [British army] at Richmond Barracks were in action within an hour of the Uprising's commencement.

By one o'clock in the afternoon, the men in the shed were taking fire from the upper stories of houses across the road that faced the Rialto gate. Though the gate itself was well fortified, Lt. Ramsay discovered a secondary entrance, a small wooden door built in the Union's encircling wall.

Ramsay led the first assault and was killed almost instantly. Next, a Captain Warmington organised another breach of the opening. He too was shot to death before his men could establish a foothold inside the Union's perimeter.

But with increased firing from the houses to the west of the Rialto gate and also from buildings across the canal, paralleling the back wall of the Union, the men in the shed were trapped, in a hopeless situation.

To make matters worse, British soldiers had breeched the Union's wall in other locations and were rapidly closing in on the trapped men in the shed.

With a sudden lull in the firing and now surrounded, one of the trapped Volunteers distinctly heard an educated English voice demand, "I will count to five. Either surrender or we are coming in." [26]

Moments later, Captain George Irvine surrendered.

Led out into the open by Irvine, Volunteers Jimmy Morrissey, Willie Corrigan, Seán Dowling and James Burke were taken into custody while Paddy Morrissey, his leg badly wounded, was given much-needed medical treatment.

The 1916 Easter Rebellion and the battle for South Dublin Union had begun.

※

[**Author's note:** For a comprehensive overview of the 1916 Easter Rebellion & for a detailed description of the battle for South Dublin Union, I recommend reading Michael Foy & Brian Barton's The Easter Rising, (2000) & Paul O'Brien's Uncommon Valour: 1916 & the Battle for the South Dublin Union, (2010).]

Back of Dublin Castle

#58 South Circular Road, Dublin

East Pier, Howth, Dublin

#26 Landerdale Terrace, New Row South, Dublin

Emerald Square, Dublin

IRISH REBELLION, MAY, 1916.

CAPTAIN WILLIAM COSGRAVE, T.C.
(DUBLIN).
Sentenced to Death.
Commuted to Penal Servitude for Life.

Lt William 'Willie' T. Cosgrave, c. 1916

The Nurses' Home, South Dublin Union

Mount Brown & north wall of SDU

Back of St. Patrick's Park along Bride St., Dublin

Stonebreaker's Yard, Kilmainham Gaol, Dublin

1916 leaders' mass grave, Arbour Hill Cemetery, Dublin

3

"WE SEEM TO HAVE LOST. WE HAVE NOT LOST."
– PATRICK HENRY PEARSE, IRELAND'S PRESIDENT-
ELECT, RICHMOND BARRACKS, DUBLIN

The tension in Emerald Square was palpable as the bell in a nearby church struck the quarter hour. Tom Cullen double checked his 7.92 mm Howth Mauser G98 [1898] rifle. He had to. His nerves were about to explode and his fine breakfast, recently consumed, felt like a stone in the pit of his stomach.

– Jaysus, I'm not going to throw up right here, am I?

He tried swallowing several times, but his mouth was dry.

– Bloody hell. I can't even spit.

Again, turning his attention to his rifle helped. It took his thoughts off his fear of being sick…it calmed him, helped him feel less anxious.

He'd examined and cleaned the weapon many times.

His particular import was obviously used. Both the butt and stock were nicked up and scratched, but the barrel was unmarked. It gleamed steel-black in the sun shining down on Emerald Square.

– Combat in the Transvaal or maybe just used in training? There was no way of telling.

One thing he did know, it fired straight and true.

Though ammunition was hard to come by, he'd taken full advantage of what there was on the two dozen or so training exercises he'd participated in over the past year and a half. While he wasn't the best shot in the company, he was good enough.

Tom often wondered how hard it would be to hit a man at fifty yards or a hundred. Would his hands shake or his finger refuse to squeeze the trigger? Would the bolt-action work smoothly or would he jam it up? Last month, on his unit's final training excursion in the Dublin Mountains, he suddenly realised he wouldn't have to wait long to find out.

Gripping the barrel, he lifted the Mauser's butt off the ground. It weighed almost nine pounds and was about four feet in length.... well more than half his height.

He checked...the safety was on and the five-round magazine was well slotted. The webbed sling was just as he liked it. He could feel the bayonet in its scabbard, hanging from his belt.

He tugged at the bandoleer across his chest. It was heavy too. He'd been issued one hundred rounds of 8mm ammo and an extra three full magazines, each with its allotment of five shells. They were the newer 'spitzer' bullets with the pointed tips instead of the older blunt, round-shaped ones. They had better long-range ballistic accuracy.

On his back, Tom carried a haversack containing a day's food rations, a flask of water, a change of underwear, a pair of socks and one clean shirt. Additionally, according to orders, he'd added a billy can with knife, fork, spoon, a tin cup for drinking and his rifle's cleaning outfit. Finally, there were several dry sticks squirreled way for starting a fire.

The Wicklow man felt smart in his recently purchased uniform. It fit comfortably, but standing around in the springtime heat, he was sweating and wished he could take off the tunic.

In the jacket's pockets he'd stashed his clasp-knife, a small notebook and pencil, matches in a tin box, boot laces, a good length of stout cord, a candle and coloured handkerchief. Nothing white or shiny could be worn.

Instead of a soft-brimmed Cronje-hat, Tom preferred his old tweed cap and the hobnailed boots on his feet were well broken in.

Looking around the square, Tom nodded to a few of his friends. He'd just walked over to say a word to Billy, when Lt. W. T. Cosgrave suddenly blew his whistle.

– Mind yourself, Billy and for God's sake keep your fecken' head down when the shooting begins.

They both smiled at one another and shook hands. Turning and facing
Cosgrave, they snapped to attention.

※

At 11.35 a.m., the battalion moved out in two parties. The plan was to occupy the South Dublin Union
workhouse as battalion headquarters, along with three
strategically located outposts: Roe's Distillery in Mount
Brown, Watkins' Brewery at Ardee Street and Jameson's
Distillery at Marrowbone Lane. [1]

Thirty-five-year-old Commandant Éamonn Ceannt, a member
of the IRB's Supreme Council, a part of Ireland's newly-organised
provisional government and a signatory of the Proclamation of the
Irish Republic, stepped out with the first group of Volunteers while
Willie Cosgrave headed up the second assemblage. [The five other
4th Battalion companies A, C, D, E & F were mobilising at other
nearby, pre-arranged locations in south Dublin.] As for Coy B:

In order to avoid detection by the authorities, this main
group of Volunteers was led [by Cosgrave] through a
warren of side streets until they reached the front gates
of the South Dublin Union. Lieutenant Cosgrave was
thirty-six years old, a Dublin city councillor and a local
man. [Cosgrave, in fact, lived just across the street from
the Union's entrance at #174 James Street.] Accompa-
nying him was forty-two-year-old Vice-Commandant
Cathal Brugha. A man of great vigour, he was driven
by a relentless determination and his position as vice-
commandant of the 4th Battalion would be crucial in
the coming days. He was known as a patriot and soldier
dedicated to the cause of Irish independence.

As this second group marched to its destination,
small parties detached from the main column and took
up their posts along the route. Each outpost consisted

of an officer and about twenty Volunteers; Captain Con Colbert was detailed to Watkins' Brewery in Ardee Street, Captain Séamus Murphy took up position at Jameson's Distillery in Marrowbone Lane and Captain Thomas McCarthy occupied Roe's Distillery in Mount Brown. These positions were chosen with the aim of preventing British troops from entering the city from the southwest. It was planned that military movements could be checked and halted along the quays of the River Liffey, at Kingsbridge Railway Station (now Heuston Station), and at the headquarters of the British commander-in-chief in Ireland, the Royal Hospital, Kilmainham. [2]

Paul O'Brien in his recently published and well-detailed description of the battle for SDU painted a fine picture of the complex's physical layout:

St. James's Hospital started life as a poorhouse constructed in 1667, becoming a foundling hospital in 1727. In the early nineteenth century the hospital was closed and the structure then became a workhouse called the South Dublin Union, a place for Dublin's destitute, infirm and the insane. The complex was spread over fifty acres and consisted of an array of buildings that in April 1916 housed 3,282 people, including patients, doctors, nurses and ancillary staff. The area, enclosed within a high stone wall, consisted of living quarters, churches, an infirmary, a bakery, a morgue, acres of green space [some of them cultivated as a market garden] and many stone hospital buildings connected by a labyrinth of streets, alleyways and courtyards. [3]

❧

Tom Cullen along with Billy King and about twenty other men followed Cosgrave and Brugha through the main gate from James Street into the vast acreage and complex of buildings known to all as the South Dublin Union. Despite the SDU's vast dimensions, the main entrance, built into an arched, two-story, stone-block opening, was rather modest in size.

Unlike the Rialto entrance, there was no one to overpower on the James Street side. With the gate unmanned, Willie Cosgrave's men entered without a challenge.

Though the first stages of the battle were at the opposite end of the huge compound, already medical staff and white-robed patients in dressing gowns could be seen running in and out of buildings.

Cries and shrieks from a nearby structure, housing mentally ill patients, could be heard. Tom imagined the terror they must be experiencing with the Volunteers' unexpected advance.

A man, probably a doctor or medical supervisor, rushed up to Lt. Cosgrave and demanded to know the reason for this incursion. Between shouting out orders to his men, the Volunteer officer curtly explained that his men were following orders and it would be best if he directed his personnel and patients to seek cover and stay clear of all windows.

– For your safety and the safety of your people, don't interfere. Move to the protection of basements or inside rooms. In a short time, the British army will be attacking these grounds and there'll be armed combat in this very square. If you disregard my orders, you and many others likely will be killed or seriously wounded.

The man stared wide-eyed at Willie. Suddenly, disbelief turned to understanding and he ran off, shouting his own orders to some unseen persons.

Tom Cullen and a group of others immediately occupied the administrative rooms above the Union's wooden gate. To the right of this suite of offices was the South Dublin Rural District Council headquarters. Also forming part of the surrounding stone-wall perimeter were other adjacent buildings, housing patient wards, a paint shop and bakery.

Following orders, the invading Volunteers broke out the glass windows and barricaded their openings with office furniture, ledger books, mattresses and anything else that might stop a bullet. Next, they began tunnelling through the block's walls to facilitate free access from one area to the next. This meant the Irish rebels could roam from one end of the stone-block complex to the other without ever going outside. Doing so would've meant exposing themselves to British-enemy gunfire.

Other members of the invading party blocked and barricaded the main gate. They unloaded a horse-drawn dray filled with hand-grenades, barbed wire for fencing and construction tools, and then used the heavy, sideless cart to help block the entrance. Next, soil from the adjacent gardens was shovelled into waiting boxes and empty sacks, all to strengthen the gate's fortification.

Cosgrave's Witness Statement, given over three decades later, noted that unlike his charges, Captain Irvine and his men assigned to hold the Rialto Gate were engaged by the enemy almost immediately. Many of the other Volunteers, who'd poured through that south-western end of the complex at Ceannt's command, advanced forward to occupy the open ground known as McCaffrey Estate and further on to the northwest corner of the Union, to a point overlooking the main road into Dublin along Mount Brown.

[**Author's note:** It was common practice in the 1700s to name a street after its most respected or successful resident. Mr. Valentino (also spelled Valentine) Browne, a brewer and the richest businessman in Dublin, resided in this Kilmainham neighbourhood.]

Of McCaffrey Estate, the future first-President of the Executive Council of the Irish Free State said:

> These fields, 8 or 10 acres in extent, were a series of irregular elevations, tapering down steeply to Mount Brown and frontaging practically all Mount Brown (which connected Old Kilmainham with James's St.). Volunteer instructions were to engage any British military entering the city. They had not long to wait and the story given to us of the fight was that the first fire of the Volunteers caused panic, which was shortly checked by a non-commissioned officer. Numbers were unequal. Volunteers had no cover; the British soldiers had the houses opposite the McCaffrey Estate. Here we suffered our first casualties.... Nurse Keogh, attached

to the hospital, S.D.U., was killed by British fire – it was generally conceded – accidentally. [4]

Lt. Cosgrave further noted:

Vice-Commandant Brugha did not go with this section towards McCaffrey's fields or Rialto. He had taken up a position some 200 yards east of the main gate in a wooden structure, apparently quarters for some of the staff of the workhouse. Having pointed out how vulnerable this position was he wanted to find better. Eventually I suggested the Nurses' Home, a three-story stone structure in a commanding position. To this he agreed and we went into occupation; some time afterwards we heard that the enemy had rushed the area first vacated by the Vice-Commandant and that some of our Volunteers carried out a hasty retreat. [5]

With the main gate barricaded and its upper suite of offices overlooking James Street occupied, attention turned to readying the Nurses' Home for defence.

Tom, Billy and a score of others repeated their window-breaking and barricading efforts just completed across the building's small courtyard, facing the main entrance.

All the energy Tom had expended in hauling supplies and barricading windows seemed to settle his nerves. In fact, he began asking after if there was any tea about or possibly some sandwiches.

❧

With their HQ situated perpendicularly to the main gate and its surrounding wall, the Volunteers stationed at the front of the building could cover the main entrance and its courtyard. Those Irishmen posted at the rear of the building had a fine view of most of the Union's vast acreage…from the far Rialto Gate, down through the grounds of McCaffrey Estate, the Orchard Fields and the Master's Fields with their gardens bordered on the north by Mount Brown. This road headed east into Dublin and west past

Kilmainham Gaol on the hill, through the village of Inchicore and eventually out to Richmond Barracks about two miles away.

Just off to the north, the occupying Volunteers could see the massive Royal Hospital, Kilmainham. This grand seventeenth-century, classically designed building with its considerable courtyard had been home to infirmed, maimed and/or retired Irish soldiers who'd served in the British army since 1680. Unceremoniously nicknamed 'the Old Man's Home,' it also served as GHQ for the British army in Ireland. Now with the outbreak of the noon Uprising, a machine gun had been installed on its roof. Early on after its occupation, the South Dublin Union Volunteers began taking deadly fire from the building's lofty perch.

Amazingly and to their great credit, the Union's staff carried on their duties of caring for patients under what became one of the most dangerous duty stations imaginable. The sick, the elderly and the confused were organised into small groups under the supervision of the Union's staff. Making sure everyone was properly clothed, the patients were moved to the safest possible accommodation. Those unable to walk stayed in their wards, but staff members covered the windows with mattresses to protect them from possible flying glass.

The calm, dedicated reassurance of the Union's personnel saved the day, allowing both patients and staff to function as normally as possible.

As Paul O'Brien aptly noted:

> Within the Union, officials and hospital staff remained at their posts and nurses removed the patients to safer quarters. Red Cross flags were draped from the windows of the buildings that still held staff and patients. Throughout the week the work of the institution continued, despite the chaos. [6]

❧

With defensive preparations completed, Tom and Billy took up their top-floor posts at the rear of the Nurses' Home. The battlefield lay before them. The sounds of gunfire and the rhythmic tat-tat-tat of the machine gun on the Royal Hospital were punctuated with the periodic explosions of hand-grenades. Occasionally, they could hear someone shouting out an order or the scream of a combatant who'd likely been wounded.

The 1966 *Capuchin Annual* noted that at no time during Easter Week did Commandant Ceannt have more than sixty-five Volunteers under his command within the confines of SDU. Besides facing a lack of manpower, the volunteers were desperately short of ammunition. Initially, their three thousand rounds seemed extravagant to the Volunteers, who'd often done without during training exercises, but with the battle becoming more intense, it became clear they might soon run short.

[**Author's note:** If Éamonn Ceannt had had his full complement of the seven hundred Volunteers at his disposal instead of the roughly one-hundred-plus 4th Battalion men who turned out on Easter Monday, he very well could have held out indefinitely.]

❦

As the afternoon wore on and more British troops flooded in from the west, the battle for the Union reached a fevered pitch.

> The rear of the Volunteer headquarters in the Nurses' Home was raked by a terrible concentration of rifle fire, and at the same time the [British] attackers swept into the grounds from Rialto and several other points and, covered by repeated volleys, converged rapidly on the insurgent H.Q. There was also a very brisk exchange of shots with the Marrowbone Lane Distillery garrison which opened a murderous and heavy fire on the party advancing along the opposite canal bank where the stretchers were soon busy carrying off the many casualties. There were many casualties, too, as the attackers advanced, for the Volunteer snipers at the windows fired repeatedly, perforce recklessly exposing themselves, so terrific and constant was the concentration of British rifle fire on their position. The volume

of fire poured into the rear of the Nurses' Home was almost overwhelming, the din was ear-shattering and unnerving, and no man felt his chance of survival could be estimated in more than minutes.[7]

Billy had just returned from a fruitless search for more ammunition when he was hit. Possibly distracted for a moment, forgetting where he was, or maybe just the victim of an unlucky, random shot, Tom heard the bullet hit soft flesh...'thud.' Instantly, the West Wicklow man jerked his head around to look in Billy's direction.

– *Oh my God, NO, NO, NO...,* thought Tom.

Billy opened his mouth to scream, but no sound came.

But even in that instant, it was too late. Billy's eyes had glassed over. A gargle of air rushed from his throat and his knees sagged. In less than a handful of heartbeats, his friend of five years collapsed on the floor...dead.

Tom couldn't believe what he'd just witnessed. Stunned and horrified, he stared at Billy's lifeless body. With the room spinning before his eyes, Tom crawled to his friend's side, laid his head on Billy's chest and cried.

His tears stained Billy's unbuttoned tunic and ran into the ever enlarging circle of red spreading across his khaki shirt. Softly, Tom whispered a Hail Mary and said an Act of Contrition.

Turning to look into Billy King's face, he reached up and closed the dead man's eyes. After straightening his friend's body and placing his hands together across his stomach, Tom edged to the room's door and yelled out, – Help! Billy's been hit. He's dead. Can someone get a priest? Please God, and hurry....

Billy's tragic, unexpected death shook Tom to the core. It was one thing to dislike, even hate the Sassenach, their cursed colonial overlords, but looking down and seeing his friend lying dead on floor, just a few feet away, knowing that an English bullet had robbed him of life, brought a sense of reality to the abstractions that served to define his reason for being part of this fight.

Ten or fifteen minutes passed. A constant spray of machine-gun rounds pinged off the outside wall of the Nurses' Home, many around his window. When the projectiles hit the heavy wooden table Billy and he had jammed into its opening, they made more of a 'splatting' sound as opposed to the sharper 'zinging' reverberations they made glancing off the building's granite-stone blocks.

Two Cumann na mBan girls and a hospital-staff attendant dressed in a white coat finally arrived to take Billy's body away. Quickly crossing himself, Tom watched the stretcher bearers carry his friend down the hall.

Alone for the first time in his third-floor room, Tom thought, — *My God, what thankless bravery these three just showed. Daring this unceasing fusillade of ricocheting death that's raining down on this buildings while never flinching a moment. Their unremitting courage and gallantry are certainly beyond measure. We, the Volunteers, have stoked the fires of death, and moments later, they're face to face with its bitter residue.*

Tom's admiration for the tasks these women and Union staff undertook, all in the face of their own deaths, touched him deeply.

— *They are living and fighting for Ireland's cause just as gallant Billy fought and died for it too. God bless them one and all.*

Suddenly thoughts of Billy's family back in King's County grabbed at Tom's attention.

— *If I ever survive this, I'll write and tell them all about our friendship, the grocery and his unquestioned bravery.*

❦

Trying to clear his head, Tom returned to his window. Kneeling on the floor, he peered through the small crack between the desk and the window frame. The narrow loophole offered a view of Mount Brown and some of the houses lining its road.

There was no foot or motor-vehicle traffic to be seen, but occasionally puffs of white smoke would erupt from one of the opposing houses' windows. Taking careful aim, Tom squeezed off an answering shot. He had no idea if his projectile hit home from that distance, but he hoped it had…for Ireland and for Billy's sake.

❦

Throughout Monday afternoon and evening, the fighting became general. Some of it was conducted at long range while other attacks involved hand-to-hand combative encounters.

On Monday, about 5 p.m., some fifty [British] soldiers attacked the women's Catholic hospital from which the patients had been cleared. Ward 17, which intersects ward 16 at right angles, was occupied by the Volunteers. Entering ward 16, the military, approaching the closed door at the point of intersection, called upon the Volunteers to surrender, at the same time firing several shots through the wooden partition which separated the parties. The officer in command stipulated he would count five before bursting in. As he proceeded to count, the Volunteers rushed to the other end of the ward, burst open a door by firing into the lock, and retreated through another vacated building, No. 4. The military followed, firing as they went; but the whole part of Volunteers safely reached headquarters, whilst the [British] military occupied wards 16 and 17 all Monday night.

On Monday and Tuesday, the military partially occupied the south of the Union and penetrated for some distance into the main group of buildings, but appeared to have withdrawn altogether on Wednesday. [8]

❧

Communicating between groups of Volunteers was virtually impossible. Asking men to move from building to building or cross open ground was just too dangerous.

During the Union's first twenty-four hours of occupation, the attackers gradually began retreating from their initial scattered positions toward the Nurses' Home and its adjacent buildings facing the front-gate courtyard. The obvious exceptions were those who'd been killed, wounded or captured. Thus, the number of men inside the HQ had increased significantly. One count totalled forty-two.

❧

On Tuesday evening, Ceannt sent two messengers outside the Union's wall in an effort to make contact with the men stationed in

Roe's Malt House across the road in Mount Brown. After a daring sprint, they arrived to learn that Captain Tom McCarthy and his men had vacated their post. With no rations, little am- munition and feeling isolated, the twenty men disbanded, knowing they could not hold the building. Instead of remaining in the fight and reinforcing Ceannt's men inside the Union, most of the Mount Brown men simply melted away into the night.

Likewise, Captain Cornelius 'Con' Colbert and his Volunteers at Watkin's Brewery on Ardee Street left their post under cover of darkness early on Wednesday morning.

According to the July, 1918 issue of *The Catholic Bulletin*:

> Com. [Commandant] Colbert who was stationed at Watkin's Brewery in Ardee Street, had learned on Tuesday that the men of the 2nd Battalion holding Barmack's factory at Blackpitts, had retired. Considering his own position ineffective, he sent to Major [John] McBride, at Jacob's [Biscuit Factory on Bishop Street], for instructions. The Major directed him to reinforce the party at Marrowbone Lane. Consequently about 6 a.m. on Wednesday the garrison at Jameson's Distillery was augmented by Colbert's command consisting of about fifteen men. [9]

Of Colbert's move to Marrowbone Lane, Desmond Ryan added:

> [They] joined the Marrowbone Lane garrison, which included seven Fianna boys and twenty-three members of Cumann na mBan, and about 100 Volunteers or more towards the end of the fighting through various additions, although the original party which took over the place [Marrowbone Lane distillery] on Monday numbered only twenty. [10]

The most impenetrable outpost was the Marrowbone Lane Distillery. It was the second largest distillery [Jameson Whiskey] in the city, with its name a corruption of St. Mary Le Bone.

Robert Holland, a Volunteer who'd fought at the distillery during Easter Week, described the outpost in his Witness Statement:

> It was about 3 p.m. [Monday afternoon] when we arrived in the Distillery. They were all in good spirits there and they had posted the small garrison that they [Captain Séamus Murphy & others] had to the best advantage, one man to each room. The rooms were like dormitories about 80 feet long by about 40 feet wide. These rooms were used as stores for kiln-drying wheat. The building lay between Marrowbone Lane at one end, Forbis (sic) Lane on one side and the [Grand] Canal in front. At the right-hand bend side was the 'Back of the Pipes'. There were eight windows on each side of each room with ceilings about 9 feet high. There was a lot of air ventilators in each wall about 12 inches from the floor level and these had small wooden shutters which could be pulled to one side. The walls of the buildings were about 2 feet thick, and we used the ventilators as port holes to fire out through. [11]

The massive building was described in the July, 1918 issue of *The Catholic Bulletin* as being "...the giant sky-scraper, the malt house which stands at the Harbour." It offered an excellent view of the back end or southern perimeter of the Union. With British soldiers rushing into the SDU grounds via the Rialto Gate or by scaling the surrounding back wall, Holland and his comrades easily picked them off one by one.

Those troopers strategically positioned in houses outside the walled perimeter were not as vulnerable. They continued raining rifle fire down on the Volunteers positioned inside the Union.

> The battle went on with retreats and advances by the [Irish] invaders. On Monday and Tuesday the British had occupied the southern part of the Union grounds

and advanced on the main group of buildings, and then retired confused and uncertain on the Wednesday. Over the wide spaces of the South Dublin Union and through the many buildings the bloody games of hide-and-seek went aimlessly on. There was tunnelling and counter-tunnelling through walls, and unexpected meetings, with hand-to-hand encounters of the British and the Volunteers. Ceannt, Mauser in hand, took part in several of these fights. Sometimes both sides occupied the same building with only a partition wall between them. Fatal shots lurked round every corner of the many intersecting passages. Sometimes the advancing British soldiers lost their way and ran into a burst of rifle fire from Volunteer guards at some window beneath which they passed unsuspectingly. [12]

❊

Tom was near exhaustion on Wednesday. He'd had very little sleep, only a catnap here and there. The incessant, mind-numbing reverberations of gunfire never seemed to stop. Scarcely a minute of quiet would pass before another round of angry outbursts would erupt. On occasions his Mauser's barrel became so hot he couldn't touch it. At those times, he used Billy's. Though they were identical, his felt differently and Tom was always glad when his cooled enough to safely handle again.

On Wednesday, during an early morning lull when he was fighting sleep, a motor car rolled to a stop as it neared the top of Mount Brown. There it was…a perfect target right before his eyes. At first he thought it was a dream then a mirage. But no, three soldiers jumped out and tried to push the vehicle backwards down the gradual incline. Obviously, they realised they were in grave danger of being shot and wanted to retreat with the auto and their lives intact.

Tom wasn't the only one to see the stranded men. Maybe the car was out of petrol, but why risk running such a gauntlet? Had the men taken drink and lost their senses or were they carrying some vital message that required immediate delivery? Tom didn't take the time to answer his own queries, he just squeezed the trigger.

The moment his rifle spoke...four, five, six other shots rang out.

The three khaki-clad interlopers fell like saplings from the swing of a woodsman's sharpened axe.

Tom wasn't sure if he'd hit one of them, but it didn't matter. Those three were out of the fight, maybe permanently.

There was just one more piece of unfinished business. Taking careful aim at the windscreen of the vehicle, exactly where the outline of its driver might be, he fired again.

He saw the glass shatter. Moments later, the head and shoulder of a soldier, slumping against the door, appeared in the vehicle's open window.

Almost imperceptibly, the auto inched backwards a few more feet and gently came to a halt against the curb.

Someone from the floor below yelled, – Up the Republic, you bastards.

The cry rang out again followed by – Up the rebels!

Tom turned and slid to the floor, his back up against the wall.

– *So that's it! An eye for an eye,* he thought to himself.

– *That one's for you Billy and may there be a good few more.*

❧

The handful of the Cumann na mBan women who'd managed to make their way into the Nurses' House on Monday deserved medals...all of them. Besides organising the kitchen and providing a limited menu of boiled meat and potatoes supplemented by buckets of tea, they cleaned and loaded rifles for the men, stood guard duty and some even took turns on the firing line as men rested.

> Even behind the Volunteer defences it was difficult to maintain proper contact between the defenders as the hurricane of bullets howled in through the windows at all angles. Even to pass up and down the stairs meant

taking a dangerous risk, a risk which could be only taken by making a desperate dash for it. [But] the spirit of Ceannt and Cathal Brugha dominated the determined Volunteer defence, which was not broken at headquarters until circumstances gave the British on Thursday an unusually capable commander who hemmed in the Volunteers and held them until the surrender [on Sunday, the 30th]. Of Ceannt it was remarked that he asked no one to carry out an order that he would not readily have obeyed himself from the moment he raised the Tricolour over the Union [on Monday, the 24th] until the moment he surrendered. His Vice-Commandant, Cathal Brugha, had had such a spirit and indifference to danger that those who shared his risks said of him that he walked into death-traps with a jest, and a force radiated from him that scorched up the very fear of death. [13]

❦

Tired, hungry, weary of war and the victims of poor communication, the twenty-seven officers and men inside the Nurses' Home almost made a fatal error on Thursday evening. Confused about one of Ceannt's orders and reacting to the cry, "*They're in!*" most of the defenders in the Union's HQ began withdrawing to the rooms over the main James's Street gate.

Surreptitiously, the British had managed to successfully tunnel into the Volunteers' headquarters from an adjacent building composed of patient wards. Breaking through, the British found themselves in the front hallway of the Nurses' Home.

The Volunteers, anticipating such an incursion, had built a five-foot-high barricade below an archway leading to a hall that extended down both to the left and right.

Brugha, the last man following the erroneous evacuation order, was passing a kitchen door when a soldier lobbed a grenade over the barricade. Its explosion blew a hole in the barricade as well as showering the Vice-commandant with shrapnel.

Severely wounded, he dragged himself through the kitchen and outside into a small courtyard. With his back propped against the yard's brick wall, Cathal Brugha, gripping an automatic Mauser pistol in one hand, could see through the open kitchen door out into the front hallway.

As the British tried advancing on his position, Cathal fired. The soldiers fired back.

Though wounded numerous times, Brugha managed, single-handedly, to beat back the enemy's attack.

Ceannt waited and waited for his second-in-command to join the rest of his men in the adjacent building. Finally, from the Nurses' Home a weak but determined voice could be heard singing the words to a familiar song: *God save Ireland said the heroes, God save Ireland said we all....*

Desmond Ryan described what happened next.

> A scout was sent back towards the singer, and returned with the news that Cathal Brugha was in the yard and still alive. The Volunteers, headed by Ceannt, rushed back. He was sitting in a pool of his own blood, which... must have covered some four square yards. Brugha's uniform was splashed with blood around his many wounds [25 of them] and he was still singing in a weak but defiant voice, stopping at intervals to challenge the British to come on, promising them he would always find a bullet for them no matter how wounded he was, demanding to know whether there was any British officer brave enough to come out and fight a Volunteer.
>
> [Later] Brugha was carried away, his wounds still bleeding, still speaking bold words of encouragement to his comrades. (On Friday he was removed to the Union hospital on a stretcher, and later arrested by the British, taken to Dublin Castle hospital from which he was released uncharged as his captors imagined his wounds were incurable.) [14]

❧

With the Volunteers back in control of their HQ, the British again tried storming the Nurses' Home. For two hours Thursday evening, the two sides went at each other with such ferocity that Tom thought the building would collapse from the number of the explosions set off within its granite confines.

In total darkness, the two sides waged a war with one another of titanic proportions. As Ryan stated:

> There was bombing and volleying, and counter bombing and volleying in the darkness between the British and the Volunteers, and the combatants could not see each other. Volunteers lay flat on the landing of the stairs blazing away with revolvers at the top of the barricade in a continuous barrage to keep the storming party from crossing. Canister bomb after canister bomb was hurled towards the spot from which the British alone could enter. In the end the Volunteers were the victors and the British once again withdrew.
>
> From Thursday night until the general surrender, Ceannt and his men remained in the South Dublin Union in comparative peace. There was no further general attack nor was it until Sunday morning that the garrison knew that the insurrection was over. [15]

Those two hours of living through the fires of hell influenced Tom Cullen's thinking for the rest of his days. He would never forget the ferociousness and wanton disregard for human life that the British displayed that night. He knew if he was ever to survive any future encounter with the 'forces of the crown,' he would have to battle them with an equally determined dedication or they would surely destroy him and Ireland in an all consuming flame, a living Dante's Inferno.

❧

There was a general lull in the fighting on Friday.

On Saturday the 29th the British military vacated the immediate area, pulling back all their forces from any contact with the

4th Battalion Volunteers in both the Union and the Marrowbone Lane distillery.

In the Nurses' Home, Ceannt and Cosgrave and the other Volunteers made hurried attempts to reinforce their battered barricades and defences.

Tom Cullen was assigned to inventory the unit's nearly depleted munitions. Canister bombs, unspent shells, serviceable rifles and revolvers were tallied. The results were alarming. Every man had at least one weapon, but the number of available rounds totalled little more than a dozen per Volunteer.

Rumour told them the Sassenach were girding their loins for one more all-out assault, one the Volunteers were afraid they'd not be able to repulse.

When Tom reported his findings to Ceannt, his OC simply smiled and said, – Sure we'll give them a good run for their money, won't we, Tom?

Not only had communications within the Union been nearly impossible during the week, Éamonn Ceannt had received no communiqués from GHQ positioned in the GPO on Sackville Street since Tuesday.

Alarmingly too, something the men of the 4th Battalion couldn't fail to notice, was the reddening glow radiating from the city centre after nightfall. By Thursday evening the intensity of the eerie light had grown brighter as had the sounds of artillery shelling. On Friday night, flames could be seen dotting the skyline. The hope of rumoured German forces landing in Dublin harbour or of Volunteers from down the country coming to their aid had all but disappeared. Despite Ceannt's noble efforts to buck up their spirits, a growing sense of doom spread throughout the Nurses' Home.

❧

But with Saturday's British withdrawal, the feeling in the Marrowbone distillery remained optimistic. Their fighting numbers had slowly increased during the week. From the initial twenty or so occupying Volunteers on Monday, the weekend count showed almost one hundred men and some forty Cumann na mBan women.

On Wednesday, men and women from Colbert's Ardee Street brewery helped swell the distillery's numbers as did the arrival of others who'd finally decided, now at the last minute, to take part despite being previously assigned to other areas of the city.

In fact, the mood of those within the distillery was so positive that a céilidh had been planned for Sunday evening. But all that changed dramatically on Sunday.

In the words of Lt. W. T. Cosgrave:

> On Low Sunday Comdt. [Thomas] MacDonagh with a flag of Truce, and Very Rev. Augustine and Aloysius came to the South Dublin Union. MacDonagh gave Kent [Ceannt] information about the military situation, which briefly was to the effect that Pearse and Connolly had surrendered when it was no longer possible to hold the Post Office nor to escape. My recollection, which is hazy, is that Ceannt was not favourable to surrender, and found support amongst some of the Volunteers. A conference took place and it was pointed out that with the limited resources available, resistance was useless and would involve loss of life to no purpose. While leaders might receive scant consideration, there was at least a prospect of the lives of the general body of Volunteers being saved. Eventually there was a general acquiescence to surrender. [British] Captain Rotheram accepted our surrender. [16]

Of the surrender at Marrowbone distillery, Annie Ryan, in her book *Witness: Inside the Easter Rising*, noted, "Half an hour later, Ceannt, a British army officer [possibly Captain Rotheram] and a priest [Fr. Aloysius] arrived. The ritual of surrender commenced."

Annie Ryan continued by quoting Robert Holland's Witness Statement.

Colbert blew his whistle to assemble his Company in the yard when all came down…. He brought us to attention and numbered us off. Ceannt, the British army officer and the priest had withdrawn to the front gate. Colbert then announced that we were surrendering unconditionally and that anyone wishing to go or escape could do so. [17]

❧

Volunteer Liam Ó Flaithbheartaigh, a member of Tom Cullen's B Coy, briefly described the Sunday afternoon surrender scene in the courtyard in front of the Nurses' Home.

On Sunday a Capuchin Priest accompanied Commandant [Thomas] MacDonagh to speak to Commandant Ceannt. That afternoon our Commandant [Ceannt] told us of the Order. We marched out of the South Dublin Union with our full equipment across to Marrowbone Lane, where we joined that garrison; thence to Bull Alley Street [adjacent to St. Patrick's Park] where we were all assembled [including members of the 2nd Battalion stationed at nearby Jacob's Biscuit Factory]. Our names were taken by a British Officer, our rifles and revolvers and all equipment left on the ground. [18]

Poignantly, Paul O'Brien provided more detail of Ceannt's surrender.

A British officer, O'Brien speculated it may have been Major Sir Francis Fletcher Vane of the Royal Munster Fusiliers stationed at Portobello British Barracks, and a priest were seen conversing with Ceannt. Supposedly, the officer complimented Ceannt on his choice of headquarters.

The Galwegian was heard to reply, "Yes, and we made full use of it. Not alone did we hold your army for six days but shook it to its foundation." [19]

Earlier, Paul O'Brien had aptly observed:

Members of the 4th Battalion of the Irish Volunteers under the command of Commandant Éamonn Ceannt, had successfully repulsed numerous attacks by superior numbers of British crown forces and held their position within the South Dublin Union and its outlying posts for six consecutive days. Sunday would be their seventh. [20]

Of the surrender scene at SDU, Piaras F. Mac Lochlainn wrote:

McDonagh (sic) having returned and having informed Lowe [Brigadier-General William Lowe, OC of British forces in Dublin] of the decision to surrender, and having formally surrendered himself, it was agreed that he should go back to the South Dublin Union and call also to Marrowbone Lane Distillery to arrange the surrender of those Garrisons. "When we returned to the South Dublin Union," continues Father Aloysius, "Éamonn Ceannt, speaking to the officer at the door of the Union, remarked that it would surprise him to see the small number who had held the place."

Desmond Ryan, referring to this incident, quotes Sir Francis Vane, who was in command of the British forces in the area, as having asked Ceannt "in amazement whether the main building had been held with only forty men" and Ceannt as having replied gently: "No. Forty-two." [21]

[**Author's note:** A few weeks after the Easter Uprising's collapse, Major Francis Vane, the officer in charge of defending the SDU was relieved of his command and unceremoniously dismissed from the British army.]

With Commandant Éamonn Ceannt marching at the head of his band, forty-one Irish soldiers [the forty-second being Vice-commandant Cathal Brugha, who presently lay in hospital] left the Union grounds via the Rialto gate. They crossed the Grand canal over the Rialto bridge and marched east to the grounds of the Marrowbone Lane distillery. Waiting for Ceannt were Captains

Séamus Murphy and Con Colbert and their one hundred or so Volunteers.

[**Author's note:** Little is written of the fate of the Cumann na mBan women posted to Marrowbone Lane or the SDU. When queried, Paul O'Brien explained: "Rose McNamara was the officer in charge of the women. At the time of the surrender, the Volunteers told them 'to make a break for it.' They refused. Instead, McNamara approached a British officer and told him who she was. The man accepted her surrender and the women were marched to Richmond Barracks/Kilmainham Gaol." O'Brien concluded his reply by stating: "I'd say a few ended up at the (St. Patrick's) park."] [22]

O'Brien's speculation was confirmed by the observation of Fr. Aloysius, O.F.M.Cap. (Order of Friars Minor Capuchin), who was present at surrender.

> When we [Fr. Augustine & himself] reached St. Patrick's Park, we saw Éamonn Ceannt's contingent arrive from the South Dublin Union and ground their arms under his command. *It included girls, some of them armed.* (CL's emphasis)] [23]

❧

From the Jameson Distillery, Ceannt led his men down Marrowbone Lane, up Cork Street, over Ardee Street to The Coombe. From there, the men turned left onto St. Patrick's Street, passed the cathedral and park to their right and made a right wheel at Bride Road, stopping to ground their arms either in front of the Iveagh Baths [Bride Road] or around the corner on Bride Street at the back of St. Patrick Park. The surrendered weaponry was loaded into hand carts then quickly transferred to waiting British lorries and driven off.

So it was there on a little-used, Dublin backstreet, in the shadow of Dean Jonathan Swift's cathedral, Ceannt's proud men joined Tom MacDonagh's loyal Volunteers from Jacob's, as both Dublin's 2nd and 4th Battalions collectively surrendered.

In her Easter Rising book, Annie Ryan added her own description of the surrender scene:

On either side of Bride Street, the British soldiers stood two deep, with fixed bayonets. Machine-guns were posted facing them, and more British soldiers closed in behind them. At Iveagh Baths, Colbert surrendered his command, and a British officer gave the order 'for us to lay down all our arms on the road in front of us.' [24]

In his Witness Statement, William Cosgrave remembered:

At Bride Road a British Officer and a junior Officer came to enquire and to record the names of each Volunteer who was unarmed. This was the method adopted at the subsequent Courtmartial (sic) to prove that those whose names were not on this "unarmed" list were armed. After having deposited arms, orders were issued… [25]

Another Capuchin priest, intimately involved in the surrender negotiations, was Father Augustine. Dramatically he wrote:

They did not arrive [at St. Patrick's Park] and I began to wonder what was causing the delay. In about fifteen minutes, however, we saw the South Dublin Union Garrison marching in, and at once my eye caught sight of the 'magnificent?' [possibly, but a word is missing from manuscript] figure of the leader.

The whole column marched splendidly with guns slung from their left shoulders and their hands swinging freely at their sides. They wore no look of defeat, but rather of a victory. It seemed as if they had come out to celebrate a triumph and were marching to receive a decoration. Ceannt was in the middle of the front 'row?' [again, a word is missing from manuscript] with one man on either side. But my eyes were riveted on him so tall was his form, so noble his bearing, and so manly his stride. He was indeed the worthy captain of a brave band who had fought a clean fight for Ireland. [26]

W. T. Cosgrave recorded that immediately following the grounding of their weapons, the large group of Volunteers reversed and, now under British military escort, marched up Werburgh Street to Christchurch Place and on to High Street, Thomas Street, James Street, past his family home and the main entrance to South Dublin Union. They then tramped on to Richmond Barracks.

[**Author's note:** Volunteer Robert Holland remembered marching to Richmond via Patrick Street, Nicholas Street and then on to Christ Church Place before entering the High Street, Thomas Street, etc. These differences in remembrances are of little consequence.]

On their journey to detention at Richmond British military barracks, Cosgrave remembered only the occasional 'non-complimentary' observations from by-standees while Holland stated the Volunteers around him were 'jeered at.'

> This was the first time I ever appreciated the British troops, as they undoubtedly saved us from being manhandled that evening, and I was very glad as I walked in at the gate of Richmond Barracks. [27]

❧

Sean O Mahony stated there were approximately 1,650 men and women 'out' in Dublin in 1916. Among some of the deployed garrisons were 412 at the GPO, 312 around the Four Courts, 188 at Jacob's, 120 in Marrowbone Lane and 57 at SDU. Of the 1,650, about 150 women were actively involved, "…cooking, dispatch carrying and first aid." [28]

❧

Tom Cullen marched with his comrades near the front of the Volunteers' column. Just ahead of him was Con Colbert. The youthful-looking officer was only two years his senior. Like himself, Colbert had joined the IV in November, 1913. Several years prior, he'd joined the Fianna Éireann and, after meeting Patrick Pearse, had served as a drill instructor at St. Enda's school, helping train the students. Though they'd met on several occasions,

Tom knew little about him, except that Colbert was a Pioneer [the Pioneer Total Abstinence Association of the Sacred Heart] so he neither drank nor smoked. What he did know was that Colbert was well liked and respected among the men in the ranks.

Bone weary and thoroughly crestfallen, Tom managed to keep up a good false front. He knew Ceannt, Cosgrave and the others were doing the same.

The months before had been full of hope and national pride. The thought that England might knuckle under and grant Ireland its independence, especially in light of the war going on in Europe, now seemed naive. Sure, the might of the British Empire wasn't going to concede feck-all to little, old Ireland even though England said one of the reasons she was fighting in France was for the 'rights of small nations.'

– *Wasn't Ireland a small nation…?*

– *Well, listen you bloody Hun-hunters*, thought Tom, *Ireland IS a small nation and we deserve to be free of your damn interference. Enough of your bloody 'Rule Britannia.'*

Looking around him, he could see the dejection on the dirt-stained faces of the others.

– *I can only guess they're thinking the same thoughts I am…God bless them one and all….*

– *Sure we put up a good fight; gave the Tommies all they could swallow and more, but in the end, what did we achieve? Not much. Yes, we did make a political statement to the world that we deserve our freedom, but who really cares? Who's listening to our plaintive cry?*

As the column of prisoners passed St. Catherine's church on Thomas Street, some Volunteer began singing *The Soldier's Song*. Soon, the entire body of Irish soldiers joined in. It had become the 'national anthem' of the Union during the week and its verses sung many times.

Passing the church, Tom and most of the others crossed themselves. For it was on this spot in September, 1803 that the British hanged Robert Emmet for organising his ill-fated rebellion against the Crown earlier that summer.

– *Would he and these men around him suffer the same fate? Hanged or shot to death for their Easter Week actions?*

Somehow, Tom thought the world wouldn't permit the English to execute thousands of men and women for their part in this week's aborted Uprising.

– No, they wouldn't…could they? No, no, no…impossible. Such behaviour was unthinkable. But what they could do and probably would do is cull out a few of the leaders and put them on the block, as an example to the world that 'might win out over right.'

Too tired to carry on a conversation with himself, Tom simply concentrated on putting one foot in front of the next. He knew where he was going…Richmond Barracks. At least he might have something to eat and a soft floor to sleep on. Tomorrow would come soon enough. He longed to have another crack at the sons-of-bitches. This week had transformed him…from a simple grocer's clerk and part-time Irish nationalist to a hardened, much more determined Irish revolutionary.

❧

Willie Cosgrave remembered well his first night of incarceration at Richmond Barracks.

> On arrival at Richmond Barracks some 60 of us were put into a barrack room in which there was no furniture and no ventilation. On opening the door in the morning the British Sergeant was almost overcome by the atmosphere. For breakfast a bucket containing tea and a basket with hard biscuit rations were brought in. The biscuits were tumbled out on the floor; empty corned-beef tins were used as tea-containers. Later, prisoners were marched to the gymnasium, placed on the righthand (sic) side of the room and told to sit down. A tall staff-officer, 6'2" came in, looked over everyone and directed most of the younger prisoners to "fall out". They were released later in the evening, marched down from the Barracks to the city. Passing by the South Dublin Union outpost they were singing the "Soldiers' Song." [29]

Volunteer Liam Ó Flaithbheartaigh had a similar remembrance.

> That evening [Sunday, 30 April] we were marched back
> by the South Dublin Union up to Richmond Barracks.
> We lustily sang "God Save Ireland" as we passed by our
> old fortress and on arrival at Richmond Barracks were
> put in groups of forty in a barrack room, without lava-
> tory accommodation.
>
> On Monday morning I saw Pádraig Pearse march-
> ing under escort to his courtmartial (sic). On Tuesday
> Éamon de Valera marched into the Barrack Square with
> his men, his height and stature making him conspicuous
> among his captors.
>
> The prisoners were gathered into the Gymnasium
> for inspection and identification. The Dublin policemen
> were officious in picking out the Volunteers known to
> them. It was a matter of separating the sheep from the
> goats. [30]

Tom Cullen shared these experiences with Cosgrave and Ó
Flaithbheartaigh. He remembered the exercise of 'separating the
sheep from the goats.'

Piaras Béaslaí, too, was one of the surrendered Volunteers.
He served as Captain Edward 'Ned' Daly's Vice-commandant
of Dublin's 1st Battalion. Their unit, badly short-handed due to
MacNeill's countermanding order, was delegated to hold a line
extending from Cabra Road in the north down to the Four Courts
on the Quays.

Greatly disappointed as well, they were forced to lay down their
arms on Saturday evening. Most of the 1st Bn spent the night on
the green in front of the Rotunda Hospital with the surrendered
forces from the GPO.

Stacked like cord wood and bounded in on all sides by 'a ring
of bayonets,' the prisoners were subjected to the abuses of the
officer-in-charge, Captain Lee Wilson, a fellow Irishman no less!

> On April 30th, 1916, when we marched helpless, dis-
> armed, prisoners through the streets of Dublin, amid

the silence or the hostile demonstrations of the people, the national outlook seemed black indeed.

While thinking in this strain in the gymnasium of Richmond Barracks, where we were being sorted out for trial or internment by the detectives, I found myself in company of Tom Clarke, the old Fenian, who had served sixteen years in English convict prison, only to come out and face death in a fresh effort against British rule. He spoke cheerfully, confidently. "This insurrection, though it has failed, will have a wonderful effect on the country," he said. "We will die, but it will be a different Ireland after us."

Seán MacDiarmada spoke in a similar strain. "There will be executions; I suppose I will be shot; but the executions will create a reaction in the country which will wipe out the slavish pro-English spirit."

Fortunately for the cause of Irish separatism, the cowardice and brutality of the English ruling classes triumphed over their political sagacity. Panic reigned and shrieked for blood. [31]

Béaslaí graphically remembered the 'gymnasium exercise.' Though he stated the culling process took place on Sunday morning, he likely meant he arrived at the barracks on Sunday, which he did, while the 'G-men' made their entrance the following day, Monday, May 1st.

On Sunday morning the prisoners were brought to Richmond Barracks. They were placed sitting on the floor of the Gymnasium, and the political detectives of the "G" Division of the Dublin Police came like a flock of carrion crows to pick out "suspects" as victims for court-martial. I was one of the first picked out, and for the rest of the day could watch the detectives passing to and fro among the two thousand prisoners studying their faces for victims for the firing squad. Anybody who had seen that sight may be pardoned if he felt little compunction at the subsequent shooting of those same "G" men. [32]

Piaras's unspoken sentiments were imagined by many including Tom Cullen and Michael Collins...words that echoed and re-echoed inside their heads for years to come. It became part of their justification for what would follow...living with the consequences of the use of violence.

Tim Pat Coogan added depth and insight to what happened in that gymnasium on the 1st day of May, 1916.

> Of the men picked out by the 'G' men for court martial, those who did not merit death sentences were condemned to penal servitude in British prisons like Dartmoor or Portland. Those who received death sentences, subsequently commuted to life imprisonment as a result of public opinion, were also sent to hard labour in England. It was in Richmond Barracks that [Michael] Collins had one of the luckiest escapes of his life. The 'G' men initially selected him for inclusion amongst those severely dealt with, but after Collins had been some time with the selected batch of prisoners, he heard his name being called from the further end of the building. Looking, he could not see who was calling and decided to risk a walk across the room. And once there, he stayed. It was for him probably the luckiest escape of his career. [33]

Tom Cullen was also one of the lucky ones. As an unknown Irish Volunteer, another faceless revolutionary, he was one of those not chosen to be tried, court-martialled or shot.

Three or four days later, he and a group of other prisoners were moved the short distance from Richmond Barracks to Kilmainham Gaol, Dublin's 1796 'Bastille' and notorious 'hell-hole.'

[**Author's note:** Arbour Hill Military Detention Barracks, near Phoenix Park, was also used as a temporary billeting centre to help relieve the overcrowding at Richmond Barracks.]

❧

[**Author's note:** According to the 1916 Easter Rebellion Handbook, the most comprehensive accounting of the facts, figures and details surrounding the 1916 Uprising to date, as of Thursday, 11th May (1916), a total of 300 persons had been killed, 997 wounded and 9 were still missing. Of the week's 1,306 victims, 469 (103 killed, 357 wounded, 9 missing) were members of the British military and 43 [17 killed & 26 wounded] were RIC and DMP policemen. The vast majority of the remaining 794 casualties (180 killed & 614 wounded) were civilians or 'insurgents.' Of this later group the Handbook said, "Many of the rebels were not in uniform, and it was not possible to distinguish between them and civilians, hence they are all included in the last figures given. Since these figures were issued the deaths of wounded persons have increased the total death roll considerably, but no complete official list is available."] [34]

Niamh O'Sullivan, historian, writer and former head guide and archivist at Kilmainham Gaol, explained that because the British had such large numbers of prisoners to deport, they used a few locales in Dublin as 'stopping off points' prior to transporting them to England. [35]

[**Author's note:** Again, quoting from the 1916 Easter Rebellion Handbook, "Over three thousand persons were arrested in connection with the outbreak and detained for various periods at various places. The majority were transported to prisons across the Channel, and considerable numbers were released and allowed to return to Ireland after a short period of detention."]

In support of O'Sullivan's comment "...the British had a large number of prisoners to deport...", the *Rebellion Handbook* noted that 3,226 prisoners (3,149 men & 77 women) passed through Richmond Barracks in early May, 1916. Of that three-thousand-plus, 1,104 men & seventy-two women were released; one hundred sixty were convicted by court-martial; twenty-three were acquitted by court-martial; 1,852 men & five women were interned in Britain.

[**Author's note:** Between 12 May & 7 June 1916, the British military authorities in Dublin announced that after careful investigation 986 men were absolved of charges and released. On 29 May, these same powers announced that sixty-four women had been exonerated and were released on 22 May 1916.] [36]

Piaras Béaslaí put a fine point on this business of prisoners and courts-martial.

> Of the surrendered prisoners in Dublin, the seven signatories, and the seven others – Major John [Seán] Mac-Bride, Commandant [Michael] Mallon of the Citizen Army, Ned Daly, Seán Heuston, Con Colbert, Michael O'Hanrahan and Liam [William] Pearse, were shot in cold blood by order of General Maxwell. Seán Heuston and Colbert were mere boys; Liam Pearse was apparently shot for being the brother of Patrick. A large number of others were sentenced to death, but their sentence was commuted to penal servitude. One hundred and twenty-two men and a woman (Countess Markievicz) (sic) were sentenced to penal servitude, eighteen men to terms of hard labour, and the remainder of the captured prisoners were "interned" at first in English jails, and later in a camp at Frongoch in Wales. Sir Roger Casement was executed in England later [3 August 1916]. [37]

❧

Tom Cullen's surrender experience was typical of the treatment that hundreds of other Volunteers received. The fact that suddenly there were several thousand Irish prisoners arriving for processing caught the British authority off-guard. Men were kept in cramped, unfurnished quarters with little or no toilet facilities except for stinking slop-pails. Accommodations for bathing were non-existent unless you count the odd bowl of water sans soap a bath. The food wasn't worthy of a dog's dinner. Sleeping was done lying on a floor or sitting up against a wall. That was one of the motivating forces for relocating the prisoners, especially the women, to Kilmainham Gaol.

There were a few exceptions. James Connolly, Cathal Brugha and a dozen or so other wounded were confined in Dublin Castle's small hospital. Only Patrick Henry Pearse, the Uprising's Commandant-General and President-elect seemed to receive 'special' consideration.

At the top of Moore Street, where it intersected with Great Britain Street [later renamed Parnell Street], he unconditionally surrendered to Brigadier-General William Lowe and his officer-son John. The proud teacher and Gaelic scholar was accompanied by his earlier intermediary, Elizabeth Farrell, a nurse. At the brief ceremony, Pearse handed over his officer's sword, an automatic pistol in its holster, a pouch of ammunition and his canteen.

Moments later he was driven by motor car to British Military Headquarters, Irish Command, Parkgate Barracks in Phoenix Park, Dublin. It was in the company sergeant-major's office that Pearse wrote out his letter of unconditional surrender which James Connolly and Thomas MacDonagh later endorsed prior to its distribution to the battalions scattered around the city.

[**Author's note**: At this point, I disagree with the several accounts that state while at Parkgate Military HQ, General Sir John Grenfell Maxwell, the newly arrived Commander-in-Chief of British forces in Ireland, called in to meet the revolutionary leader.

A British general, certainly not one with an ego as big as Maxwell's, wouldn't have gone across town from his official HQ at the Royal Hospital, Kilmainham to Parkgate to meet a 'school teacher,' the leader of a band of rabble, who'd the audacity to challenge the mightiest army and empire in the world. He would've had Pearse brought to him...to his office, at his pleasure. Additionally, street travel would've been too dangerous...especially for the British Commander-in-Chief. Rebel snipers populated the city and four of the five Dublin battalions had not yet retired. Besides, it was Maxwell who reportedly said, "Hanging was too good for that lot (the leaders). My solution is court-martial and shoot!"

Later that evening, Pearse was transferred from Parkgate to Arbour Hill Detention Barracks, less than a mile distant. That is when I assert he detoured and was driven to the Royal Hospital to meet Maxwell.]

Paul O'Brien, among others, agreed with me. The author of two books centred on the events surrounding the 1916 battles for Mount Street Bridge and South Dublin Union, believed Pearse was interviewed, no doubt, in rooms in the hospital's north range.

In a personal communiqué, O'Brien, who works in an office on the hospital grounds, stated: There is a panelled, oak room in that north wing which was likely Maxwell's office. Nearby, at the top of a staircase, were a series of reception rooms. This likely is where Maxwell and Pearse would have met.] [38]

Later, on Saturday evening, Pearse was taken to Arbour Hill Detention Barracks. It was there he wrote a letter to his mother, which was never delivered.

Maxwell kept it and used its confession against him at his court-martial. A copy of it was finally discovered in a collection of PM Hebert Asquith's personal papers in 1965. Pearse also wrote three short business letters and four poems, three of which were entitled: *To My Mother; To My Brother* and *A Mother Speaks*.

The President-elect remained in Arbour Hill until Tuesday morning when he was transferred to Richmond Barracks for court-martial.

It was at Richmond that Desmond Ryan repeated a brief story, possibly a fable, of Pearse meeting Joseph Plunkett.

Plunkett was believed to have said, "I suppose this means twenty years?"

Pearse replied, with a gesture of his hand round his neck, "No, it means this!" [39]

At his court-martial, Pearse declared, "We seem to have lost. We have not lost. To refuse to fight would have been to lose; to fight is to win. We have kept faith with the past, and handed on a tradition to the future." [40]

After his trial and sentencing, he was again transferred, this time to Kilmainham Gaol where he spent his last night.

Patrick Henry Pearse was executed, by firing squad, at 3.30 am the following morning, Wednesday, 3 May 1916, God bless his soul.

❧

Tom Cullen spent two or three nights in a cell in Kilmainham.
Early in the morning on Friday, 5 May, he would've heard the shots
fired that executed Major Seán McBride, May he rest in peace.
In the words of Niamh O'Sullivan:

> All fourteen of the executions [including Major Seán
> McBride] were carried out in the Stonebreakers' Yard
> of Kilmainham Jail at about 3.30 AM on the allocated
> mornings. This yard was chosen as it is surrounded on
> all sides by high walls. None of the windows from the
> prison buildings overlook the yard, ensuring complete
> seclusion. The firing squads were formed by men of the
> Sherwood Foresters, and attempts were made to have
> each man serve in only one squad. However, with twelve
> to a firing squad and fourteen men to be executed, it
> is thought that some could have been called on more
> than once. Each of the executed leaders had a small
> piece of white paper pinned over his heart, and all were
> blindfolded. There were no crowds gathered outside the
> jail to lend support, as a month-long curfew had been
> ordered by the Lord Lieutenant, Lord Wimborne, in a
> proclamation dated 25 April 1916.... [41]

❧

On that same day, Tom and eighty-seven other Irish prisoners
left Kilmainham Gaol for internment in Wakefield Detention
Barracks, West Yorkshire, England. They arrived the following
day, 6 May. At the time, Wakefield Prison was being used as
a British army detention centre. During the next thirty days,
approximately seven hundred fifty Volunteers were deported to
Wakefield.

Volunteer Liam Ó Flaithbheartaigh, one of Tom's fellow
SDU comrades who was deported from Richmond to Knutsford
Detention Barracks in north-western England on 2 May, briefly
described his experience that would've been similar to Tom's.

In the evening [2 May] the prisoners were marched out of the Barracks down Kilmainham through the Royal Hospital (where a great field of artillery was gathered for battering down Dublin) down the Quays (a fire was still burning at the end of Bridge Street) to the North Wall. The crowds who lined the route did not seem very fond of us (the exceptions were our own immediate friends). That night we travelled by cattle boat to England and eventually reached Knutsford Gaol. After a few weeks solitary in the cells we were allowed out for exercise in the compound and were allowed to write home and receive letters and parcels. [42]

O Mahony noted that most of the twenty-five hundred deported prisoners were lodged in their respective detention barracks for the next month.

During this time nearly 650 men were released and allowed return to Ireland. The remainder amounting to 1,863 men were served with internment orders under the Defence of the Realm Act and presumably suspected of having honoured, promoted or assisted an armed insurrection against His Majesty. [43]

❧

Sometime during Tom's arrival at Richmond Barracks and prior to his deportation to England on 5 May, he was 'interviewed' by unknown British military authorities. Beside name, rank and Volunteer posting, Tom was asked for a 'contact' address. According to the *1916 Easter Rebellion Handbook*, 'a' Thomas Cullen listed #26 Landerdale Terrace, New Row (South), Dublin as his address.

[**Author's note**: The 1911 census lists a family of 'Cullens' residing at that address and yes, there was a Thomas Cullen among its nine occupants. The 'head-of-family' was Kate Cullen, a fifty-two-year-old widow with eight children. The listed 'Thomas' was thirty-two and an electrician who was, as were all the other family members, born in 'Dublin City.'

Through a stroke of luck, Anne-Marie Ryan, an archivist at Kilmainham Gaol, passed on the name and address of a Mr. Christopher E. Duffy who believed he was the great-great-grandson of the Landerdale-Terrace Thomas Cullen.

Mr. Duffy's research found that his relative 'Thomas' was an Irish Volunteer in 1916, serving with the 1st Battalion in the Four Courts area. He would have been approximately thirty-seven years old and likely would have known or had met Edward 'Ned' Daly, Piaras Béaslaí and Liam Tobin, among others, who were 1st Bn leaders.

So clearly, the Thomas J. Cullen, 4th Bn, from West Wicklow and the Thomas Cullen, 1st Bn, of Landerdale Terrace are two different people.

Amid all the turmoil and confusion caused by the Uprising and mass surrender, it is likely a few individuals slipped through the cracks. It is my contention that the thirty-seven-year-old Thomas was one of those. But why did Thomas J. give the Landerdale address to the British? Three possible alternatives come to mind. (1) Kate Cullen and her family were related to Tom, maybe an aunt or cousin. If so, he could have visited #26 Landerdale or possibly even resided there for a short time after 1911. (2) Because of his family relationship with the Landerdale Cullens, he purposefully gave #26 as his address, knowing they would hold messages and that it might confuse the British authorities by having two persons named Thomas associated with that address. (3) Rather than involve Pat Dowling and the grocery, fearing the British might take their revenge on Pat by cancelling their Portobello-business arrangements, Tom gave the #26 address instead of the #58 South Circular Road one. But it must be remembered that given Tom's state of mind while he was at Richmond, #26 may have been the only street address he could think of on the spur of the moment.

Later, in 1921, Tom chose St. Nicholas of Myra Church for his marriage. It was the local parish church for Landerdale Terrace and one where he may have attended Mass while associated with #26. It is only a few blocks distant. On the other hand, St. Nicholas may have been chosen for his wedding as it is set back from the main road, Francis Street, and because its entrance steps are in a dark courtyard, making the ceremony a less obvious one to the authorities. At the time, the War for Independence was raging. Tom, his best man Liam Tobin, and guest Michael Collins were all wanted men on the run from the British and police. Sure we'll never really know, will we?]

※

Tom Cullen spent just over a month at Wakefield Detention Barracks. As with his friend Liam Ó Flaithbheartaigh, he spent his time in an isolation cell. Near the end of May, the officials relaxed the rules and he was permitted to exercise in the prison yard and receive post.

During the early weeks of June, Tom and the other prisoners throughout the country were transported by rail to Frongoch Internment Camp in North Wales. It was near the small town of Bala. The surrounding land was an isolated, heather-covered moorland and sparsely populated.

Previously, the internment camp had been a whisky distillery, but with the outbreak of war in 1914, it was closed. Soon it was converted to a German prisoner-of-war camp. Then, following the Irish Uprising, the British authorities moved the Germans out and readied the facility for the Irish internees.

Again, historian and author Sean O Mahony commented:

> If the execution of the leaders was a major mistake by the British in reaction to the Rebellion, the second major mistake was Frongoch. Here were housed nearly 1,900 of the finest of their generation and it became a veritable political university and military academy, aptly described elsewhere as a 'University for Revolutionists'. [44]

And so for the next six months Tom Cullen, Michael Collins, Joe O'Reilly, Piaras Béaslaí, Terry MacSwiney, Tomás MacCurtain, Richard Mulcahy and hundreds of other men who were to play important roles in Ireland's renewed fight for independence, lived in close proximity to one another...waiting for their day of retribution.

On 21 December 1916, the camp closed and the 1916 Easter Rebellion prisoners began making their way home to Ireland.

The Easter Uprising had ignited a fire inside of Tom. Soon his actions and the heartfelt deeds of others would turn Patrick Henry Pearse and James Connolly's flickering flame of freedom into a raging fire storm.

❧

[**Author's note**: For additional reading, I heartily recommend Sean O Mahony's *Frongoch: University of Revolution*, (1995) & Niamh O'Sullivan's *Every Dark Hour: A History of Kilmainham Jail*, (2007).]

4

"Six months for drilling."

—Mr. W. Sullivan, Resident Magistrate

The clanking of bottles and the banging of a door woke Tom Cullen from a night of fitful sleep. The narrow bed was strange and uncomfortable. The thin mattress sagged badly and he could find no comfort in it. Whenever he turned over, its few wire bedsprings complained. Each squeak sounded an alarm, robbing him of much needed rest.

Now awake in the pitch-black room, the West Wicklow man felt a moment of disorientation. Rubbing the sleep from his eyes, his hand felt the two-day growth of beard on his face.

– *Ah yes,* he thought, *I remember now…I'm in Wicklow, beginning my life over again.*

Tom smiled at his own cynical sense of humour.

Feeling no need to crawl out from under the cocoon-like warmth of the bed covers, he let his thoughts drift.

– *Sure this bed, despite all its inadequacies, is better than most I've slept in these past months…best be still, you eejit, and be thankful for what I have.*

He consciously dismissed the sounds of gentle snoring emanating from the two other men sharing the sleeping room on the building's first floor. Five beds lined one wall while three others were squeezed in between a large dresser and a tall wardrobe on the opposite side of the room. He'd taken the bed at the far end across from the room's single window.

Sinking deeper into the fold of his mattress, Tom realised he'd much to be thankful for and said a silent prayer for having survived his recent ordeals.

April last seemed as if it was just yesterday while at other times it felt like a lifetime ago. Vivid memories of mustering in Emerald Square on Easter Monday morning flooded back. The air was still that morning and the sun shone warm on his back as he stood waiting to march into action. Alarmingly, only one hundred twenty of the battalion's seven hundred Volunteers were present. Commandant Ceannt had expected at least five hundred, but didn't seem dispirited by the paltry numbers. Those present stood huddled together in small groups talking quietly. All appeared confident, but upon careful observation, Tom noted signs of tension, or maybe it was fear, etched in their faces.

As the men of 'B' Coy waited patiently, Lieutenant W. T. Cosgrave, his unit's OC, checked equipment and offered words of encouragement. A rumour passed among the ranks that more men would join their numbers at the Union.

Like a kaleidoscope of changing images, Tom's thoughts suddenly turned to remembrances of the week's fighting. In his mind, the sounds of machine-gun fire competed with the shouts of embattled men.

Lying in the bed, he took a deep breath. He could almost smell the acrid stench of cordite mixing with the intense aroma of antiseptic disinfectant. He also couldn't dismiss the recurring knot of fear in the pit of his stomach that, throughout the week, had produced periodic waves of nausea which he'd, thankfully, managed to suppress.

These and a myriad other memories he vividly remembered, still almost daily, since B Coy took sanctuary in the Nurses' Home at South Dublin Union.

If he listened carefully, he could still hear Commandant Ceannt's voice amid the uproar…orders intermingled with words of support.

– *He'd been absolutely brilliant…a rock of a man if there ever was one…someone to lay down his life for,* he often thought.

As if turning the page of a photograph album, the battle scene changed and he was thrown into the jumble of confusion amid the smell of unwashed, sweat-stained bodies at Richmond Barracks. Fear was replaced with anxious annoyance.

— What were the fecken' Sassenach going to do with the hundreds of exhausted men they'd corralled here?

This dramatic saga continued unfolding before his mind's eye. Several nights in Kilmainham, the overnight cattle boat to England, five weeks of imprisonment in Wakefield, the train ride to Frongoch followed by six months in that holy hell hole.

Tom pinched himself to see if he was awake. Was it all really behind him now?

He almost answered his own query out loud, *— It was!*

❋

Two days after Christmas, Tom Cullen walked into his father's house in Co. Kildare. He'd lost almost two stone since it'd all began, but despite the loss of weight his body felt taut, hardened by resolve and demanding activity. The anger that had enveloped him for the first months after the Uprising had slowly subsided. It'd been replaced by sheer determination. Yes, he wanted another go at the bloody bastards who'd dare think they could deprive him and Ireland of the freedom they both rightly deserved.

He wasn't alone with those feelings. A thousand Irishmen had just returned home from internment, all harbouring similar thoughts and emotions. No, he'd be back on the 'battlefield,' some 'battlefield' sooner, not later, and this time things would be different.

His father welcomed him with open arms. They embraced for the longest moment. He'd often wondered what this reunion would be like…experiencing his Da's welcome home. It wasn't quite what he'd expected, but sure he really had no idea. All he knew was it was good to be back…to feel his Da's love and to happily respond in kind.

Tom missed his mother every day, but especially around his birthday and at Christmas. She'd been the centre of his life growing up back in Blessington and later after they'd move to Queen's County. But all that was in the past. Now, little Annie and young James were around the table in her absence. He knew the three of them were almost strangers, growing up without him at home as they had. Of course, there were the age differences. He'd just turned twenty-six. Annie was fourteen and looked more like their mother every day, while James stood shoulder to shoulder with him, even without boots on.

Mannie had made him feel very welcome, though he sensed they too were strangers. Tom held no resentment. She'd made his father's life happy, filling the void as best she could. The woman was a good mother to her two stepchildren and kept a fine house. His father was a lucky man to have met and married her. But no matter how Tom tried, memories of his mother and her death always came flooding back.

❧

Patrick and Andy arrived into the house on the twenty-ninth. It was almost like old times again. The three brothers united after years of being apart.

Each took turns telling their stories, and with their father in tow, they drank pints at a nearby pub. But no matter how exciting or routine their lives had been, talk always turned to their mother and their two sisters. Maria was living in England...married to an Irishman working in Liverpool. Margaret, now in her thirties and a mother herself, lived in Galway with her husband and three boys.

On New Year's Eve, Andy and Tom went for a long walk. After a mile of kicking stones and small talk, Andy wanted to know what Tom's plans were.

He told his brother a week at home was enough for him. He longed to be out on his own again...to taste the freedom that had been so harshly denied during the last nine months.

Unsure of what lay ahead, he told Andy he was going back to Dublin. Maybe his old boss Pat Dowling would have something for him.

Before Tom could elaborate, Andy interrupted. He had something for him, a sure thing.

– Now, it's not the greatest job in the world, but one you're well suited for, said Andy.

– Doing what?

– Grocer's assistant. You'll like Wicklow Town. Larry Byrne's a good man. He's just opened up a new place last year...Fitzpatrick's. You can sleep upstairs over the grocer – bar. He won't pressurise you. You can take your time...besides the Volunteers are just getting reorganised in town...you'd be the perfect man for the job. I'm one of them, just like you were once.

In silence, Tom kept on studying the road...lost in thought.

– It will give you a chance to collect yourself...see what you want to do...what do ya think, Tom?

❧

Two days after New Year's, Tom Cullen, carrying an old, half-empty leather case, walked into Maynooth and caught the train for Dublin.

He first called into Dowling's grocery. Pat welcomed him like a long lost brother and returning hero.

– Begad, it's good to see you, Tom. Sure you look none the worst for wear.

Smiling at one another, the two men warmly shook hands. Suddenly turning, the grocer pointed to a hook in the corner of the shop that held a white grocer's coat.

– It's been waitin' for ya lo these many months, Tom. Sure Mrs. Curtis gave it a good washing and you're welcome back here...anytime.

Tom nodded.

– Ah Pat, I knew I could count on you. It's as if I never left, said Tom, looking around the shop.

– Terrible news about Billy. You knew he died in the fighting?

– I saw him fall, Pat. I heard the bullet hit him 'thump.' He turned to look at me, but his eyes already had a glassy stare about them. He didn't make a sound...just the 'swoosh' of air escaping from his mouth. Suddenly, his knees buckled and he dropped to the floor. He was gone in a handful of seconds...God rest his brave soul.

Almost instinctively, both men crossed themselves.

Several moments of silence passed, before they were interrupted.

– Mr. Dowling, what are ya asking for these apples?

※

Tom accepted Pat's kind offer of a bed and told him he needed some time to think about the job.

The next day, he called in to express his regrets to Mrs. Ceannt and to inquire how she and Rónán, her only child, were getting on. Later, he walked over to the Cosgrave house on James Street to pay his respects. W. T.'s mother had no idea when her son would be freed.

– You know he'd been sentenced to death.

Tom nodded.

– But thanks be to God it was commuted to penal servitude for life. He was first sent to Portland Jail, but later was transferred to Lewes Prison. I do receive the occasional letter from him, she said.

W. T.'s brother Phil and their stepfather, Thomas Burke, were also arrested and served sentences in England. Tom had met Mr. Burke in Frongoch. He'd just returned home two weeks ago as Tom had.

Over tea, Willie's mother and Tom talked of the Uprising, prison life and speculated about when the other internees would be freed. Tom thought it wouldn't be long as England's war effort was flagging in Europe. He suggested they might use a prisoner amnesty to curry favour with American politicians, hoping they'd choose to enter the war sooner rather than later.

Though the Cosgrave house and shop were almost directly across the street from the entrance to SDU, Tom felt no compulsion to revisit the walled fortress he'd called home for that historic week during April last.

Anthony J. Jordan, William T. Cosgrave's biographer, summed up the mood of newly returning 1916 prisoners:

> When the internees were released back to Ireland, they returned in triumph to their welcoming families and communities. Internment had transformed them by its injustice, into formidable radicals, intent on continuing the struggle, but this time to a successful conclusion.

They were still Volunteers, not Sinn Féiners, but it was via the latter body, which they regarded with some disdain as being too moderate, that they would gradually turn down the political road. Their initial entry into politics was motivated by their desire to defeat the IPP, rather than with any long-term coherent plan. [1]

❈

Tom made a number of discrete inquires asking after the whereabouts of Michael Collins but to no avail. He knew the Big Fella had planned to head for home in Cork upon his release, but hoped he'd returned to Dublin by now. Mick had been one of the Volunteer leaders at Frongoch and had told him to be sure to look him up when he was back in town.

Tom met with other disappointments too. None of his close comrades from the 4th Bn or recent associates from the camp seemed to be around either.

One thing he did notice was the town had changed a good bit since last spring. Much of Dublin was still in ruins. Even now, the shelled remains of Connolly's Liberty Hall attracted the attention of the odd passerby. The lower half of Sackville Street had been knocked but little rebuilding was under way. And there in the middle of town, the GPO stood like a silent, roofless relic of a defeated, broken dream.

Coupled with the city's destruction, there was the strong presence of armed military on the streets. Dublin's helmeted DMP were much in evidence too. In pairs, the helmeted coppers paraded about with an air of smugness, looking down their noses, acting victorious, as if they'd singlehandedly taken the city back from the insurgent 'Sinn Féiners.'

There was even a detail of bloody soldiers bivouacked outside of Larkfield, Count Plunkett's home in Kimmage.

– *Guarding the chicken coop after the hens had flown,* chuckled Tom to himself when he walked by their encampment.

Tom clearly remembered those early days in 1916. Larkfield had been the focal point for the many Irish Volunteers who'd returned home from any number of British cities that spring. Rather than being swept up into the ranks of the British army, they'd elected to come back and fight for Ireland. In retrospect, Tom guessed the authorities chose to ignore the Volunteers' activities in deference to the Count's respected status in Dublin.

Piaras Béaslaí reminisced about those days too:

> A large number of Volunteers from London, Liverpool, Manchester, Glasgow, and other centres in England and Scotland, arrived in Dublin at the same time. They had come to Ireland not to evade military service through any personal fear, but because they regarded it as the basest of treachery to their country to serve in the Army of Ireland's oppressors. Instead of occupying the less dangerous position of "conscientious objectors" in England, they elected to join their fellow Volunteers in Ireland in armed resistance. As proof of the faith that was in them they founded a camp at Kimmage, near Dublin, where they lived under military conditions, with sentries always on duty, showing their determination to resist with arms any attempt to raid their stronghold. These men were known jocosely as "the refugees," a name they resented. [2]

Besides first meeting Michael Collins at Kimmage, Tom recalled meeting others including a man he took an instant liking to by the name of Frank Thornton. He'd been the captain of the Liverpool Volunteers and exuded an air of confidence, even at Richmond Barracks after the surrender. Frank had spent much of Easter Week stationed inside the Imperial Hotel on Sackville Street, just opposite the GPO.

❧

Despite wandering the streets of Dublin for the better part of a week, Tom was not discouraged. Though unable to reconnect with old friends, he felt a new sense of confidence and determination burning inside him. In just his few short months of incarceration, a growing maturity had replaced the youth, inexperience and uncertainty that characterised his being prior to Easter Monday, 1916.

With time on his hands, he thought about Andy's offer. The more he mulled over heading down to live in Wicklow Town, at least for awhile, the more it made good sense. Yes, it had practical appeal. Settle down a wee bit, enjoy living life again, earn a few bob and put his knowledge and experience to good use with the local Volunteers. It would be a good step toward settling the score with England.

The more he thought about it, the more he liked the idea of heading south. This dream of freeing Ireland wasn't going to happen overnight and he certainly couldn't do it on his own. He'd let things settle down and sort themselves out. In the interim, he'd bide his time and ready himself.

❧

Sean O Mahony's detailed description of the Easter internees' experiences in Frongoch and their renewed determination to strike for national independence captured well the mindset of men like Tom Cullen:

> And so the men returned home for Christmas. They came back as heroes to a land that earlier in the year had spurned them. In the struggle for national liberation, 1916 was a momentous year – the Easter Rising had sparked the flame of freedom. The men who had organised the Rebellion were clear of mind and firm of purpose; but they were dead. The others who ended up in Frongoch were uncertain and hesitant, but in the camp a new certainty, and a new purpose evolved. In their shared experiences, a common perception of what lay ahead was formed. From disparate elements a national amalgam was forged. [3]

❧

After a quick wash up at the bowl on the dresser, Tom headed down the stairs for his first breakfast at Fitzpatrick's, the grocery-cum-bar on Abbey Street in Wicklow Town.

Andy had made all the arrangements. Mr. Edward M. Collins owned the building and had let it to Larry Byrne. It was Larry who had the job for Tom. He'd divide his time between waiting on customers in the front grocery and serving pints in the pub at the back.

The Fitzpatricks were a good family in town. Arthur and his son Jimmy ran a bakery just down the way on Bridge Street and were active supporters of the Volunteers.

After a breakfast of eggs and rashers, Tom studied the main street through the grocery's front window. The daylight was just coming up on this January morning and people were beginning to stir.

The street and footpaths were hard-packed clay. A handsome drain made from loose stones brought up from The Murrough divided the walkers from the motor cars and horse-drawn wagons. Some enterprising merchants had paved over the footpath in front of their shops with flagstones or wooden planking. Just down the way a polished granite obelisk caught the first rays of the sun. It stood in memory of Robert Halpin, a local man and master mariner, who'd laid the first transatlantic cable back in the 1860s.

As Tom stared out the window, his brother Andy unexpectedly came into view. He had a young lady on his arm. Pausing, he held open the door to the newsagent shop directly across the street. The woman smiled at her escort and entered the premises on her own.

Moments later, Andy turned and walked across the street. Seeing his brother standing in Fitzpatrick's window, he came through and stuck out his hand in greeting.

Returning the gesture, Tom said, – And who's the lucky lady?

– Ah sure, she's the daughter of the Mrs. Considine. You remember, the Considines…I told about them. They're the family I'm staying with here in town.

Tom smiled for suddenly his brother seemed nervous.

– Uh-huh, said Tom.

– Ah no, said Andy. – I was just being polite. Sure I want you to come over and meet the family…they're lovely people.

Tom nodded.

– But now I must run or I'll be late for work.

Halfway out the shop door, Andy turned. – Are you alright here? Sleep well?

– Everything's grand. Now, be off wit ya or they'll be after you with a cleaver.

※

Good to his word, Andrew Cullen brought Tom around to call on the Considines the following Sunday afternoon.

The house sat down just below the level of St. Patrick's Road, directly opposite the new Gothic-designed St. Patrick's Church. The impressive granite façade of the building, dedicated in 1844, stood part way up a steep hill with a commanding view of the Wicklow Mountains to the north.

Next to the Considines' eight-room home with its six front-facing windows was the former St. Patrick's Church. Tiny in comparison to its successor on the hill, the simple cruciform-shaped structure had served the town's Catholic community for fifty years from the late 1700s.

[**Author's note**: Though the strict penal laws of the eighteenth century finally were being relaxed, church construction was only reserved for back streets and other obscure locations in an effort to avoid 'offending' the Protestant 'upper classes' of the day.]

Prior to his death, Jacobus 'James' Considine, originally from Co. Clare, used the deconsecrated church building as a school. He called it Hill View Private School. In the 1901 census, he referred to himself as 'head' of the family and a 'national school teacher.' He gave his age as thirty-six. [**Author's note**: The date and cause of James's demise is unknown. He was alive in 1901 but missing from the 1911 census. It is interesting to note his wife, Marianne, still referred to herself as 'married' and 'head of family' instead of 'widowed' in 1911.]

When Tom first came calling in early 1917, there were five persons living in the residence at #9 St. Patrick's Road. [The house has since been knocked.] Marianne Considine would have been in her mid-fifties. In 1901, she gave her age as forty-two, but ten years later she stated she was just fifty! Additionally, she listed her

1901 and 1911 occupation as 'organist.' [She was the organist at St. Patrick's Church across the road.]

Also living at home in 1917 was James Joseph 'J. J.' Fallon, now thirty-two. Born in Co. Wicklow, he described his occupation as being a 'clerk.' In point of fact, he worked at the newsagent on Abbey Street, across from Fitzpatrick's. He was Marianne's son from a former marriage. [Later, J. J. bought the newsagent business and renamed it 'Fallon's'.]

Also residing at #9 was J. J.'s half-sister, Maria Bedilia 'Delia' Considine, who was born in Co. Wicklow on 3 April 1890. On the 1911 census, she listed her occupation as 'clerk' like her step-brother.

By 1911, several other family members noted on the 1901 form had either died or moved away. Edith M. Fallon, aged twenty-one in 1901, stated she too was an organist and had been born in Co. Kildare. Three other children, all born in Co, Wicklow, were Donald Jacobus Considine, born 8 January 1892; Cecilia Maria Considine, born 26 February 1894; and Maria Considine, born 24 April 1897. Each was listed as residing at #9 St. Patrick's Road in 1901, but were absent from the 1911 census report.

Two additional persons lived at #9 in 1911. They were Dermot McMahon Byrne, a twenty-one-year-old 'pressman,' listed as a 'boarder' and Andy Cullen, a 'lodger.' Tom's twenty-four-year-old brother was employed as a 'foreman butcher' right there in town.

[**Author's note**: With her husband gone, it seems apparent Mrs. Considine was forced to take in boarders to help make ends meet. Donald, Cecilia and/or Maria may have died or were being raised elsewhere.]

As was common practice in the early 1900s, the property had a piggery and fowl house adjacent to the house…again, seemingly another cost-saving measure adopted by the family.

❧

From their first introduction, it became apparent to Andy that Tom and Delia were attracted to each other. Though careful to hide any outward signs of personal feelings for Delia, months later Tom confided to his brother that he could grow 'sweet' on the young lady.

Though twenty-six years of age, Tom Cullen had never paid a great deal of attention to the opposite sex. He enjoyed the company of women, but making a romantic commitment to one was just not a priority. Irishmen often married late in life back then and Tom saw no reason to rush things. If Delia was to be in his future, sure things would work out in their own good time.

※

Settling down in Wicklow Town, working for Larry Byrne, proved to be just the thing for Tom. As Andy had mentioned, there was an interest in reorganising the Irish Volunteers in Co. Wicklow. One of the men spearheading the movement was Christopher M. Byrne of Ballykillivane, Glenealy, Co. Wicklow. In his Witness Statement, dated 27 September 1954, he described in detail his initial efforts going back to the Volunteers' inception in the autumn of 1913:

> After the Irish Volunteers were organised in Dublin in October (sic), 1913, I proceeded without any authority from anyone to organise Wicklow, but could make very little headway until January, 1914, when I got Companies in Ashford, Glenealy and Roundwood. I continued the efforts during the Spring of 1914, but it was not till April and May that my efforts produced any great results. Then Companies sprang up all over East Wicklow, from Arklow to Bray. All during the Summer there was continuous marching and drilling in every town and village. [4]

But by the autumn of 1914, the mood changed. John Redmond, a barrister, the leader of the IPP and an Irish MP in the House of Commons, had taken control of the IV leadership by flooding its Provisional Committee with his own men.

With the outbreak of the war in Europe in August, 1914, Redmond, hoping to assure that the British government would

follow through on its Irish Home Rule pledge, issued an appeal
for the Volunteers to join Irish regiments in the British army.

Needless to say, the founding organisers of the Volunteers,
men like Patrick Henry Pearse, Bulmer Hobson, Eoin MacNeill,
Joseph Plunkett, The O'Rahilly [Michael Joseph O'Rahilly],
Liam Mellowes, Éamonn Ceannt, Thomas MacDonagh, Seán
Mac Diarmada, Piaras Béaslaí and Sir Roger Casement among
others balked.

The resulting division proved disastrous. The Volunteer
movement split with the vast majority siding with Redmond.
Approximately 180,000 men followed him, supporting Britain's
war mobilisation. They renamed their ranks the National
Volunteers, while the remaining initial 12,000-14,000 men retained the original label, Irish Volunteers [IV].

Chris Byrne commented on this historical split:

> ...after Redmond's nominees entered the Provisional
> Committee, the great majority of the male population
> in East Wicklow was either in the volunteers or support-
> ing them, and after his [Redmond's] declaration in the
> House of Commons even the Unionists were friendly
> disposed to join up, while the genuine Volunteers, who
> had no intention of joining the British Army, were
> dispirited. East Wicklow, needless to point out, had a
> big Unionist population, being the most planted part
> of Ireland outside Ulster, and those who were not defi-
> nitely Unionist were for the most part Shoneen, and,
> when the split came in September-October, the whole
> movement collapsed and there wasn't an Irish Volunteer
> Company active. [5]

After the Easter Uprising in 1916 and the return of the internees in December, 1916 and June, 1917, Christopher Byrne again
picked up the threads of the shattered Volunteer movement:

> I started off again organising both Sinn Féin and the
> Volunteers. In every district where I got a Sinn Féin
> Cumann, I saw that I got a Company of Volunteers
> and vice versa. We soon had sufficient Companies to

form two Battalions, one operating from Wicklow town known as the East Wicklow Battalion with Tom Cullen, afterwards so well known as an I.R.A. man in Dublin, as Commandant of this Battalion. Tom was a Cullen from Blessington and was managing a business house in Wicklow Town. And another Battalion with Headquarters in Rathdrum was known as the South Wicklow Battalion with Seamus O'Brien, a Rathdrum business man, who had been out with the boys in Enniscorthy in 1916, as Commandant. Subsequently we had a Brigade with O'Brien as Commandant, T. Cullen Vice Commandant, myself as Quartermaster, and L. Daly of Wicklow as Adjutant. [6]

❧

Tom Cullen's 1917 promotion to captain and commandant of the East Wicklow battalion suited him well. Most of the men, be they teenagers or older, looked up to Tom. His experiences as an IV in Dublin from the group's inception to his active service in '16 and his internment in Frongoch quickly became the stuff of popular legend. His association with the Uprising's leadership also counted in his favour.

Much to Tom's delight, Andy, his brother, was elected battalion quartermaster.

The battalion's membership, certainly at least part of them, gathered together in the early morning hours several times a week. It became a common sight in town to see thirty, forty, sometimes more men training, drilling or marching along The Murrough under Captain Tom Cullen's command.

[**Author's note**: The Murrough is a flat strip of land, much of it grassy, but with some marshy areas, that stretches ten miles from Wicklow Harbour north toward Bray Head. The shoreline, between the Irish Sea and The Murrough, is rocky with a narrow ribbon of sand liberally dotted with small smooth stones and large boulders.]

The year 1917 proved historic in many ways. Ireland's infant political party, Sinn Féin, embarked on becoming the island's dominant force by adopting republicanism and abstention from taking any seat electorally won in London's House of Commons as its political platform. Arthur Griffith's faction, formerly a small, separatist, Irish-monarchist party, won by-elections in Roscommon [Count Plunkett], South Longford [Joseph McGuinness], East Clare [Éamon de Valera] and Kilkenny [W. T. Cosgrave] at the IPP's expense. Michael Collins, emerging from national obscurity, played an important role in helping Sinn Féin succeed in these by-elections.

But Tim Pat Coogan put these events in a sobering context:

> But behind the cheering at the hustings it was brought home to [Michael] Collins that there was a harsher side to the power struggle. It was an aspect of this that first brought him to the public's attention. To counter the growing disaffection in the country the authorities made copious use of the Defence of the Realm Act (DORA) which amongst other provisions allowed for deportation, and trial by court martial for offences such as illegal drilling or making speeches likely to cause disaffection. [7]

In August, three of Collins's friends, well-known Sinn Féiners, were arrested pursuant to Dublin Castle's enforcement of DORA. One of those men, Thomas Ashe, president of the IRB from Kinard, Lispole, Co. Kerry [near Dingle Town], with whom Mick had campaigned, joined other DORA victims on hunger strike in Mountjoy Prison. In response to this protest tactic, the prison authorities resorted to drastic measures. They forcibly inserted a tube down into a prisoner's stomach and pumped a mixture of milk and eggs into the physically restrained man. Tragically, after three days of forced feeding, Tom Ashe died in Dublin's Mater hospital.

[**Author's note**: Later, a coroner, looking into the details of his death, found Ashe had died unlawfully.]

Sean O Mahony, in his tribute to Tom Ashe, wrote:

> An inquest into the causes of his [Ashe's] death began on the 27 September and it was to last until the 1 November 1917. It sat for eleven days in all. Tim Healy

KC [King's Council] acted for the Ashe family. The jury found in accordance with the medical facts but censured the authorities for allowing forcible feeding and recommended its discontinuance. [8]

Again, Tim Pat Coogan described what happened as Ireland paid tribute to this brave Kerryman, a proud surviving 1916 commandant of the Dublin Brigade's 5th Battalion:

> A combination of spontaneous feeling and IRB organisation made his death the subject of a national demonstration of mourning and protest. Clad in a Volunteer uniform, the shirt of which had been given to him by Collins, the body lay in state while some 30,000 people visited the hospital to pay their respect. Public bodies from all over the country were represented at his gigantic funeral. For a short time, as they marshalled the crowds, and marched in the funeral procession wearing their Volunteer uniforms, the Dublin Brigade, under the command of Dick McKee, took over the city.
>
> At the graveside [Glasnevin Cemetery] three volleys were fired and then Collins, in Volunteer uniform, stepped forward and made a short and revealing speech in Irish and English. His English words were: 'Nothing additional remains to be said. That volley which we have just heard is the only speech which it is proper to make above the grave of a dead Fenian.' [9]

※

Tom closely followed the events surrounding the death of Tom Ashe from Wicklow Town. Several days later, Captain Cullen led a representative number of men from the East Wicklow Battalion to Ashe's funeral. Afterwards, Tom spent an hour in the Gresham Hotel bar conversing with Michael Collins, Gearóid O'Sullivan, P. S. O'Hegarty and Dick McKee. O'Sullivan and O'Hegarty were old Co. Cork friends of Collins while McKee was a Dublin man and a printer by profession. With the reconstituting of the

Volunteers, beginning in 1917, Dick soon became the OC of the Dublin Brigade. Under his leadership, this unit became the most redoubtable quasi-military unit in Ireland. Until his tragic death in 1920, McKee was second only to Collins as the recognised leader of the Irish Volunteers, whose name would soon change from Volunteers to the Irish Republican Army.

Tom told Michael about his move to Wicklow Town and his volunteer work there.

The Big Fellow only smiled and said, – Don't become too attached to the country life, my friend. There's more important work to be done here in Dublin.

❧

Two other events of 1917 that would prove central to Tom Cullen's life occurred at the end of October. On the 25th, Sinn Féin's annual Ard Fheis (convention) was held in Dublin. In historian James Mackay's words:

> At this meeting, de Valera was elected to the presidency of Sinn Fein (sic). Arthur Griffith would probably have won the presidency if it had been forced to a vote, but he was aware that the IRB was backing de Valera and in the interests of solidarity he generously gave way, accepting the vice-presidency instead. Michael [Collins] and his close friend Harry Boland were among the two dozen elected to the Executive Council. This Convention set the seal on the emergence of Sinn Fein as the potent force rallying all shades of Nationalist opinion, from the ultra-conservative Irish Nation League to socialists and Marists, from the moderate constitutionalists to the 1916 revolutionary wing led by de Valera, Collins and [Cathal] Brugha. [10]

Two days later, the annual Irish Volunteer Convention took place, also in Dublin. Again, de Valera was elected president of this organisation, taking the country's lead as both its political and military head. Additionally, Cathal Brugha, the hero of South

Dublin Union who'd miraculously survived his multiple-1916 wounds, was selected Chief of Staff. Dick Mulcahy was appointed as his deputy while Michael Collins became Director of Organisation, an honour thanking him for his help in revising the Volunteer Constitution.

[**Author's note**: Prior to his death in 1916, Patrick Henry Pearse, the first president of the 'Irish Republic' also held the post of Director of Organisation.]

❦

In the spring of 1918, Tom's life took a sudden turn. He was arrested by the local Wicklow Royal Irish Constabulary. The Saturday, 20 April 1918, issue of *The Wicklow News-Letter* gave a full accounting of his arrest and subsequent trial. Its headlines read:

Six Months For Drilling

Exciting Scenes in Wicklow

Police v. Civilians. – Co. Inspector Injured.

Train Held Up.

(Passed by Censor).

Scenes of an exciting character occurred in Wicklow on Monday following the arrest of Mr. Tom Cullen, Abbey Street, Wicklow, on a charge of illegal drilling on [Sunday] April 7th. The accused, who had been at eight o'clock Mass and who visited the altar rails, was arrested by Head-const. [constable] Plower and Sergt. [Sergeant] Fitzroy on returning from the church [St. Patrick's]. Having been allowed to take his breakfast, he was brought up at a special court before Mr. W. Sullivan, R.M. [Resident Magistrate], in the courthouse shortly after nine o'clock. About three dozen sympathisers, who had got wind of the affair, assembled in the market Square, and a majority of them gained access to the court. The prisoner was put sitting beneath the dock. He refused to take off his hat, which was thereupon removed by the police.

District-inspector Britten, who prosecuted, read an information made by Constable [James J.] Malynn to the effect that on the Sunday in question he saw Cullen drill 40 men. [11]

The 'information' or police report made by Constable James J. Malynn that District-Inspector Britten read to the court was as follows:

The Information of Constable James J. Malynn of Wicklow, Royal Irish Constabulary who saith on his oath that I am a Constable of the Royal Irish Constabulary and stationed at Wicklow: On Sunday the 7th day of April 1918 I was on duty at the Murrough, Wicklow at about 10 ¾ am. I saw about forty young men on the Murrough Wicklow, with Thomas Cullen of Abbey Street, Wicklow in Command. They "fell in" in Military Formation, "Two Deep." I heard Thomas Cullen giving the following commands "Form Fours" "Right" "Left Turn" and several other similar commands all of which the young men obeyed. He marched them down the Murrough. I saw them returning in Military Formation at 12.45 p.m. They crossed the Railway Bridge marching towards Wicklow Town. I heard Cullen blow a whistle and saw the men "doubling." They proceeded to Wicklow Town. In the Town Cullen gave the Command "Company Halt, Right Turn, Right Turn Dismiss." [12]

The wording of the official complaint report, entered into evidence at Tom's trial on the day of his arrest, stated:

Complainant: The King at the Prosecution of Frederick A. Britten, District Inspector, R. I. [Royal Irish] Constabulary

v.
Thomas Cullen, Defendant.
Petty Sessions District of Wicklow
County Wicklow

Whereas the Defendant in this case has been duly charged before the Justices assembled at Wicklow Special Petty Sessions, on the 7th day of April 1918, of having unlawfully with other evil disposed persons to the number of three or more did unlawfully assemble and gather together to the disturbance of the public peace and in contempt of Our Lord the King and His Laws with intent to drill and practise military evolutions without lawful authority and being as unlawfully assembled and gathered together did drill and practice military evolutions without lawful authority, against the Peace of our Lord the King and His Laws at Wicklow in the said County of Wicklow, on the 7th day of April 1918. And it was ordered by the said Justice that he, the said Defendant, should be bound by Recognizance to be of good behaviour towards all His Majesty's liege subjects, for the period of twelve Months. [13]

Once the complaint had been read into the record and Malynn verified its accuracy, Mr. W. Sullivan, the presiding court officer, asked [Cullen] if there were any questions for the witness [Malynn].

Suddenly, Tom displayed an unaccustomed belligerence in Wicklow's courthouse. Granted, he'd committed hostile acts in the past in defiance of Britain's rule in Ireland. Certainly joining the Irish Volunteers in 1913 could be construed as an anti-British act, but he was only one of thousands who'd enlisted.

Though the Volunteers were a military organisation created by Irish nationalists to counter unionist actions that established the Ulster Volunteer Force in 1912, it was, on the surface, seen as a 'defensive' measure "to secure and maintain the rights and liberties common to the whole people of Ireland." [14]

But the sub rosa purpose for the IV organisation, as seen by many of its founders, was 'offensive.' They hoped the Volunteers could establish a military toehold, striking for Ireland's independence while Britain was occupied with the war in Europe. Inspired by the old Fenian motto, 'England's difficulty is Ireland's opportunity,' the IRB and its military council prepared to rebel against their island neighbour, secretly supported with German and American help.

Of course, Tom's participation in the 1916 Easter Uprising was a very bold move, a declaration of war against England, and he'd paid the price for doing so. He'd been arrested, deported and had served eight months' internment for his rebellious beliefs.

Now, in a subtle but somewhat obvious attempt to enflame anti-British sentiments, Captain Tom Cullen undertook to prepare his military charges for another go at 'The Empire.' He knew his actions were in violation of DORA, but marching and drilling were going on all over the country. Sure it was a bit of a gamble. Thinking that sleepy, little Wicklow Town was safer than most places in Ireland to flaunt the authority's law, he pressed ahead with a training regime. Sure, he'd been doing so for the better part of a year with no repercussions.

For some reason, however, he'd pushed the question a step too far. Maybe, he'd a run in with James Malynn over another matter. Possibly, he'd been short with the constable in Fitzpatrick's or had made him wait for his pint longer than the man thought reasonable. Perhaps it had nothing to do with him but with his brother Andy. The two could have had a recent disagreement in the butcher shop and Malynn was taking it out on him. Or perchance, the constable and his wife had had words that morning and arresting Tom was his way of striking back, enforcing the letter of the law so often blatantly disregarded in the past.

One other issue may have influenced the RIC to act as it did. The war in Europe was dragging on, despite America's entrance into the conflict during the previous year. Lately, Germany's spring offensive had broken through Allied lines at several points in France. Britain, facing serious troop limitations, was threatening to impose military conscription in Ireland. Needless to say, this threat was unpopular and strongly opposed by most including the

Irish bishops and Ireland's dominant political parties, including the IPP and Sinn Féin.

Britain, in an attempt to fill its war ranks, threatened to link the implementation of the Government of Ireland Act of 1914 (the Third Home Rule Act) with a conscription bill. This further galvanised Irish anti-conscription feelings. Irish political parties walked out of Westminster, returned home and began an active campaign opposing such 'blackmail.'

Maybe these generalised, anti-British feelings were enough to trigger RIC retaliation. If the Irish weren't going to support the war effort, then the police would begin enforcing DORA to the 'letter of the law.'

Surprised, irate and rebellious, Tom Cullen struck back. In the four-plus years since he'd first taken his defiant, obstructive stance, he'd matured. Harden by war and prison, Tom was more convinced than ever Ireland deserved its independence. No longer was he going to play the game of bowing down to King and Empire. The lessons he'd been taught at his father's knee had taken on new meaning. Now in 1918, he was going to stand up and be counted. No more would he opt to play the 'safe' card, choosing to sit back and be a passive pawn. He was going to strike out as Pearse, Connolly and Ceannt had in 1916.

At this juncture, *The Wicklow News-Letter* detailed what happened in the courtroom when Mr. Sullivan asked Tom if he had any questions:

> The prisoner, who remained seated, intimated he had not, and said, "I don't recognise the court; I haven't a dog's respect for it" (laughing). [15]

At this point, Mr. Britten and Mr. Sullivan discussed the possibility of bail as it was known that Tom was employed and in charge of 'a grocer's shop.'

> Mr. Sullivan said he would bind him over, himself in the sum of £50 and two sureties of £25, to be of good behaviour for 12 months, in default to go to jail for six months. He asked prisoner did he intend to give bail.

Prisoner (laughing) – I don't recognise this court; it is farce. Mr. Sullivan – Very good. Do you wish to find bail or not? Prisoner – I tell you again I haven't a dog's respect for the court.

There was applause in court, and a number of Volunteers called down from the gallery, "We will see you again, Tom, when the six months are up." Prisoner (laughing) – The Germans will be here before then.

There was further applause and remarks from the gallery, and the district-inspector called to have these people removed. Mr. Sullivan – Put them out.

The police proceeded to eject the occupants of the gallery, who started cheering and singing the "Soldier's Song."

It is understood that the police again asked Cullen was he going to find bail, but he refused. The Resident Magistrate was groaning as he left the court. A number of sympathisers surrounded the prisoner in the hall shaking his hand and clapping him on the back. The police attempted to put back the crowd, when some of them, both men and women, struck the district-inspector and some other members of the force.

A large number of people assembled by this, and the police, having extricated the prisoner and removed him from the building, attempted to prevent the crowd from following by shutting the doors, but they were rushed in a scuffle which ensued and the doors were forced open. The prisoner and his escort were followed to the barracks by a large and hostile crowd carrying a Sinn Féin flag. Other flags were displayed from the window of the Sinn Féin Club and from Mr. Wm. O'Grady's* house [#12 Main Street]. A number of people remained in the neighbourhood of the [RIC] barracks [#3 Church Street], and the head-constable

---

* Re: Mr. William O'Grady... See Author's note at end of chapter.

returning from the post-office about 10 o'clock, came in for attentions of a hostile nature by a small section, some of whom brandished sticks over his head. Sergt. Roberts, however, arrived on the scene with his baton drawn and the incident terminated. [16]

Despite living in Wicklow for only a little over a year, it is apparent that Tom Cullen was well liked and respected by many in town. Working at Fitzpatrick's and heading the local IV battalion, Tom came into contact with many Wicklow residents. It is doubtful someone of questionable character would have garnered such liking and support despite the growing national anti-British sentiments spreading throughout the countryside. Indeed, it is apparent Tom's emergent reputation as a community leader and man worthy of national standing had surfaced.

❧

But the riotous scene at the courthouse in Market Square and the hostile row at the RIC barracks in Church Street, less than a block from Fitzpatrick's, was only the beginning of the confrontation.

> Fully four hundred people gathered outside the barracks before 12 o'clock, and the matter assumed a threatening aspect when the prisoner was brought out to be taken to the [Dublin] train. Business in the town was at a standstill, the men employed in the manure works and practically everywhere else having left work after breakfast.
>
> The police drew a cordon across the top of Church Hill [two blocks distant], and, with batons drawn, attempted to hold the crowds in check.
>
> A rush was made despite the efforts of a number of Volunteers, and stones and sticks, with which many of the people were provided, were freely used on the police, who retaliated with their batons, and in the melee which ensued Co. Inspector Morrell, who had arrived

on the scene, was injured by a blow on the head, while a Volunteer named Jas. Smullen was badly cut about the head by a baton stroke. The police retreated, followed by the crowd, by this time in a very excited state, and stones were thrown after them as they proceeded along Church Hill. When the 12.25 train drew up at the platform some of those present cut the air brakes, and some of the carriage windows were broken with stones. [17]

Matters continued to deteriorate. Prior to the failed attempt to deliver Tom to the early afternoon train for Dublin, the police had tried to secure the rail station and its northbound platform. All RIC efforts in this regard failed. A crowd surged forward and gained access to the station by forcing open its doors. After the train's brakes were cut, both engine driver and fireman were threatened with bodily harm if they tried moving it.

Despite the violence on Church Hill and Brickfield Lane, a short cut leading to the train station, the police, headed by Sergeant Duff and Constable Morrissey managed to put Tom onboard one of the carriages. It was obvious the crowd planned to rush the train and effect Tom's rescue. But despite their obvious loyalty to their captain and fearing his injury, a group of Volunteers, organised by Andy, managed to maintain order and control the crowd.

With much of its emotions vented, the mood of those at the station relaxed. Some went home to have their noontime dinner, but many who left returned later.

Around 6 o'clock that evening, the temper of the station crowd surged forward again. Tom, now without his handcuffs, was physically separated from his guards and removed from his carriage by some well-meaning supporters.

Surrounded by his rescuers, Tom was pushed and shoved back up Brickfield Lane toward Church Hill. At this point, the police charged and managed to recapture their prisoner. Despite a renewed shower of stones and blows, the RIC managed to return Tom to their barracks, back down in the town.

During this three-quarters-of-a-mile journey, Sergeant Jones and Constable McCormack sustained severe head wounds. To their credit, though, some Volunteers and members of Sinn Féin did their best to prevent further violence.

Again, the crowds in front of barracks grew in number and the two-story building was attacked with stones. Most of windows were broken. A ladder was hoisted up along the side of the building in an attempt to gain access to the first floor. Resident Magistrate Sullivan's motor car, parked unattended in the barrack's yard, was stoned, breaking its windscreen.

At this point in the re-escalating battle, District-Inspector Britten emerged from the RIC barracks with some constables armed with carbines. With the eminent threat of deadly gunfire, the crowd quietly retreated to the bottom of Church Street and the adjoining Fitzwilliam Square.

At 7.30 pm, a special military train with approximately two hundred armed soldiers arrived into the Goods Yard which was parallel to The Murrough and was on the far side of the River Vartry about three-quarters of a mile from the barracks.

The military formed a cordon from the train to the RIC HQ. Despite the presence of the armed military, more stones were thrown and the angry crowd showered British soldiers with boos and derisive shouts. Eventually, surrounded by the rifled men, Tom Cullen was escorted out the back way, across the Wooden Bridge [1860-1964] over the Vartry and safely placed onboard the special train.

Finally, at 9.15 that evening, the military train with Tom in tow pulled into Westland Row Station [later renamed Pearse Station]. On the platform stood a large force of Dublin Metropolitan Police directed by Detective Johnny Barton. Under close guard, Tom was taken to Mountjoy Jail.

The Wicklow News-Letter concluded its report of the day's events with the following observation:

> The whole affair created intense excitement in the district and was unprecedented in the history of the town during recent years. While it was primarily a demonstration of sympathy with Cullen, who, during the couple of years he has been in Wicklow, has made

himself popular with all classes, the amount of heat displayed also marked the people's resentment of the conscription proposals at present before Parliament. [18]

Christopher Byrne, in his Witness Statement, described the day's proceedings as well.

> All business was at a standstill in Wicklow Town that day and it was an illustration to the British of the difficulty they would have enforcing conscription on an (sic) united people. The R.I.C. were chasing round, sending wires and running to and from the station all day. Eventually they got a train with at least 200 soldiers to take one man. They brought this train to the goods station and from there Tom Cullen to Dublin where he was handed over to a few more soldiers and Detective Johnny Barton in a cab. [19]

❧

Refusing to recognise the authority of a British court was nothing new to Irish nationalists or their more radical counterparts, Irish Republicans. Just two years earlier, the 1916 leaders and their associates had stood up against the might of General Sir John Maxwell, Britain's newly appointed Irish Commander-in-Chief, at his sham courts-martial. Tom, like those before him, only did what his conscience told him was right and just.

❧

Michael Collins found himself in the similar predicament. James Mackay recounted what happened:

> In March 1918 Michael had been in Longford again, doubtless combining business with pleasure.... At Legga near Granard he made a speech that was deemed to be particularly inflammatory. The law finally caught up with him on 3 April when he stepped out of his office in Bachelor's Walk, straight into the arms of waiting G men. At first Michael strenuously resisted arrest and the

resultant brawl soon attracted a large and sympathetic crowd. [20]

The little drama could have become a serious matter had not a friend turned up and convinced Mick to go along peacefully to the nearby Brunswick Street police station.

Charged and arrested for seditious speech making at Legga in Co. Longford, Michael was transported to Longford Town and formally arraigned. Refusing to post bail, he was imprisoned in Sligo Gaol.

Piaras Béaslaí, in jail himself, described what happened next:

> Michael Collins was at this time in jail owing to his refusal to give bail. It was felt that, in view of the approaching fight, it was absurd that so essential a man should be kept out of it by so trivial a matter. He was asked to give bail, did so, was released and returned to Dublin. [21]

The approaching fight that Béaslaí referred to was The Conscription Crisis. He succinctly summarised the determination of nationalist Ireland at the time:

> Like other bodies, the Executive of the Irish Volunteers met to consider the situation [The Conscription Crisis]. Their course seemed clear. If the English decided to enforce military service on the people of Ireland, it could only be regarded as a declaration of war; and it was the duty of the Volunteers to resist by force of arms. It was decided to devise plans for the most desperate resistance and the most drastic measures of retaliation, in view of the outrage which the English Government proposed to inflict on the Irish people. [22]

Meanwhile back in Dublin's Mountjoy Jail, Tom Cullen and Piaras Béaslaí were cooling their heels behind bars. Due to prison overcrowding, prisoner hunger strikes and a general climate of unrest, some inmates were transferred to Belfast Jail. The authorities felt they had more control of the 'rebels' there, away from Dublin.

Béaslaí expressed the feeling of others in similar situations:

> Tom Cullen and I had been fellow-prisoners in Mount-
> joy and Belfast. When I received the order to give bail
> I hesitated for some days, as I feared my action might
> be misunderstood.... [23]

Tom too, received orders, but his came directly from the top: Michael Collins, who was now also acting as Adjutant General of the Volunteers in addition to his official duties as Director of Organisation.

After Cullen's removal from Wicklow Town on 8 April, Collins called Chris Byrne to Dublin:

> Shortly after that I was called to Headquarters where I
> met Michael Collins, Michael Staines and Austin Stack,
> and they told me to go to Mountjoy and get Tom Cullen
> to come out on bail. This I did, having wired Cullen's
> boss [Larry Byrne] to come up to bail him. He did so
> but Cullen refused to come out. I came back and found
> Stack and told him of Cullen's refusal. He said he would
> have to come out. I said, "Very well, but I am going
> home. I have business to look after and I also want to
> see what the Volunteers are doing." Meanwhile Cullen
> was transferred to Belfast from where they took him out
> on bail. He returned to Wicklow but was recalled to
> Dublin where he was kept for the rest of the struggle. [24]

At this point, Béaslaí noted:

> It was decided to issue orders to all Volunteers who
> were in jail in lieu of bail to give bail and secure their
> release in order to be out for the coming fight. Among
> the prisoners affected by this was Tom Cullen, Captain
> of the Wicklow Volunteers. Collins had been already in
> touch with this young man, and had conceived a high
> opinion of his capacity. He was very insistent on Cul-
> len giving bail; and when, reluctantly, he did so Collins
> persuaded him to stay in Dublin and take a position on
> his staff. This was the beginning of an association which

was to last up to the death of Collins. [25]

No doubt the letter he received, signed Míceal Collins, Adj. Gen [Adjutant General] on Oglaig na h-Éireann official stationery helped Tom make up his mind to post bail. The letter was addressed to Commandant Thos Cullen, Mountjoy Jail.

The communiqué, its receipt delayed because of Tom's transfer to Belfast, clearly stated:

To Commandant Thos Cullen
Mountjoy Jail

In accordance with a decision of the Irish Volunteers Executive you are hereby instructed to give bail so as to secure your release from prison at this critical time.

For & on behalf of Headquarters Staff,
(Signed) Míceal Collins, Adj. Gen [26]

❧

Whether Tom returned to Wicklow Town to resume his Volunteer duties and his employment is unknown. Chris Byrne's Witness Statement indicated he did, at least for a short time. Maybe Tom put in a brief appearance to collect his personal belongings and say 'thank you' to Larry Byrne for going his bail. Additionally, a few goodbyes were certainly in order, especially to his brother Andy and to Delia Considine, the woman who'd recently become his 'unofficial' sweetheart.

On the other hand, if we are to believe Béaslaí, Tom's visit to Wicklow must have been a very short one, as he wrote:

...he [Collins] badly felt the need of a capable assistant. He already had Joe O'Reilly as an assistant, but in a different capacity. I do not think Joe's job was ever defined. He had to do a thousand things; but the nearest definition I can find for his position is confidential messenger and aide-de-camp. Cullen, at this time was wanted for office work in Bachelor's Walk. [27]

❧

Thus, sometime in late April or early May, 1918, Tom Cullen began working for Michael Collins. At first, his Dublin duties entailed being an Honourable Secretary of the Irish National Aid Association with offices at #10 Exchequer Street and, just a few weeks later, he gained another title, 'Assistant Quarter-Master General,' as his growing portfolio of responsibilities doubled or tripled. For security reasons, he began using rooms at #32 Bachelor's Walk on the Liffey Quays for his quarter-mastering responsibilities.

❧

[Author's Note: William 'Bill' O'Grady, a long-time resident of Wicklow Town, was another remarkable individual who passionately believed in the cause of Irish freedom and would've been intimately acquainted with Tom Cullen. In fact, I believe he'd have cut Tom and Andy Cullen's hair on numerous occasions.

Bill was born on 13 July 1872 at #30 Castle Street, Dublin. His parents, William and Anne Walsh O'Grady, were life-long residents of Dublin Town. In the late 1800s, Bill left Dublin and moved to Wicklow Town. By the 1901 census, now aged twenty-eight, he was living on his own and resided at #11 Main Street. With his marriage just three weeks away, the Dubliner had already begun a successful career as a hairdresser. He was well liked and respected by the town's residents.

The 1911 census finds Bill O'Grady a married man of ten years. He and his wife, Henrietta, whose parents owned a fish-monger shop with their residence above just a few doors away from William's business, were married on 21 April 1901 at St. Patrick's Church in Wicklow.

Ten years later, they were the parents of eight young children. William Patrick, aged nine; Robert, eight; Dermot, seven; Edward Terence, six; Kathleen Mary, four; Séamus, three; Kevin, one; and a newborn named Sheelah, who sadly died about a year later, 27 June 1912. The O'Gradys went on to have nine more children with Eileen O'Grady, born in 1925, the eighteenth and last child.

Out of necessity, William and Henrietta moved into the larger residence next door at #12 Main Street by the time the 1911 census information was collected. Again, the family lived upstairs, occupying the dwelling's five rooms while the ground-floor space served as his hairdresser's shop which he'd opened in c. 1905. (I should point out that William's handwriting on the census documents of the day was as handsome and confident as his physical appearance portrayed him to be.)

Both O'Gradys were devoted nationalists. William, a keen supporter of the burgeoning Irish language movement in the early twentieth century was also a prominent, local supporter of Sinn Féin as well as holding membership in the IRA. (I would guess he also was a member of the Gaelic League and possibly the Gaelic Athletic Association. His obituary stated he helped organise 'Gaelic' concerts.)

It is uncertain if Bill joined the Irish Volunteers in 1913-1914. His interest and activities seemed to follow Irish cultural and political lines instead of military ones.

Bill's name was prominently mentioned in the newspaper coverage surrounding the events of Monday, 8 April 1918, the day of Tom Cullen's trial and subsequent deportation to Dublin. To quote from his obituary published in an unnamed newspaper (likely *The Wicklow People*):

> With so many of his fellowtownsmen (sic), in April, 1918 he was involved in the protest made against the arrest and imprisonment of Tom Cullen, who was at that time commandant of the Wicklow company of the I.R.A. and principal organiser of the volunteer move-ment in the county. After Tom Cullen's trial and sentence to imprisonment, there were disturbances, which led to baton-charges, and so serious did the situation develop that the train which was to take the prisoner to Dublin was held up at the station, the police were besieged in their barracks, and eventually, a special train brought a company of fully-equipped soldiers into the town to enforce order, with a curfew put into force for several

days, and certain men on the run for weeks to follow. Several of them were eventually rounded-up, including William O'Grady, and they were tried and sentenced. Later on, in the I.R.A. campaign (Ireland's War for Independence) he was again arrested and imprisoned in the old Wicklow Jail, where his health became affected. He was elected a Sinn Féin representative on the Urban Council and sat for several years. As his health deteriorated, he retired from public life, and later still from his own occupation, and since then he had been an invalid. Mr. O'Grady was respected by and popular with everyone, irrespective of political outlook. [28]

Regarding *The Wicklow News-Letter*'s reference, in the body of this chapter, to "flags flying from the window of the Sinn Féin Club and Mr. Wm. O'Grady's house..." Bonnie Jean O'Grady, his granddaughter-in-law, believes the two were actually one in the same.

In support of her contention, I quote from *From Under The Stairs: The Story of Sheelah O'Grady*, "I was far too young to know what went on at meetings held at our house...." and "Even though Father addressed meetings and the local 'action' Committee met in our front parlour...." [29]

On the other hand, I'm inclined to believe that though the O'Grady home was an obvious hotbed of nationalist support and activity, I believe there were one or more *other* residences in Wicklow Town equally supportive of pro-Irish/anti-British sentiments. I offer the fact that 'hundreds' of town's people turned out in protest of Tom Cullen's April arrest.

Throughout the several pages of excerpts authored by Sheelah O'Grady, the family's seventeenth child who was born 17 November 1920 and died 4 January 2007 in Essex, England, I wasn't surprised by her portrayal of the Black and Tans' cruelty and vindictiveness.

On the 17th November 1920 my mother, Henrietta, was in labour when the Black and Tans burst their way into our house on Main Street Wicklow, in search of arms and my father who was the local leader of Sinn Fein. To force her to reveal his hiding place they snatched away my little wet body almost as soon as it was delivered and, as far as she knew, my little life was over even before it had begun. [30]

And…

As it was I was found alive and presumably well under the stairs by the front door whilst father was frog-marched up the street to Wicklow Jail with a pistol at his head and steel-tipped boots hacking at his ankles. The Black and Tans were not the most gentle of mercenaries. [31]

Her brother Paul wrote from London:

But I do remember our house raided many times. Of course Father…was a prime target. Take the shop window for example: I remember it when it was tarred.

I remember when our house was raided. I recall well they didn't give him time to dress, just in his shirt, & marched up to the Market Square & tried to get him to sing *"God Save the King,"* at least that is what we heard. [32]

Sheelah's older sister Patricia O'Grady also remembered:

When the Black and Tans came, they covered our house with tar, got my Father out of bed, and pushed him (pricking his heels with their bayonets) to the Market Square, where they tried to get him say where some members of the "I.R.A." were hiding. He never did and we never knew how much he knew. [33]

Lastly, Edward Terence 'Ted' O'Grady reminisced:

…about Pop and the Sinn Féin, let me say that he was a true and dedicated Irishman, and I think I follow in his footsteps. I remember that the Tans came to our house and took him out of bed in his PJ's. They brought him out on the sidewalk, made him kneel down and sing *"God Save the King."* If it weren't for his wife and family, I believe he would have said, "Shoot me!" They made him stand up and walk; and while he was walking, the Tans were kicking him on his heels until they were bloody, scraped and blistered. I don't remember how long Pop was in jail. [34]

According to Sheelah's memoir, her father was incarcerated in Wicklow Gaol on several occasions. She and her other siblings recalled visiting him there often. His last imprisonment was in cell #19. To this day, a hand-carved chess board of his is there on display. (The old Wicklow Gaol opened in 1702 and finally closed its doors as a prison in 1924. Today, it is a museum and historical site.)

William wasn't the only 'rebel' in the family. On 24 May 1918, likely from the residue still percolating in town after the Cullen trial and deportation, Henrietta O'Grady, his wife, was arrested and brought before the Wicklow Petty Sessions. She was accused of spitting at police officers in Wicklow Town. Allegedly, while passing several RIC in the street, some of her spittle landed on one of the policemen's tunics. (On 10 May 1918, William had been arrested, tried and imprisoned for his involvement in the Cullen affair. According to *The Wicklow People*, "he'd been charged with unlawful assembly and sentenced to two months hard labour in Mountjoy Prison Dublin.")

Mrs. O'Grady, encouraged by her sister who was present in the courthouse on the 24th, defiantly stated, upon being found guilty and order to pay a fine, – Well, I will pay no fine. I will go to jail.

In response, District Inspector Egan said, – Give her into police custody immediately. (Three-quarters of a century later, memories of the Cullen riot plus William and Henrietta O'Grady's involvement are still remembered. The spitting incident was told to me on two different occasions.)

In the popular lore, William's involvement is less clear. One person, however, told me he clearly recalls being told that Mr.

O'Grady was seen on Church Hill swinging a golf club in 'a threatening manner' at a policeman. (Bonnie Jean O'Grady had not heard of the golf club story and could not confirm or deny its authenticity.)

In conclusion, two things struck me about Patricia O'Grady's remembrances. Remembering her father, she said:

> He was not against England. It was her [England's] occupation of his beloved Ireland with no more justification than arguments of irrelevant history. A kinder, more gentle man could not have been found. He was far removed from the stereotype image of a freedom fighter. [35]

And...

> He loved Ireland and De Valira (sic), and filled my life with belief in magic, fairies, and the beauty of nature. I still have the ornate gold decorated green sash and medal he so proudly wore in procession, both religious (St Patrick's Day) and political. [36]

After a long illness, William O'Grady died at home on Main Street, Wicklow Town on 28 May 1955...God bless his soul.

Christopher M. Byrne, his WS quoted at length earlier in this chapter, and his wife were among the many old friends who attended William's funeral. The proud and devoted Irishman was buried (grave #614-K-11) in the New Cemetery, Rathnew, Co. Wicklow...the same graveyard as was Tom Cullen...may they both rest in peace.]

❦

[**Author's Note**: Additional reading would include Ernie O'Malley's *On another Man's Wound* (1990) and Ulick O'Connor's *The Troubles: The Struggle for Irish Freedom 1912-1922* (1992).]

1916 SDU garrison signatures

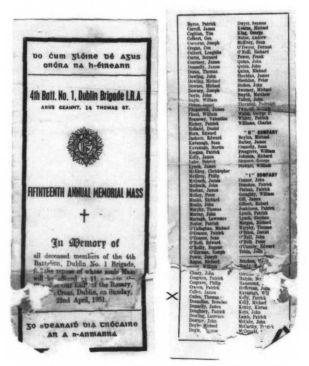

15th Anniversary, 4th Bn memorial Mass card

Fitzpatrick's public house, Wicklow Town

[Fallon's] Earl's newsagent shop, Wicklow

Old St. Patrick's Church, Wicklow

St. Patrick's Church, Wicklow

Tom Kilcoyne, Tom Cullen, Joseph Lalor [l to r], c. 1917-1918

Tom Cullen's IV uniform buttons

Courtroom, Wicklow Town

RIC barracks, Wicklow Town

Church Hill, Wicklow Town

Brickfield Lane, Wicklow

Rail station, Wicklow

The Wood Bridge, Wicklow

5

"KILMAINHAM JAIL...STANDS TO-DAY A SILENT MONU-
MENT TO THE GREAT MEN WHO HAVE HELPED TO MOULD
THE DESTINY OF IRELAND'S POLITICAL FUTURE."
— BROTHER HUBERT O'KEEFFE, CLERK,
ST. JAMES CHURCH, DUBLIN

Tom Cullen's arrival back into Dublin Town from Wicklow occurred amid the Irish 'Conscription Crisis' of 1918.

With the war on the Western Front dragging on and on, British army troop levels became increasingly hard pressed. To date, Great Britain alone had witnessed the loss of over 500,000 lives in a conflict originally thought to be over in five months... Christmas, 1914.

By spring, 1918, a renewed German offensive broke through several sectors of the front line in France, pushing the forces of the Allied Powers backwards. As a consequence, the British government, seeking to increase its pool of fighting men, extended conscription to Ireland.

Conscription was first introduced in Britain with the passage of the Military Service Act of January, 1916. It targeted single men aged eighteen to forty-one, with a few exceptions. On 2 March 1916, the first conscripts were called up. Three months later, on May 25th, the law was extended to include married men. By the war's end, the conscription age had been raised to fifty-one.

In Ireland, the bill's passage met with strong opposition.

Britain's attempt to involve more Irishmen in its European conflict proved extremely unpopular, despite the fact that thousands of Irishmen already had voluntarily enlisted. [**Author's note:** In fact, by the war's end in November, 1918, 200,000-300,000 Irishmen had fought for its island neighbour with c. 51,000 giving their lives.]

On 18 April, the British Military Service bill became law in Ireland. Hoping to soften its impact, the British government continued dangling Home Rule before the Irish people, if only they'd support conscription now.

The linking of Home Rule and conscription infuriated the Irish Parliamentary Party seated in London. Headed now by John Dillon, a Dublin man and Irish Home Rule activist, he'd succeeded John Redmond as party leader after Redmond's unexpected death just one month earlier.

As a show of strength and solidarity, the IPP along with the newly organised All-for-Ireland League, a non-sectarian, pro-Home-Rule, pro-nationalist party, walked out of the House of Commons in a united show of protest and returned to Ireland. Their intent was to support an organised opposition to conscription.

> On 18 April 1918, acting on a resolution of Dublin Corporation, the Lord Mayor of Dublin (Lawrence O'Neill) held a conference at the Mansion House, Dublin. The Irish Anti-Conscription Committee was convened to devise plans to resist conscription, and represented different sections of nationalist opinion: John Dillon and Joseph Devlin for the Irish Parliamentary Party, Éamon de Valera and Arthur Griffith for Sinn Féin, William O'Brien and Timothy Michael Healy for the All-for-Ireland Party and Michael Egan, Thomas Johnson and W. X. O'Brien representing Labour and the Trade Unions. [1]

That same evening, the Catholic bishops, holding their annual Bishops' meeting in Maynooth, met with a delegation of representatives from the Anti-Conscription Committee. This powerful coalition of politicians, labour and religious leaders endorsed the taking of an 'anti-conscription pledge' at each Catholic Church in every parish of Ireland on the following Sunday, 21 April 1918. The oath read:

> Denying the right of the British government to enforce compulsory service in this country, we pledge ourselves solemnly to one another to resist conscription by the most effective means at our disposal. [2]

On Tuesday, 23 April, Irish labour leaders called for a general one-day strike throughout the country. Virtually all work in Ireland came to a dead stop, even in munitions factories. This work action proved a huge, unprecedented success.

W. B. Yeats captured the thoughts and feeling of many Irish when he declared, "...it seems to me a strangely wanton thing that England, for the sake of 50,000 Irish soldiers, is prepared to hollow another trench between the countries and fill it with blood." [3]

During the beginning of May, large, anti-conscription protest meetings were held throughout the country with one of the largest staged in Co. Roscommon at which two predictable political opponents shared the same platform. John Dillon, leader of the IPP, and Éamon de Valera of Sinn Féin spoke as one against Britain's conscription bill before a crowd of some 15,000 people.

In a vain attempt to quell the rising tide against forced enlistment, David Lloyd George's government, through its British representative Lord John French, the Viceroy or Lord Lieutenant and its Supreme Military Commander in Ireland, concocted some incriminating evidence against members of its political opposition. The fraudulent scheme accused representatives of Sinn Féin and Germany of masterminding a treasonable plot for the purpose of overthrowing the resident British government.

So, on the night of 17 May, during the height of the Conscription Crisis, Dublin Castle authorities, with the help of their agents, local police and the military, rounded up a large number [c. 73] of Sinn Féiners including de Valera, Griffith, Count Plunkett, W. T. Cosgrave and Countess Markievicz.

Two days earlier, one of Michael Collins's Dublin Castle 'spies,'

Ned Broy, had obtained a list of those the government planned to 'lift' and passed it on to Collins.

On the night of the scheduled raids, Collins, at a meeting of the Volunteer Executive, warned those present of the planned arrests.

De Valera, Volunteer president and always one to play the 'political card,' advised the others against going into hiding and touted the benefits of being detained. He too knew the British charges were a gaffe, the result of trumped-up information and faulty intelligence gathering, all designed to blacken the cause of the Irish secessionists.

"In the end, we'll gain a great measure of sympathetic press. It'll help rally Irish nationalists to our cause here at home and focus the spotlight of world attention on England's bully-boy tactics," Dev said.

Collins, Harry Boland, Eamonn Duggan and Michael's newest protégée, Tom Cullen refused Dev's urgings. They were joined by a handful of others. Sleeping away from home that night, they all woke up free men the following morning.

In the meanwhile, those who took de Valera's advice found themselves deported and interned in English prisons for the next nine or ten months.

[**Author's note**: Several important results spun out of the events of May, 1918. Sinn Féin's cause for uniting Ireland gained ground. Coupled with its past association with the 1916 Uprising and its present-day public stance against conscription, Griffith's party popularity rose dramatically, spelling the final death knell for the IPP.

By arresting much of Sinn Féin's moderate leadership, effectively taking them out of action, its more extreme followers surged to the fore. Led primarily by Michael Collins, this core of revolutionaries began to exert their influence and reshape Ireland, putting it on the road to armed rebellion.

The commanding control Michael gained after the German-Plot arrests assured him that it would be his policies and his alone that would dominate Irish political thought until Éamon de Valera finally wrestled control back after his successful election in 1932.

On the negative side of the ledger, Sinn Féin's association with the tainted events of the German Plot and its anti-Conscription Crisis stance resulted in Ireland being ignored by the victors at the Paris Peace Conference in 1919. Wishing to have its desired freedom from British rule recognised and its stature as an Irish Republic established, Ireland was denied on both counts.

The events surrounding the rise of Collins's authority and his tragic, untimely death; the delay, the decline and the eventual rise of de Valera's influence; a costly Irish War for Independence; the signing of a contentious treaty with Britain; the copper-fastening of Ireland's partition; a divisive, bitter Irish Civil War; and finally the gradual establishment of Ireland's two present-day, dominant political parties were all still waiting in the wings to play out their hand. When they did, however, history dealt the Irish another cruel blow. Instead of delivering a independent, united Ireland, it meted out a flawed Irish Republic in 1949...one composed of twenty-six not thirty-two counties.]

❀

Tom Cullen, along with his brother Andy, stood out on the Dublin footpath looking up. Sure the number over the door said '32' but no one answered their knock. The door leading up the stairs to the offices above was locked. The haberdashery shop on the ground floor didn't open until ten.

With thirty minutes to wait, the two men headed down Bachelor's Walk looking for a cup of tea.

It was a mild morning. The warm sun played off their backs as they walked along the Quays. Tom couldn't help but think that the day's weather was much as it had been two years ago, almost to the day. Easter had come early this year, at the end of March, but in Tom's mind, April 24th held a special significance...that was the day he'd first taken up arms against the Sassenach.

Taking their seats in a small café, the two ordered a pot of tea and sweet buns. They'd left Wicklow early that morning. Andy had borrowed a motor car from one of his friends for the journey up to Dublin. Though Tom hadn't many belongings to transport, the comfort of the auto made the journey enjoyable.

With the two Sugar Loaf peaks behind them, the brothers

knew the village of Enniskerry was at hand. From there it was up and over the Dublin Mountains and down into Dublin Town.

Earlier that month, when Tom returned to Wicklow from his brief stay in Belfast's Crumlin Road Gaol, there was a note waiting for him from Collins. Michael wanted him in Dublin no later than the end of the month. In it the Big Fellow clearly restated there was much work to be done and the sooner he'd 'come up' the better.

Mick said to call into him at #10 Exchequer Street if he arrived before the 22nd. If not, he'd find him at #32 Bachelor's Walk.

Tom had only a vague understanding of what he'd be doing for Collins. They'd known each other briefly before the Uprising. Michael had joined the other 'refugees,' Irish Volunteers who'd left England in early 1916 under the pretext of going home to join the British army. Yes, they were going to join 'an army,' but it wasn't British; it was a fledgling Irish army.

Upon his arrival back in Ireland from London, Collins took a position with "a well-known firm of chartered accountants, Craig, Gardner and Co., of Dame Street." [4] He also handled Count Plunkett's bookkeeping as well as trained with the other Kimmage lads at Plunkett's Larkfield estate. That's where Tom and Michael first met.

Though Collins spent a good deal of his time at Larkfield and was considered a member of their 4th Battalion unit, he didn't live there as many of the others did. Considered a criminal by the British for actively evading conscription, he found it necessary to change his residence from time to time. Prior to the Easter fighting, he rented a room from the Beltons in their family home at #16 Rathdown Road. That was the address he gave to the British authorities upon his arrest at the end of April, 1916.

Tom and Michael met up again in Frongoch. During their six-month internment, the two became good friends. Just prior to their release at the end of December, Michael said he'd like Tom to come work for him after things were sorted out. The Wicklow man told him such an arrangement would be most welcomed.

So during the time Tom was living and directing Volunteer activities in East Wicklow, Michael was heading up the work of the Irish National Aid and Volunteers' Dependents' Fund organised by Kathleen Clarke, wife of Tom Clarke and sister of Ned Daly, two of the executed 1916 leaders.

> On 19 February [1917] Collins became Secretary to the Irish National Aid Fund. The Fund had been set up by Mrs. Kathleen Clarke to alleviate distress amongst the dependents of those killed or imprisoned as a result of the Rising. It was funded both by public subscription and by money from the Clan na nGael in America. The Christmas release of the internees and the less heinously regarded prisoners from Reading [Jail], including Arthur Griffith, meant that suddenly a great deal more work became attached to the post so it was decided to make it salaried, at the princely sum of £2 10s [2 pounds 10 shillings] a week. Collins was the favourite candidate. [5]

[**Author's note**: The Irish National Aid Association was initially led by its directors…Dublin solicitor George Gavan-Duffy, son of Sir Charles Gavin-Duffy, and Dublin Alderman Patrick Corrigan. Within a year it merged with Mrs. Clarke's Irish Volunteers' Dependents' Fund to form the Irish National Aid and Volunteers' Dependents' Fund. Kathleen Clarke enlisted the help of some other family members of those executed to serve on its board: Áine Ceannt (wife of Éamonn), Margaret Pearse (mother of Patrick & William), Muriel MacDonagh (wife of Thomas), Eily O'Hanrahan (sister of Michael), Madge Daly (sister of Edward) and Lila Colbert (sister of Cornelius).]

※

His appointment as Fund secretary marked Collins's further entry into Ireland's underground world of subversive Republicanism with the goal of overthrowing the British yoke of colonial imperialism. Initially, his membership in the soon-to-become militant Irish Volunteers and the secret Irish Republican Brotherhood were Collins's first step down the road to revolution. Later, during his internment in Frongoch, his newly developed friendships and contacts with others sympathetic to the 'cause of

Ireland' only increased his sphere of influence and stretched his thinking.

Those opportunities, coupled with his new relationship with Kathleen Clarke and the Fund's network of like-minded people willing to come to Ireland's aid, opened new doors. In a short time, Michael suddenly found himself in the enviable position of national prominence. He was quickly becoming a lightning rod for revolutionary change in Ireland.

> Apart from running the National Aid Association with great efficiency, Collins took an active part in the reorganisation of the Volunteers, the IRB and Sinn Féin, and established strong links with Clan na nGael through John Devoy in New York. He also began making trips to various centres in England such as London, Liverpool and Manchester, setting up the arms-smuggling network which was later to work so spectacularly well. Even more importantly, as time progressed, he made secret contact with figures who…would be of crucial importance in the coming onslaught on Dublin Castle four of its trusted detectives, Joe Kavanagh, James MacNamara, David Neligan and above all, Ned Broy.
>
> Most of this activity was hidden from the public. What people saw was a powerfully built, extraordinarily efficient young man with a big heart and sometimes, a big mouth.
>
> He never missed an appointment. Never lost a file, or a piece of paper. Kept meticulous accounts and, most important of all, the fund's beneficiaries were treated like heroes of the revolution, not objects of charity. It was in the National Aid Association's offices in 10 Exchequer St. that, building on his GPO and Frongoch reputations, his mythic status began to emerge. [6]

This was the exciting, bold, new world that Tom Cullen stepped into upon his arrival into Dublin at the end of April, 1918.

❧

Finishing their tea, Tom and Andy headed back up the Quay to #32.

As they approached, they could see the door leading upstairs was ajar.

– Hello, called out Tom, pushing the door open.

No answer.

– Hello, Tom called out again but louder this time.

– Hello yourself, came a reply from above.

– Michael?

– Well, for feck sake. Is it the Wicklow warrior himself?

Moments later, the building seemed to shake as Michael Collins came bounding down the stairs.

– Jaysus wept, it's good to see you again, Collins said.

But before he'd a chance to reply, Tom was engulfed in a suffocating bear hug.

– God almighty, Michael, you're none the worse for wear.

– And yourself too. I heard it took an entire train load of Tommies to bring you up to Dublin.

Now standing at arm's length, the two men studied each other's faces carefully. Several moments passed.

Breaking the silence, Collins said, – ...and I suppose this is your brother Andy?

– Yes, he's been looking forward to meeting you. I've told him all about you.

– Fecken' lies...all of it. Not one word of truth in the whole lot.

– Well, Mr. Collins or is it Michael, I'm sure there were a few bits and pieces of exaggeration...

Before Andy could finish, Collins turned and with a nod of his head motioned them to follow him up the stairs. Taking the steps two at a time, the Corkman called back over his shoulder, ...and it's Michael...glad to make your acquaintance.

❧

Michael Collins was in the process of opening a second office for the National Aid Fund at #32. He'd already set up a finance office for himself on the building's second floor [the third floor by US standards] some months earlier. But with increased activity and public interest in the Fund, he planned to install Tom Cullen in the first floor office just below his.

Michael was a bit vague about Tom's duties, but assured him he'd be kept busy, maybe busier than he'd like.

As the three men surveyed the empty space, Collins pointed out where desks, bookshelves, storage cabinets, etc. would go. The small entry room off the hallway would be for reception.

Tom, as one of the Fund's four 'Honourable Secretaries,' would occupy the larger, adjoining office. A door off of it opened to a small kitchen and dining area with a door leading down some back steps to street level.

Opening the back door, Collins said, You never know, Tom, when you'll want to slip out the back way or leave the building unnoticed. I've a door just like this on the second floor. That's one of the reasons I leased these rooms. Besides, it's smack in the heart of the city...lots of people around all hours of the day and night...and you can approach or leave the building from all angles.

Tom and Andy nodded in agreement.

– Oh, one more thing. I'll have a day bed brought in...just in case you decide to spend a night, but in the meantime, it's off we go. I want to reintroduce you to a friend of mine.

Down on the street, the three piled into Andy's borrowed machine. With Collins giving directions, they headed across town to Donnybrook and #1 Brendan Road.

Much to Tom's surprise, the man who answered the door was none other than Batt O'Connor. They'd met in Frongoch, but hadn't seen each other since the autumn of 1916.

Tom remembered Batt being one of the luckier ones. He'd been released in September after a British government Advisory Committee interviewed him and found him innocent of direct involvement in the Easter-Week fighting.

As Batt explained later that morning:

> It was quite plain that the examination [by the Advisory Committee] was a mere formality, and that the British authorities had made up their minds to get rid of all

the Irish prisoners, except those who had been actually caught 'red-handed' in the fight. I daresay they were finding it rather difficult to keep us prisoners while they were fighting a war for the freedom of small nationalities in other parts of Europe. [7]

※

[**Author's note**: Bartholomew 'Batt' O'Connor (1870-1935) was a stonemason from Brosna, Co. Kerry. He later moved to Boston, Massachusetts, becoming a bricklayer and an Irish republican. Upon returning to Ireland, Batt became a successful builder in Dublin, a member of the Gaelic League and the IRB. He also became a close personal friend of Seán MacDiarmada and was devastated by Seán's execution in May, 1916.

Batt himself was not in Dublin at the time of the Uprising. On Mundy Thursday, the IRB ordered him to travel to Co. Kerry and await further instructions. Unfortunately, it was then that the IRB's Rebellion plans began to unravel. With Sir Roger Casement and other IRB arrests in Tralee compounded by the news of the *Aud*'s scuttling, he was at a loss as to what to do. On Easter Monday, news of the fighting in Dublin reached Batt at his mother's home in Brosna.

With travel disruptions being what they were, it took him most of the week to reach the outskirts of Dublin. Unfortunately, because of the military's cordon around Dublin, Batt was arrested trying to slip back home. He was imprisoned first in Dublin, then in England's Wandsworth Jail and later interned in Frongoch. In September, 1916, he finally returned to his wife Maire and their house in Dublin.

Soon, it was his skill as a carpenter and his association with the IRB that copper-fastened his relationship with Michael Collins. Batt and Michael became close friends and the Kerryman built many concealed compartments and special hidden spaces in buildings throughout Dublin for Collins to secret away important documents. Additionally, Michael often used Batt and Maire's home at #1 Brendan Road as a safe house. On those occasions when he wasn't lodging in, he'd often come to #1 Brendan Road for dinner.]

※

After tea and some light sandwiches, Maire took Tom upstairs and showed him what was to be his room for as long as he wished.

Surprised and flabbergasted, the Wicklow man graciously accepted her kind offer.

Later, unloading his two cases from the motor car, Tom said good-bye to Andy. Promising to come up on the train soon, Andrew Cullen bid the O'Connors, Michael Collins and his brother adieu.

※

Tom Cullen had a most unusual experience soon after returning to Dublin to work for Michael.

On Sunday, 12 May, the two-year anniversary of the final executions of the Easter leaders at Kilmainham Gaol, Tom, accompanied by his brother and his former comrade W. T. Cosgrave, attended a special commemorative Mass very near Cosgrave's home. It was held at St. James Church in James Street to mark the solemn occasion. [**Author's note**: Kilmainham Gaol is within St. James's parish boundaries.]

After Mass was over and the three were walking out of the church, a man approached Tom and W. T. He introduced himself as Brother Hubert O'Keeffe, clerk of the church.

Stating that he recognised the two men from their incarceration in the jail two years earlier, he thanked them for attending the Mass and wondered, if they'd the time, would they join him for tea in the presbytery.

Thanking him for his offer, the three nodded and followed the man into the nearby house.

After briefly bringing Br. O'Keeffe up-to-date on the events of their lives, they enjoyed his hospitality of tea and sandwiches.

As they prepared to leave, Br. O'Keeffe bid them wait.

Addressing Tom and W. T. specifically, he said, – There is something I want to tell you…something I want you to know.

Exchanging curious glances, the three guests sat back down.

– As you know, a myth…a legend has begun to grow, not only here in Dublin but, I dare say, around the world, about the deaths of the executed leaders of the 1916 Rebellion.

The three men acknowledged his assertion with nods.

– I don't know if you realise this or not, but your friend and commandant, Éamonn Ceannt, was not shot standing at attention in Stonebreakers Yard.

Without pausing, O'Keeffe continued, – I'm certain this story is true. I've heard it from two eyewitnesses…the two priests who were there. They saw his execution take place.

Tom glanced over at W. T., but said nothing.

– I don't know if either of you were visited by a Father Augustine or not while you were in Kilmainham. He's a Capuchin from the Friary in Church Street. It was he who told me this story.

In a conscious effort to be true to Fr. Augustine's words, Br. O'Keeffe said, – To the best of my recollection this is what the Father told me:

> Then on a certain morning [8 May], he [Ceannt] sent for me. The very first moment I entered his cell [in Kilmainham Gaol] I saw a beautiful white paper with some lines of ink upon it. We spoke for some little time, and did something else, and he said to me: 'Father, you have to make other visits, haven't you?' 'Yes,' said I, 'I have.' 'Well, Father,' said he, 'I would like you to come back to me again.' And then, taking out his watch, he looked at it and said: 'Father, I have yet an hour, have I not?' And I turned to the wall before I said: 'Yes, Éamonn, just another hour.'
>
> I went away across the hall to minister to poor [Michael] Mallin and when I came back again [to Ceannt] we prayed together as long as we could. I remember the Irish saints we invoked….We invoked them all. And then, as I was going out, I said to him, leaving him my

own crucifix: 'Éamonn, keep that, and I will be with you to the last.'

And so, when with another priest [Fr. Eugene McCarthy?], I had gone out to the verge of the outer courtyard outside, I left him quickly and shot back and I saw Éamonn coming towards me down the hall, and my soul leaped to him, and my heart embraced him, and we went out together, he to die for Ireland, and I to live for my country.

I had to stand a short distance away, and what I am going to say now I have never said and I will never say again. I have never said it even to his dear heroic wife, Mrs. Ceannt. I am just as I have never had the heart, to say it to her.

They [British soldiers] brought out a soap-box there and they asked Éamonn to sit down on the soap-box, and an officer came forward, and, when Éamonn was sitting there, asked him to stretch his legs out and, bearing my cross in his tied hands, and with his eyes blind-folded, the poor, sweet, gentle soul, the dying saint, who died with forgiveness of his enemies on his lips, and telling of the kindness of a British officer, he put out his feet, and the firing squad took their aim, and shot....

When poor Ceannt tumbled over from the soap-box I stooped to take the crucifix which he was bearing in his hands and I saw that it was spattered with blood.... [8]

[**Author's note**: Captain Seán Heuston, a twenty-five-year-old Volunteer commandant, was stationed at the Mendicity Institute along the Quays at Usher's Island on Easter Monday. Attached to Dublin's 1st Battalion, whose HQ was across the Liffey near the Four Courts, Heuston and a group of twenty-six young Irishmen held their vulnerable position for two incredible days of fighting. They finally surrendered on Wednesday, after being asked by James Connolly on Monday to hold the building for only three or four hours. Upon retiring to a vastly superior detachment of

Crown forces, the red-faced British officers demanded to know where the rest of his men were. To this demand Heuston simply declared, "There are no others!"

Embarrassed at being out-battled by the youthful Seán Heuston and his boy soldiers, Seán also was shot sitting on a soap-box. They were the only two executed leaders to die in such a way. To this day, I've often wondered if embarrassed revenge wasn't the motivating factor dictating the manner in which their executions were carried out.]

❧

After Br. O'Keeffe's concluded retelling Fr. Augustine's story, the four men crossed themselves unable to speak.

Seconds passed, maybe a minute...even more.

W. T. finally broke the silence, – Thank you Br. O'Keeffe for relaying that story to us. I've not heard it before. Had you, Tom?

Tom shook his head no.

Again, the men returned to the comfort of silence.

Then, unexpectedly, Tom stood up.

– Commandant Ceannt was a grand man and officer. Dedicated...determined to the core he was...there was never anyone braver inside the Union that entire week. By marching out with us, he knew his life was forfeit, but that didn't matter. It was the cause of Irish freedom that mattered and he was going to lead by example.

– But tell me one thing, Br. O'Keeffe, continued Tom, – what was this business of sitting on a soap-box all about? Something to break the monotony? To give the bloody Tommies a better line of sight? Or was it simply to belittle and demean a brave Irish revolutionary? Sometimes I just don't understand the damned Sassenach's mentality.

– Maybe all of those things, Tom, Willie said, – ...maybe all of those things.

The three rose to thank their host once again, but Br. O'Keeffe held up his hand.

– If you've the time, there's one other story I'd like to put right.

Before they could offer an objection, Br. O'Keeffe began talking.

> As clerk of the church it was my duty to accompany the priests on "their visits" and in this connection I found myself often in direct contact with the leaders. [9]

After pausing to make certain his guests were comfortably reseated and their tea cups refilled, Br. O'Keefe continued his revelations.

> The leaders were soon tried and the executions followed each other in quick succession. Father Eugene McCarthy officially attended at each execution, being taken from bed each morning at four o'clock. The prisoner having been placed against the wall and the firing party having fired, his duty was to anoint the body where it fell. On the morning of Joseph Plunkett's execution he was taken away earlier than usual and told he was to perform the marriage ceremony of the prisoner and Grace Gifford prior to the execution, which ceremony he performed in the dark prison cell in the cold chill of early morning. Mrs. Plunkett afterwards visited him at the Presbytery, during which time the place was raided by the military. [10]

– Such traumatic events you witnessed, Brother O'Keeffe, murmured Willie. – It must be hard for you not to be bitter and angry.

– My faith in God sustains me. It gives me the strength to carry on, though I must admit England's cruelty to the Irish is often unfathomable.

– You're right, Brother O'Keeffe. Shooting Joseph an hour after his marriage is a cowardly act...one completely without merit. Their insensitivity to the dying man and his innocent bride can only turn public opinion and personal sentiment against them, said Tom.

– Ah Tom, you're giving the Tommies too much credit. They're a mindless lot. Steeped in their own sense of self-righteousness,

Maxwell and his bloody lackeys could give a damn. They wanted to purge the land of anyone willing to stand up to their brand of contemptuous injustice for fear a noble Irishman would rally the people around the cause of true liberty...someone in the mould of Emmet or Lincoln or William Wallace.

– That's right Andy, answered Tom, – but the story of Joe and Grace will endure forever. In song and in legend, their union and his death, thanks to Sassenach stupidity, will long be remembered as a symbol of '16. Other names may be lost in the mists of time, but not theirs.

– A living symbol of British short-sightedness, added W. T.

The contemplative silence descending on the foursome was short-lived.

Br. O'Keeffe edged forward in his seat, clearing his throat before he spoke.

–What you've said goes without saying, however, British Easter Week malice didn't end there. The executions continued. You know that. But would you like to know what really happened. Sure it's not the story reported in the newspapers. I'd like to put the record straight, at least to you men. It's about the death of James Connolly, the labour man. Sure you remember him so?

The two Cullens and Willie Cosgrave nodded in the affirmative.

> In giving a description of Connolly's execution Fr. McCarthy told me that the prisoner, who was in a bad condition, elected to stand like the rest, but failed. He was then tied to a chair but slumped so much that he overbalanced. Finally he was strapped on a stretcher and placed in a reclining position against the wall. In this manner he passed into the ranks of Ireland's roll of honoured martyrs. The sight left an indelible impression on Fr. McCarthy. Describing the scene to me afterwards he said: "The blood spurted in the form of a fountain from the body, several streams shooting high into the air." The possible explanation of this may have been the tightening of the straps about the body. [11]

Again, the men crossed themselves.

– Connolly's death, like Joe Plunkett's, will be a lasting symbol and remembrance of this country's quest for freedom and justice, said Andy.

– He was such a giant of a man, someone who would stand up to anybody, sure it seems fitting he died upright...not sitting in a chair, said Tom.

– You're right about that, Tom. The courage it took to face up to William Martin 'Murder' Murphy and the rest of his lot during the Lock-Out will not soon be forgotten, said Willie.

Rising from his chair, Br. O'Keeffe clasped his hands and asked his three guests to bow their heads in prayer. After giving thanks to God and asking for His blessings on the three brave Irishmen before him, he said:

> Kilmainham Jail...it stands to-day a silent monument to the great men [and women] who have helped to mould the destiny of Ireland's political future. [12]

Amen.

❧

Somewhat mystified by their visit with Br. O'Keeffe, the three walked down the street towards W. T.'s house.

Nothing about Ceannt or Connolly's death surprised them. They all knew that the British authorities and certainly the military in Dublin were a small-minded, insecure yet arrogant lot who'd never hesitate to discredit an Irishman...especially one who would dare defy their rules or offend their sensibilities.

[**Author's note:** Gerard MacAtasney in his biography of Seán MacDiarmada wrote: "Little is known of the actual mechanics of the executions which took place in the stonebreakers' (sic) yard of Kilmainham Gaol. Various attempts have been made over the years to depict what transpired and legends have grown as to what may have happened." [13]

MacAtasney also related an emotional and upsetting account of Seán MacDiarmada and James Connolly's executions on 12 May 1916. The story, a first-hand accounting of the day's events, was told to William Gogan, a Dublin shopkeeper, in the autumn of 1916 by a British soldier, albeit inebriated, who was at the jail that day. According to Gogan's statement, the original transcript of which is now in the possession (as of 2004) of Piers Gogan, describes the soldier's mood as greatly relieved to be leaving Dublin. He was so distressed by what he'd witnessed that the man rejoiced when he learned he'd be leaving for France and the western front the next day.

The British soldier told Gogan that on the morning of May 12th, he'd been sent to Kilmainham, driving a 'pioneer's' wagon, one used for transporting mud.

In Gogan's transcribed words:

> When he drove into the prison he was told that Mr. Asquith, the English prime minister, was in John Mc-Dermott's [Seán MacDiarmada's] cell and it was likely that no one would be shot that morning. But after a while a number of officers came out of the governor's office and among them was an old gentleman whom he was told was Mr. Asquith. Presently an ambulance drove into the yard, a stretcher to which a man was strapped was drawn out and laid on the ground. Just then guard (sic) marched into the yard; they had a prisoner, a dark, young man who walked with a halt. He was marched over to the wall and left standing there with some officers grouped around him, then the stretcher was lifted up and brought to the wall where it was placed upright beside John McDermott. The officers moved away, the firing party were formed up. The next thing a volley rang out. McDermott fell a huddled mass on the ground. Connolly drooped down on the stretcher with his head hanging forward. [14]

Gerard MacAtasney concluded his telling of William Gogan's account of the soldier's words:

> The firing party were marched away. He was ordered to bring his wagon over to where the bodies lay on the ground. Four men of a fatigue party took John

McDermott's body by the arms and legs and pitched it into the wagon. James Connolly's body was handled the same way when it was removed from the stretcher. The two bodies were covered up with straw and he was told to drive to Arbour Hill prison. He drove into the prison yard where there was a shallow grave dug. The two bodies were put into the grave, lime was thrown on top of them. The earth was filled in and rammed down, then the gravel was spread evenly as if there was nothing unusual there. [15]

Of these and the other executed leaders' burials, Michael Foy and Brian Barton in their book *The Easter Rising*, repeated the promise of General Sir John Grenfell Maxwell, Ireland's new military governor, who arrived on Easter Friday, 28 April 1916: "Irish sentimentality will turn these graves into martyrs' shrines to which annual processions etc will be made. (Hence) the executed rebels are to be buried in quicklime, without coffins." [16]

❧

Unlike the death of his mother which stayed with him always, Tom forcibly struggled to put thoughts of Easter, 1916 out of his mind. Remembrances of Billy King, of Éamonn Ceannt, of the fighting at South Dublin Union, of prison and internment at Frongoch, of the brutality, humiliation and execution of the Rebellion's leaders, especially in light of the news regarding Ceannt, Heuston, MacDiarmada and Connolly's deaths, would continually haunt him if he'd let them. But burning resentment of British-government policy or their inhumane treatment often meted out by their representatives, be they military, police or undercover operatives, had to be set aside. If not, it would poison him, cause him to become careless and lose focus. Eventually, if he weren't careful, it would destroy him all together.

Tom Cullen knew that well. But intellectual understanding and keeping control of your emotions were two different things. Thankfully, working for Collins was a great outlet for the internal fury that still bubbled up, sometimes without warning.

Now, as if in answer to a prayer, he and Michael and the others were finally taking action that would return tit for tat...'equivalent retaliation,' as Michael liked to say.

– We're on course to show our unwelcome Anglo-Saxon tenants the meaning of 'the consequences of the use of violence,' Mick often said.

Tom had been in Dublin only a few weeks when Michael told him he was resigning as Secretary of the Volunteers' Aid Fund. Now, with all the 1916 prisoners released and the fund financially secure, it had raised almost £200,000 since its inception, Collins had other undertakings demanding his attention.

Then on 3 June, unwittingly or not, a Dublin Castle directive was issued, calling for 50,000 Irishmen to join the British army by the autumn. [**Author's note**: The Allied war crisis of spring, 1918 had dissolved. During the summer, the earlier German spring offensive had been reversed. With the help of American troops, the Allied forces counter-attacked. They won the 2nd Battle of the Marne River and would soon launch the Hundred Days' Offensive.]

Still, with the war only months away from a successful conclusion, the London government continued demanding an additional 2-3,000 Irish enlistees per month, over and above the 50,000, 'to maintain division troop quotas.' These English declarations were viewed as merely implied threats in Ireland and were largely ignored. The real beneficiaries of this British enlistment coercion were the Irish Volunteers. As a counter-reaction, they saw their ranks swell.

According to some reports, the Volunteer numbers soon reached 100,000 strong. Pathetically, however, only a small percentage of the enlistees were armed and many joined for the wrong reason: avoiding possible British compulsory conscription.

With their heads squarely screwed on backwards, the Sassenach ploughed stubbornly forward. Béaslaí astutely noted:

On the 3rd July the English Government issued another "proclamation" solemnly declaring "the Sinn Féin
Organisation, Sinn Féin Clubs, the Irish Volunteers,
Cumann na mBan and the Gaelic League" suppressed,
on the grounds that "the said organisations in parts of
Ireland encourage and aid persons to commit crime
and incite to acts of violence and intimidation, and
interfere with the administration of the law, and disturb
the maintenance of law and order." It would be hard to
conceive a proceeding more farcical or more calculated
to bring the English government into contempt and
ridicule than this "proclamation." All the organisations named in it carried on their work as usual after
its publication. One of them, the Gaelic League, was
simply an organisation for the revival and spread of the
Irish language.

Next day appeared a fresh proclamation, from
the English military General Headquarters in Ireland,
prohibiting the "holding or taking part in meetings,
assemblies, or processions in public places within the
whole of Ireland," unless such meeting or assembly was
authorised in writing by the Chief Commissioner of the
Dublin Metropolitan Police, or the County Inspector
of the Royal Irish Constabulary. [17]

❧

It was about this time, shortly after the German Plot 'round
up' that Collins began putting together, at least in his mind, the
framework for his 'intelligence team' on which Tom Cullen would
play such an important role as his Assistant Director.

With Tom already onboard, Mick began casting about for
persons to fill other key positions. The name Liam Tobin caught
his attention. A fellow Corkman, born in 1895, Tobin was destined
to become Michael's Assistant or Deputy Director of Intelligence,
his number-two man.

Piaras Béaslaí, who knew Tobin well, wrote:

Tobin was still a very young man. He began life as a
clerk, and took part in the Easter Week Rising when he
was barely twenty years of age. He was sentenced to ten
years' penal servitude, and was one of the Portland and
Lewes convicts. He first came into contact with Collins in connection with the work of the National Aid
Association. After his release he became associated with
the New Ireland Assurance Society, then a new venture.
[The insurance company was founded in 1918.] He had
become Intelligence Officer of the Dublin Brigade, and
thereby came under the notice of Collins as a particularly good man at Intelligence work. [18]

❧

With Collins free of his Fund responsibilities, Tom Cullen
also found himself with less to do, but that was soon rectified.
Michael began using Tom as his Assistant Quartermaster General
assigned to "...superintending the import and distribution of
arms, ammunition and military equipment, and the circulation of
'An tÓglách,' the official organ of the Volunteers." [19]

Still using the offices at #32 Bachelor's Walk, Tom took ad-
vantage of the groundwork Collins had laid down as early as 1908.
While living and working in London, Mick had made friends with
Neill Kerr, an active Liverpool IRB member.

After the Uprising, Kerr succeeded in making the necessary
contacts and obtained sizeable amounts of arms and ammunition.
As an employee of the Canard Steamship Company and a friend
to many sailors, the Liverpool man was responsible for seeing the
weaponry was delivered into Collins's and later Cullen's hands.

Michael took full advantage of his early contacts and worked
hard to develop new ones. Arming the Volunteers was one of his
highest priorities.

Both men made visits, particularly to Liverpool, to keep the
arms-pipeline flowing. They also met important contacts, usually

at Vaughan's Hotel, to plan and exploit future deliveries.

Collins was also a master of utilising both the English and Irish postal systems as a source for intelligence gathering. With the help of his former London friend and fellow Corkman, Sam Maguire, Mick often knew the Sassenach's plans before they were issued. Through his associations with fellow Frongoch internees and later with contacts made while he was the secretary of the Volunteers' Fund, Michael was able to ferret out citizens sympathetic to Ireland's causes. As a result, The Stranger's administrative, as well as its military and police cipher messages, were opened and decoded before they ever reached the hands of those they were intended to reach.

Additionally, the Big Fellow succeeded in establishing relationships with compassionate jail and prison warders. With hundreds of Irish nationalists and republicans passing through both Irish jails and the British prison system, many since the spring of 1916, prisoners were able to develop associations with sympathetic officials who were in position to aid Collins's future causes.

Another cog in Michael's bourgeoning, sub-rosa intelligence planning was his success in developing associations with several Dublin Castle political detectives who shared his pro-Irish aspirations.

Again, because of Béaslaí's close relationship with and his first-hand knowledge of Collins and Cullen's activities, the historian provided much detailed information.

> By June or July [1918] Collins was in direct contact with several political detectives. One of these was Joe Kavanagh...who died [in hospital of heart failure] early in 1920. Another was James MacNamara, who was destined to do much important work for him, and narrowly escaped detection during the Black and Tan period [1920-1921]. Another was Ned Broy, who was arrested by the English in 1921, and at a later stage Collins came in touch with David Neligan. There were other detectives who rendered assistance, but the four mentioned were the principal ones. [20]

Beginning in the summer of 1919, the paths of Tom Cullen and these four men crossed many times.

❧

As 1918 came to an end, so too did the war in Europe. An armistice dictated by the Allies was signed by the Germans at five o'clock in the morning, 11 November. Six hours later, at the eleventh hour of the eleventh day of the eleventh month, World War I officially ended.

With the conflict finally over, Ireland expected England to release the Sinn Féin leadership it had interned back in May. Instead, The Stranger undertook further arrests and deportations of Irish nationalists. This action confirmed what Collins and many others long suspected. England's May arrests had nothing to do with Germany and the Allied war effort. It was simply a political manoeuvre to sterilise Ireland's struggle for self-governance.

The arrest warrants for Michael Collins, Tom Cullen and the many others remained in effect. They were still wanted men...men on-the-run whose daily lives were lived in fear of being arrested and imprisoned.

[**Author's note**: During the run-up to the December, 1918 election, there was the ambiguous belief, more a hope than anything else, that Sinn Féin candidates were safe from arrest as long as they were canvassing in their own constituencies.]

❧

Soon after the armistice was signed, the British government called for a snap general election scheduled for 14 December. Confident their internment actions and arrest intimidations had stymied the 'rabble-upshots' of any ballot-box successes, the powers-to-be in Dublin and London were in for a surprise.

When the election results were announced on Monday, 30 December, Sinn Féin had swept to victory, winning seventy-three of the one hundred five Irish MP seats. The Irish Parliamentary Party was devastated, its political future virtually destroyed.

The election finally provided Arthur Griffith's party with the national opening it had long sought to establish: the creation of an 'Irish' governmental assembly that would meet in Dublin. It would be the first time an Irish parliament had met there since 1800 when a Protestant Irish legislative body, meeting in College Green, voted itself out of existence and copper-fastened Ireland's 1800 Act of Union with its island neighbour.

The 1918 election victory also affirmed Sinn Féin's refusal to recognise the British House of Commons and avowed their pre-election pledge not to take any seats, if victorious.

※

Just prior to this election victory, Béaslaí spotlighted Collins's behaviour as he ran for elected office for the first time.

> Although Michael Collins was still working only behind the scenes, and had attained little or no prominence, he was sufficiently known in his native district to be selected as Sinn Féin candidate for South Cork. He is-sued his election address in Irish and English, but he was unable to visit South Cork during the election owing to more pressing claims of his work in Dublin. The victory of Sinn Féin in South Cork was regarded as certain. [21]

Tom Cullen, also living and working behind the scenes, main-tained his non-political stance, keeping his electoral involvement to a minimum: he simply cast his ballot on polling day.

※

Finally, Piaras Béaslaí brought the year to a close with an intimate, personal look at the Big Fellow.

> At this period Collins was rarely seen without a ciga-rette in his mouth. He admitted once that he smoked between forty and fifty cigarettes a day. A year later he suddenly gave up smoking altogether, but he retained the habit of carrying boxes of cigarettes around in his

pocket, offering them to his friends but never touched them himself a striking instance of will power. From 1919 onwards he drank only a little sherry, though on a few occasions, when nearly in a state of collapse from overwork, strain and neglect of meals, he took brandy. He was a very moderate drinker. I mention this because I am aware that lying statements and scurrilous cartoons on this point were circulated by his political opponents at the time of the Treaty debates [December, 1921-January, 1922]. It is quite clear to any man of common sense that only a very temperate man could possibly have got through the enormous amount of work which Collins transacted daily and nightly, with the strictest punctuality and system. I was his constant companion in his convivial moments, both in the period of prolonged tension before the Truce, and the period of reaction which followed, and my testimony on this point is emphatic and unequivocal. [22]

In conclusion, Tim Pat Coogan put a fine point on Collins's life during this same period.

Michael Collins, in 1918-19, was responsible for a number of initiatives: the setting-up of two underground newspapers, the building of an intelligence network, an arms smuggling route, the organisation of a national loan, the creation of his elite hit unit, the 'Squad', a bomb-making factory, and a variety of other schemes. [23]

All the while, Tom Cullen, working undercover, waited in the wings for the moment when his talents would be more fully utilised.

❧

[**Author's note**: For additional reading, I suggest Piaras F. Mac Lochlainn, *Last Words: Letters and Statements of the Leaders Executed after the Rising at Easter 1916,* (1990) & Batt O'Connor, TD, *With Michael Collins: In the Fight for Irish Independence,* (undated).]

6

"Tall, gaunt, cynical, with tragic eyes, he looked
a man who had seen the inside of hell."
—David Neligan's description of Liam Tobin,
Deputy Director of Intelligence

Tom Cullen spent much of the Christmas and New Year
holidays in Wicklow Town. It was good to relax, to spend
time with Andy and friends. Together, the two of them drove to
their father's house in Co. Kildare for a brief family reunion on
New Year's Day, 1919.

He enjoyed these occasional breaks from the pressures of
Dublin. Michael Collins kept him busy, but it was the looking
over his shoulder that prayed on his mind. The ever-lurking danger
of the bloody Peelers and the 'G' Division detectives kept him on
his toes. The last thing Tom wanted was to be caught up in some
police raid or apprehended by a British military dragnet.

Since his return to Dublin over seven months ago, he'd heard
from more than one respected authority that his name had moved
up on the list of men 'wanted for questioning' by Castle authorities. Tom thought they probably had a photograph of him, back
from the time of his arrest in Wicklow Town, and certainly they
had his description. But luckily he was just one of many men the
rozzers were trying to keep their eye on. If he took the necessary
measures, he was confident he'd be alright, unless of course they
turned up the heat.

Tom's ring of latchkeys was growing. After spending most
nights during the summer sleeping in #1 Brendan Road, thanks
to the hospitality of the O'Connors, he started moving around.

Sometimes he slept in his Bachelor's Walk office. Other times he stayed in Mrs. McCarthy's Munster Hotel at #44 Mountjoy Street and occasionally across the street with the Dickers. Madeline 'Dilly' Dicker, a girlfriend of Mick's, and her father Edwin, a died-in-the-wool republican, kept a room for the odd guest in need of a bed for the night.

Once in a while he knocked on Commandant Ceannt's door. Mrs. Ceannt always had a smile, a hot meal and a place for him to sleep. She and her son Rónán were getting on without Éamonn, but they missed him terribly. The pain of his death never went away.

Tom also spent many nights sleeping in the basement of Patrick Pearse's first school, Cullenswood House, at #21 Oakley Road, and even occasionally in Sinn Féin offices at #6 Harcourt Street near Stephen's Green. Another of his favourite lodgings was Vaughan's Hotel. Just a few blocks from #32, both Michael and he spent many comfortable nights sleeping peacefully in Rutland Square. For some reason, the authorities had overlooked it as a sanctuary for revolutionaries.

Every so often, Tom bunked in with W. T. Cosgrave who was now living in digs at #173 James Street, next door to his boyhood home.

Bill's pending marriage to Louisa Flanagan was a frequent topic of conversation, but without fail, talk always turned to how the Dubliner took the wind out of the three British officers who came into his cell at Kilmainham after the Uprising.

He'd been court-martialled on 4 May and, immediately afterward, was transferred to the old Gaol. It was on the following day that he learned his fate…a day of very mixed blessings. Phil Cosgrave [Willie's brother], Major Seán MacBride and he were lodged separately in adjoining cells.

In W. T.'s own words:

> At daybreak on Friday morning [5 May] I heard a slight movement and whisperings in the Major's cell. After a few minutes that was a tap on his [MacBride's] cell door. I heard the word "Sergeant", a few more whispers, a move towards the door of the cell, then steps down the corridor, down to the central stairs. Through a chink

in the door I could barely discern the receding figures; silence for a time; then the sharp crack of rifle fire and silence again. I thought my turn would come next and waited for the rap on the door, but the firing squad had no further duty that morning.

Fr. Augustine came into [my] cell in the afternoon and told [me], Major MacBride was shot at daybreak. He died like the soldier he was, R.I.P. [1]

W. T. broke the mood of reverence and reflection as he continued:

Shortly afterwards, three officers come to [my] cell and announced that the verdict, "You William Thomas Cosgrave, have been found guilty and have been sentenced to death and to be shot." [Then] the officer paused for effect. [I] did not comment. The surprised officer continued, "The sentence has been commuted to penal servitude for life." [My] reaction, to the surprise of the officers, was to inquire as to when [I] could see [my] solicitor. [2]

[**Author's note**: In August, 1917, Kilkenny Town saw W. T. Cosgrave, recently released from prison, sweep to victory in its local by-election, becoming another member of Sinn Féin to stand for his party. Now, as an MP in the House of Commons, he adhered to Sinn Féin's policy of refusing to take his elected seat in London.]

❧

Spending time with Michael and their small circle of close friends often offered a false sense of security. Precautions always had to be taken...lookouts posted. Never meet or dine in the same place on consecutive evenings. Never travel the same streets two days in a row. Always keep your eye on the door and don't make the mistake of failing to have an alternative exit close at hand. Enter through the back door and leave by the front or vice versa. Patronise establishments operated by those sympathetic to Sinn Féin's cause and avoid places run by known touts or Shoneens.

❧

One of the other reasons Tom enjoyed returning to Wicklow so much was having time to spend with Delia Considine. There was no doubt about it, they fancied each other. Whether walking out along the grassy slopes by Black's Castle or borrowing a motor and driving up to Greystones for the day, they enjoyed each other's company more and more.

Though he wasn't able to tell Delia much about his day-to-day activities in Dublin, she knew he worked for Michael Collins and that his involvement with the Volunteers was risky business.

She'd met Michael on two occasions and they enjoyed each other's company. Quiet and not too talkative, Delia was a great one for playing the piano. To top things off, she'd a wonderful singing voice. With her shy, beguiling smile, infectious laughter and excellent taste in fashion, Delia caught everyone's eye upon entering a room. Together, Tom and she made a fine-looking couple. Though he wouldn't discuss it with others, Tom began contemplating marriage.

❧

The impact of December's general election was taking hold in Ireland. Newspapers reported the stunning results and politicians, especially those in the IPP, still were dazed by its outcome.

Imagine, less than three years ago, prior to the Easter Uprising, the Irish Parliamentary Party was the unquestioned political power in Ireland. The vast majority of Irish citizens followed its dictates without giving it as much as a by-your-leave. If last month's polling had been held prior to April, 1916, the IPP could well have won every seat up for election from Sinn Féin.

Piaras Béaslaí provided wonderful insight into the mood of the Irish people immediately after the polling outcome was published.

> This result must not be taken as indicating a sudden and complete conversion of the Irish people to Republicanism. The basis of all national and patriotic movements in Ireland, whether "moderate" or "extreme," political

or cultural, had been a desire for a separate national existence for Ireland, independent of England; but the majority of the people had no reasoned political theories on the subject, and were always most interested in the removal of those grievances or disabilities which weighed most heavily on them. The desire of nationhood had been allowed, no doubt foolishly, to crystallise itself into the formula of Home Rule. The betrayal of Home Rule by the English Government, the surrender to Carsonite threats, and the obvious weakness of the [IP] Party, the heroism and sacrifices of Easter Week, and the subsequent coercion and persecution by the English Government, had changed the mind of the people; and the passing of the Conscription Act had proved the final blow. [3]

❧

Michael Collins slagged Tom Cullen about his absence from work upon his return to Dublin four days into the New Year.

Not one to take such treatment seriously, the Wicklow man gave as much as he received. To the unwitting stranger, overhearing the two men going on at one another, he'd have thought that one of them would surely end up dead...strangled by the other. But no. Their twinkling eyes and broad grins betrayed their real intentions. Mick and Tom, like brothers, were just letting off steam and having a good laugh at the same time. Such bouts of verbal abuse simply strengthened their relationship not weakened it.

❧

With Tom back at his desk in Bachelor's Walk, Michael aggressively launched a new scheme, hoping to accelerate the realization of the dream that finally Ireland would be free of its colonial overlord's tyranny.

Upon consultation with a few close confidants, Collins put into motion the beginnings of a bold new plan. Acting without official authority, the Big Fellow decided to challenge Britain's venerable spy and intelligence systems that had helped it dominate Irish life for many, many decades.

At the present time, the Director of Intelligence was Eamonn Duggan, a Dublin solicitor and politician. Born in Co. Meath, he'd fought with the 1ˢᵗ Bn, Dublin Brigade during the Uprising. Arrested, he was sentenced to three years penal servitude, but was released in June, 1917 under the general amnesty. He returned to his Dublin law practice, and as part of the Volunteers' reorganisation, took over as head of intelligence in 1918.

Unfortunately, with only one assistant, Christopher Carbery, and a growing legal practice, Eamonn wasn't able to devote much time to his added responsibilities. Collins, on the other hand, saw the need of establishing an aggressive, all-embracing intelligence network to counter Dublin Castle's well-oiled, two-headed devil: the DMP and the RIC.

Within the parameters of Dublin Town and its bordering county, the Dublin Metropolitan Police were the immediate authority. Modelled after the London Metropolitan Police, both units wore similar uniforms and were unarmed. Both recruited physically tall, imposing young men to uphold the law.

Dublin Town itself was divided into fourths with each area given a letter 'A' through 'D'. Divisions 'E' and 'F' were responsible for governing the surrounding county population. The seventh was the 'G' Division. Its province was routine crime, political investigation and carriage control. Officially, its single-letter abbreviation stood for the Department of Political Investigation and Information of the Dublin Metropolitan Police. Its force consisted of approximately fifty plain-clothes detectives, mostly assigned to division headquarters at #1 Great Brunswick Street [later renamed Pearse Street]. The 'G-men' were headed by a commissioner, Colonel Walter Edgeworth-Johnson, who spent most of his time in his office in Dublin Castle, also headquarters of the RIC.

Down the country, law enforcement was another matter all together. Often called 'policemen,' the RIC were not. They were a military force and were stationed in 'barracks' not police stations as were the 'police' in England and in other 'law-abiding, free countries.'

England didn't view Ireland as being an idyllic, peace-loving country. Weren't the Irish always rising up in armed rebellion against their authority? Weren't they the sort who needed to be 'watched' and 'controlled'?

Béaslaí, the master of hitting the nail on the head, had it right when he wrote:

> The "R.I.C." were a military force, armed with rifles and living in barracks. Their primary and essential purpose was to hold the country in subjection to England. In furtherance of this aim, the force was kept at a strength out of all proportion to the requirements of a normal police force. In districts where crime was practically unknown, where the only case that came before a magistrate in the course of a year would be an odd case of a drunken travelling tinker, barracks full of strapping young men, armed with rifles, were maintained at the expense of the people of Ireland. Every village had its barracks, with its garrison holding the post for England, and dominating the countryside. [4]

Without compunction, he continued:

> The R.I.C. were recruited from the ranks of the [Irish] people for the purpose of spying on the [Irish] people. To ensure that no personal sympathies or friendly ties would influence them, it was a regulation of the force that no constable could be stationed in the county of which he was a native. The R.I.C. had established an elaborate system of espionage which was carried to a wonderful pitch of perfection. In every town or village all the movements of persons were watched and reported upon. All popular organisations were kept under observation, and all persons who expressed patriotic opinions were the object of surveillance. Even their activities in such matters as teaching Irish, or acting in Irish plays, were duly reported; and Dublin Castle, as the result of these reports, had the most exact information as to the personnel, strength and methods of all national move-

ments in the country. So perfectly was this done that the people concerned had not the slightest idea of the extent to which they were being spied upon. [5]

This in a nutshell was a first-hand description of the intrusive role the RIC played in the daily life of Irishmen and women during the time prior to and immediately after the Uprising.

Seán Moylan, the Co. Cork republican leader, painted a more moderate picture of the RIC.

> It would be incorrect to say in the years before 1916 the RIC were unpopular. They were of the people, were inter-married among the people; they were generally men of exemplary lives, and of a high level of intelligence. They were a moderating influence that kept within some bounds the responsibilities and criminalities of the Black and Tans. [6]

[**Author's note:** As with so many diverse opinions, I'm sure the truth, at least in most instances, lies somewhere in the middle between Béaslaí's and Moylan's characterisations. I know some families whose RIC fathers or grandfathers were fine men caught up in a very difficult situation. Older members of the Constabulary, who might have wanted to resign for various reasons, simply were financially unable to face losing their pensions, accrued after years of service. But on the whole, I'm inclined to agree with Piaras. I think his accounting of the RIC's role in 'taking the King's shillin' is more likely the accurate one. Seán's portrayal seems a bit too sugar-coated to suit my fancy.]

❦

The RIC were the 'brainchild' of Sir Robert Peel, British Conservative PM from 1834-1835 and again from 1841-1846. With the passage of the Irish Constabulary Act of 1836, this 'force' became a fact of life in Ireland. The word 'Royal' was affixed to the organisation's name after their 'heroics' in helping put down Ireland's Fenian Rising in 1867.

Both Britain and Ireland kept alive the memory of Robert Peel's legacy long after his death in 1850. As the 'father' of the 'modern' police force in both lands, the British adopted the nickname 'Bobby' for their policemen while in Ireland, the term 'Peelers' became a common reference for these erstwhile guardians of the peace.

Without the Irish Constabulary and later the Royal Irish Constabulary, the British administration in Ireland, centrally housed in Dublin Castle, wouldn't have been able to govern. Besides being the strong arm of the law, the Peelers were England's eyes and ears on the ground. The information gleaned from these uniformed custodians of the countryside allowed the Castle to operate successfully. Unless the Irish cut off the head of this British 'snake in the grass,' little would change. Michael Collins understood this and was determined to eradicate the imposing 'Judas blight,' hoping the local government's elaborate system of information and controls would implode.

❧

Collins decided to begin with the Castle and its operatives first. Once he'd had a good understanding of who was working for whom, he'd tackle the RIC next.

Irish historian Ryle Dwyer said it succinctly:

> Collins set up a far-reaching network, incorporating intelligence gathering, counter intelligence and matters relating to prison escapes and smuggling (both arms and people). He was the brain behind the whole network and his industry was phenomenal. He retained personal control over work similar to that done by three different intelligence agencies in Britain: MI5 [domestic], MI6 [foreign] and MI9 [military].
>
> An intelligence office was set up over the print shop of J. F. Fowler at 3 Crow Street which was just off Dame Street and right under the nose of Dublin Castle. Collins generally stayed away from that office.

Joe O'Reilly acted as his main courier to the office and everyone in it. Members of the staff were supposedly 'manufacturing agents' [Irish Products Company], but they spent much of their time in the office decoding intercepted messages. [7]

David Neligan, the 'G' Division man turned Castle spy for Michael, provided a good description of the men Collins chose for his intelligence network's inner circle.

I knew Joe's [O'Reilly] appearance well, indeed all the G-men did. He could be seen at all hours pedalling an old bicycle furiously. The G-men never attached any importance to Joe, but they were wrong. He was Collins' confidential courier and often carried important despatches. As Frank O'Connor said in his readable book, *The Big Fellow*, Joe lived only for Collins. Like him, he was a Corkman, a thin, eager, sparely-built youth with lively movements, a very dynamo of energy. He was also innocent, ingenuous and intensely religious; altogether an admirable person. A poor labourer, he had given up his work to take on a life of drudgery far worse than labouring, for Collins was a hard taskmaster, sparing none, himself least of all. [8]

Next, Michael chose Liam Tobin as his Deputy Director…his number-two man, the one in charge at #3 Crow Street.

Tall, gaunt, cynical, with tragic eyes, he looked a man who had seen the inside of hell. He walked without moving his arms and seemed emptied of energy. Yet this man was, after Collins, the Castle's most dangerous enemy. Like all of us, a poor man, an ex-shop assistant, he had a great flair for intelligence work, and was Collins' chief assistant. He ran a secret intelligence office within a stones throw of the castle. It was never discovered by the British. Untrained or self-trained as he was, he was an efficient counter-espionage agent and I believe would have been worth his place in any intelligence bureau.

It was a measure of the G-men's impotence that they never had tagged Tobin.... [9]

Of Tobin, James Mackay added:

Tobin, in particular, had a genius for gathering and collating the seemingly unconnected trivia which enabled him to build up a picture of the enemy's movements and intentions. Using such unlikely sources as *Who's Who* and the social column of *The Times* and *The Morning Post*, Tobin constructed elaborate profiles of the movements, haunts, hobbies, appearance and social connections of everyone remotely connected with the British administration of Ireland. From this building [#3 Crow Street]..., the intelligence machine of the infant republic operated with deadly and devastating efficiency. [10]

Tom Cullen was Michael's pick to be Liam Tobin's assistant and the network's third in command. Tom's new duties were simply added on to his continuing responsibilities as Assistant QMG. As Collins's Assistant Director of Intelligence, he worked closely with both Mick and Liam; with the Wicklow man and Liam Tobin soon becoming fast friends.

Michael Foy in his comprehensive look at Collins's intelligence network, Michael Collins's *Intelligence War*, commented that it was Tom's "...loyalty, discretion and bluff common sense [that] Collins valued highly." [11]

Frank Thornton completed Collins's intimate troika of intelligence chiefs.

Again, Foy's research uncovered other important details.

The 28-year-old Thornton was from a fiercely republican Drogheda [Co. Lough] family. In 1912 he moved to Liverpool, worked as a shipyard painter, joined the Irish Volunteers and met Collins, who initiated him into the IRB. An excellent organiser and conspirator, Thornton smuggled weapons to Ireland before returning to Ireland in 1916.... Subsequently in prison he met [Liam] Tobin, with whom he established the New Ireland Assurance Society [1918-1919] in order to challenge foreign domination of the Irish insurance industry. When Collins sent him to Longford in late 1919 to resuscitate the county's Volunteer organisation, Thornton used the Society as a front for his clandestine activities. [12]

While in Liverpool, Frank became the leader of the local Volunteers. Then, in early 1916 Collins, Thornton and a group of others returned to Ireland. They quickly became valued members of the Kimmage contingent. During Easter Week, Thornton, like Collins, was a member of Headquarters Battalion. While Michael was positioned inside the GPO, Frank was stationed across the street in the Imperial Hotel.

Of Collins's intelligence trio [Tobin, Cullen & Thornton], Peter Hart wrote:

> In practice these three men acted as a triumvirate and effectively ran the department from their offices in [#32] Bachelor's Walk and then from [#3] Crow Street near Dublin Castle, consulting Collins on a nightly basis. Collins was the boss, but the success enjoyed by IRA Intelligence is at least as much attributable to their canniness and hard work as to his direction. [13]

Béaslaí further noted:

> The Intelligence Staff was built up slowly, as suitable men were not easily found. Among the earlier members were Joe Dolan, Frank Saurin, Joe Guilfoyle, Charlie Dalton, Paddy Caldwell, and Frank Thornton. Later additions, about the end of 1920, were Peter Magee, Ned Kelleher, Dan MacDonnell (sic) Charlie Byrne, and Paddy Kennedy. [14]

Of Frank Saurin, Ryle Dwyer wrote:

> ...Frank Saurin, who stood out as one of the best-dressed men in the movement. He turned out in an

impeccable suit and often wore lavender gloves. Some of the British made the mistake of assuming he looked too respectable to be a rebel, with the result that his sense of dress often amounted to a pass allowing him to saunter through enemy cordons. [15]

Dwyer also added important organisational detail to Collins's new endeavour in his book *The Squad.*

Each company of the Volunteers had its own intelligence officer [IO] and they reported to a brigade IO, who, in turn reported to the intelligence headquarters under Tobin. Each IO was encouraged to enlist agents in all walks of life, but especially people in prominent positions who boasted of their British connections.

Intelligence was divided into two areas. First there was the gathering of information on the movement of British forces, and second, information on the activity of British agents, whether they were members of the special intelligence service, military intelligence or members of the various police intelligence units. [16]

Each of Michael's Volunteer intelligence officers had his own territory or area of responsibility, e.g., hotels, restaurants, public houses, newsagents, sport grounds, rail stations, racecourses, etc. In each locale, the IO was responsible for developing contacts that were in position to observe and later pass on information about the comings and goings of interested persons, government officials, military officers and known enemy agents…all for the purpose of eliminating the offending parties if and when it became necessary.

The members of the intelligence staff were essentially aides of Collins. Their initial task was to gather as much information as possible about the police, especially G Division. Information such as where they lived and the names of members of their families would prove invaluable to Collins in the coming months. His agents were a whole range of people, with no one too humble to be of use.

Maids in guesthouses and hotels, porters, bartend-
ers, sailors, railwaymen, postmen, sorters, telephone
and telegraph operators, warders and ordinary policemen all played an important part. Certain sorters and
postmen intercepted mail for British agents undercover,
and Collins and his men had mail sent to them under
cover-names at convenient addresses. The Big Fellow
had the splendid ability of making each of the people
helping feel important, even though he rarely, if ever,
thanked them for what they were doing.

'Why should I thank people for doing their part?' he
would ask. 'Isn't Ireland their country as well as mine?' [17]

The dapper Frank Saurin described how he became a valued
member of Crow Street in his Witness Statement given in the
1950s.

About 1919, I was appointed Company I.O., and a
recommendation was put forward for my promotion to
Battalion I.O. However, this did not materialise, and I
was transferred to G.H.Q. Intelligence Section of the
Irish Republican Army in August 1920. This was a paid,
whole-time job, directly under Michael Collins, and my
immediate superiors were, Liam Tobin, Tom Cullen and
Frank Thornton. Our headquarters at the time was at
No. 3 Crow Street. Each member was given a number
to cover his identity for reference in Correspondence
and to sign reports. Through our agents I was enabled
to get to know by sight a number of enemy personnel
– the object being their extermination if and when the
opportunity offered. [18]

Charlie Dalton, another early member of Collins's intelligence
staff, related the following:

One of our greatest sources of information in the trac-
ing of movements of prominent personages was the
society columns of newspapers, covering banquets,
dinners, etc. Also "Who's Who", which enabled us to

trace clubs, hobbies, etc., of these people, as well as Press photographs taken at Castle or similar functions. In our Crow St. office we kept an alphabetical card index of all known enemy agents, Auxiliary Cadets, R.I.C. men, etc. Any information as to their movements, whereabouts or intentions obtained from the Press in this manner was tabulated and circulated to the country Volunteers, if it concerned them. Photographs were studied by our staff, and, in many instances our identification, on the street or elsewhere, of these individuals was made possible through a study of their photographs.

During the daytime Michael Collins worked from an office of his own, and at no time did he visit the Crow St. or Brunswick St. offices. Inter-communication was maintained by his special messenger, Joe O'Reilly. In the evening time Michael Collins used to meet Liam Tobin and Tom Cullen at one of his numerous rendezvous in the Parnell [Rutland] Square area these were Jim Kirwan's, Vaughan's Hotel and Liam Devlin's.

In the early years Michael Collins used to meet these men at 46 Parnell [Rutland] Square and at [Mrs. Myra T.] McCarthy's in [#44] Mountjoy St. They were all on the run and on many occasions they stayed together, sometimes at Joe O'Reilly's lodgings, Smith's of Lindsay Road, and on other occasions at Paddy O'Shea's house in Lindsay Road. [19]

In his Witness Statement, Dan McDonnell, another GHQ intelligence man, added important detail about how the Tobin-Cullen-Thornton operation worked.

When we joined the Intelligence staff, we all got numbers – my own particular number was 101 – and when I had any written report to make, which was rarely, I just signed it '101'. My first assignment was to go to Leeson Street at 9 o'clock on a Monday morning and to report on all British personnel, whether in cars or on foot, that passed up Leeson Street Bridge. Along came three or four staff cars with staff officers, etc., and with brass hats, red bands, etc. I did this morning after morning. At the same time another member of our staff had been detailed to watch these fellows from another place, and what we saw, between us, tallied. Nothing that I know of was done in these particular cases.

We were next taken into the office and our first job was (at this time there had been a couple of raids made on the G.P.O.) to go through every letter from wherever it came, that went to the Castle. [**Author's note**: Because of the massive devastation done to the main GPO in Sackville Street, an auxiliary GPO was established up the street in the Rotunda Rink, next to the Rotunda Hospital, in Rutland Square. This was the same building in which the Irish Volunteers held their first organisational and sign-up meeting in November, 1913. The O'Connell Street GPO didn't officially re-open until July, 1929.]

Our office was in 3 Crow Street. We were known as manufacturing agents. We also built up and checked up on the codes used by the British forces between Dublin and [down] the country. They used two kinds of codes: one was the simple letter code which was changed monthly. Another code which was more complicated and much harder to break down was a number code which was changed frequently. What happened was, we got the letters of the first 25 per cent of the message from our sources within the Castle, and as the messages came through we worked them out. We were not as efficient with this code as with the letter code; the reason being by the time we had it broken down and had it working, the system was changed again. [20]

Miss Lily Mernin, Piaras Béaslaí's cousin, was a young typist who worked for British army command HQ. Working for Colonel Hill Dillon, the chief intelligence officer in Ireland, she was in a unique position to funnel important information to the GHQ intelligence staff. Her loyalty to the cause of Ireland can't be underestimated. She often risked her life to pass on copies of key documents.

She remembered how it all began.

I was employed as a shorthand-typist in the Garrison Adjutant's office, Dublin District, Lower Castle Yard, during the years 1914 to 1922. Piaras Béaslaí, who is a relative of mine, used to visit my house, and during the course of conversation I may have made some reference to the work on which I was engaged in Dublin Castle.

Apparently, Béaslaí spoke to Michael Collins about me, because some time in 1918, Michael Collins asked to meet me and Piaras Béaslaí brought him to my home and introduced him to me as a Mr. Brennan. I did not know he was Collins at the time. He asked me would I be willing to pass out to him any information that might be of value which I would come across in my ordinary day's work. I remember he produced letters that he had intercepted concerning some of the typists and officers in the Castle, and things that were happening generally. I cannot remember exactly what they were. I promised to give him all the assistance that I possibly could. [21]

Sometime in 1919, Lily Mernin met Tom Cullen.

On various occasions I was requested by members of the Intelligence Squad to assist them in the identity of enemy agents. I remember the first occasion on which I took part in this work was with…Tom Cullen in 1919. Piaras Béaslaí asked me to meet a young man who would be waiting at Ó Raghallaigh's bookshop on Dorset St. and to accompany him to Lansdowne Road. I met this man, whom I learned later was Tom Cullen, and went with him to a football match at Lansdowne Road [Ballsbridge]. He asked me to point out to him and give him the names of any British military officers who frequented Dublin Castle and G.H.Q. I was able to point out a few military officers to him whom I knew. [22]

Lily also accompanied Frank Saurin, among others, to cafés,restaurants and the like on similar identity-parade missions.

Collins was determined to have at least one individual in every British cum Irish office, sympathetic to the nationalist cause, supplying information directly or indirectly to GHQ intelligence agents.

In Tim Pat Coogan's insightful book, the famed historian wrote of Michael Collins:

> Behind his handful of detectives, his porters and clerks and postmen and warders and train drivers, his Tobins and his Cullens, he [Michael Collins] had the spirit of the people [with him]. [23]

If he could prevent it, the Big Fellow would never let eighteenth-century, Irish statesman and philosopher Edmund Burke's curse come to pass on his watch: "Bad things happen when enough good men do nothing."

❦

Tom Cullen sat in the gallery of Mansion House's Round Room on 7 January 1919 as twenty-four of the recently elected Sinn Féin MPs took an oath in support of establishing an independent Irish Republic. Michael Collins was one of those present. Addressing the issue of why so few delegates were present, he stated that thirty-six of the candidates were still in English prisons, victims of the May last German Plot round-up, three were essentially permanent exiles and six were on the run.

Though Michael voiced his objection to initially launching the assembly with so many of its members in English jails, the enthusiasm for pressing on was contagious. Collins was overruled for one of the few times in his life.

Committees were drawn up to make arrangements for the initial session of the new assembly, Dáil Éireann, which was scheduled to convene in two weeks' time. Others agreed to draft a provisional Constitution, a Declaration of Irish Independence and an agenda for the momentous inaugural of Ireland's national government, the first since the late 1700s.

❧

Dublin was abuzz with anticipation. Reporters from all over, even from the United States, planned on attending. Everyone wondered what the British would do. Would they allow the meeting to proceed or would they interfere? With an international audience of visitors packing the Round Room, it was likely the authorities would stay away, not wanting to further embarrass their government. Cathal Brugha was nominated to preside.

Two days later, with both Collins and Cullen eager to carry on with their plans for enhancing Ireland's bourgeoning intelligence network, the two made their separate ways to #5 Cabra Road, the home of Michael Foley. The arrival of Ned Broy was much anticipated. Collins had wanted to meet him ever since he'd received the list of the men that the authorities were planning to lift in May, 1918.

Broy too was eager to meet this 'growing myth' of a man… supposedly the most wanted person in Ireland.

Ryle Dwyer recounted the meeting, using many of Broy's own words recorded in Ned's three lengthy Witness Statements.

> Would this Michael Collins be the ideal man I had been dreaming of for a couple of years? Looking up the police record book to see what was known about him, I discovered that he was a six-footer, a Cork man, very intelligent, young and powerful. There was no photograph of him at that time in the record book.
>
> Steeped in curiosity, I went to 5 Cabra Road and was received in the kitchen by Foley. This was a place where every extreme nationalist visited at some time or another.
>
> I was not long there when…Michael Collins arrived. I had studied for so long the type of man that I would need to act efficiently, that the moment I saw Michael at the door, before he had time to walk across and shake

hands, I knew he was the man. [24]

This meeting between Collins and Broy was the beginning of a genuine friendship. Michael thanked Ned for his past help and asked him to continue funnelling information his way.

During their conversation, it became apparent to Mick that Broy was an out-of-character political detective. It seemed he despised the British government and the stranglehold it had on the Irish people as much as the Big Fella did.

During their almost four-hour-long meeting, Ned cautioned Michael that if the Volunteers didn't begin resorting to violence, he feared the fledging movement would collapse. On the other hand, if they did elect to strike out against the police and the military, there'd be serious consequences to pay all around.

Nodding his head in agreement, Collins told him he realised what the costs of such a plan could easily be, but clearly stated he was prepared to take those risks. In fact, the seeds of such as a scheme were already germinating.

[**Author's note**: Dwyer noted in his book, *The Squad*, that Michael had spoken with Timothy 'Tim' Michael Healy, a prominent Irish constitutional nationalist, politician, barrister, writer and controversial Irish House of Commons MP.

Healy told Collins that he and his followers didn't have a ghost of a chance of freeing Ireland if they resorted to violence, but on the other hand, they were most likely to fail as well if they followed the constitutional pathway to national reform.]

Originally, Healy was an avid supporter of Parnell, but the O'Shea divorce crisis soured him and he turned against Ireland's Uncrowned King.

With the IPP leader's death and the establishment of the anti-Parnellites, led by John Dillon, he felt isolated and under appreciated. Losing interest in politics, he buried his energies in his law practice. More embitterment followed with the negative treatment that his brothers, his followers and John Redmond received at the hands of their fellow IPP party associates.

With the collapse of the Easter Uprising, Healy recognised that the IPP was doomed and threw his support behind Arthur Griffith and Sinn Féin but was opposed to any physical force movement.

In 1917, he acted as legal counsel to the family of Thomas Ashe, the dead hunger-striker, and additionally, he provided legal services to post-'16 Sinn Féiners in both England and Ireland.]

❧

Now standing up from the kitchen table, ready to leave Foley's house, Broy turned and again pleaded the DMP's case. He emphasised that 'the cop on the beat' was almost entirely apolitical. For the vast majority, they didn't involve themselves in anti-Sinn Féin activities, unlike members of the RIC. If possible, the Corkman would be doing everyone a big favour if he'd do nothing to alienate or provoke members of the DMP.

Motioning Ned to sit back down again, Michael briefly outlined a strategy of using the Volunteers to attack outlying RIC barracks, relieving them of their weapons and burning their buildings. Such a tactic would force the RIC to seek the protection of RIC barracks located in larger towns. This tactic would eliminate their poisonous presence in much of the Irish countryside. It would concentrate them in limited areas where they could be observed and contained more easily.

Agreeing, Broy once more stated the obvious…that 'ruthless war' should be targeted only against those who were hostile to Ireland's independence movement.

> No attack should be made on the uniformed service, and no attack should be made on the members of G Division who were not on political duty and active on that duty. In this way, the DMP would come to realise that, as long as they did not display real zeal against the Volunteers, they were safe from attack. In the case of any G man who remained hostile, a warning was to be given to him…before any attack was made on him. [25]

With their talk concluded, both men stood up and again warmly shook hands.

Tom, who was an interested but silent observer, wished Ned good luck and God's blessings.

– I'm sure this will be the first of many exchanges between the three of us. There's much work to be done, Tom said.

– Much work indeed…and the sooner we start, the happier I'll be, Broy said.

– …and the better off this country will be, Collins empathically added.

With Broy heading out the front door, Michael and Tom slipped out the back way. Both men left with a good feeling about their meeting with Broy.

❧

Dressed in his Sunday-best suit, clean shirt, starched collar, neck tie, waistcoat and polished boots, Tom Cullen again sat in the front row of the visitors' gallery at Mansion House on Dawson Street.

Cathal Brugha gavelled the first session of Dáil Éireann to order on 21 January 1919. As hoped, the authorities didn't interfere. Twenty-seven of Ireland's newly-elected members attended.

Tom couldn't help but chuckle to himself when he heard that Michael Collins's and Harry Boland's names were read into the register as being present. In fact, the two republicans were in England at that moment, making arrangements to free Éamon de Valera and others from Lincoln Prison, east of Manchester.

The proceedings opened with a prayer by Father Michael O'Flanagan followed by the Ceann Comhairle reading the roll. Béaslaí noted that one of the clerks replied to several of the names read: "Fé ghlas ag Gallaibh." [Imprisoned by the English.]

Next, the Provisional Constitution was read by Brugha. Part of its directive provided for an Executive or ministry of five: a president and four ministers including Finance, Home Affairs, Foreign Affairs and Defence.

The title of the state was declared to be the Irish Republic or Soarstát na hÉireann in Irish and this pronouncement was followed by the reading of the Declaration of Independence in Irish, French and English.

Éamon de Valera, Arthur Griffith and Count Plunkett were nominated, seconded and agreed to as Ireland's representatives to the pending Paris Peace Conference.

Finally, a radical Democratic Programme was read into the record, again in Irish, French and English. Its language, communistic in tone and thought to reflect the thinking of Ireland's first president, Patrick Pearse, was seconded and approved.

At this point, a motion to adjourn until the next day was approved. The historic first meeting of the Dáil Éireann was history.

While this momentous event took place in Dublin, history was also being made on a lonely, narrow bit of a dirt road in the heart of Co. Tipperary. Eight Irish Republican Army Volunteers, lying in wait for five days, stopped a horse-drawn wagon carrying gelignite to the nearby Soloheadbeg stone quarry. The two Irish RIC policemen guarding the shipment, Constables James McDonnell [Co. Mayo] & Patrick O'Connell [Co. Cork], raised their rifles. As a consequence, the two men, refusing to surrender, were shot and killed by their *agents' provocateurs*.

Dan Breen, one of the eight, recounted the events of the day in his book, *My Fight For Irish Freedom*.

> The Volunteers were in great danger of becoming merely a political adjunct to the Sinn Féin organisation. [Seán] Tracey [another one of the eight] remarked to me that we had had enough of being pushed around and getting our men imprisoned while we remained inactive. It was high time that we did a bit of the pushing. We considered that this business of getting in and out of jail was leading us nowhere. This action of ours would proclaim to the world that there still lived Irishmen who made up their minds not to allow free passage of an armed enemy.
>
> The moral aspect of such action was vigorously criticised after the event. Many people, even former friends, branded us as murderers. We had thoroughly discussed the pros and cons and arrived at the conclusion that it was our duty to fight for the Irish Republic that had been established on Easter Monday, 1916. We had decided also that when the smoke of battle had cleared away we would not leave Ireland, as had been the usual practice.

We would remain in our native land in open defiance
of the British authorities. Our only regret was that the
escort had consisted of only two Peelers instead of six.
If there had to be dead Peelers at all, six would have
created a better impression than a mere two. [26]

Though the killings generally are credited as marking the
beginning of Ireland's War for Independence, the Volunteer GHQ
in Dublin was enraged, or so the 'popular' view stated at the time.
Did the attack have their approval or not? If not, were egos bruised?
Was Dublin's leadership trying to instil a measure of control and
authority on a vastly dispersed Volunteer paramilitary body? A
few even imagined Collins had given it his tacit approval. But
regardless of the hurt feelings or lack of 'official' authority, it was
the Soloheadbeg incident, not the initial meeting of Dáil Éireann
that captured the headlines in the next morning's newspapers.

In contradiction to this 'popular' view of the Soloheadbeg
Ambush being 'unauthorised' or 'illegal,' Piaras Béaslaí spoke for
many when he editorialised in the next issue of *An tÓglách*:

> The Irish Government claims the same power and au-
> thority as any other lawfully constituted Government;
> it sanctions the employment by the Irish Volunteers of
> the most drastic measures against the enemies of Ireland.
> The soldiers and police of the invader are liable to be
> treated exactly as invading enemy soldiers would be
> treated by the native army of any country.
> *England must be given the choice between evacuating
> the country and holding it by a foreign garrison, with a
> perpetual state of war in existence.* She must be made
> to realise that a state of war is not healthy for her. The
> agents of England in this country must be made to
> realise that it is not safe for them to try to 'carry on' in
> opposition to the Irish Government and the declared
> wishes of the people. [27]

[**Author's note**: In the days to come, Michael Collins would
use the same sentiments, expressed so eloquently by Béaslaí, as

justification for his ruthless actions against the Sassenach's spies, touts and quislings in Ireland.]

❧

Besides Collins's growing network of intelligence men, one man deserved special mention...Dick McKee, the Commandant of the Dublin Brigade.

Meetings of the GHQ, McKee's command, and the Volunteer Executive, with Éamon de Valera as president and Michael as a member of its leadership board, were often held in Cullenswood House in Ranelagh, the site of Patrick Pearse's first 'St. Enda's school' [1908-1910] and briefly reopened [1917-1919] as a school, operated by Pat's mother Margaret Pearse. They also met at the Dublin Typographical Society, a printers' trade union at #35 Lower Gardiner Street. Because many of the same men belonged to both organisations, there was often an overlapping of responsibility and agreed upon action. [**Author's note:** In theory, the Volunteer Executive was accountable for making policy while the GHQ was in charge of military operations.]

De Valera, affectionately nicknamed 'Dev' or 'the Chief,' and many of his followers often missed meetings. They were either in jail or in America [June, 1919 – December, 1920]. As a result, Griffith took the lead at Volunteer Executive gatherings in 'the Chief's' absence. This vacuum allowed Collins to play a greater role than he might have with Éamon present.

With a keen eye, Cathal Brugha saw what was happening and resented it. Fearing that he'd be pushed aside, Brugha let others know that he thought Collins and his closest followers were trying to take control of the movement in Dev's absence.

Despite being a recognised leader of Ireland's quest for independence, Cathal was unable to do anything about the unfolding dynamics. Rather than confront Michael, he allowed his resentment to fester. It marked a dramatic change in their relationship. Rather than friendship, jealously and even open hostility came to dominate their association.

But again, Piaras Béaslaí, ever the keen observer of the personalities and the evolving events of the day, zeroed in on who the key figures were in early 1919. The policy makers were de Valera and Griffith. Military operations were headed by McKee and Collins, while Intelligence was the domain of Collins and Tobin.

> But the man calling for most notice was Dick McKee, who, after Collins, was certainly, from a military point of view, the most energetic and efficient member of G.H.Q. He was a printer by trade, in the employment of M. H. Gill and Son, who had acquired a wide range of technical knowledge which he was able to apply effectively. In planning elaborate operations with a minute attention to details he showed extraordinary capacity; and the formation of the "flying columns," which played such a big part in the later guerrilla warfare, was largely due to his initiative. Dick McKee was tall, dark, slight, good-looking, with a very gentle manner. He gave a general impression of resourcefulness, energy and practical efficiency. Collins had a very high opinion of his capacity, and reposed great confidence in him. [28]

❧

Michael Collins's return to Ireland was brief. Harry Boland and he were again back in England at the beginning of February, preparing to 'spring' Dev, Seán McGarry, a top IRB man, and Seán Milroy, a leading Sinn Féiner who'd been arrested back in May, 1918 as part of the 'German Plot' arrests.

After some fits and starts over improvised keys that threatened to derail the escape plan, Collins and Boland were in place, outside Lincoln Prison on the evening of 3 February. As prearranged, they lit a lamp and waited for the three inside to answer in kind.

Béaslaí described what happened next.

> At the appointed time the signal was given and replied to, and Collins and Boland rose and proceeded to the door [in the prison wall]. When they reached it they found that outside the door there was a second iron

gate. Collins had brought a duplicate key with him, and this he inserted in the gate. It fitted in easily enough, but, when he attempted to turn it, it broke off in the lock. At the same moment the door at the other side of the gate swung open, and they could see De Valera, MacGarry (sic) and Milroy on the other side; but all egress was barred to them by the gate with the broken key in the lock.

Boland, in describing the scene to me, dwelt on the feeling of utter despair which seized him at this juncture. Collins said, in a heartbroken tone, "I've broken a key in the lock, Dev." De Valera uttered an ejaculation, and tried to thrust his own key into the lock from the other side. By an extraordinary piece of luck he succeeded in pushing out the broken key with his own, and opening the gate. [29]

Much to Michael's consternation, Dev, now free of confinement but still 'on the run,' had decided to journey straight on to America from England. The Chief believed it was only with Irish-America's pressure and President Wilson's endorsement that Ireland could gain its long-sought independence...based on England's 'fighting for small nations' promise.

This was contrary to Ireland's wishes to celebrate de Valera's prison release and his return as their elected leader. The country's political leadership wanted to bring their 'Chief' back home with a triumphal demonstration while, at the same time, thumbing their noses at Britain's government. But if he ducked out and made for America straight away, it might give the impression he was acting selfishly, maybe even cowardly, and set back 'the movement' which finally was gaining some momentum.

Despite all the pleading and pending adulation, he still insisted on going abroad. So after being smuggled back into Ireland, Dev was secretly returned to England where he awaited final arrangement for his clandestine journey to America.

Whether it was because of a sudden change of heart about his trip to America, or the fact that the British government abruptly decided to release all the German Plot prisoners, no one can be sure, but Éamon de Valera and the others [c. 70] returned to Ireland on 26 March as truly free men.

Uncharacteristically, Dev chose his return sans fanfare while the others gratefully accepted the plaudits of the country's citizenry.

❈

In the meantime, Cullen was busy. Following Michael's orders Liam Tobin, Dick Mulcahy, Rory O'Connor and Tom, with the help of some others, made arrangements to free Robert Barton from Mountjoy Jail on Sunday, March 16th.

The Big Fellow had become friends with Barton. Five months earlier, in 1918, the two of them plus Seán T. O'Kelly and George Gavan Duffy had ventured to London, hoping to meet with visiting President Woodrow Wilson. The American leader rebuffed their attempts and, half-jokingly, Mick talked of kidnapping the man in order to plead their case for Irish independence.

Of his relationship with Collins, Barton remembered:

> I was on very friendly terms with Michael Collins and we used to see one another almost every evening. Collins had an office under [in the basement of] Cullenswood House, which was known as the "Republican Hut". Here he was relatively safe and Tom Cullen and Joe O'Reilly could always find him at 9 p.m. and bring persons he wanted to see. [30]

The heady elixir of Barton's successful escape only fuelled Michael's desire to free others, particularly Piaras Béaslaí, a well-known thorn in Dublin Castle's side. He'd been arrested by some Castle detectives and DMP on the evening of 4 March.

Again, with Cullen, Tobin, Thornton, Mulcahy and others, a plot was hatched and the date of Saturday, the 29th was set.

Saturday at Mountjoy was an ideal time to schedule a breakout. The criminal population was confined to their cells in the afternoon and usually only two or three warders were on duty in the exercise yard.

Unfortunately, it snowed that day and the men orchestrating the escape thought the prisoners might not be allowed outside. But no, at the appointed hour, the men emerged, and taking full advantage of the unusual conditions, created a diversion by throwing snowballs at one another.

With the rope ladder now over the outside wall, several prisoners pounced on the guards and restrained them. Actually, two of the three warders were nationalist sympathisers and offered no resistance. The other was subdued with a blow to his jaw. Intentionally torn prison tunics later testified that all the prison officials had tried their best to stop the escape, thus securing their continued employment at the jail.

In all, twenty men scampered over Mountjoy's inhospitable wall.

The only regret in the entire affair was that the men restraining the guards were unable to join their comrades on the other side.

Michael was ecstatic when Joe O'Reilly brought him word that he thought 'the whole jail is out.'

As usual, Tom Cullen and Joe O'Reilly were with the Big Fellow at the Republican Hut after all the excitement of the day had died down.

> As he sat in his office in Cullenswood House that night, Collins put down his pen and burst out laughing. They had brought off a coup and boosted party morale and (sic) more than offset whatever damage had been done when they cancelled the [initial] welcoming ceremonies of de Valera. [31]

※

Dáil Éireann met in private session on the 3rd and 4th of April.

De Valera was selected to be President or First Minister [Príomh-Aire] of the assembly. The recently ratified constitution made his newly elected position unambiguous. Dáil Éireann would not or should not elevate itself to the lofty heights of appointing or electing a 'President of the Irish Republic.'

In another matter of importance, it was decided to increase the number of Dáil ministers from five to nine with the addition of extern ministers who'd sit in executive session but wouldn't be voting members of the cabinet.

Dev appointed Michael to serve as Minister for Finance in his new eight-man ministry. The Chief also chose Arthur Griffith for Home Affairs, W. T. Cosgrave for Local Government, Cathal Brugha for Defence, Count Plunkett as Minister for Foreign Affairs, Countess Markievicz as Labour Minister, Eoin MacNeill for Industries and Robert Barton as Agriculture Minister.

The Dáil also sanctioned the opening of embassies in France [Seán T. O'Kelly] and Washington, D.C. [Dr. Pat MacCartan].

※

Up to this point in time, the Irish Volunteers, now more popularly renamed and referred to as the Irish Republican Army, were viewed as a 'defensive body' not an 'offensive' one. Part of this image was a throwback to its founding purpose in 1913 and partly due to its failure to wrestle independence from the British in 1916.

With its reorganisation and gradual arming, thanks in large measure to Collins and Cullen's efforts, that impression was changing. Though still poorly trained and equipped, more Irish citizens looked to it as a force, hopefully, to be reckoned with and capable of delivering independence.

If the idea of waging war with England was lurking in the back of Michael's mind, it wasn't in Dev's. Just prior to his June departure for America, the Dáil publicly endorsed the idea of social ostracism against the RIC.

[**Author's note:** Memories were reborn of Michael Davitt's first use of the term 'boycott' during Ireland's Land War of the 1880s.]

Béaslaí quoted some of Éamon de Valera's acerbic words

delivered on 10 April.

It is scarcely necessary to explain what is meant by this motion. The people of Ireland ought not to fraternise, as they often do, with the forces which are the main instruments in keeping them in subjection. It is not consistent with personal or national dignity. It is certainly not consistent with safety. They are spies in our midst. They are England's janissaries. The knowledge of our sentiments and feelings and purposes, which they derive either from their own hearts, because they are of our race, or from intercourse amongst us, they put liberally at the disposal of the foreign usurper, in order to undo us in our struggle against him. They are the eyes and ears of the enemy.

They are no ordinary civil force, as police are in other countries. The R.I.C., unlike any other police force in the world, is a military body, armed with rifle and bayonet and revolver, as well as baton. They are given full licence by their superiors to work their will upon an unarmed populace. The more brutal the commands given them by their superiors, the more they seem to revel in carrying them out, against their own flesh and blood be it remembered!

Their history is a continuity of brutal treason against their own people. From their very foundation they have been the mainstay of the privileged ascendancy, and the great obstacle to every movement for social as well as national liberty. [32]

Unbeknownst to de Valera at the time, these were the exact words Michael Collins wanted to hear. They offered a justification for taking action against the Sassenach...not the passive, social ostracism Dev was advocating, but rather licence to act boldly and decisively against the Forces of the Crown.

❦

[**Author's note:** Additional reading would include T. Ryle Dwyer's *The Squad and the Intelligence Operations of Michael Collins,* (2005) & Michael T. Foy's *Michael Collins's Intelligence War: The Struggle Between the British and the IRA, 1919-1921, (2006).*]

William O'Grady's residence & shop, #12 Main Street, Wicklow

William O'Grady, c. 1920

Wicklow Town Gaol

Michael Collins's letter to Tom Cullen, April, 1918

#10 Exchequer St., Dublin

#32 Bachelor's Walk, Dublin

Crow Street, Dublin

#21 Oakley Road, Cullenswood House, Dublin

Church of St. Nicholas of Myra, Dublin

Main Alter, Church of St. Nicholas of Myra

Michael Collins [seated ctr. next to] Harry Boland & Tom Cullen, Armagh, 1921

7

With Liam Tobin, Tom Cullen and Frank Thornton functioning as loyal lieutenants, Michael Collins was finally
on the brink of establishing an intelligence network worthy of
challenging Dublin's G Division and the Castle's assortment of
undercover operatives.

A man of great organisational ability, energy and unflagging
determination, the Big Fella gathered about him competent
individuals who were "...strong-willed team players, courageous
risk-takers whom he liked testing to the limit." [1]

Michael Foy further described Collins and his rapidly expanding spy system.

> Collins liked organisational flexibility and luckily for
> him his intelligence machine was created from virtually
> nothing, staffed by men lacking professional experience
> and free of rigid bureaucratic attitudes, concern for
> hierarchy or boundaries of responsibility. Crow Street's
> agents [Tobin, Cullen & Thornton among others] learnt
> on the job, and the organisation's relatively small size
> meant that they frequently performed tasks outside their
> designated area. Deputy Director Liam Tobin func-
> tioned as officer manager, field agent and triggerman. [2]

Michael often worked sixteen to twenty hours a day. Besides
being 'officially' appointed [Volunteer] GHQ Director of
Intelligence as well as its Director of Organisation and its Adjutant

General, Mick tackled with his usual vigour his new post as Dáil Director for Finance. From the middle of 1919, he embarked upon organising and running a nationwide National Loan appeal. Originally designed to accomplish its objective through the sale of bonds, he hoped to raise £250,000 in Ireland in support of funding its new government. [A corresponding £250,000 was targeted for American fund-raising led by Dev.] Collins's Irish efforts eventually raised almost £400,000...an astonishing accomplishment in light of the 'troubled' times. [De Valera reportedly raised $5,000,000 during his eighteen-month stay in America.]

To top matters off, sometime during June or July, Michael was elected leader of the IRB...the Chairman of its Supreme Council.

In his book on Collins, Foy stated:

> But Collins's tremendous self-assurance, his belief that he could do almost anything   certainly better than anyone else   combined with a compulsive need for absolute control, created the danger of a one-man band. He also loved accumulating offices and responsibility, occupying four important government and army posts simultaneously for most of 1919. [A fifth, if you add his IRB presidency.] ...he lived at a headlong pace, constantly overstretching his physical and emotional resources and cramming a dozen lifetimes into one relatively brief career. [3]

❄

In the early morning hours of 7 April 1919, Collins had an eye opening experience.

With the assistance of police detective Ned Broy, Michael's double agent inside #1 Brunswick Street, Collins and his IRB comrade Seán Nunan were smuggled into the bowels of G Division HQ.

Ned, who'd previously advocated driving the RIC from their outlying barracks to eliminate their intrusive presence and domineering manipulation of Ireland's rural population, was often assigned to night duty. He admitted the two republicans and took them upstairs to the division's political office. Armed with candles and matches, the policeman unlocked the vault-like, windowless records sanctuary of the 'G-men.'

For five hours, Collins and Nunan read file after file. Being a bit of a curious egotist, Collins even found his own folder and was chuffed to learn that at the end of 1916, a West Cork RIC official noted he belonged to a 'brainy family' who was 'disloyal and of advanced Sinn Féin sympathies.' [4]

Luck was on Michael and Seán's side that night. Thanks to Ned's willing risk-taking, the two walked out of G Division HQ just as the sun was rising. Breathing sighs of relief, they headed to their own separate lodgings.

Walking across the Liffey and up Sackville Street on his way to Mrs. McCarthy's, Michael was trembling with excitement. Prior to his night's adventure, he'd only a vague idea of G Division's organisation…its ways and means and depth of knowledge.

> After five hours reading and taking notes, Collins emerged…a changed man whose questions had been answered, whose ideas had crystallised and who now knew what G-men knew – and did not know – about the republican movement. Having entered and toured his enemy's mind, Collins was now in a position to create 'his own G-Division' – one that would emulate and finally outclass the original model. [5]

Ryle Dwyer added his own touch to the night's events.

> The various files gave him an invaluable perspective on what G Division knew, and who were the most active detectives. He also got an insight into the people who were providing information. Before leaving, Collins pocketed a bound volume of all telephone messages received by G Division during the week of the 1916 Rising. Some of the messages were from loyalists pro-viding information about where Irish Volunteers had occupied positions in small numbers, or where rebel snipers were posted on roofs or in windows. Other mes-

sages were from people who later posed as republican sympathisers. Collins had many cynical laughs listening to protestations of patriotism by some of those who had sent messages to G Division. [6]

James Mackay saw it this way:

> Michael carried away an old detective daybook as a souvenir – and in his head the details of the RIC intelligence system. Now he knew exactly what he was up against and how he could best fight it. With the slender resources in men and arms at his disposal he realised that he could never hope to combat the British on their own terms; but if he could eliminate the enemy's intelligence he could paralyse its police and military or at least severely limit their effectiveness. [7]

❧

With his newly-discovered insights, Michael sent his key men down the country to urge the Volunteers into action.

Consequently, Tom Cullen was sent to Wicklow, Kildare, King and Queen's counties where his reputation preceded him. He was on a first-name basis with many of the local IRA leaders.

The attitude of the men outside Dublin varied. Some units were anxious to have a go at the Sassenach as most hadn't been out in '16. Others were reluctant, wanting to wait for the RIC to make the initial move. Their reasoning said, if the Peelers assailed the civilian population first, the IRA would gain a new-found respect as 'defenders of the people' instead of their being viewed as the aggressors...upsetting the cart. A few simply were hesitant to leave families and farms for economic reasons or had had their four-year fill of death and violence and sought the peace and tranquillity of 'home.'

Tom met with these varied responses, but in the end his message from GHQ in Dublin was simple and straightforward: attack the bloody RIC.

– Consider it a training exercise, sharpening your military skills.

Tom's acerbic words bristled with defiance and controlled anger.

– It also will provide you an opportunity to collect some much needed military hardware, he said.

– If you should meet with strong resistance, answer it in kind.

Whether you realise it or not, Ireland's at war with England. Now is the time to break their connection with us.

The Wicklow man hoped his visits would serve as a wake-up call. It was time to shake the lads from their self-imposed lethargy and have them rise up in righteous revolution. Pearse and Connolly and Ceannt had done that in '16. Now, Collins and he were taking their turns...shaking the tree of liberty again.

– *Please God*, he thought, – *the outcome will be different this time.*

His departing watchwords to his countrymen were always the same: 'Remember '16' and 'Up the Republic.'

❧

Late one evening as Tom and Michael walked from Kirwan's public house around to Vaughan's, they finished discussing the current state of affairs.

– There's no doubt in my mind...full-fledged war with England is inevitable.

– I'd say it's immediate, not inevitable, Michael said, – but regardless of when the IRA springs into country-wide action, I want to be sure we have every advantage possible on our side. No going off half-cocked and having their fecken' boot end up in our arses.

– Shyte, no! But even today, with some ground work already laid, most republicans, let alone the general population, aren't in the mood for war. The memory of what happened in France is still fresh in their minds. Fifty thousand or more of our countrymen... dead. Sure that's not easily forgotten, Tom said.

– And it shouldn't be, but I'll tell you…three years ago we both witnessed a revolutionary takeover by a tiny minority of determined men. It almost worked.

– Yes, with a little more luck and some better planning…

– …this time, Tom, we'll make our own luck, Michael retorted.

– A democratic mandate? Tom asked.

– No fecken' mandate, Tom. If we're to wait for an 'All in favour of…,' we'll both be long dead and in the ground. No, let's lead and show the people what's possible. If we're successful, they'll follow us so, mark my words.

– We'll lead and the people will follow…that's what the men and women of '16 did, Tom said.

– God rest their souls, Tom, that's what they tried, but we won't make the same mistake. First, we'll strike at England's soft, yellow underbelly. One by one, we'll eliminate their agents of cruel oppression …we'll ferret them out and cut off their serpent-like heads. Without their fecken' intimidation to cow the people, maybe just maybe, they'll see what freedom from a colonial overlord is truly like.

> His [Michael's] strategy in 1919 was to first create a radical coalition – a war party – by winning over Volunteer GHQ and the Dublin Brigade, then create a war atmosphere by exploiting British Government mistakes and increasing popular frustration at political stagnation before bringing the crisis to a head through calculated acts of provocation. [8]

❦

By the spring of 1919, Michael had established an important working relationship with Dick McKee, a fellow IRB man and, like himself, a determined revolutionary. It wedded McKee's Dublin Brigade military assets with Collins's burgeoning intelligence capabilities. Together, the two men possessed the capability of inflicting great damage upon England's long-standing hold on Ireland.

It also opened the door for a closer friendship with McKee's ally, Richard 'Dick' Mulcahy, the Dublin IRA's Chief of Staff, whose opinion carried considerable weight.

The 33-year-old Chief of Staff was originally a post office engineer who had joined the IRB and the Irish Volunteers in Dublin before the war [WWI] and whose coolness and tactics as Thomas Ashe's second-in-command had really won the Battle of Ashbourne in 1916. Superficially the reserved, bookish Mulcahy had little in common with Collins, but both were products of the British civil service who brimmed with organising ability, and they complemented each other perfectly. Mulcahy was clearly enthralled by the slightly younger man and revelled in their almost symbiotic relationship.... [9]

Dick crossed the line from nationalist to republican when Ireland's case was rejected out of hand by the leadership of the Paris Peace Conference. Not only was its request for independence denied but Dublin Castle increasingly pressurised Irish republicans by raiding the homes and businesses of Volunteers and Sinn Féiners.

The Chief-of-Staff viewed these increasingly hostile and deliberate provocations as a prelude to Britain making a pre-emptive assault against the Irish people and its newly installed government. It seems the Sassenach were trying to push the Irish into a corner with their belligerent, aggressive tactics.

This apparent menacing scheme was the final straw, convincing Mulcahy that Collins's approach was the right one. The Big Fella was itching to strike a telling blow, an anticipatory assault against the Castle's daunting intelligence operation.

❧

It became apparent to Tom Cullen that Michael's plan was coming together and quickly. Almost to his surprise, he felt an unexpected sense of pride at being an important part of it.

In the run-up to '16, he felt overwhelmed and, even at times, confused about his role in the struggle. But being a part of that heroic defence of South Dublin Union, and experiencing firsthand the enemy's willingness to take what didn't belong to them had changed him. He was fully convinced that the English would ask no quarter and would with pleasure give none either. This was going to be dogfight to the bitter end. There'd be no turning back...no surrendering. The Sassenach didn't take prisoners...1916 had taught him that lesson. What was it Maxwell said, – *Court martial and shoot? Or was it trial and quicklime? It didn't matter... sure it was all the same in the end, wasn't it?*

Looking ahead instead of back, Tom liked being around Dick McKee. Dick and Mick, as he sometimes joked, were men of action. Deeds not words were their unwritten motto.

Michael had introduced the two of them to each other almost a year ago. If fact, they'd met in the Keating Branch of the Gaelic League in Rutland Square on the very evening the Big Fella swore Tom into the ranks of IRB. Now that seemed a lifetime ago, but the words Michael spoke and Tom repeated and agreed to uphold were still fresh in his mind:

> In the presence of God, I, Tom Cullen, do solemnly swear that I will do my utmost to establish the independence of Ireland, and that I will bear true allegiance to the Supreme Council of the Irish Republican Brotherhood and the Government of the Irish Republic and implicitly obey the constitution of the Irish Republican Brotherhood and all my superior officers and that I will preserve inviolable the secrets of the organisation. [10]

Michael Foy painted a brilliant picture of McKee in his book about Collins.

> A 26-year-old bachelor, McKee was already an iconic figure to the Dublin Volunteers: a tall, imposing natural leader whose languid exterior and soft beguiling drawl concealed a driven and ruthless personality. At Brigade headquarters McKee had assembled a like-minded inner

circle typified by Mick McDonnell, the quartermaster of 2nd Battalion, a firebrand who was constantly baying for action. But McKee's closest confidant was his future vice-brigadier, Peadar Clancy, who ran an outfitter's shop in [#94] Talbot Street [whose name, Republican Outfitters, printed in bold letters above the door, was an in-your-face brazen challenge to the British authorities] that doubled as a revolutionary drop-in centre. These [three] inseparable friends had grown up, conspired, fought [in 1916] and been imprisoned together. [11]

Dick McKee knew that war with England was just around the corner. He reorganised and re-equipped the Dublin Brigade with that thought in mind. He delegated men to buy or steal weapons and grenades from British soldiers. In March, 1919, some of his men participated in a spectacular arms raid at the British military aerodrome at Collinstown [today the site of Dublin International Airport north of the city]. The bold manoeuvre saw the IRA capture nearly one hundred rifles and thousands of rounds of ammunition.

McKee was also a great one for providing sanctuary for fellow freedom fighters from down the country. Some were men who'd been forced to abandon their homes because the local citizenry objected to their harsh tactics. Two examples were Dan Breen and Seán Treacy, ostracised by the general population for their killing of the two RIC at the Soloheadbeg ambush.

❧

Michael's team of dedicated, talented men was taking shape… Tobin, Cullen, Thornton and now McKee and Mulcahy. But Collins's impatience was eating away at him. He feared he hadn't much time. Sure, with the Dáil strutting its stuff before world public opinion, how much time did he have before the Sassenach lowered its boom of repressive condemnation and vitriolic rebuttal? Irish belligerence was bad for Britain's colonial image. Benevolence and forgiveness were not part of their royal vocabulary in 1919.

Creating a proper Volunteer Intelligence Department
would have daunted anyone less confident and resilient
than Collins. He started with only a nucleus of police
moles and IRB helpers and weighed down by a conviction that time was rapidly running out, that once G
Division had completed gathering intelligence on republicans, the British would destroy Dáil Éireann, Sinn
Féin and the Irish Volunteers. Collins believed the Irish
nation faced a stark choice between the obliteration of
its legitimately elected government and an Anglo-Irish
War in which victory would be attainable [only] through
an effective Volunteer intelligence system. But building
such an organisation would take months, whereas Collins's immediate priority was destroying G Division. [12]

❧

The time for action had arrived. In mid-July, Collins called
Tom Cullen and Liam Tobin together with Dick McKee and Mick
McDonnell. They tooth-combed a short list of Volunteers who
might be fitting men to have as the nucleus of a 'murder team'
for the purpose of assassinating odious 'G-men' who were bent
on destroying Ireland's quest for freedom.

Collins was both surprised and uncertain with the results of
that first meeting. He was taken aback by the reluctance some
of the invited men expressed about fully committing to such an
idea. But his overriding concern was how would the murdering
of a 'policeman' be viewed by the body politic of Volunteers, by
the members of Sinn Féin and by the Irish population as a whole?
It had only been six months since the Soloheadbeg attack and
emotions still ran high. Clearly, murder was murder and could
not be passed off as a mistake or an unfortunate accident. No,
political assassination was murder and there was no way around
it. Would his brazen plan collapse before it could be objectively
viewed? Michael had no idea, but he was about to find out.

❧

This 'hit-team,' soon to be nicknamed 'The Squad' and often later referred to as 'The Twelve Apostles,' indicating the team had grown to include twelve men, became destined to bring the G Division to its knees.

Michael Foy stated: "Most who signed on, like Paddy O'Daly [sometimes written as just Daly], Joe Leonard, Tom Keogh and Jim Slattery, were from McKee's old and super-militant 2nd Battalion."[13] Later, he wrote: "Paddy Daly claimed that Collins initially appointed four full-time Squad members – Daly himself as leader, Joe Leonard, Ben Barrett and Seán Doyle – while another four Volunteers were soon to be allocated important responsibilities.[14]

Tim Pat Coogan, in his biography of Michael Collins, noted that the 'Squad' was officially formed on 19 September 1919, but said it had seen action during the previous two months. Its inaugural meeting was held at #49 Rutland Square, headquarters of the Keating Branch of the Gaelic League.

> The first recruits were warned by Dick McKee that their work would not be suitable for anyone with scruples about taking life, so they had no illusions as to what they were going into. Collins impressed on the Squad members that no organisation in Irish history had had a unit to deal with spies and the members of the Squad regarded themselves as being part of an elite. Its first leader was Mick McDonnell, a former Frongoch man, who was later succeeded by Paddy Daly.
>
> The first members of the Squad were Joe Leonard, Seán Doyle, Jim Slattery, Bill Stapleton, Pat McCrae, James Conroy, Ben Barret, and Daly. Then in January 1920 Collins added Tom Keogh, Mick O'Reilly and Vincent [Vinnie] Byrne.[15]

Time and egos have a way of rewriting history. Some personal accounts have become 'unintentionally' altered or confused. Wonderful historians battle with these inconsistencies all the time. T. Ryle Dwyer, a most careful researcher and exacting writer, described the Squad's formation in these words:

Jim Slattery recalled a meeting at 35 North Great George's Street around the middle of July 1919. A number of men were selected by Dick McKee and Mick McDonnell and brought to an inner room. McKee asked if any of them objected to shooting enemy agents.

'The greater number of volunteers objected for one reason or another,' Slattery said. "When I was asked the question I said I was prepared to obey orders...I recall that two men, who had previously told Mick McDonnell that they had no objection to being selected for special duty, turned down the proposition at that meeting...McDonnell seemed very annoyed at them and asked them why they had signified their willingness in the first instance."

Among the men who agreed that night were Tom Keogh, Tom Kilcoyne, Jim Slattery and Joe Leonard. These four, together with Tom Ennis and, later, Paddy O'Daly, were to become the nucleus of the famous Squad, but there was no mention of this that night. [16]

Further along in his book, *The Squad*, Dwyer reported:

Paddy O'Daly had not been at the original meeting in July...[he was in Mountjoy Jail until 2 August]. 'Dick McKee told Joe Leonard and myself [O'Daly] to report at 46 Parnell Square [then known as Rutland Square] – the meeting place of the Keating Branch of the Gaelic League – on 19 September 1919,' O'Daly recalled. Mick McDonnell, Joe Leonard, Ben Barrett, Seán Doyle, Tom Keogh, and Jim Slattery were at this meeting, which Michael Collins and chief-of-staff Richard Mulcahy addressed.

'They told us it was proposed to form a Squad,' O'Daly said. 'The Squad would take orders directly from Michael Collins, and in the absence of Collins, the orders would be given to us through either Dick McKee or Dick Mulcahy. We were told that we were not to discuss our movements or actions with Volunteer officers or with anybody else. Collins told us that we were being formed to deal with spies and informers and that he had authority from the government to have this matter carried out.'

Collins gave 'a short talk, the gist of which was that any of us who had read Irish history would know that no organisation in the past had an intelligence system through which spies and informers could be dealt with, but that now the position was going to be rectified by the formation of an intelligence branch, an Active Service Unit or whatever else it is called.'

Collins only picked four of us for the Squad that night – Joe Leonard, Seán Doyle, Ben Barrett and myself in charge,' according to O'Daly. [17]

Finally, Piaras Béaslaí, writing in the middle 1920s and who knew all of these men personally, wrote:

It was in the month of July, 1919, the "The Squad" was formed, a body that played a big part in the subsequent fighting in Dublin. The "Squad" consisted of a small band of Volunteers attached to the Intelligence Department, specially selected for dangerous and difficult jobs. They were required to give their whole time to the service of the Volunteers, and to be always available, but they were not mercenaries. They were paid only the salaries which they had been earning in their ordinary occupation from which they had been withdrawn.

The first commanding officer of "The Squad" was Mick McDonnell. The second in command was Paddy Daly…. He afterwards succeeded McDonnell as "O.C." Early members of the "Squad" were Tom Keogh (half brother of McDonnell), Jim Slattery, Vincent Byrne, Joe Leonard, Eddie Byrne, Ben Barrett, Paddy Griffin and Seán Doyle. Tom Keogh was also employed in the Volunteer "Munition Factory," but later left it to give all his time to the "Squad." Other members of the "Squad" were Frank Bolster, Ben Byrne, James Conroy,

J. Brennan, Pat McCrae, Paddy Drury, James Connolly, and Bill Stapleton. To the courage, loyalty and secrecy of the members of this small body was due the success of many of the operations in Dublin, which wrought such damage to the English machinery of coercion and oppression. [18]

But in the final analysis, Collins, McKee and Malachy had two charges for each Squad member: Kill without question or hesitation and be ready to die yourself…either on the street or at the end of a British rope.

⁂

With Michael's intelligence cum active service unit (ASU) expanding, he was able to create a division of labour among his IRA Volunteers.

The Intelligence Corp, working out of #3 Crow Street and headed by Tobin, Cullen and Thornton, were responsible for gathering and interpreting information on many key subjects… "[they]…analysed [Dublin & county IRA brigade] intelligence officers' reports, evaluating their reliability, completeness and significance." [19]

The Crow Street 'Three' and their associates collated information from a wide array of sources. They ascertained patterns of behaviour, put names to faces and soon were able to positively identify 'offending' British agents that included: 'G-men,' RIC policemen and their reinforcements [Auxiliary Cadets and the Black & Tans], British military spies and secret service agents.

Foy, quoting from the Witness Statements of Dalton, Thornton and Dan McDonnell, reported:

> At Crow Street Tobin, Cullen and Thornton functioned as line managers, training and supervising a corps of paid, full-time intelligence officers, whose activities they coordinated with the Squad. Most intelligence officers were IRB members whom McKee had recruited for Collins, and all were Dublin Volunteers. Initially there were

only three intelligence officers: Joe Dolan, Joe Guilfoyle and Paddy Caldwell, whom Tobin, Thornton and Cullen assisted for some months. But, as the war [Ireland's War for Independence] intensified, others joined in July and August 1920. The new recruits included Charlie Dalton, Frank Saurin, Charlie Byrne, Peter McGee, Dan McDonnell, Ned Kelleher, James Hughes, Con O'Neill, Bob O'Neill, Jack Walsh and Paddy Kennedy. By the end of 1920 Crow Street's expanding personnel and workload necessitated a departmental sub-office, which Thornton ran from rooms situated above a Great Brunswick Street cinema. [20]

Later, during 1920, Peter Magee, Ned Kelleher, Dan MacDonnell, Charlie Byrne and Paddy Kennedy were added to the mix at #3 Crow Street. [21]

One of Crow Street's principal duties was identifying targets for members of the Squad to assassinate. These included Peelers, British soldiers, intelligence secret agents, Auxiliaries, government civilian employees and anyone in the general population who posed a real threat to the Irish government, members of Sinn Féin or IRA Volunteers. Through a prearranged system of signals, the intelligence officer would point out who the intended victim was, and their fellow Squad members, usually working in pairs, would fire the fatal shots.

Tobin, Cullen or Thornton had no authority to order an execution, but based on their studied information, they'd make recommendations to the Big Fellow. Assassinations were Collins's responsibility, but his three deputies did manage all the counter-intelligence schemes employed against British agents who'd tried to surreptitiously penetrate IRA ranks in Dublin or, if necessary, expose fellow IRA men who'd 'taken the King's shillin' in town.

Initially, once the Dublin intelligence operation was launched, it became apparent it had no counterpart down the country. As the war throughout Ireland hotted up, it became vital that local information be collected regarding troop movements, RIC personnel activities, allocation of weaponry and supplies in addition to every enemy installation's security measures. To rectify this deficiency, Michael Collins issued orders that brigade commandants be responsible for amassing intelligence information from each of their company commanders or intelligence officers. These individual reports would be forwarded to brigade HQs for assimilation, and then they'd be sent on to his Intelligence HQ in Crow Street.

When Mick did order the elimination of an enemy agent, he tried to do so unemotionally and based his decision on hard evidence. Usually, the intended target had been warned to stop his offensive activities or he'd suffer the consequences. Sometimes, the agent provocateur was told to leave Ireland if he valued his life. Occasionally, as a warning, a spy or tout was handcuffed to a railing in front of a local police barracks or tied to one of the gates of Dublin Castle.

Michael's carefully orchestrated killings were not thoughtless acts of a frightened foe, but rather, deliberately entered into with the intended purpose of eliminating one of Ireland's enemies who was a full participant in the ongoing struggle against seeing Ireland achieve independence. Importantly, Michael was not acting in a vacuum. His decisions to attack the enemy had the full approval and support of both McKee and Mulcahy.

Initially, Michael ordered that the executions take place in the early evening hours when the likelihood of involving innocent civilians was minimised, but in response, when the authorities reduced their law enforcement presence at night, Mick was forced to change tactics and send his Squad out during the day.

> When the Squad started operating full-time, its members had to be permanently available. Crow Street ordered them to leave home and live in groups at safe houses, subsisting on an allowance of £4 10s a week – a tradesman's average wage.
>
> Half a dozen Squad members were permanently available at short notice in their headquarters, originally a private house in [#100] Seville Place off Amiens Street. [Later]…the Squad shifted to Upper Abbey Street, six or seven minutes away from Crow Street via the Liffey [Ha-penny] footbridge. [22]

The new digs to accommodate full-time Squad operations were disguised as George Moreland cabinet makers and builders. The premises were well shielded from the street and with sundry tools and wood shavings scattered around, any inquisitor would have been duly impressed. If someone inquired about having work done, they were politely put off, saying the carpentry firm had projects backed up for months.

Squad members posed as carpenters, but each had a revolver squirreled away under his apron. Their other weapons, safely hidden in a bricked-up lavatory, were close at hand.

In his intelligence book, Michael Foy described the individual personal characteristics needed for Squad membership. First, a recommendation by Collins or McKee was essential.

> The Squad's work best suited strong and fit young men and most were bachelors in their late teens or twenties. Paddy Daly, a widower in his early thirties, was an exception, while the balding 40-year-old Mick McDonnell was positively ancient. They needed agility for rapid attacks and retreats.... Proficiency with handguns, a marksman's keen eyesight, steady hands and natural shooting ability were essential.... Physical courage was vital, but so too were personal stability and sound judgement: emotionally brittle, volatile and erratic individuals threatened the Squad's cohesion and even survival. [Acting ability also came in handy at times.] [23]

❧

Tragically, it was the Squad's first OC, Mick McDonnell, who failed to survive his own internal turmoil. Divorce, the death of his close friend, Martin Savage, and an unfortunate love affair took its toll on this gallant warrior. Finally, it became apparent McDonnell was unfit to lead. In the summer of 1920, two of his Squad comrades went to Tom Cullen, and persuaded him to intervene with Collins on their friend's behalf.

As a result, the compassionate Corkman concocted a story

that the British were on to Mick and arranged for him leave the country. [**Author's note**: Sadly, his temporary departure for northern California turned into a lifetime of exile for this brave Volunteer leader.]

❧

Tom, an intelligence man who also had quartermastering responsibilities, was a master of juggling several responsibilities at a time. On one occasion, he'd fondly remembered a personal encounter with W. A. Tynan, an IRA officer and the quartermaster of the 5th Battalion, Laois Brigade. To his credit, Tynan was also an active Sinn Féiner and took great pride in raising money for Michael's National Loan.

Once when he was in Dublin, he met with Tom about a request he'd made regarding a shipment of weapons for his unit, but Mick's frequent criticism that some counties and battalions weren't carrying their weight in the conflict must have rubbed off on Tom.

After listening to Tynan reiterate his request for more rifles, the Wicklow man lost his temper. Knowing GHQ was in receipt of a recent report that his 5th Battalion had scored a small success in the taking of a local RIC barracks, Tom wanted to drive home the point that one success wouldn't win the war and it didn't warrant an extravagant issuance of weapons on his part.

Annie Ryan noted the details of the meeting in her book *Comrades* and described what happened.

> [The successful RIC raid]…was a promising start, and GHQ felt justified in letting Tynan have some small arms — but not before [he] enduring a lecture from Tom Cullen, a member of GHQ, when Tynan went to collect the guns. Tynan reports: 'We [Tynan and others of the battalion] discussed the question of rifles with Tom Cullen, who accused us of not doing our bit in Laois. We pointed out that there were no rifles in the whole Brigade.'

Cullen relented, and the rifles were to 'be sent on within a week, probably by canal.' By the time they arrived, Tynan was in custody. [24]

After Tynan's arrest for possessing incriminating documents, he was court-martialled on 18 September 1920 and sentenced to two years' hard labour. Finally, on 23 December 1921, prior to actually completing his full sentence, he was released by the British authorities, largely because of the agreed-upon Anglo-Irish Treaty.

Despite Tynan's bad luck, Tom felt justified in telling off some of the lads down the country. If Ireland was going to win its struggle, everyone had to do their part regardless of the hardships facing them. The Wicklow man wasn't one to accept excuses and easily reward slackers.

※

With police reinforcements and additional British military pouring into Dublin, one of Tom Cullen's closest associates described just one of many close calls they'd experienced. In Frank Thornton's own words:

> On a couple of occasions we had exciting experiences. One night the British decided to raid Parnell [then Rutland] Square, house by house. Needless to remark, none of us went to bed in Devlin's [pub] on that particular night. We kept a sharp lookout and about an hour after they started the raid one of our party reported that they could hear the movements of men on our own roof. This was too near to be healthy but the raid continued and without any attempt on the part of the enemy to search the houses on our side of Parnell Square. From what we discovered afterwards, it would appear that the party on the roof were a covering off [backup] party for the raiding party in the Square. Little [did] they know that what they were looking for was right underneath them all the time. [25]

❧

At the end of July, 1919, the Squad received its first 'assignment.' They were ordered to kill Detective Sergeant Patrick Smyth. In his early fifties, Smyth had assisted in identifying some of the leaders of Easter Week, 1916. Recently, despite several warnings to cease his aggressive inquiries into Volunteer activities, the detective blatantly refused, thinking he was invincible and the admonishments were a bluff.

Receiving his orders from Michael Collins, Squad OC Mick McDonnell ordered fellow ASU members Jim Slattery, Tom Keogh, Tom Ennis and Mick Kennedy to shoot the man. After a fortnight's delay, caused by the uncertainty they'd the right man, the four Squad members confronted Smyth on the street near his home on the evening of 30 July.

Ryle Dwyer described what happened.

> They waited that night with .38 revolvers, which they soon found were not powerful enough. They had expected that Smyth would fall as soon as he was shot. 'But after we hit him he ran,' Slattery noted. 'The four of us fired at him. Keogh and myself ran after him right to his own door and I think he fell at the door, but he got into the house.'
>
> Smyth was hit four times, the most serious wound was from a bullet that entered his back, passed through a lung and lodged in his chest, just above the heart. At the time Smyth's wife and three of their seven children were in the country on holiday. In the commotion his six-year-old second son raced from the house vowing 'to catch those who shot Dada'. He returned later saying that the men had run off.
>
> 'Was it not a cowardly thing to shoot him in the back without giving him a chance of defending himself?' Smyth's sixteen-year-old daughter said the next day. 'He always carried a revolver,' she added, 'but he hadn't it with him last night, so he could not put up a fight against his would-be murderers.'

'We made a right mess of the job,' McDonnell complained the next day.

'But I can assure you,' Slattery said, 'I was more worried until Smyth died than Mick was. We never used .38 guns again; we used .45 guns after that lesson.' [27]

[**Author's note**: Smyth died in Dublin's Mater Hospital on 8 September.]

※

On 7 September, a detachment of British soldiers on their way to church in Fermoy, Co. Cork, was attacked by a unit of IRA Volunteers dressed in mufti. It was the first British military fatality in Ireland since the 1916 Uprising. With the death of Detective Smyth the following day, the British government suppressed Dáil Éireann. King George V expressed his anger over the soldier's death as did British Prime Minister David Lloyd George, Britain's Chief Secretary in Ireland Ian Macpherson and its viceroy to Ireland Field Marshal Lord John French.

Macpherson announced that this action was tantamount to a declaration of war but wouldn't shirk from what he saw was his vested responsibility. Then, to compound insult to injury, he proscribed Sinn Féin, the Gaelic League and Cumann na mBan as well.

Reflecting on this folly, a high-ranking British civil servant, Sir Warren Fisher, commented, "Imagine the result on public opinion in Great Britain of a similar act by the executive towards a political party (or the women's suffrage movement)!" [27]

Collins, McKee and Mulcahy, among others, viewed the British suppression of Ireland's infant assembly tantamount to a declaration of war. The gloves were coming off on both sides. Britain began their crackdown with renewed vigour while de Valera's hope of a peaceful assertion of Irish national constitutional rights collapsed. Dev's leadership absence coupled with the Dáil's political hamstringing opened the door for bitter recriminations between the Long Fella and Collins.

❧

While the British authorities were flexing their political muscles, the DMP was raiding Sinn Féin headquarters at #6 Harcourt Street under the direction of Detective Constable Daniel Hoey.

With no advance warning of the police's incursion from Broy, Michael Collins was trapped in his upstairs office.

Controlling his anger over his possible arrest, Mick waited calmly for a constable to enter his office. When the District Inspector Neil McFeely appeared, Collins, in a theatrical display of annoyance, vented his irate feelings of righteous indignation at the offending party.

The man was immediately cowed and taken aback. After a cursory search of the room, he left. Collins had successfully bluffed his way out of a dangerous predicament.

This episode would prove to be only a dress rehearsal for future such encounters, as it wouldn't be the last time the Corkman was forced to use his mouth instead of a gun in defence of his life.

That very evening, 12 September, the Squad was in action for the second time. Their target was Detective Constable Daniel Hoey, the man who'd coincidently led the day's earlier search at #6 Harcourt Street.

Hoey had long been a thorn in Collins's side as well as a nuisance to Dublin's Volunteers even prior to 1916. In his thirties, the 'G-man' knew who Collins was and could identify him. He'd missed his chance earlier that day and wouldn't have another.

Additionally, Hoey had taken the lead in conducting raids around town, and the Big Fella feared it would be only a matter of time before the detective struck gold. Besides, both Sergeant Smyth and now Hoey had ignored earlier warnings as they continued pursuing aggressive actions against the Volunteers.

Mick McDonnell, Jim Slattery and Tom Ennis drew the short straws and shot the man dead in front of Great Brunswick Street police headquarters as he was about to enter the building at 10 o'clock that night.

❧

Towards the end of 1919, Piaras Béaslaí noted that the 'curious title' of IRA had become part of the popular vernacular.

> Strictly speaking, this popular name had no justification. The official title of the body so designated was always "Óglaigh na h-Éireann," or, in English the "Irish Volunteers." On the election of Dial Éireann, however, which the Volunteers recognised as the lawful authority in the country, and the submission of their control to a Minister of Defence [Cathal Brugha] elected by the Dáil, "An tÓglách" began to refer to the Volunteers as "the Army of the Irish Republic," and this phrase became popularly transmuted into "Irish Republican Army" and regularly abbreviated to "I.R.A." [28]

With violent incidents accelerating on both sides of the ledger, Michael Collins's name became an admired and respected one in Dublin. With more public acclaim, the Corkman found that people were willing to come forward, offering their help.

Batt O'Connor was one of them. After the September raid on Sinn Féin HQ, the Big Fella opened another office down the street at #76 Harcourt Street. In an effort to help secure a place for hiding sensitive documents, Batt built some hidden storage spaces at the new office.

They didn't have long to wait to test the new construction. On 8 November, the police raided #76. Again, Collins was in his office when the invasion occurred. Fleeing through a skylight, he found sanctuary in the neighbouring Standard Hotel. Minutes later, he walked out its front door and boarded a south-bound tram. Over his shoulder, he could see the rozzers still milling about in front of #76.

With just enough time to hide the incriminating evidence, Michael's staff had placed the papers and ledger books safely behind Batt's sliding door.

On 10 November, Detective Officer Thomas Wharton, who often patrolled along Harcourt Street, was shot and wounded as he and three other detectives walked down Cuffe Street along the top of Grafton Street.

Luckily for the 'G-man,' Paddy O'Daly's parabellum jammed and he could only fire one shot.

But Detective Sergeant Johnny Barton was not as fortunate. He was shot at 'knocking-off time' on College Street as he stepped off the footpath, preparing to cross over to the Brunswick Street police station. Jimmy Slattery and Vinnie Byrne fired the fatal shots.

Ryle Dwyer filled in the details.

> He [Barton] was shot in the back from such close range that there were powder burns on his overcoat. As he crumpled down on his right knee, he said, 'Oh, God what did I do to deserve this?' He pulled out his gun and fired up College Street.
>
> The wounded detective was helped to the door of a nearby club. The fatal bullet had gone right through his body, through his right lung.
>
> 'They have done for me,' he said. 'God forgive me. What did I do? I am dying. Get me a priest.'
>
> Barton received the last rites upon his arrival at hospital and died minutes later. [29]

David Neligan described Detective Barton as one who wore 'weird clothes' and could easily have been taken for a simpleton. But that would've been a mistake. He was, in actuality, a fine policeman with many undercover operatives working for him. Apparently, financially well off, rumours abounded that he'd extorted money from Englishmen seeking refuge from conscription in Ireland during the war. Supposedly, Barton wasn't afraid of Collins or his intelligence men either. With that in mind, Michael viewed the man a menace to the terror crusade he was waging against the Sassenach.

[**Author's note**: Detective Johnny Barton also had a Tom Cullen connection. It was Barton who'd met Tom's military train at Westland Row rail station on the evening of 8 April 1918. His assignment was to escort Tom to prison in Mountjoy.

Today, I've often wondered if Barton's death wasn't Collins's way of retaliating for the man's role in Cullen's arrest and brief incarceration. Supposedly, settling personal vendettas played no part in the Mick's political assassinations, but the Corkman's loyalty to his closest friends could've easily become a mitigating factor in this case.]

When discussing the events of the day in his inner sanctum with Liam Tobin and Tom Cullen, Michael was quick to point out, — The death of Barton exemplifies the consequences of the flagrant use of violence, my friends, and yes, their dastardly deeds and their eventual consequences must never be forgotten.

Needless to say, the actions of Collins's men drew the ire of the authorities. Resorting to old tricks, they tried to engineer another mass arrest similar to the one undertaken in May, 1918. Again, Collins foiled their plans. With advanced information and well heeded warnings, only two men were picked up. But that wasn't the end of it. After several fruitless raids on #6 and #76 Harcourt Street, the British ordered the two Sinn Féin offices closed and their doors nailed shut.

Unperturbed by the increase in British and RIC activity throughout Ireland, the IRA stepped up their attacks on military and police barracks. To compound the RIC's problems, the local authorities were having a difficult time attracting new recruits to their ranks. The time honoured policy of de Valera's social ostracism against the RIC had taken its toll. As a result, outlying police barracks were closing. Gradually, the Peelers were losing control of the countryside, forced to relocate their policemen into larger towns.

❋

On 29 November, the British Field Marshal and Viceroy Lord John French publicly offered a reward of £5,000 to anyone who could offer up evidence sufficient enough to obtain a conviction for those responsible for the deaths of policemen Smyth, Hoey and Barton. [**Author's note**: Béaslaí noted it was never claimed.]

But three weeks later, it was French's life that was on the line as the Squad and Michael's intelligence men conspired to kill the Viceroy.

On a tip from Ned Broy, Collins learned the Field Marshal would be returning to Dublin around noon on 19 December. He'd be arriving at the Ashtown Station by private train from his rural estate in Co. Roscommon. The little rail station was the closest one to his Phoenix Park residence.

With only a day's advance notice, an ambush was quickly planned. Liam Tobin and Tom Cullen along with Dick McKee cycled out to Ashtown to reconnoitre the situation.

Quickly, plans were drawn up and members of the Squad were in place on the Friday morning in question.

From the station, French would be met by three especially armour-reinforced motor cars. Next, the procession would head down the Ashtown Road, cross over the Blanchardstown Road at a juncture know as 'The Ashtown Cross.' Proceeding straight ahead, the convoy would enter the Ashtown Gates into Phoenix Park, a distance of just less than half a mile.

[**Author's note**: Dan Breen noted that four military lorries drove up from the Park Gate and halted nearby. Each carried a full complement of soldiers in full 'battle array.']

Beside the Ashtown Cross was Kelly's public house, known as the 'Half-way House,' which was bordered by a growth of shrubbery. The hedge offered some cover and the attack on the Viceroy would commence from there.

Collins picked fourteen men [Breen & Béaslaí say eleven while Foy says fourteen] for the ambush including Mick McDonnell, Paddy O'Daly, Tom Kilkoyne, Joe Leonard, Tom Keogh, Vinnie Byrne and Jimmy Slattery, all well-tested men who wouldn't lose their nerve. For the occasion, Leonard had brought along another volunteer, Martin Savage. In addition to this mix, Michael added Dan Breen, Seán Treacy, Seamus Robinson and Seán Hogan, four of the eight Tipperary men who'd staged the Soloheadbeg attack back in January. They had been forced to leave their homes as a result of their unpopular actions. They were in effect 'men on the run' who'd sought refuge in Dublin. They'd been welcomed by McKee and Collins who valued their fearless devotion to seeing the British driven from Ireland.

Thinking that French would be in the second car, the IRA men planned to stop it by pushing a large cart out onto the road prior to its crossing the main Blanchardstown thoroughfare.

With the sound of the train arriving earlier than expected, O'Daly's men rushed out the back of the pub, taking up their positions along the hedge row. Meanwhile, McDonnell's group hurriedly began pushing the cart, parked in the pub's front garden, out onto Ashtown Road.

Unfortunately, it proved unusually heavy and regrettably became stuck in the ditch bordering the road. Struggling to finish the job, the men were interrupted by the unexpected arrival of a policeman who'd been assigned to stop traffic at the crossroad.

At that moment, one of Squad members threw a bomb at the advancing convoy. The party struggling with the cart were knocked down as was the policeman.

With the three cars speeding toward them, the IRA began firing their revolvers and throwing grenades.

Concentrating their fire at the second vehicle, the first motor sped past. Unbeknownst to the IRA, Lord French was inside and escaped unscathed.

The Squad successfully disabled the second car and its driver surrendered while the third machine sped past, exchanging fire with the attackers as it went. In the intensive hail of bullets, Martin Savage was killed. Unable to take his body with them, Breen and others carried Martin inside Kelly's.

Thinking that French was in the second motor car, the one riddled with bullet holes, the IRA imagined they'd accomplished their mission. The men quickly mounted their bicycles and headed for town.

Suddenly, while pedalling as fast as he could, Breen noticed one of his trouser legs was soaked with blood. Dismounting, he discovered he'd been badly wounded. Taking a shoe lace from his boot, he tied off the bottom end of his trousers. He didn't want to leave a trail of blood for the British to follow.

With the exception of Martin, all Squad members escaped, as did Lord French.

Piaras Béaslaí summarised this affair with the following words:

It was inevitable that Lord French, as the representative of a usurping Government, and the head of the armed forces which were waging war on the Irish people, should be attacked. All the acts of violence against the nation to which I have referred, from the advent of French, were done in his name and by his authority. It is difficult to grasp the mentality of those who have described this daring attack as an "attempted assassination." It was an attack by a tiny handful of men — eleven all told – on a strongly armed body of soldiers and police in armour-plated cars, who were perfectly aware that they were liable to such an assault; and those who carried it out faced a double risk, the risk of death in action, and the risk of death if captured.

From his advent in Ireland [May, 1918] Lord French was attended by a bodyguard – a precaution which, despite all the fables of English journalists, was never taken by Collins – not even during the [Irish] Civil War. It is stated that after the attack at Ashtown, and up to his departure from Ireland [c. April, 1921], Lord French, the representative of British royalty, never travelled by train and never ventured abroad, save in an armour-plated car with a strong escort. In fact, it was justly remarked at this time that "Lord French, who cannot go anywhere without an escort, is much more 'on the run' than Mick Collins, who goes openly round Dublin alone." [30]

❧

With the dawn of 1920, G Division detectives and undercover operatives, who were pressurising the IRA, abruptly grew more cautious. As a result, Squad members were forced to adapt.

By early 1920 the Squad's modus operandi involved open-air killings in broad daylight carried out by two gunmen, in case one shooter missed or his weapon jammed. After a waiting intelligence officer [#3 Crow Street personnel such as Tom Cullen, Liam Tobin, etc.] had indicated the target to them by a prearranged signal like a waved handkerchief or raised hat, the first killer would down the victim while the second [shooter] finished him off with shots to the head. A three-man covering party was never more than 50 yards away to prevent soldiers, policemen or civilians intervening – though, in fact, this almost never occurred. Most of Dublin's uniformed policemen quietly sympathised with the Volunteers, remained ostentatiously neutral or had been cowed into submission. Occasionally one intervened but got little assistance from bystanders. [31]

❦

Tom Cullen was eager for an assignment when Michael approached him with one.

As can be imagined, Lord French was enraged that he'd been targeted and had barely escaped death just before Christmas. He felt the G Division was in tatters and needed stronger leadership. Morale was low, recruiting numbers were down and many veteran officers were resigning. Its current commissioner, Colonial Walter Edgeworth-Johnstone was a comfortably well-off, career bureaucrat in his fifties who seemed to lack imagination.

French wanted to bring in a new man, but instead of abandoning Johnstone, the policing board created a new position, an assistant commissioner. With the move, Lord French promptly forwarded his replacement choice to the committee.

In short order, District Inspector William C. Forbes Redmond, a tough, aggressive policeman from Belfast with a sterling reputation, was appointed. He moved to Dublin and reported for duty on 1 January 1920. [**Author's note**: David Neligan remembered Redmond arriving and meeting the 'G-men' in November, 1919.] Neligan described the new man.

He [Redmond] was a neatly-built man of about forty, nattily dressed and wearing a bowler. He looked more like a stockbroker than a policeman. He gave us a pep talk. It was extraordinary, he said, that we, who knew Dublin so well, could not catch Michael Collins, whereas a man who had only just arrived from England had managed to meet him more than once. [32]

❀

Ryle Dwyer stated that though he arrived with a good reputation, "…he showed himself to be incredibly naïve and his appointment further undermined the morale of the DMP." [33]

Redmond quickly made two mistakes. First he brought some of his own Belfast detectives with him to Dublin. This immediately caused resentment within the local ranks. Secondly, he boldly announced he was going to make the capture of Michael Collins his #1 priority.

He called all DMP detectives from sergeants up and told them 'that they were not doing their duty, that he would give them one month to get Michael Collins and those responsible for shooting the various detectives, or else he would order them to resign." [34]

To further compound matters, Redmond, a stranger to Dublin, needed someone to chauffeur him around town. By some strange coincidence, he picked James McNamara for the job.

Unbeknownst to Castle authorities, McNamara was one of Collins's four 'G-men' double agents. The son of a policeman himself, McNamara was a clerk for the assistant commissioner of the DMP in Dublin Castle. A jovial sort, he was well liked and trusted by his colleagues and supervisors. It was those same qualities plus his pro-Irish convictions that had won over Collins. As a result, Michael knew Redmond's next move almost before the man did himself.

Upon first learning of Redmond's appointment, the Big Fella sent Frank Thornton up to Belfast to procure a photograph of the man. When he returned, #3 Crow Street made sure each member of the Squad had a good look at it.

In mid-January, Tom Cullen took a room in the Standard Hotel on Harcourt Street. His task was to watch Redmond who was residing there. Tom methodically tracked the man's every movement. By now, the Wicklow man had become deft at following a subject without their becoming aware of his stalking presence.

Several nights later, a Redmond-led raid searched Batt & Maire O'Connor's home at #1 Brendan Road in Donnybrook. Only Maire was home at the time and, thankfully, nothing incriminating was discovered.

On Tuesday evening, 20 January, Tom Cullen was tipped off that Redmond's men were planning to raid Cullenswood House that very night. With Thornton in tow, the two cycled over to Oakley Road to warn Collins, whom they found working away in his basement office.

Mick left immediately while Tom and Frank hurried upstairs to alert Dick Mulcahy who'd recently taken a top-floor flat in Pearse's former school building.

Awaking the GHQ's chief-of-staff, the three men headed off only minutes before the raiding party arrived in four lorries.

That was enough for Collins. The following morning he ordered the Squad to kill Redmond.

His words to Mick McDonnell were likely spot on. – Either we get the bastard first, or God help us, he'll get us!

Taking Michael at his word, Paddy O'Daly shot and killed the Belfast policeman as he crossed Harcourt Street in front of the Standard. Knowing the man wore a bullet-proof waistcoat, he aimed for his head. "The first shot shattered his jaw and he [Redmond] tried to draw a gun, but the second shot in the forehead killed him." [35]

Tom Keogh, O'Daly's backup partner, delivered the coup de grace, but Redmond was already dead.

Ryle Dwyer wrote a fitting conclusion to the Forbes Redmond affair, a death that ended the effective use of the DMP as a political undercover force against Sinn Féin and the Dublin Volunteers.

Following Redmond's death, his own undercover detectives pulled out and returned to Belfast, and therefore G Division 'ceased to affect the situation', according to British military intelligence. Redmond's post was not filled....

Dublin Castle offered £10,000 rewards for information leading to the arrest and conviction of the person responsible for Redmond's death.

He [Collins] was behind the killing of Redmond. Rewards of £5,000 had already been offered in connection with the deaths of the three other DMP detectives, Smyth, Hoey and Barton, and these rewards were now doubled. Collins had ordered all four killings, so there was a handsome cumulative reward for the evidence to convict him, though the reward was never specifically offered for his arrest and conviction.

Many of the detectives and policemen knew him by sight, but their failure to arrest him could not be explained by fear alone. Like the police who were working for him, others were undoubtedly passive sympathisers. One night as Collins was cycling before curfew, a couple of uniform policemen were standing by the road, and one of them shouted, 'More power, me Corkman!' [36]

❧

On Saturday evening, 24 January 1920, the Baltinglass [Co. Wicklow] RIC barracks was attacked. Details of the events are sketchy. Paul Gorry, author of the book, *Baltinglass Chronicles 1851-2001*, described what happened. The one name he left out was that of Tom Cullen.

The last train from Dublin arrived into the Baltinglass rail station about 7 o'clock that evening. Several dozen passengers, returning home, disembarked and headed down Station Road and into Mill Street.

About that time twenty-four-year-old Maggie Doogan collected the evening newspaper and, along with her

teenage sister Essie, headed for the police barracks in
Mill Street to deliver it, as she did regularly. She tapped
on the window. Inside were Sergeant Kavanagh and
three constables, Bellew, Malynn and Robinson. James
Malynn went to open the door, expecting Maggie as
usual. Before she had time to hand him the paper
a group of men rushed at the door. A man shouted
'hands up' and Maggie was pushed into the hall where
she fell. She heard shots and as she tried to crawl into
the dayroom Malynn fell to the floor, saying 'Maggie,
I'm shot.' She heard more shooting and then the door
was shut. [37]

The attack was well planned. This was not a random act of
violence or an unprovoked incident. It had all the markings of a
deliberate, carefully thought-out attempt to kill RIC Constable
James Malynn.

If this had been a group of IRA men seeking weapons with
the ultimate aim of destroying the barracks, as had become a
common occurrence in the past six months, the attackers would
have behaved differently. No weapons were seized and the building was not torched.

Gorry noted in his report that six or seven men carried out the
actual attack, but that forty or fifty others were involved. These
additional men acted as lookouts on the roads leading into and
out of town. Others served as drivers for the three or four motor
cars used in the operation. Additionally, the telegraph wires into
town were cut prior to the attack.

It certainly appears Malynn was the target, but Francis
McPartlan, an off-duty constable, standing in the doorway of his
house next to the barracks, received two superficial wounds while
Willie Wall, a jaunting car driver, was grazed in the leg by a stray
bullet. Young Essie Doogan, standing in the street, was told by
the attackers to 'keep back.' She later said, "Shots were fired right
over my head."

The following day Fr. Brophy, a local priest, stated, "...the
misdeeds of those in authority were not a justification for the
shedding of innocent blood...." [38]

In his account of the incident, Gorry said he thought men from Wexford were involved. Later, seven men were arrested but they refused to recognise the court. In shackles, they all were transported to Dublin's Mountjoy Jail. Only one served time in an English prison [four months] while the other six were released from jail and returned to Baltinglass a month later to 'an enthusiastic welcome.' It seems the seven were never convicted of any crime.

James Malynn was critically wounded in the attack. A single bullet penetrated his right lung and severed his spine. The following day, he was taken to Dublin's Mercer's Hospital. Later, he was released but died the following November in his home in Moate, Co. Westmeath.

But why would Tom have been involved? There are several reasons for that assumption. The attack took place in Co. Wicklow... his turf. He would have known many of the IRA men involved from his days as captain of the East Wicklow Volunteers. The sophistication of its planning suggested the raid was staged by an experienced person or persons. The attention to detail had all the earmarks of a Crow Street operation with the probable assistance of men from McKee's Dublin Brigade. Either Michael or Dick would've had the IRA contacts from other districts to call upon for help, if in fact some of those involved were from neighbouring Co. Wexford. They also would have been able to arrange for three or four motor cars to be available, especially after the authorities in November had issued an order prohibiting the possession of a car without an authorised permit. The fact that only one man, Malynn, was singled out was reminiscent of the 'jobs' carried out by the Squad. Additionally, Tom easily could have been on that evening train from Dublin.

Finally, the big clincher, Constable James Malynn was the same RIC man who'd arrested Tom Cullen for 'drilling' Volunteers in Wicklow Town back in April, 1918. Since then, Malynn had been a constant thorn in the side of the IRA. Though likely warned to back off on several occasions, he persisted. As a result, many, beside Tom, wished him ill.

[**Author's note**: I don't believe Tom was one of Malynn's attackers. That was not his style, at least not yet. But I do believe he planned or helped plan the undertaking. He likely arrived in Baltinglass on the evening train. When he saw everything was ready and the men were in place, he gave the operation its go-ahead.]

❧

Though the DMP and 'G-men' of Dublin Castle were pressurised by the workings of Crow Street and the actions of the Squad, the British authorities weren't. The Sassenach decided to turn their Dublin secret service operation over to Mr. Basil Thomson and his London Special Branch section. His first priority was penetrating the IRA's top ranks and uncovering information about their leadership personnel, the very ones who'd been wreaking havoc with the Castle's G Division.

Military raids on suspected IRA hangouts, safe houses and places of business increased in Dublin as well as throughout the country. Some days a dozen or more raids were conducted. An 11 pm – 6 am Dublin curfew was in place and rigorously enforced. Motor vehicle permits were required and, if upon questioning one was not forthcoming, the motor was confiscated and its driver arrested.

In England, the British government was advertising for individuals willing to face the 'rough and dangerous task' of reinforcing the RIC in Ireland. With enrolment at an all-time low, Dublin Castle desperately needed to find men to rebuild its depleted policing ranks. By the end of March, Ireland began seeing the first of these police replacements arrive. Nicknamed the 'Black & Tans' by the Irish, they'd soon shower the countryside with their own brand of terror.

In addition to drafting new policemen, the British were busy enlisting the aid of their own spies, hoping to unseat Dublin's republican leadership and particularly Michael Collins including his three intelligence officers, Tobin, Cullen and Thornton.

The first man to surface, an unlikely spy, was Henry Timothy Quinlisk, a Co. Wexford man. He'd been an Irish prisoner-of-war in Germany and was recruited unsuccessfully by Roger Casement for his ill-fated Irish Brigade prior to Easter Week, 1916.

Quinn, as he liked to be called, was a fine dresser and very much a ladies' man. He boasted he was a close personal friend of Michael's and knew all his secrets.

Soon after his arrival in Dublin, he visited G Division HQ, where coincidentally, Ned Broy typed his confidential statement in which he divulged his wish to inform on Sinn Féin and tell all he knew about that 'scoundrel' Michael Collins.

[**Author's note**: Collins had, in fact, helped Quinlisk with financial aid following his return to Ireland after the European war and had found him a room at #44 Mountjoy Street, the Munster Hotel. Mick felt the man's knowledge of German and his military experience might be useful to the Volunteers.]

In due time, Broy forwarded a copy of Quinn's 'confession' on to Michael.

Realising what Quinlisk's real intentions were, Mick smuggled a message into Dublin Castle where the man now was holed up. Stating that the two of them should meet at Wren's Hotel in Cork City because Dublin was becoming 'too hot' for him, Quinn immediately took the bait and informed the Cork authorities prior to making plans for travelling there himself.

Unbeknownst to Quinn, his coded message from the Castle to the chief constable in Cork, informing him of Collins's 'supposed' arrival, was intercepted and decoded.

On the prearranged date, Mrs. Wren's hotel was duly raided by the local RIC only to find Collins wasn't there.

When Michael learned of the raid, confirming his growing suspicions, he sent Quinlisk another message, informing him that Tom Cullen would be arriving into Wren's on the evening of 18 February. Once there, arrangements would be made for both men to rendezvous with Collins.

On the appointed Wednesday evening, Quinlisk was in the hotel lobby decked out in his best suit. But on the contrary, it was not Tom Cullen that called for him at Wren's that evening, but members of Cork's #1 Brigade. They took him outside of town and shot him eleven times.

Ryle Dwyer described what the Cork authorities found when they discovered his bullet-riddled body the following morning.

There was one bullet wound through the socket of the right eye, two bullet wounds between the right eye and right ear, and three further bullet wounds on the right side of the forehead, as well as five other bullet wounds to the body. The Cork Examiner concluded, 'the medical evidence was that they could not have been self-inflicted.' [39]

※

Basil Thomson, the highly educated son of an Archbishop of York had led an adventurous life. He'd farmed in Canada, been the prime minister of Tonga and taught the King of Siam's son. Now the most powerful person in British intelligence circles, he'd been enlisted to run Irish secret service from his London office.

Thomson's first offering in establishing an intelligence offensive in Ireland was a British agent named John Charles Byrnes, alias Jameson, a thirty-five-year-old Londoner [some reports have him born in Limerick] whose only Irish connection was a grandfather who'd come from Wexford. Piaras Béaslaí described the *modus operandi* of this very clever British Secret Service agent. [Béaslaí recorded 'Burn' instead of 'Byrnes.']

Burn, who, under the name of "Jameson," had been posing in English Labour circles as Bolshevist. Burn, or Jameson, was a remarkable type of the agent provocateur and had been admitted into the counsels of organisers of the British Police strike. He was an ex-soldier, and succeeded in winning the confidence of Art O'Brien, our representative in London, by offers to secure arms "to help the revolution in Ireland." He got from O'Brien a letter of introduction to Collins, armed with which he proceeded to Dublin. Collins received him favourably, and, for a time, was quite impressed by his "schemes." He pretended to be in touch with the Soviet Government in Russia and to have large sums of money at his disposal. He offered to obtain a number of machine

guns, and gave the names of soldiers in various barracks in Dublin and other parts of Ireland, who, he
said, would help.

Although trusting him and recommending his services to G.H.Q., Collins had the wisdom to deal with
him chiefly through his lieutenants, Tobin and Cullen,
and this precaution probably saved his life. Cullen, at
his very first meeting with Jameson, conceived a distrust
of the man. [40]

For several weeks, Jameson pressed Liam Tobin and Tom
Cullen for a meeting with Michael. They effectively put him off,
but his insistence only confirmed in Tom's mind that the man
was not to be trusted under any circumstances.

Suddenly, Jameson was nowhere to be seen. In actually, he'd
returned to London to report to his superiors at Scotland Yard.

Upon his return to Dublin, Collins decided to put Jameson to
the test, as he was intrigued by any man who said he could supply
all the Dublin Brigade with weapons.

Jameson was blindfolded and taken to a room populated with
four men: Collins, who called himself McCabe, Dick Mulcahy,
Liam Tobin and Rory O'Connor, Volunteer GHQ Director of
Engineering.

> Collins described British military pressure on the IRA
> and expressed his interest in Byrnes's idea of winning
> [British] soldiers over by fraternising with them at
> dances and other social functions. He also handed over
> a detailed list of British troop strength in Ireland, which
> identified those units most antagonistic to the Volun-
> teers. He asked Byrnes to find out how well equipped
> British forces were and by which routes and methods
> reinforcements would be sent to Ireland. [41]

Meeting Michael Collins, aka McCabe, and some of his insid-
ers delighted Byrnes. It was clear to him that Collins was the chief
architect of Ireland's insurgency and that he'd supplanted Éamon
de Valera's authority during Dev's extended absence from Ireland.

Upon his return to London, Byrnes reported directly to Thomson. In his report, Byrnes felt that it was Collins who was responsible for ordering the murders of the Castle's G Division detectives, but he felt Collins had taken no part in the actual shootings.

Needless to say, Thomson was pleased with Byrnes's progress. Having a meeting with Collins and establishing a personal relationship with the 'most wanted man in Ireland' was a major breakthrough. Now that they had Collins's attention, it was time to arrange for his death.

Upon returning to Dublin once again, Byrnes tried to schedule another meeting, but repeatedly was told that Collins was out of town. He continued to press Tobin and Cullen about the matter so Collins decided to set a trap for Byrnes to see if Tom's initial impressions of the man were correct.

Frank Thornton said in his Witness Statement that Tom, "… had forcibly expressed his dislike of the man from the beginning, and possibly this had reactions on myself. In any case there were none of us impressed." [42]

Béaslaí described the plot Collins and Crow Street devised to test Byrnes.

> Jameson had given Tobin a pass purporting to admit the bearer to [British] military barracks. He was now pressing for its return. Tobin told him Collins was in the country, but had written to him, and he showed him Collins's reply, in which he told him the pass was to be found in File No. 31, Box No. 5, on the third shelf at an address in Iona Drive, where he kept all his papers. The address given was that of an ex-Lord Mayor of Dublin, J. J. Farrell, who during his term of office, had insisted on receiving the King of England [George V in 1911], in violation of his pledge given when elected. Mr. Farrell did not obtain his expected knighthood, but it was exceeding unlikely that the British forces would ever dream of raiding his house in the ordinary course of things. [43]

256 of 512 • FEAR NOT THE STORM

That evening, Farrell's house was raided and thoroughly searched. Blinded by his initial success, Byrnes was exposed by his own greedy stupidity.

Tom was delighted his initial intuition was correct and that he'd been able to protect Michael from the likes of a bumbling eejit.

The end of the 'Jameson affair' came quickly.

Upon Byrnes's recent return from England, he'd brought over a case of Webley revolvers for Tobin as a show of good faith. Now, with his fate sealed, Liam, carrying the case of revolvers, took Byrnes to #56 Bachelor's Walk, offices of New Ireland Assurance Society.

There they met Frank Thornton who took possession of the case. Later, Frank stated, "When the coast was clear I handed the portmanteau of revolvers over to Tom Cullen who was waiting at 32 Bachelor's Walk, which was the Quartermaster General's stores." [44]

That same morning, Michael contacted James McNamara and asked him to let him know if the Castle was planning any raids in the immediate future. About noon, McNamara sent back word that #56 was listed for a 3 pm raid.

At three that afternoon, Mick Collins, with Tom Cullen and Liam Tobin in tow, watched from the opposite bank of the Liffey as Crown forces raided the Bachelor's Walk building.

> They first went into the cellar and ransacked it. They then searched the whole building, but found nothing other than an Irish Volunteer's cap. They returned at 1 o'clock the following morning and smashed in the front door. They had picks and shovels and proceeded to dig up the basement looking for a secret passage. Byrnes fate was sealed. [45]

That evening, Tuesday, 2 March, Paddy O'Daly met Byrnes in the Granville Hotel at #17 Sackville Street Upper. On the pretence of taking him to meet Collins, they walked out in the direction of Glasnevin.

Along the way, the two men were intercepted by Squad members Ben Barrett and Tom Kilcoyne. They searched Byrnes who tried to bluff them about his 'supposed' friendship with Collins and Tobin.

Having none of it, they asked, – Do you want to pray?

– No, he replied.

– We're only doing our jobs, Barrett said.

– And I did mine, Byrnes replied.

Mick McDonnell and Jimmy Slattery shot him once in the head and again in the heart while Tom Keogh and Vinnie Byrne, acting as backups, covered their two comrades.

Immediately after Daly and Byrnes had departed the Granville, Cullen and Tobin went to his room and removed all the man's personal effects. They discovered among his belongs some 'very incriminating documents.'

❧

Piaras Béaslaí brought this chapter of Britain's attempt to infiltrate Ireland with its secret agents to a close.

> Yet another British spy had meanwhile got in touch with Collins – Fergus Bryan Mulloy, ostensibly an Army Sergeant, stationed in the [British] Pay Office, G.H.Q., Parkgate, who declared himself able and anxious to give Collins much valuable information. Collins met him at [Batt and Maire] O'Connor's house, and, unlike the case of Jameson, distrusted him from the first. He made great promises, but performed nothing. He proposed that Collins should give him genuine information, and enable him to bring off some capture so as to place him higher in the confidence of his English employers. Collins saw through the man, played him, and had him watched until evidence was accumulated of his treachery. Mulloy was shot dead [24 March 1920] in Wicklow Street, in broad daylight. He was the last British spy to get into touch with Collins up to the truce. [46]

[**Author's note:** At one point during his short career as a British undercover spy, Mulloy invited Tobin, Cullen and Thornton to come with him to Dublin Castle so they could 'obtain' some important information. The three wisely declined his offer.]

※

Sometime in early to mid-March 1920, Michael decided to put all Squad members on paid, full-time duty. He also amalgamated the two 'separate' elements of the Squad into one.

Originally, the Squad began as two units which were unaware of the other's existence. This strategy sprang from Collins's obsession with secrecy and for letting only those involved in an operation know the details.

[**Author's note**: This may explain the confusion of Squad leadership. Some reports indicated Mick McDonnell was the Squad's first OC while others stated it was Paddy O'Daly. In fact, it appears they were, for all practical purposes, co-leaders.]

With Squad members serving as unpaid, part-time Volunteers who worked other jobs during the day, the British intelligence service was free to operate with little interference from 8 am 'til 6 pm. But as the English ramped up their activities, Mick needed to respond in kind to their increased threats.

※

On 13 January 1920, Field Marshal Sir Henry Wilson, the Chief of the Imperial General Staff reportedly said, "The state of Ireland is terrible."

Both Wilson and Secretary of State for War Winston Churchill wanted to reinforce the flagging RIC while keeping the British military presence in Ireland at a minimum, likely for public appearance sake. Churchill proposed raising a 'special force' of former British soldiers for this purpose. It would help eradicate two growing problems: Reducing the rolls of unemployed British ex-military men and fortifying the depleted ranks of the RIC.

> Churchill refined his pet scheme so that the new force
> consisted of two distinct elements – one, former enlisted
> men [the Black & Tans], and the other, former officers,

who became known as auxiliaries. The enlisted men were so hastily recruited that they did not have proper uniforms, so they wore a blend of military khaki and the dark green uniforms of the RIC. They acquired the sobriquet Black and Tans. They made little or no pretence to be policemen. They were an irregular military force with little or no discipline. Some stole everything they could lay their hands on, and as a force they committed terrible outrages, often against non-combatants. [47]

[**Author's note**: Contrary to popular belief, the Tans and Auxies who arrived in Ireland in 1920-1921 were *not* the sweepings of British jails. However, by the time they left at the end of the War for Independence, they *were* criminals, guilty of many heinous crimes.

Much is written and remembered of their despicable deeds and rightfully so, but before final judgement is passed, I offer one possible explanation for their vile contemptuousness.

Ex-soldiers, down through the ages, are a unique breed. Some become addicted to war. Having the power of life and death over another is intoxicating liquor indeed. Life, overshadowed by combat, laced with fear and death, can lead to an opiate-like addiction...an appetite for more of the same. I imagine many of these British imports, arriving in Ireland, suffered from post-combat withdrawal after the Armistice in November, 1918.

Finally, home from the front, the ex-soldiers, many now jobless civilians, struggled with emotional malaise and economic frustrations. They yearned for the thrill of the hunt (battle). They longed for the close comradeship war triggers. Absent too was the sense of power, the ability to dictate the terms of life and death. They hungered for the adrenalin-induced excitement of danger now missing in their lives...lives envisioned with no immediate prospects of fulfilling their missing desires.

Suffering from varying degrees of emotional and psychological posttraumatic stress, the ex-soldiers received an unexpected reprieve. Presented with an opportunity to feed their craving for adventure, they headed for Ireland.

Often viewed as an inferior, ungrateful lot with an insubordinate, revolutionary penchant, the Irish suddenly became the targets for their present life's dissatisfaction. With Ireland 'on the stir,' what better calling was there than satisfying their troubled psyches while restoring order in the 'offending' colony. So over the Irish Sea they came by the thousands...Englishmen to 'put things right' in Ireland.

Away from Mother England, absent of family and friends and lacking the normal inhibitions of human restraint, the Tans and Auxiliaries went about satisfying their own selfish, anti-social needs in an uncontrolled setting. Backed by the 'authority' of the State, they took off the gloves and ran amuck.

Unequipped to analyse or deal with the complex human dynamics suddenly brought to bear on them, the IRA reacted in ways that might be expected when lives, families and country are threatened...they fought back...tooth and nail. Blurred standards of right and wrong quickly emerged on both sides of the struggle. Self-survival became paramount. What choice did either party have as the consequences of the use of violence further escalated matters, inflaming the conflict even more?

I offer the foregoing not as justification for the Tans' and Auxies' actions, but simply as one possible explanation for the mayhem these transitory, quasi-military policemen engaged in during their brief but violent stay in Ireland.]

Ireland didn't have long to wait for the Tans to demonstrate who and what they were all about. On 20 March 1920, the newly elected [30 January] Lord Mayor Tomás MacCurtain of Cork City was shot to death in his home in front of his wife, Muriel.

Tim Pat Coogan described what happened next.

> Around 1 am a party of armed men with blackened faces forced their way into his house and shot him dead in the presence of his wife. IRA intelligence subsequently established the fact that a group of civilians entered King St RIC barracks shortly afterwards. One of the group was further identified as looking suspiciously like the man in a photograph which Crow St (had obtained)....
>
> Collins was hard-hit by the death. He wrote to [Terry] MacSwiney, 'I have not very much heart in

what I am doing today thinking of poor Tomas. It was surely the most appalling thing that has been done yet.' It was also a thing which would have far-reaching consequences in another highly sensitive part of the country, Northern Ireland. Collins took no retaliatory action until after the inquest which was in effect a trial of British policy. Despite efforts by Lord French and [David] Lloyd George [British prime minister] to claim that MacCurtain was murdered by his own extremists the jury, which had been selected by the police, brought in a verdict that was a comprehensive indictment of both Westminster and Dublin Castle. [48]

❄

With the sudden and unexpected deaths of Quinlisk, Byrnes and Mulloy, Basil Thomson tried a different tack. If his secret agents couldn't penetrate Collins's invisible wall of impermeability then he'd tackle the problem from a different angle…a monetary one.

Thomson knew Collins was Minister for Finance and was in receipt of thousands of pounds collected for the Dáil's bond fund that he'd organised.

Michael's strategy in securing the monies was to open numerous bank accounts around the country in the name of respectable persons who acted as fronts for Mick's deposits. No doubt the various bank managers were aware of what was going on, but because of either their nationalist leanings or their fear of interfering, they stayed out of the Corkman's way.

As a result, Thomson's next move was to call upon Mr. Alan Bell to track down Collins's secret Dáil accounts. Mick was particularly incensed when he learned of resident magistrate Bell's intended actions to uncover where he had squirreled away the bond funds.

This money, collected in dribs and drabs from poor farmers and shepherds, 'the tips of servant girls and baccy money of old men', was not only hard cash but symbolic of the national will, and Michael was damned if he would let Mr. Bell get his sticky fingers on a single penny. [49]

Bell was from Banagher, King's County. Previously, he'd served for many years in the RIC before becoming a magistrate. In 1919, he'd been brought out of retirement and sent to Dublin from Belfast.

Piaras Béaslaí, eminently qualified to comment, summarised Basal Thomson's attempt to employ Bell, hoping the man could uncover where Collins was hiding the Dáil's money. Thomson's thinking was if he couldn't uncover and kill Collins or his henchmen, then the next best thing to do was to cut off their source of funding.

> One of the measures taken by the English against Dáil Éireann was an attempt to trace and seize its funds by holding an inquiry into accounts held in the different banks. A gentleman named Alan Bell, who had conducted a similar investigation in the Parnellite days [He'd also investigated the December ambush of Lord French.] was appointed to carry out a search for the Dáil Funds and National Loan. Bank officials were compelled to appear before him in the Castle, produce their books, and face a searching enquiry into the affairs of their customers. The funds entrusted by the people of Ireland to Dáil Éireann were in grave danger of being stolen by the English. [50]

Crow Street obtained a photograph of Mr. Bell and Collins issued the order to eliminate him as quickly as possible. But Mick's demand was easier said than done.

As the Squad soon discovered, his house at #19 Belgrave Square North was well guarded by 'G-men.' Detectives also met him when he stepped off his Dalkey tram at Nassau Street and personally escorted him to his office in Dublin Castle. In the evening, they'd return him safely to the tram that would take him to his Seapoint residence.

The only time he was left unguarded was on the bloody tram, surrounded by scores of innocent commuters.

On Friday morning the 26th of March, Mick McDonnell ordered Jimmy Slattery, Vinnie Byrne, Joe Guilfoyle, Paddy O'Daly and Tom Keogh out to Monkstown, along with the Deputy Director of Intelligence Liam Tobin and his lieutenant Tom Cullen. Their assignment was to intercept Bell as he rode into work and kill him.

O'Daly remembered:

> None of us, except Tom Cullen, knew Alan Bell by appearance, but we got his address out in Seapoint [Belgrave Square] and Tom Keogh and myself used to go out every morning to try and locate him. We got a very good description of him from Tom Cullen, and we found out that he used to leave his house at about half-past nine every morning and get the tram into the city. [51]

Joe Dolan picked up the story at this point.

> [A group of Squad members]…and I waited at the corner of Ailesbury Road to carry out the job. After waiting for some time we saw Tom Keogh cycling towards us as fast as he could go, and he reached us just before the tram did. He was breathless and pointed out the tram to us. I got on the tram and went inside and Vinnie Byrne went on top [of the open-topped, double-decked tram]. Joe Guilfoyle was with me, and Mick McDonnell and Tobin were together. Mick McDonnell and Tobin were sitting opposite Alan Bell and McDonnell leaned across and said to Bell, "Are you Mr. Bell?" ["I am, he said, but…"] He didn't get time to say any more before McDonnell said, "Come on Mr. Bell, we want you!"] Tobin and Mick McDonnell caught him by the shoulders immediately and brought him out to the platform of the tram. Joe Guilfoyle pulled the trolley off the wires and stopped the tram at the corner of Simmonscourt Road. I jumped off the tram to cover it in case any detectives would interfere. Tobin and Mick McDonnell

shot Bell, and we escaped down Simmonscourt Road into Donnybrook. [52]

Ryle Dwyer added some fascinating detail in his book, *The Squad*.

The conductor had just finished collecting fares on top and was about three steps down the stairs. 'I noticed three men having a hold of Mr. Bell,' he said. 'Mr. Bell had his hands on either side of the door of the car, but the three men broke his grip, and they all came out struggling on the platform together. One of the three men was behind Mr. Bell pushing him and the other two were in front.' None of them were saying anything.

'Then I noticed one of the three men putting his hand in his pocket and taking a revolver from it,' the conductor continued. 'When I saw the revolver I went back to the top of the car. I passed a remark to some gentlemen there that "something terrible was going to happen downstairs." I felt very weak and sat down and saw no more.'

'Let me down off this tram,' [Vinnie] Byrne cried as he cut the trolley rope. 'Joe Guilfoyle pulled the trolley off the wires and stopped the tram at the corner of Simmonscourt Road....'

[As the Squad members ran down Simmonscourt Road]...a motorbike with a sidecar passed them. 'We should have stopped that fellow on the bike,' Tom Cullen cried. Some of them ran for the Donnybrook tram. [53]

Béaslaí summed things up.

There were no further inquiries into the affairs of Sinn Féin customers of the Irish banks. Another political detective named [Laurence] Dalton was shot dead in Mountjoy Street. A second one, Sergeant Revell, attacked later, was luckier. Protected by bullet-proof armour under his coat he was only wounded. From this time the political detectives practically ceased to function on the streets. [54]

[**Author's note**: Liam Tobin was at the Broadstone rail station that day to point out Detective Larry Dalton to members of the Squad. Mick McDonnell, Tom Keogh and Jimmy Slattery were assigned to kill Dalton while Joe Dolan, Vinnie Byrne and Joe Dolan were the Squad's covering party.]

❧

Alan Bell's murder sent a warning to the British authorities: Don't interfere with Ireland's national loan contributions.

Michael Collins's administrative skills proved unmatched. The Dáil's £250,000 loan fund was over-subscribed by forty percent. Despite all their conniving and secret service interference, the British only succeeded in discovering £18,000 of the almost £400,000 eventually collected…donated by Irishmen and women who wished to break the connection with England. [55]

The year 1920 was proving to be the bloodiest one in Ireland since the 'Year of Liberty,' the Rebellion of 1798. But the worst was yet to come. Michael Collins and his three Crow Street intelligence men were ready and willing to take on all that the Sassenach would deliver.

❧

[**Author's note**: Additional reading would include Joseph E. A. Connell's *Dublin in Rebellion: A Directory 1913-1923*, (2009) & Dan Breen's *My Fight for Irish Freedom*, (1993).]

8

Ah, to breathe the air of freedom.
    Again, Tom Cullen repeated the words to himself, – *To breathe the air of freedom...*
    – It had a ring to it alright, he thought. *– If only I was a poet, maybe I could make something of it, but no...I'll press on and leave the poetry to others.*
    Walking up the square to Vaughan's, he glanced over his shoulder to make sure no one was following him. It was Holy Saturday evening. Few people were on the street. Most were either at home or in church, preparing for tomorrow, Easter Sunday.
    Satisfied, the Wicklow man hurried into the small lobby and up the stairs.
    For some unknown reason, British intelligence had incorrectly ascertained that Sinn Féin planned to 'celebrate' Easter Week by staging a 'mini' repeat of 1916.
    – Béaslaí's right, thought Tom, recalling the words of his esteemed friend. Why it was only yesterday that the Director of IRA Publicity had made the astute observation, "It was odd that such an absurd suspicion should have taken root in their minds... it was obvious that our present methods of guerrilla warfare were proving far more effective than the chivalrous gesture of Easter Week, 1916." [1]
    – Ah yes, the bloody Sassenach seldom has it right any more. We've taken them to task and given 'em more than they bargained for, thought Tom, reaching the second floor landing. *– The fecken' lot of them are on the run, sure they are.*

Tom Keogh was on the door at the end of the hall.

With a nod of his head, he said, – They're inside…waitin' for ya, Tom.

As the door opened, the men seated around the table looked up. Mick Collins lowered the revolver he'd raised when Tom's footsteps announced his arrival seconds earlier.

With the Big Fella were a handful of friends including Gearóid O'Sullivan, Diarmuid O'Hegarty,Liam Tobin and Piaras Béaslaí.

Tom knew they'd all just arrived. Cigarette smoke hadn't filled the room yet.

He took the empty seat as Béaslaí poured him a healthy splash of whiskey from the bottle decorating the table.

– Any news? he asked, raising his glass in salute to the others.

– Too early, replied O'Sullivan.

– Ah sure, the amadáns are running around without a notion, said Piaras.

Tom knew what he was referring to.

> …once again the inefficiency of their [British] Intel-
> ligence Service and the ineffectiveness of their military
> measures were demonstrated. [During the preceding
> week, Holy Week]…military cordons with barricades
> were placed on all the main roads approaching Dublin,
> Cork, Limerick, Thurles, and other cities and towns.
> Passengers by train were searched, and their luggage
> examined. Troops patrolled the streets, and warships
> patrolled the coast. [2]

In the days leading up to Easter, 1920, with the British military organising their pre-emptive build-up, IRA battalions through-out Ireland were preparing for their own 'special' celebration: a country-wide, coordinated strike against Income Tax Offices and RIC barracks.

Again, Béaslaí chronicled the moment when the IRA took the initiative away from the British.

> On the night before Easter Sunday a number of raids
> by Volunteers was made on almost all the Income Tax

Offices in Dublin, Cork, and every city, town and centre in Ireland; the offices were set on fire, and all documents, books and records relating to income tax were destroyed. Where necessary the residences of Income Tax officials were raided. Even the Belfast Custom House did not escape.

In practically every case the raids were entirely successful, and the collection of Income Tax in Ireland was paralysed, as it was said, "for months to come." As a matter of fact, practically no more income tax was collected in Ireland from that time until the Free State began to function, except what was deducted from official salaries.

On the same night, no less than 315 evacuated R.I.C. barracks were destroyed by fire. It was no wonder that the "Freeman's Journal" humorously remarked that the "Irish problem" had become "a burning one." [3]

❧

Michael Foy's astute comments put the events of late March and early April into perspective.

[Alan] Bell's assassination [and the tax offices' and RIC barracks' burnings] was part of an escalating IRA campaign.... Although [Lord] French had not exactly promised six months earlier that troops would be home before the leaves fell from the trees, the situation, far from improving, was getting worse. Now there was just a rapidly receding light at the end of a tunnel, visible to the Viceroy only through his field-marshal's binoculars. [4]

❧

Suddenly, the intimate gathering at Vaughan's Hotel on the 'Night of the Burnings' was rudely interrupted. Christy, 'the

Boots,' the hotel's junior night porter, rushed upstairs to announce a large party of British soldiers had just encircled Rutland Square.

Michael and three others raced out of the building, through the back garden, over the wall and spent a chilly night in the open under the shadows of Dominick Street Chapel.

On the other hand, Tom, Liam and Piaras faired better. They too beat a hasty retreat from the hotel. After clambering over rooftops, they luckily gained entrance to an unoccupied building further down the square. With the aid of some comfortable matting, the three passed a relatively restful night.

Upon returning to Vaughan's the following morning, Easter Sunday, they learned that the military hadn't searched the hotel at all. In hindsight, there'd been no reason to flee, but the displacement was a small price to pay for their continued freedom.

Collins and his comrades, on the other hand, were less philosophical. They were tired, chilled to the bone and in no mood for Tom and Piaras's slagging. Mindful of their friends' sour moods, Cullen and Béaslaí walked down the square and over to the Pro-Cathedral for Mass.

❧

In March, 1920, just prior to the 'Night of the Burnings,' the intensity of the War for Independence ratcheted up several notches in Dublin.

The city was infected with spies, touts and informers of all sorts. Added to this list, the British military and its network of undercover agents became increasingly aggressive. While Michael and his intelligence team, backed up by the Squad, concentrated their efforts on ridding the town of all varieties of Castle spies, Dick McKee and his Dublin Brigade focused their attention on holding the military at bay.

Ryle Dwyer, in his book *The Squad*, provided important insight into a new crowd pressurising the Dublin Republicans.

> A new threat began to grow in the form of the so-called Igoe Gang. The Igoe Gang was a group of undercover RIC men whose job it was to identify republicans

from Dublin and from the provinces who had set up in Dublin, such as Dan Breen, Seán Treacy and their gang. Their leader was Head Constable [Eugene] Igoe from Galway.

Even though they wore civilian clothes, they were heavily armed. They began moving about on the footpaths, covering each other on both sides of the road, walking some yards apart so that they would be inconspicuous as they looked for wanted men from Dublin or the country. IRA intelligence never fully identified the personnel of Igoe's party, beyond establishing that they comprised members from different 'hot spots' in the country. They were nearly all Irishmen with considerable experience and service in the RIC, and they were effective in picking up volunteers. Igoe's gang became a difficult and dangerous force in the eyes of the Squad and IRA intelligence. [5]

Michael Collins quickly recognised Igoe and his 'Murder Gang,' RIC officers from down the country who'd been driven out of their barracks by increased IRA aggression, as a real threat.

In Dublin their ruthlessness and combative mentality inspired fear among Volunteers. An evocative photograph shows them armed to the teeth, smiling and relaxed in an open-topped car, eerily reminiscent of Western desperadoes. And indeed they regarded Ireland as England's Wild West, a land where rough frontier justice prevailed. A superior of Igoe's acknowledged that he had a freewheeling attitude to legality since he 'found it necessary to be handier with his gun than the gunmen were with theirs. Hence his extreme unpopularity. There is no doubt that, whilst the Police Officers in Dublin were filled with the utmost admiration for Igoe, he is regarded by the IRA as a murderer and that his life will be in danger wherever he goes.' [6]

[**Author's note**: Neither Collins's men nor Igoe's 'Murder Gang' succeeded in eliminating the other. At one point, Michael, frustrated by the Galway man's tactics, had Liam Tobin bring a Galway IRA man who knew Igoe to Dublin. After several weeks of searching, the Galwegian, Tom Newell, accompanied by Squad member Charlie Dalton, spotted Igoe in Grafton Street. But before other Squad members could be alerted, Igoe and some of his men had the two Republicans surrounded. Igoe had recognised Newell as well.

Dalton acted 'the innocent' and fortuitously was sent on his way. Newell, on the other hand, played the aggressor and paid dearly for his belligerence.

With Igoe and several others, Newell was driven to the north side of the Liffey and shot several times. Badly wounded, he was hospitalised for an extended period. Luckily, he lived but remained a cripple for the rest of his life.

With the Truce ending the War for Independence in July, 1921, Colonel Ormonde Winter, head of British intelligence in Ireland, promoted Igoe as a reward for his efforts, but his reputation as a marked man in Ireland dogged him. Both the Head Constable and his wife were forced to flee Ireland forever.]

❧

The month of March marked the arrival of the Black and Tans in Ireland. Tomás Mac Curtain, Lord Mayor of Cork City, would be their first victim, as the battle of wits and the persistent danger of arrest escalated that spring. Tom Cullen and Liam Tobin, never ones to shy away from the lure of outsmarting the enemy, conspired with Dave Neligan to infiltrate the very heart of danger.

Again, Tim Pat Coogan captured the essence of the moment.

>...Neligan had managed to get himself accepted as a member of the British Secret Service. He then proceeded to introduce Tobin, Thornton and Cullen to his Secret Service colleagues. They generally met either at the Rabbiatti Saloon in Marlborough St. or in 'Kidd's Back', a famous bar off Grafton St. at the back of what is now the Berni Inn in Nassau St. The British modus operandi was to have each member of the Secret Service surround

> himself with a number of touts, or minor informers. Some must have been worse than useless to their employers. They were generally English and completely at sea. One day in Rabbiatti's, Cullen and Thornton found themselves sharing a table with a group of them. One of whom suddenly exclaimed wonderingly: 'Gor blimey, how did you learn the Irish brogue. We're here in Dublin for the last twelve months and we can't pick any of it up. You fellows have it perfect.' The Irishmen solemnly explained that there was an art in such matters. [7]

Tim Pat in his Collins biography noted that the three Republican intelligence men played a most dangerous game. He quoted Frank Thornton, who said, "A lot of our information was picked up by taking a very big risk." [8]

Again, Neligan introduced Collins's top men to senior British intelligence officers, who commonly populated the more socially chic Kidd's Back bar. Tom along with Frank Thornton and Frank Saurin became recognised as 'regulars' to the elite of British intelligence.

> Some of the most dangerous men in Europe met in that bar, from both sides. One day some of the British agents were chatting with the three Irishmen [Cullen, Thornton and Saurin] when an officer suddenly said to Cullen: 'Surely you fellows know Liam Tobin, Frank Thornton and Tom Cullen. These are Collins's three officers and if you get those fellows we should locate Collins himself.' That conversation in Kidd's was a tribute to the effectiveness [and the daring] of the campaign Collins and his men were waging against the Castle's hitherto invincible intelligence system. At least one of the battles in that campaign was fought out in Kidd's. [9]

❧

Michael Collins was under great pressure as the War for Independence hotted up. Beside his intelligence operations, his

Sinn Féin obligations, his Dáil finance responsibilities and his Volunteer-IRA oversight, Mick was a wanted man. In addition to his Republican comrades and personal friends wanting his company and counsel, the Big Fella was number one on the British military, the British intelligence, the RIC and the DMP's wanted list. These enemy contingents vied for the honour of being the responsible party for the arrest of the most wanted man in Ireland…reward or no.

Naturally, Michael's burdens impacted those closest to him. All but one seemed to feel the weight. Tom Cullen was the exception. His bright, optimistic and vivacious personality seemed to protect him as if he was wearing a steel-clad breast plate. Mick treasured his friendship with Tom. It was as if a breath of fresh air arrived into the room when the Wicklow man walked in. The two were often seen huddled together, off to one side, engaged in animated conversation. Serious dialogue was occasionally interrupted with the nod of a head and the odd laugh. It was clear to those nearest the Corkman that Tom Cullen was more than a friend. He acted as confidant, confessor and sounding board…a safety valve when the pressures of life reached the boiling point.

Cullen needed his release too. With the coming of spring and the advent of summer, Tom and one or two of his close friends always managed to find time to slip out of town and spend several afternoons a month at the racetrack. Tom's fascination with race horses and the excitement of thoroughbreds going head to head over a green, rolling Irish race course was just the therapy he needed.

Between races, Tom and his comrades enjoyed a pint while studying the sleek animals parading around the paddock. With their mental notes carefully made, it was over to the tick-tack men for a bet. His friends often queried him as to which horse caught Tom's fancy. Sometimes they'd listen to him and other times not. Those who did usually arrived home with more pounds in their pockets than when they left.

Beyond office work spent examining purloined letters and pouring over newspapers for innocuous enough social announcements, Tom Cullen divided his time between the track and rendezvous with unsuspecting amadáns in places such as Rabbiatti's

Saloon or along Baggot Street. If time permitted, he'd slip out of town, taking the train down to Wicklow to visit Delia and Andy.

Occasionally, Delia would come up to Dublin. Tom put her up in the Munster Private Hotel run by Mrs. Myra McCarthy in Mountjoy Street or across the way at Dilly Dicker's. Once in a while she took a room at Vaughan's but Tom feared that place was too dangerous...too much in the thick of things as far as he was concerned. Finally, after Joint #1 was raided and Delia was put out into the street, he settled on the Clarence Hotel along the South Quays. It was a very respectable establishment and not likely to be raided or its guests disturbed. But regardless of the convenience of having Delia residing but a few blocks away, Tom always felt a sense of relief when they kissed goodbye at the Westland Row or Amiens Street Rail Station. He preferred having Delia living safely at home in Wicklow Town.

In the time since their relationship became serious, Delia had taken a real interest in supporting Tom and Michael's efforts to once and for all put an end to England's occupation of Ireland. She'd enlisted in the Wicklow chapter of Cumann na mBan.

The attractive young woman took great pride in giving lectures on the lives of the leaders of the 1916 Uprising from Bray to Arklow and even over to Rathdrum. Several of her written pieces appeared in the Republican newspaper, the *Irish Bulletin*, first edited by Desmond FitzGerald and later by Erskine Childers. The paper served as a counter-propaganda weekly, highlighting the Dáil and Sinn Féin's successes while listing British government raids and providing details about their flagrant mistreatment of Irish citizens.

Though the newspaper had a short life [November, 1919-July, 1921], it served to inform and rally the Irish people around the 'cause of liberty.' It focused public attention on Ireland's fledgling government and its brave assembly of Volunteers, both engaged in the age-old struggle to break the hated bonds of slavery that bound the two nations together.

Delia also helped organise relief aid for families whose homes, crops or livestock were damaged or destroyed by the thoughtless or wanton actions of the British military and the newly arrived RIC reinforcements, the Black and Tans.

Tom lovingly nicknamed her "The Wicklow Rebel."

✻

In mid-April, 1920, a moment of carelessness caused Tom some personal embarrassment and the focus of Michael Collins's wrath.

Though Tom spent the majority of his 'office time' at #3 Crow Street, he occasionally used his old office at #32 Bachelor's Walk. On this particular day, Tom was doing some quartermaster paperwork along the Quays when he was called away on an urgent matter. Not wishing to leave any incriminating documents in his desk for fear of a raid, he bundled them together and placed them in the bottom of a small case over which he stuffed several soiled shirts and some used hand towels.

Asking the shopkeeper below his office to mind the bag until he returned, Tom left.

As bad luck would have it, an hour later the British military arrived in four lorries. Soldiers blocked off the thoroughfare from Sackville Street down to the Ha'penny Bridge.

At first the Tommies, ignoring the shops, concentrated their ill-behaved rummaging to the lodgings and offices above. With nothing to show for their mindless searching and vengeful destruction of property, the captain in charge instructed his men to give the shops along the Quays a good going over. That's when Tom's bag was discovered, innocently tucked away below a counter.

Ecstatic with finally having found something that looked important, the British officer poured over Tom's papers which included columns of figures and a listing of items that looked suspiciously like a weapons inventory. No names or exact addresses were included but the cities of Liverpool, Birmingham, Manchester, London and Cardiff were clearly discernible.

With the bag, its laundry and incriminating evidence tucked under his arm, the captain and his band of yobs piled back into their vehicles and headed across the O'Connell Bridge on their way to the Castle.

Piaras Béaslaí made a passing reference to this incident in his Collins biography.

Dublin Castle issued an official report of the raid giving a list of articles found. The list solemnly began: "Six daggers, as used by assassins." The "daggers" were, of course, knives used for domestic purposes. The papers in Cullen's bag, which were [later] lost, included accounts of the expenditure of money on purchasing arms in England – a fact that caused sore embarrassment to Collins at a later date [during the London Treaty talks]. [10]

❧

A little over a week after 'the Night of the Burnings,' the IRA staged a re-enactment of their hugely successful and propaganda-rich Holy Saturday raids. Thirty more Income Tax Offices were attacked. Official papers were burned as were another one hundred or so evacuated RIC barracks.

At about this time, Béaslaí noted:

There was great military activity on the part of the English in Ireland. Two thousand troops landed at Bantry, and were distributed through County Cork. Buildings were commandeered for military occupation in many towns. [11]

❧

With Dublin Castle paralysed by internal tensions [the hawks vs. the doves syndrome], [PM David] Lloyd George reshuffled the Irish Executive in late March 1920. He shifted [Chief Secretary Ian] Macpherson to the Ministry of Pensions, transferred Commander-in-Chief [Sir Frederick] Shaw and offered the combined post of army and police supremo to 58-year-old General Nevil Macready, the Commissioner of the [London] Metropolitan Police. As a former Adjutant General, an admirer of the prime minister and a highly political soldier, it was hoped that Macready would faithfully implement government policy while at the same time

Irish nationalists might respond favourably to someone who had alienated Ulster Unionists before the war [WWI] when military commander in the province. But the vinegary Macready hated Ireland and every Irish faction.... [12]

The tit for tat game was on. The IRA, gaining increased weaponry thanks in large measure to the efforts of Quartermaster Tom Cullen and possessing amplified confidence in their ability to wage war against their vastly superior opponent, began staging a newly coordinated pattern of aggression.

On 20 May 1920 Irish dockers had embargoed British 'war materials' and railway workers refused to carry troops and munitions, precipitating the most serious industrial dispute since the Dublin Lockout of 1913. It was just as bitter and almost as protracted as the earlier strike. It seriously impeded the British military build-up, and the Castle put pressure on railway companies to dismiss thousands of employees refusing to cooperate. On 30 July Collins intervened by making 'non-combatant' supporters of the British Government's hardline policy 'legitimate targets.' [13]

On the other hand, the British, not to be outdone, were upping the stakes from their end. British administration in Ireland was reorganised. More soldiers poured into Ireland along with the recently recruited Black and Tans who were under the tutelage of General Henry Hugh Tudor, the self-styled 'Chief of Police.'

By the end of July, Tudor had recruited another force of soldiers whose hated reputation and taste for violence soon became the stuff of legends in Ireland. Initially, this new force of some five hundred ex-British army officers was employed to further reinforce the sagging numbers of RIC policemen. Adopting the nom de plume of the Police Auxiliary Cadets, Auxies for short, this Auxiliary Division with their stylish, military uniforms and tam-o'-shanter caps were spotted on the streets of Dublin in early August, 1920.

To complement Tudor's aggressive deployments of men and terror and in a concentrated effort to corral Ireland's recalcitrant revolutionaries, Colonel Ormonde de l'Épée Winter, nicknamed 'O' or 'the Holy Terror,' arrived in Ireland on 11 May 1920. The newly appointed Chief of British Army Intelligence and Deputy Chief of Police in Dublin, Winter, once described by Mark Sturgis, British Assistant Under-Secretary in Dublin, as looking like "a wicked little white snake," quickly upped the ante. His newly organised force of intelligence agents were determined to smash Collins's network of undercover operatives.

General Hugh Tudor was charged by his immediate superior General Nevil Macready to manage the DMP and the RIC plus revitalise the demoralised intelligence corps. Tudor focused his attentions on policing and chose Ormonde Winter to head up intelligence.

> Although Winter had no professional intelligence expe-
> rience, Tudor placed greater value on someone's profes-
> sional and social background and personal qualities.
>
> As 'O', Winter became a legendary figure in Ire-
> land, a cloak-and-dagger man of mystery with black
> greased hair and monocle, a taste for fine food, wines
> and attractive women and a proficiency in French,
> Russian and Urdu [a Hindustani language]. Aggressive
> and utterly fearless, he had had an acquittal in his late
> twenties for the manslaughter of a boy who stoned his
> boat on a river. In adulthood he still thrived on quarrels
> and stormy relationships and for a spymaster could be
> remarkably unsubtle. [14]

Winter's influence in Dublin was soon felt with the surfacing of the Cairo Gang. They were a group of a dozen or so British plain-clothes intelligence agents sent to Ireland to conduct undercover operations against the leadership of the IRA and in particular against Michael Collins and his personal team of intelligence men.

Tim Pat Coogan stated: "...a group of intelligence officers, known as the 'Cairo Gang' because of their Middle-Eastern experience rather than the fact that some of them frequented a Dublin haunt known as the Cairo Café, began to augment their spying activities by carrying out shootings in Dublin." [15]

※

With the British reorganizational and military build-up under way, the Squad remained active. Near the end of April, 1920, Detective Sergeant Richard Revell, one of the last of the Castle's 'G-men,' was followed by Vinnie Byrne from his home in Connaught Street, just off Phibsborough Road near the Royal Canal.

Revell spied Byrne trailing him and quickly sought the safe company of a nearby on-duty policeman.

Not wishing to be arrested, as the police had recently become more aggressive in trying to apprehend Collins's associates, Vinnie reported his findings to Mick McDonnell and Liam Tobin.

The three quickly decided it would be best to act immediately.

The following morning Mick and Vinnie, assigned to complete the operation or job, as they were usually referred to, stepped out from behind a garden gate and shot Revell seven times as he approached.

The 'G-man,' last seen lying in the street, was presumed dead as the two gunmen made good their escape. Tom Keogh and Paddy O'Daly, the backup cover men, were also sure the man was dead.

Later that evening, imagine their surprise as they read in the newspaper that Detective Revell survived the attack and was recovering in hospital.

From that day on, Vinnie Byrne had every reason to worry. If he was ever arrested, Revell, who later stated he could identify one of his attackers, would be waiting to pick him out of any Castle identity parade. [**Author's note:** Vinnie had cause for alarm. Squad members wore no disguises. This increased the risk that witnesses to their attacks might identify them later.]

On 22 June, the Squad missed their man again. On standing orders from Michael Collins, the Squad was always directed to avoid at all costs the involvement of innocent bystanders. Such was the case with RIC Assistant Inspector-General Albert Roberts.

The Inspector's chauffeur-driven motor car often passed through Beresford Place. The obvious means of stopping the vehicle was with a grenade, but the collateral effects of the explosion would likely wound or kill others. As a result, Paddy O'Daly, the lead man on this 'job,' was forced to resort to a volley of shots fired from his .45 revolver.

As his first round hit the windscreen, the driver expertly zigzagged through the crowded square beside the Custom House and sped on in the direction of Dublin Castle. Roberts was only slightly wounded.

On 30 July, the day the Big Fella warned the British government that their 'non-combatant' supporters of its hardline, anti-embargo policy would be considered viable wartime targets, Frank Brooke, chairman of the Dublin and South Eastern Railway company and an opponent of the rail blockage, was shot and killed in his office. If the British authorities were unsure Collins meant business, Brooke's killing changed their minds.

On that fateful day, the chairman had returned to his office from a board meeting about noontime. After pouring a drink for his associate Arthur Cotton and himself, they sat back, likely discussing the IRA's threat.

Unnoticed, Jim Slattery, Tom Keogh, Paddy O'Daly and a fourth Squad member slipped into the building and headed upstairs. In his Witness Statement, Slattery stated:

> We immediately opened fire on him and he fell. As we were going down the stairs again [O']Daly said to me, "Are you sure we got him?" I said I was not sure, and Daly said, "What about going back and making sure?" Keogh and myself went back. When I went into the room I saw a man standing at the left of the door and I fired a shot in his direction, at the same time looking across at Brooke on the floor. I fired a couple of shots at Brooke and satisfied myself that he was dead. Although I did not wound the other man who was in the room, I was informed afterwards that it would have been a good

job if he had been shot, as he too was making himself a nuisance. [16]

Michael Foy astutely summarised the impact of Brooke's death.

> Brooke, who was shot through the heart and lungs, reeled across the room and fell dying near the fireplace, just as an incoming train muffled the sound of gunfire. Newspapers noted the 'amazing precision and coolness' of the unmasked assassins, and hinted at an inside job: 'The murder must have been carefully planned and it is evident that those who carried it out had made themselves thoroughly familiar with the surroundings of the station and the location of the rooms.' Brooke's death, like that of [Assistant Police Commissioner William] Redmond six months before, was a deadly warning to hardline supporters of British Government policy, but it also struck hard at his [Brooke's] close friend the Viceroy [Field Marshal John French]. [17]

❧

Likely in response to Brooke's death and Collins's order to treat hardline non-combatants as possible targets compounded by the growing turmoil and violence of Irish daily life, Ireland's Chief Secretary Hamar Greenwood introduced draconian legislation in the House of Commons on 2 August 1920. The bill entitled 'The Restoration of Order in Ireland' passed into law on 13 August. It extended and enhanced the DORA legislation enacted back in August, 1914 at the outbreak of the Great War. The new law provided for vast powers of state control regarding the enforcement of curfews, arrests and internment without trial. It also replaced trials by jury with military courts-martial and suspended coroners' inquests, replacing them with military courts of enquiry.

Greenwood's edict was aimed at addressing the virtual collapse of British civilian administration in Ireland. It also was intended to increase arrests, convictions and imprisonment of Irish Republicans without having to declare martial law, a more severe edict.

[**Author's note**: Greenwood's administration in Ireland was a disaster, marked by the failure of the British government to rule civilly. His policies were characterised by lies, illegalities and violence as he welcomed the arrival of the Tans and Auxies to Ireland. In fact, in the Irish folklore of the day, the phrase 'to tell a Hamar' became synonymous with 'to tell a lie.']

❧

While Michael Collins and Tom Cullen were having a late evening meal in Devlin's public house, the Big Fella told his friend that the whereabouts of Lea Wilson had been discovered.

[**Author's note**: District police Inspector Percival Lea Wilson had been on duty in Dublin during Easter Week 1916. He was one of the 'officials' who'd supervised the containment of the surrendered Volunteers from the GPO and Edward 'Ned' Daly's 1st Battalion on the grounds of the Rotunda Hospital at the top of Sackville Street. Not only did Wilson 'supervise' the Irish prisoners, but he and others tormented, harassed and embarrassed several of the men. In particular, he singled out the fifty-nine-year-old Tom Clarke and polio-crippled Seán MacDiarmada, both leaders of the Rebellion and signatories of the Proclamation. Stories of Wilson having Clarke strip off before the watching eyes of the hospital staff, who observed the happenings playing out before them from the building's windows, have been repeated by many. Forced to endure the cold of the night and the derision of their captors, Clarke later (3 May, the morning of his execution), in a message given to his wife for the Irish people, wrote: "I and my fellow-signatories believe we have struck the first successful blow for Freedom. The next blow, which we have no doubt Ireland will strike, will win through. In this belief we die happy." [18]

It's also been said that Wilson took MacDiarmada's cane from him, making it difficult for Seán to stand or walk.]

As the two men dined, Michael asked Tom if he would do him a personal favour.

– No bother, Michael. You know you have but to ask.

– By asking you, I'm breaking one of my own rules.

Naturally, Tom's curiosity was aroused.

– I'd do it meself, but under the present circumstances, that's impossible.

Looking directly into the Wicklow man's eyes, the Big Fella said,

– It could prove to be dangerous.

Tom simply nodded.

– I want you to take a small party of handpicked men, go on down to Gorey [Co. Wexford] and shoot your man.

– For what he did to old Tom and Seán?

– Yes, Tom, for what he did to those two grand men. I realise others might not understand. Sure I'm opening myself up to criticism…using my friends to settle a personal score, but I've no choice. That fecken' bastard deserves what's coming to him. I think our lads will understand, and besides, I want only experienced men to handle this job…for your safety and protection and for seeing it done right so.

– Leave it with me, Michael. Consider it done, my friend. Now, give me all the details….

[**Author's note:** Of Lea Wilson, Ryle Dwyer wrote:

Wilson had been a constable in Charleville (Co. Cork) before joining the British army in 1915. He had served for a time in France and was in charge of the Rotunda Gardens while the republican prisoners were being held there following the Easter Rebellion. He became notorious for mistreating prisoners and had reportedly humiliated Tom Clarke and Seán MacDermott (Mac-Diarmada).] [19]

A week later, on 14 August, Tom headed south in the company of Tom Keogh, Pat McCrea, Jim Slattery and most likely Joe Hyland. They spent the night in a barn, owned by one of Tom's old IRA contacts, just outside of New Ross, Co. Wexford. Up early the following morning, they drove the final few miles to Gorey.

[**Author's note**: Paddy O'Daly later stated that Wicklow men were chosen for the job because they knew the countryside and might have to take to the hills afterwards.] [20]

> I was not concerned in the shooting of Lea-Wilson which took place in Wexford. Tom Keogh, Pat McCrea, Tom Cullen and other Wicklow men were picked to carry out his execution. I think it was Pat McCrea who drove the car with Tom Keogh and Tom Cullen, to New Ross. I do not know who the other men were; I would not be surprised if James Slattery was there, but I am not sure. I think Joe Hyland was there too. [21]

With information provided by two local IRB men, they parked their commandeered motor vehicle just beyond the edge of town, near some railroad tracks, on the road between the Gorey RIC barracks and Wilson's house.

There they waited patiently. It was a little after nine in the morning on August 15th. To avoid arousing suspicion, they raised the bonnet of their vehicle. Joe Hyland stayed behind the wheel while the other four leaned in, studying the engine.

Shortly before half nine, Wilson, dressed in mufti and reading a newspaper as he walked home from the barracks, happened upon the seemingly disabled car.

– What's the trouble, lads? he asked.

– You're the trouble, said Tom.

Turning to face his target, Tom pulled a revolver from the waistband of his trousers and shot Wilson twice...once in the head and again in the chest.

T. Ryle Dwyer painted a more complete picture of Wilson's death.

> Wilson was reading his newspaper as he walked so he may not have seen his assailants until the final moment. From the bloodstains and sounds it would seem that two shots were fired and that he went down but got up again and tried to run for about fifteen yards. There were bullet marks on the wall at the side of the footpath. He

then went down again and was shot repeatedly on the ground. He died at the scene. Minutes earlier, while on his way to work, Joseph Gilbert, a grocer's assistant, had noticed a car in the area. The bonnet was up and four men who he had not recognised were standing around the engine; there was another man in the car. After the shooting the car was seen going in the Ballycarnew (sic) direction. [22]

Later that evening, Michael Collins unexpectedly arrived into the bar of a Wicklow hotel, quite possibly the Grand Hotel or maybe even Fitzpatrick's where Tom used to live and work. Standing there having a drink was Joe Sweeney. [**Author's note**: Sweeney, originally from Burtonport, Co. Donegal, was currently an elected member of the Dáil as well as a former member of the GPO garrison during Easter Week.]

Upon seeing Sweeney, it was reported Collins said, "We got the bugger, Joe."

Not understanding what the Big Fella was talking about, he asked for clarification.

It took only a few words from Collins to remind Tom Sweeney who Lea Wilson was and why he'd been shot.

[**Author's note**: The matter as to whether Wilson's death was a personal vendetta on Collins's part or was justified on other grounds remains unanswered. I've stated it was personal, but that's just my opinion. Paddy O'Daly believed otherwise. He reported so in his Witness Statement given in the 1950s.

> Captain Lea Wilson was not shot because he had ill-treated Seán McDermott and other prisoners in 1916, because there were other British officers just as bad as he had been and no attempt was made to shoot them. I believe he was shot on account of the position he held at the time of his execution, and for no other reason. I am satisfied from my long experience with the Squad that no man was shot merely for revenge and that any execution sanctioned by Michael Collins was perfectly justified. [23]

Not to belabour the point, but was O'Daly defending his friend Collins or was he rebutting personal criticism levelled at him for his 'vindictive' murdering of eight IRA prisoners-of-war at Ballyseedy Cross during Ireland's Civil War in March, 1923?]

In Paddy O'Daly's defence, he related the following story in his Witness Statement.

> After the Squad was formed [in 1919, a DMP Super-
> intendent] Winters [not to be confused with Colonel
> Ormonde Winter] was still living very close to me, and
> this rumour got around that I was going to shoot him.
> There was no truth in this rumour, the thought of killing
> Winters never entered my mind. [I find this statement
> difficult to believe after Winters himself joined a Brit-
> ish military raiding party at O'Daly's house (sometime)
> after 1916. After O'Daly's four-year-old, handicapped
> daughter (she was born with only one hand) called
> the superintendent 'Traitor Winters', the police officer
> shoved the little girl and knocked her down.] The ru-
> mour got to Michael Collins' ears and he sent for me.
> He was in a towering rage. "What is this I hear about
> you going to shoot Winters?" he demanded. I answered,
> "that is the first I heard of it. I think it is a joke." "It is
> too serious to be a joke," said Collins. I told him that
> as far as I was concerned it was a joke, that the thought
> of killing Winters never entered my head and that it
> was only talk.
>
> Michael Collins then gave me a lecture on revenge
> and told me that the man who had revenge in his heart
> was not fit to be a Volunteer. [Michael's statement seems
> in conflict with his order to kill Lea Wilson (August,
> 1920), Roche and Fitzmaurice, the two Tipperary po-
> licemen who identified Seán Treacy's body (October,
> 1920) and Corporal John Ryan (January, 1921).] I
> had to convince him that I never thought of shooting
> Winters, but I passed the remark that if Winters was
> on our list I would like to carry out the job.

That lecture shows clearly that Collins or any of the
headquarters staff would not shoot merely for revenge. [24]

❧

[**Author's note**: During the 1920s, Lea Wilson's wife, Dr.
Marie Lea-Wilson purchased an unidentified painting that had
hung in the former Scottish home of William Hamilton Nisbet
since the early 1800s. In the 1930s, she donated it, still unauthenti-
cated, to the Jesuit Fathers in Dublin in gratitude for their personal
kindness to her after her husband's death. The painting remained
with the Dublin Jesuits until the 1990s when Sergio Benedetti,
Senior Conservator of the National Gallery of Ireland, happened
to see it on a visit to the Jesuits' residence. The conservator thought
he recognised the work. After much cleaning and careful research,
the painting was identified as *The Taking of Christ* by the Italian
Baroque master Michelangelo Merisi da Caravaggio (c. 1602)
which had long been considered 'lost.' Today, it is on permanent
loan to the National Gallery in Dublin.]

❧

On Thursday night, 23 September 1920, John Lynch, a Sinn
Féin county councillor from Kilmallock, Co. Cork was shot and
killed by members of the Cairo Gang in his hotel room in the
Exchange Hotel in Lower Baggot Street. He had come to Dublin to
deliver some National Loan money [£23,000] to Michael Collins.
British secret service agents claimed his death was justified because
the middle-aged man had drawn a gun on them. Michael rejected
this assertion out of hand.

A more likely explanation was inaccurate British intelligence
information. Their agents had mistaken John Lynch for another
man, Commandant Liam Lynch, who was O/C of Cork's No.
2 Brigade and wanted for a series of anti-British wartime activities including the capture of British Brigadier General C. H. T.
Lucas on June last. The age differences of the two men made such

confusion most unlikely. Rather, the fact that John Lynch was an active Sinn Féiner was more to the point. His political leanings not his name led to his death. Simply being affiliated with Ireland's Republican political party was all the British secret service needed to impose the death penalty. It became clear to Michael and his intelligence troika that the English government had accelerated its policy of reprisals in answer to the IRA's attacks on British agents, spies and touts. As both sides squared off against one another, the violence and bloodshed could only but gather speed.

Whether Michael Collins had decided to take the initiative or was just answering the British government's war challenge, is unknown. But on Sunday morning, the 26th of September, the Big Fella orchestrated the largest Squad operation to date. The plan was to kill up to a dozen senior DMP police officers as they left the protection of the Castle on their way to Mass. Tom Cullen and Mick McDonnell orchestrated the attack.

Dwyer described the event's staging using Charlie Dalton and Vinnie Byrne's words taken from their Witness Statements.

'I was instructed to accompany Paddy O'Daly and Joe Leonard and report with other members of the Squad for an operation to be carried out outside the Upper Castle yard in the maze of alleyways that approached the rear entrance of Saints Michael's and John's church,' Charlie Dalton explained. 'We took up the various positions indicated by Mick McDonnell... We were advised that a party of the political branch of G Division would leave from the Upper Castle Yard on their way to eight o'clock mass.' In addition to the Squad the Tipperary gang was present – Treacy, Breen, Hogan and Robinson – Tom Cullen of the intelligence branch, along with Hugo MacNeill and Jim Brennan. They took up positions on Essex Street, outside the back entrance of the church.

'I would say there was between ten and twelve in the group,' Vinny Byrne recalled. They were waiting for a signal from Cullen. [25]

Suddenly, Tom called off the attack. Ever the one with a keen eye, he noticed that Jim McNamara, one of Michael's key Castle undercover police operatives, was among the group of detectives.

Tom made the snap decision to abort the job. With no way of warning the others of Jim's presence, it was far better to call things off than to possibly kill one of their own.

Re-enactments of the mass attack were postponed at the last minute on the next three Sundays. A British road blockade interfered with their plans on the following week. Then for the next two weekends running, the detectives went to different churches and multiple ambushes could not be satisfactorily arranged in the short time available to the Squad. Finally, Michael called off the operation all together.

✼

Tragedies befell the Dublin Republicans in October.

On 20 September, Kevin Barry, an eighteen-year-old medical student and IRA Volunteer, was arrested, and on 20 October he was sentenced to death for taking part in an attack upon a British lorry load of soldiers, who'd stopped beside Monk's Bakery in Dublin's Upper Church Street. The Tommies were collecting bread for their barracks at Collinstown Camp north of the city.

Kevin fired only one shot before his .38 Mauser parabellum jammed. As British and Irish bullets flew, the young man, now a defenceless Volunteer, dove under the lorry, seeking its protection from the lethal gunfire.

The fire-fight lasted less than three minutes, but Kevin's fate was sealed. Trapped under the vehicle and unable to flee, he was arrested and taken to North Dublin Union. Three British soldiers died in the urban ambush and several others were wounded.

Later, he was transferred to Mountjoy Prison where he refused to cooperate with the local authorities.

[**Author's note**: By a bizarre coincidence, Kevin Barry gave his address as #58 South Circular Road to his British captors... the same address at which Tom Cullen resided when the 1911 Irish Census was taken. As it turned out, Patrick 'Pat' Dowling,

Tom's friend and former employer, was Kevin's uncle. Earlier that month, on the advice of Kevin's Volunteer superiors and because of his recent IRA activities, he'd been instructed to 'sleep away from home.' As a result, the young man had moved in with his Uncle Pat.]

Pleas for sparing Kevin's life fell on deaf ears. Also attempts by his comrades to effect a breakout were unsuccessful. Promises of a pardon, a free medical education and £2,000 a year for life did not tempt him to betray his IRA comrades. Hoping to face a firing squad, Kevin Barry was hanged on 1 November, All-Saints' Day, an Irish Catholic holy day of obligation. At eight o'clock in the morning, the prison bell began tolling to inform the vast crowd of Kevin Barry's supporters outside the prison gates that he was dead.

[**Author's note**: It is my feeling the British government picked the 1st to hang Kevin as simply another way of thumbing their nose at Irish Catholics.]

No inquest was held. The body was enclosed in a roughly painted, simple wooden coffin and buried at 1.30 p.m. in a small plot of ground inside the walls near the women's prison.

[**Author's note**: On 14 October 2001, Kevin's remains and those of nine other Irish Volunteers, executed by the British during the War for Independence, were given a State funeral in Dublin's St. Mary's Pro-Cathedral. Nine of the remains were reinterred in Glasnevin Cemetery. The tenth, Patrick Maher, was reinterred in Ballylanders, Co. Limerick at his family's request.]

On 25 October, Terry MacSwiney died after seventy-four days on his hunger strike in Brixton Prison [London] in protest for his internment and his objection to his having had a military trial rather than a civilian one.

> On 12 August, Terence MacSwiney, Lord Mayor of Cork and Commandant of its 1st IRA Brigade, was caught with a police cipher [and some seditious documents in Cork City Hall], court-martialled four days later and sentenced to two years' imprisonment. He immediately began a hunger strike, apparently on his

own initiative, intending to pit his willingness to die against that of the British Government to let him. After being transferred to Brixton Prison in London on 18 August, MacSwiney deliberately conserved his strength, buying time either for the British government to release him or for a wave of sympathy to develop at home and abroad. [26]

Arrested with three others, the four men began the hunger strike. The London men were joined by eleven other Republicans currently detained in Cork City jail, as a symbol of their support for the deported men and as a protest of Britain's demonic policies in Ireland.

After lengthy negotiations with British representatives, the three men arrested with Terry were released, but Winston Churchill, England's Secretary of State for War, refused to grant MacSwiney, a political VIP, clemency. The Secretary felt it would set an outrageous example to others and be interpreted as a reward for the IRA's anti-British activities.

Piaras Béaslaí tells the rest of the story.

> After a fast of seventy-four days Terence MacSwiney died, on October 25th, and about the same time two of the Cork prisoners who were on hunger strike also died. The event caused intense emotions throughout Ireland, and, indeed among the Irish race all over the world. The body of the martyred Mayor of Cork was brought to Holyhead for the purpose of embarking it for Dublin. Here a disgraceful scene took place. A body [group] of Auxiliaries seized the coffin from the relatives, and put it on board a boat, which conveyed it to Cork. The purpose of this unexampled act of indecent vindictiveness on the part of the English government was to prevent the honours which would be paid to the poor corpse in Dublin. A large and impressive demonstration was none the less held in Dublin on the day of MacSwiney's funeral.

Arthur Griffith, as Acting President of Dáil Éireann, wrote to the surviving Cork hunger strikers asking them to abandon their fast, saying that they had sufficiently proved their courage and devotion to Ireland. The men complied with the request. [27]

❧

As events of October unfolded, Michael Collins became particularly disturbed over the senseless death of John Lynch, the popular and well-known Kilmallock man. Mick, with the help of his intelligence network, had pasted together the events surrounding Lynch's murder by members of the Cairo Gang. A certain Captain Baggelly, a member of the General Staff at Ship Street Barracks, was a conspiring party to the shooting. It became evident to Collins that the incident was clearly a premeditated act of senseless violence.

Coogan mentioned Baggelly in his Collins biography and briefly described some harrowing moments for Michael's three intelligence comrades.

> Captain Baggelly was one of those whose fate [and pending death] would illustrate the danger of being mentioned in dispatches by Michael Collins. The Cairo Gang, though they made [possible] mistakes like those over [John] Lynch, were getting closer [to Collins and his team]. October saw all three of Collins' top intelligence agents picked up and released after questioning, Thornton being held for ten days before being released. Tobin and Cullen also got away with a grilling after being detained in Vaughan's. Collins knew that it was only a matter of time before they and he were finished. But just as the [Cairo] Gang were closing in on him he was closing in on them. [28]

With the Cairo Gang's increased activity, Michael assigned Frank Thornton the task of drawing up a list of their names including the gang's leadership. Colonel Aimes and Major Bennett headed his list...men whom Frank had become 'friends with' at Kidd's Back.

While Michael was hatching his strategy for dealing with the influx of British spies, a shoot-out occurred in the north Dublin suburb of Drumcondra. Béaslaí described what happened.

On the night of October 11th two Tipperary officers in Dublin, Dan Breen and Seán Treacy, who were "wanted" by the English since the shooting of policemen at Solo-headbeg, in January [1919], were traced to the house of Professor Carolan, "Fernside," Whitehall, Drumcondra. After midnight the house was surrounded by English soldiers, and a body of Intelligence Officers [likely members of the Cairo Gang] effected an entrance. There can be little doubt that the intention was, not to arrest the two men, but to shoot them in bed. Breen and Treacy, surprised in bed, sprang out, seized their automatics, put up a fight, and got away after killing two Intelligence Officers, and dangerously wounding another. The two who were killed, it may be added, were known to be concerned in the murders of civilians in Dublin. One of these, Major Smyth, was a brother of Divisional Commissioner Smyth, whose speech to the R.I.C., in Listowel, led to the mutiny there.

Breen, who covered the retreat of Treacy, was wounded and badly cut by the glass of a verandah through which he fell in escaping. He lost his comrade [Treacy] in the darkness, and, after wandering about for some hours, was compelled, by loss of blood, to seek shelter in a strange house. The people of the house, though they knew nothing of him, and, it is said, were not in sympathy with Sinn Féin, showed him every kindness, and he was soon put into the hands of his friends and removed to the Mater Hospital. [29]

One of Dan Breen's 'friends' that Piaras referred to was Tom Cullen. He helped coordinate the cover

operation surrounding Breen's care and safety while he
was on the mend from his wounds. [30]

In Breen's own words, he described what happened after he'd
sought safety in that 'strange house.'

> I knocked. I realised well enough what a spectacle I must
> have presented at such an unearthly hour, half-clad,
> dishevelled and blood-stained.
>
> For the second time I knocked. A man opened
> the door. My appearance was sufficient explanation; I
> mumbled that I needed shelter, and instantly swooned.
> As though from far away I heard his words: 'I do not
> approve of gunmen, I shall call the military."
>
> A woman's voice reprimanded him: 'If you do, I'll
> report you to Michael Collins.' [31]

The man and woman turned out to be a Mr. and Mrs. [Fred]
Holmes, and it was Mrs. Holmes's actions that probably saved
Breen's life. She summoned a nurse who lived nearby and his
wounds were initially dressed. Then Mrs. Holmes, deftly avoiding
the neighbouring military cordon thrown up to search for the two
escaped Republicans, took a note to Dan and Seán's Tipperary
friend Phil Shanahan. He, in turn, contacted Dick McKee.

It was the Dublin Brigade's O/C that arranged for some of
his men to collect Breen and transport him to the Mater Hospital
in Phibsborough.

All the while, Breen believed Treacy had been killed in the
Fernside gun battle. In reality, however, luck was on their side that
night. Miraculously, Seán escaped unscathed from the professor's
home while Dan's pick of 'safe houses' was heaven-sent. Black
and Tans were living in the houses on either side of the Holmes's
residence.

But luck wasn't with Treacy for long.

The funeral for the two British officers killed in the
Drumcondra Road raid, Major Smyth and Captain White, was
scheduled for Thursday, 14 October. Upon learning that Hamar
Greenwood [Britain's Chief Secretary for Ireland], General Hugh

Tudor and other high-ranking officers planned on attending, Michael Collins and Dick McKee quickly organised an ambush, hoping to kill one or all of them as they marched in the funeral procession.

Dwyer quoted Frank Thornton who said:

'With this purpose in mind Liam Tobin, Tom Cullen, Dick McKee, Frank Henderson, Leo Henderson, Peadar Clancy and I met at the back of Peadar Clancy's shop [The Republican Outfitters at #94 Talbot Street]. Receiving information that none of those whom we sought were taking part in the funeral, the job was called off.'

Thornton and Tom Cullen were almost the last to leave Clancy's shop, with Dick McKee following behind them. 'As we left, Seán Treacy arrived, and on informing him of what had happened he went on towards the shop while we went towards the Pillar [Lord Nelson's Pillar in Sackville Street nearly opposite the GPO],' Thornton continued. 'We had very nearly arrived at the Pillar when the shooting started lower down the [Talbot] street, but to all intents and purposes it looked to us like one of the ordinary incidents which were happening every day in the streets of Dublin.' 32

Piaras Béaslaí picked up the threads of the story at this point.

Breen, being badly wounded, was confined to bed, but Treacy moved freely about his usual haunts, with the result that he was again seen and shadowed, this time to the draper's shop of Peadar Clancy, known as "The Republican Outfitters," at that time a great centre of Volunteer activity. Treacy was in the door of the shop with Dick McKee and others, when a lorry full of soldiers, and an armoured car, dashed up. Seeing it coming they started to move out from the door. McKee got on his bicycle, and got safely away, but Treacy, when he had got a few yards from the shop, was recognised by an Intelligence Officer on the lorry, who sprang from the car to seize him. Seán Treacy struggled with him, and succeeded in shooting him. At the same time the soldiers in the open car fired on Treacy, regardless of the civilians with whom the street was thronged, and even of their own officer, who was grappling with him. The Intelligence Officer, whose real name was Price, but who passed under an assumed name, was killed, whether by Treacy or his own party is uncertain. Treacy was killed, and several civilians in the street were killed and wounded, including a policeman and a girl. [33]

Dwyer wrote that along with Treacy, the two innocent by-standers were Patrick Carroll, a young messenger boy, and Joseph Corringham, a tobacconist. [34]

[**Author's note**: Michael Foy added detail regarding Treacy's death that I've heard repeated more than once.

McKee got away just before the convoy, by chance or design, stopped outside the shop. While the others hesitated Treacy walked out, ignoring the raiders as they leapt down on to the pavement. Treacy then jumped on a bicycle that someone had left standing on the pavement. But it was much too big for him [Seán laboured to place his feet on the bike's pedals and propel it forward.], and, while Treacy manoeuvred it, a British intelligence officer called Christian recognised him and ran forward shouting 'This is Treacy!' Treacy shot Christian and wrestled him to the ground, where they struggled violently. Treacy got a few more shots off, which held the other British officers at bay, and tried turning his weapon inwards against the more powerful but visibly weakened Christian. But, when Christian's colleagues saw Treacy about to break free, they fired on him, and the armoured car crew joined in with machine-gun bursts. When the firing ceased, Treacy and Christian were lying dead on the pavement while nearby another British agent called Price lay fatally wounded. Two civilians had also been killed. [35]]

Tom Cullen and the others had luckily escaped, but not the dapper, gallant Tipperary gentleman, Seán Treacy.

His body was taken to the Mater Hospital for identification. Two Tipperary policemen named Roche and Fitzmaurice were brought to Dublin to identify the body.

When Dave Neligan informed Michael of their coming, the Big Fella, full of anger and regret over Treacy's death, ordered the Squad to seek its revenge and kill the two constables.

Some say Neligan was in on the job but others say he was surprised, even infuriated, that he'd been an unwitting victim to the attack. In any event, as he squired the two Tipperary policemen around Dublin the following day, Joe Dolan and Frank Thornton shot and killed Roche but only managed to wound Fitzmaurice who luckily escaped the ambush. The job's 'covering team' of Tom Keogh and Jim Slattery also fired shots at the two RIC men. Uncharacteristically, the Squad members, possibly with their minds blinded by rage and grief over Treacy's killing, wounded two innocent bystanders, a young girl and an elderly man.

❀

On the same day Seán Treacy was killed, Michael suffered another personal loss. His good friend and valued comrade Joe Vize, a Wicklow man like Tom Cullen and a former British naval officer, was arrested later that afternoon in Clancy's shop on Talbot Street. He'd been brought back to Dublin from Glasgow, Scotland to serve as GHQ Director of Purchases. His main responsibilities were to oversee the importation of arms. He was someone whom Collins had chosen to work closely with Liam Mellowes, now GHQ Quartermaster and Tom Cullen, the former quartermaster.

As Piaras wrote: "He had been one of Collins's most trust-worthy agents abroad for the purchase and importation of arms. Vize was interned in Mountjoy up to the Truce [July, 1921], and throughout that time Collins kept in close and constant communication with him." [36]

❀

With the build-up of British troops and increased aggressive-
ness of its intelligence agents, Michael Collins felt an imaginary
noose tightening around his neck. The ruthlessness of the Black
and Tans compounded by the utter mercilessness of the Auxies
only helped make up his mind. Something dramatic and extraordinary must be risked to take the pressure off of Dublin's
Republican contingent.

Foy said: "Collins believed the British threat to the IRA's
position in Dublin demanded dramatic action, and he planned to
eliminate many enemy intelligence agents in one massive swoop." [37]

Béaslaí remarked: "We [Collins's inner circle] were satisfied
that there was a conspiracy to murder Irish citizens, deliberately
carried out by the Intelligence Department of the English Forces
in Ireland with the sanction of their G.H.Q." [38]

Piaras further noted: "These Intelligence officers, living
among the citizens under disguised names in civilian clothes,
were not only spies, subject to the penalties of spies of war, but
had all directly or indirectly been concerned in the murder of
Irish citizens." [39]

Collins gave Dick McKee responsibility for the planning of
this major operation. Michael was determined to teach the British
that their dastardly and underhanded behaviours in Ireland
must stop. He felt the Sassenach had brought the storm that
was coming down upon their own heads and that Ireland would
refuse to tolerate their evil ways any longer. Violence would repay
violence...the consequences of their behaviours were to be repaid
in kind. Hate begets hate. Terror begets terror. Vengeance would
beget vengeance.

McKee called the leaders of his four Dublin battalions and
the Squad together. They were given the names, descriptions and
addresses of the British agents that Mick's intelligence men had
unearthed. It was information that Tobin, Cullen and Thornton
had carefully sifted through to assure its accuracy.

Initially, a list of some sixty names involving twenty locations
was forwarded, but Collins said no. Such an operation was too
ambitious.

...trying to kill so many enemy agents piecemeal over time was clearly futile and so Collins decided to risk a coordinated pre-emptive strike, a concept which must also have appealed to his sense of the dramatic and his willingness to play for the highest stakes. Collins's conviction that only decisive action could prevent enemy mastery of Dublin was shared by McKee.... [40]

Dick Mulcahy, who acted as Volunteer Chief-of-Staff, agreed with his two comrades. He too felt it was only a matter of time before the British would come down hard on the Dáil, GHQ and its brigade officers as well as Collins's operatives. 'On the run' since January last, Mulcahy had recently escaped arrest by fleeing through the skylight of Professor Hayes's house on the South Circular Road. But in his rush to take flight, he'd left some important papers behind. They contained the names and addresses of some two hundred Irish Volunteers. [41]

Though Dick McKee was the coordinator, the Big Fella maintained overall control. It was he who picked the date of Sunday, 21 November 1920 for the operation. Nine o'clock in the morning was the appointed hour.

※

As plans came together, Mick's three closest allies had dangerous brushes with the authorities. Those incidents only confirmed in Mick's mind that now was the time to act.

In early November, Frank Thornton had been arrested and held for ten days. Luckily, he managed to convince the agents holding him he had nothing to do with the IRA.

Then, just a week before the 21st, Tom Cullen and Liam Tobin were both awakened by a raiding party of British intelligence men at Vaughan's Hotel.

Both gave false names and addresses. [They had falsified papers with them supporting their aliases.] They were questioned, and the officers were clearly suspicious, but not sure enough of their ground to take any action. The object of the raid, judging by those engaged upon it, was to shoot the two men; but they were not sure that they had the right men, and to arrest them on suspicion would render their subsequent murder difficult [to justify]. [42]

In what can only be considered very poor judgement on their parts, Tom and Liam were back sleeping at Vaughan's three nights later. And sure enough, the hotel was raided again by the Cairo Gang. Whether they thought they wouldn't be disturbed on almost consecutive nights, or they were giving the 'two fingers' to the Sassenach or they suffered from a death wish, or whatever, the two friends fortunately made it out a rear window and spent the rest of the night in a small shed behind the hotel.

[**Author's note**: Two days later, two of the men who participated in that raid on Vaughan's were shot dead on what was soon to become known as 'Bloody Sunday.']

❈

The night before the 'big job' Tom Cullen and Liam Tobin received a warning from David Neligan and Jim McNamara. In Dave's own words he wrote:

> On Saturday night, 20th November 1920, Tobin and Cullen asked myself and McNamara to the Gaiety Theatre [South King Street, just beside the top of Grafton Street]. They told us that those agents were to be shot next morning. In a box nearby were two or three of them with women. Cullen asked me was I going to Croke Park, a hurling and football pitch, next day. There was an important match on. I said: 'No damn fear, and don't you go there either!' He asked 'Why not?' and I said that if those men got shot in the morning the Tans and Auxies would surely revenge themselves by shooting up Croke Park. [43]

Elsewhere in Dublin that evening, Piaras Béaslaí wrote:

> ...the usual crowd assembled in the smokeroom of Vaughan's Hotel. Many details of business were trans-

acted, and there was some speculation as to what the morrow would bring forth. Dick McKee [and Peadar Clancy] was one of the first to leave when the party broke up. Collins was one of the last. [44]

Ten minutes after Collins left, a troop of Auxies raided the hotel.

The Big Fella just managed to seek the safety of an apartment of a friend at #39 Rutland Square, a few doors down from Vaughan's.

Meanwhile, back at the hotel, Piaras, Seán O'Connell and a young Irish language student from Co. Clare, Conor Clune, remained behind talking.

Feeling he had nothing to fear from the raiders, Clune made no attempt to flee. On the other hand, Béaslaí and O'Connell made it out a back door, seeking the safety of the night.

As it turned out, Conor Clune had every reason to be afraid. He was arrested and taken into custody.

Elsewhere in Dublin, at #36 Gloucester Street Lower [later renamed Seán MacDermott Street], Dick McKee and Peadar Clancy, McKee's dear friend and Vice-Commandant of the Dublin Brigade, were arrested by Captain Hardy, a man whose name was linked with murder and the torture of prisoners.

[**Author's note**: #36 had long been a safe house and the home of Seán Fitzpatrick, a loyal friend of Ireland's cause.] [45]

❧

At nine o'clock the following morning, small groups of men, members of the Squad augmented by Volunteers from the Dublin Brigade, raided specific houses scattered around Dublin. They were following orders issued by Michael Collins.

T. Ryle Dwyer, somewhat humorously, wrote: "'It's to be done exactly at nine,' Collins insisted. 'Neither before nor after. These whores, the British, have got to learn that Irishmen can turn up on time.'" [46]

Nineteen soldiers, one or two of them probably not agents, were roused from their sleep and shot, some in the presence of their wives, and girlfriends, some in bed, others standing against a wall. One was 'shot in his pyjamas in the back garden.' Captain Baggelly, who died at 119 Lower Baggot St., never knew that one of the three-man party which shot him would be a future Irish Taoiseach, Prime Minister Seán Lemass. [47]

[**Author's note:** The exact number of British agents killed that morning is a continuing subject of debate.]

Historian James Mackay added:

> The raids took the British completely by surprise, and the hit squads, for the most part, managed to escape without incident. Those engaged in the raids on Mount Street and Pembroke Road, however, ran into bands of Auxiliaries and this led to a series of ferocious running battles. Though heavily outnumbered and outgunned, the volunteers succeeded in getting away, dragging their wounded with them. Only one man, Frank Teeling, fell into the enemy's hands, and Michael organised his escape before much harm could befall him. [48]

Planning the attacks for a Sunday when Dublin would be full of people from down the country, who'd come to town to attend the football match at Croke Park, would backfire on Michael. Try as he might to have the GAA cancel the event, he was told it couldn't be done. People were already massing around the sport stadium.

Tom Cullen, disregarding Neligan's warning, felt compelled to attend. Knowing that the British would likely attempt to disrupt the event by closing the stadium or staging some show of force by indiscriminately arresting people, he still headed off into town.

Initially, Tom planned to carry his small Mauser pocket pistol [7.65mm] with him, but at the last minute decided against it. It had been his trusted companion over the past months when he felt he needed a backup piece. This time, however, discretion proved the better part of valour. Sure if he did need a weapon, he knew of several 'dumps' around Dublin where he could easily obtain one.

Upon arriving at Croke Park, he found the excited crowd buzzing with news of the morning attacks.

Taking his seat, but keeping a watchful eye on his surroundings, Tom settled in as the Gaelic football match between Dublin and Tipperary began. It wasn't long, however, when word spread through the crowd that troops of Tans, Auxies and police were massing outside the entrances to the stadium.

Again, I turn to Béaslaí's description of what happened.

> As a "reprisal" the Auxiliaries rode up in lorries to Croke Park that afternoon, where a huge crowd of men, women and children were engaged in watching a Gaelic football match...and fired on the crowd, killing fourteen, and wounding about sixty. One of the players in the match [Tipperary's goaltender Michael Hogan] was among the killed. They then dismounted [stepped from their vehicles] and searched all the men in the Park. By way of justification it was alleged that they were fired on – a statement palpably absurd. It was also alleged that they had information that the shootings that morning had been done by men from the country [particularly Co. Tipperary], who came up for that purpose, under the guise of attending the match, and that this was the reason for the raid on Croke Park. If they really believed that the series of successful raids that morning had been done by strangers to the city, without local knowledge, they must have been very bad judges. [49]

Feeling trapped and fighting the urge to panic, Tom Cullen worked his way through the terrified crowd and, using all of his athletic strength and agility, managed to escape.

Neligan said of the afternoon's terror: "Hundreds of Tans and Auxies concentrated on Croke Park, opening fire with rifles and machine-guns on the densely-packed crowd, killing and wounding a great number. In spite of my warning, Cullen went there and had to climb a tall fence to get away." [50]

> That night most of the prisoners held in Dublin Castle were transferred to Beggar's Bush [a British military barracks in Dublin]. Clancy, Clune and McKee were left in the guardroom beside the canteen where, MacNamara

reported, the Auxiliaries were 'drunk and thirsting for vengeance.' Later that night the three were 'shot while attempting to escape'. Neligan and the other friendly detectives reported to Collins that all three had been tortured and that, when their bodies were being loaded on to a lorry, the officer responsible had battered their faces with his torch [flashlight]. [51]

❧

As for Dublin Castle's reaction to the morning's executions, Ryle Dwyer wrote:

Cabs, sidecars and all modes of conveyances began arriving at Dublin Castle as undercover agents sought information and refuge. 'Panic reigned,' David Neligan noted. 'The gates were choked with incoming traffic – all the military, their wives and agents.' They were seeking protection within the castle walls. 'A bed was not to be found for love or money,' he added. 'Terror gripped the invincible spy system of England. An agent in the castle whose pals had been victims, shot himself. He was buried with the others in England. The attack was so well organised, so unexpected, and so ruthlessly executed that the effect was paralysing.' Neligan continued that 'the enemy never recovered from the blow. While some of the worst killers escaped, they were thoroughly frightened.' [52]

Foy noted, "On 25 November 1920 [the same day McKee and Clancy were buried] the funeral procession of the dead British officers wound it way through the city to a destroyer waiting at the North Wall [Dublin]." [53]

[**Author's note**: Upon their arrival back in England, the bodies of the British agents were driven in hearses through the streets of London and received state funerals at Westminster Abbey.]

❧

As can be imagined, Michael Collins, Liam Tobin, Tom Cullen and Frank Thornton were filled with incredibly conflicted emotions. On the one hand, the early attacks on the British intelligence agents proved to be a spectacular success. But the exhilaration of the morning was upturned by the massacre at Croke Park which was soon followed by the terrible news of McKee, Clancy and Clune's murders.

[**Author's note**: McKee and Clancy were buried in Dublin while Clune's body was returned home to his village of Quin, Co. Clare for burial. A medical examination of his body found he'd been shot in the chest thirteen times!]

※

Dan Breen noted: "Mick Collins and Tom Cullen made the arrangements for the obsequies [for McKee and Clancy] at the Pro-Cathedral. I mention this to their everlasting credit." [54]

Tim Pat Coogan added the detail.

Collins was beside himself at the news [of McKee and Clancy's deaths]. Contemporary accounts speak of him swaying in anguish as he relived the tortures, continually repeating that all was over. He caused uproar by insisting that the bodies be dressed in Volunteer uniforms. Even the bravest of men thought he was mad and some refused to accompany him to the mortuary chapel in the pro-cathedral. However, he pushed his way through the small crowd of detectives and spies who were hanging around the gate to see who would turn up and stood in the chapel as doctors opened the coffins to examine the bodies. The stories had been so awful that the investigators were almost glad at what was revealed. Badly battered faces certainly, and bayonet thrusts, and bullet wounds, but not the mutilations expected. He took part in dressing his comrades in Volunteers' uniforms and accepted the verdict of the clergy that the coffins should be closed again because of the condition of the faces. Next morning he also attended the funeral Mass and, with no one present knowing from one moment to the next whether the Auxiliaries might suddenly burst upon the scene, made his last gesture of friendship and defiance. First, wearing a trenchcoat, he stepped out of the crowd, which, because of the threat of the Auxiliaries, was unusually small for such an occasion and pinned an 'in memoriam' message on the coffin: 'in memory of two good friends Dick and Peadar and two of Ireland's best soldiers. Míceal O'Coileain, 25/11/20.' Then he helped carry the coffins. He went to Glasnevin for the burial also and was recognised by a woman. 'There's Mick Collins,' she exclaimed. He turned round and snarled at her, 'You bloody bitch.' [55]

[**Author's note**: After the Requim Mass at the Pro-Cathedral, Mick Collins, Liam Tobin, Tom Cullen, Frank Thornton, Gearóid O'Sullivan among others helped carry the coffins of Dick McKee and Peadar Clancy to their hearses. Later that day, the Evening Herald carried a front page photograph of Michael and Tom Cullen carrying one of the coffins. Enraged, the Big Fella ordered some of his men to visit the newspaper's office and destroy the photographic plate as well as buy up all the unsold newspapers off the street. As Tim Pat noted: "…Dublin Castle missed getting a good picture of their chief enemy."] [56]

In a memo describing his reaction to the events of 'Bloody Sunday,' Michael Collins wrote:

My one intention was the destruction of the undesirables who continued to make miserable the lives of ordinary decent citizens. I have proof enough to assure myself of the atrocities which this gang of spies and informers have committed. Perjury and torture are words too easily known to them.

If I had a second motive it was no more than a feeling such as I would have for a dangerous reptile. By their destruction the very air is made sweeter. That should be the future's judgement on this particular event. For myself, my conscience is clear. There is no crime in detecting and destroying, in wartime, the spy and the informer. They have destroyed without trial. I have paid them back in their own coin. [57]

As the events of 'Bloody Sunday' played out, the British public, government officials and even King George V were horrified at the behaviour of their agents regarding the Croke Park incident. But the English papers concentrated their reporting on the stunning assassinations of their intelligence agents that morning.

Foy said: "Bloody Sunday remains a remarkable achievement by Collins. It sent a seismic wave through the British political system, shaking public faith in the government's assurances that its Irish policy was succeeding. After 21 November 1920 the credibility gap was just too wide between a claim that it had murder by the throat...." [58]

[**Author's note**: On 9 November 1920, British PM David Lloyd George told a gathering of Lord Mayors at their annual dinner in London's Guildhall that his security forces had 'murder by the throat' in Ireland.]

Despite all the catastrophic happenings befalling the victims of Ireland's thirty-month War for Independence, the horrific deaths of McKee and Clancy were likely the most dramatic and tragic single event of that brutal and bloody conflict.

Béaslaí said: "To Collins the loss [of those two men] came with a peculiar sense of poignancy. McKee had been his right-hand man in all his undertakings, and a warm and loyal personal friend." [59]

Collectively, 'Bloody Sunday' was an intelligence blow to the English government's strategy in Ireland. With the killing of many Cairo Gang members, the day proved to be a public relations disaster that did irreparable damage to England's image and the cause of British rule in Ireland. It also fuelled new support for Dáil Éireann, for Ireland's quest for freedom and self-governance and for the images of Michael Collins and Éamon de Valera.

Coogan wrote:

[Winston] Churchill subsequently stated at a Cabinet meeting that no reprisals had taken place after the Dublin murders [on 'Bloody Sunday' morning]. However the initiated amongst the ranks of British decision-makers knew that Collins had probably struck the most damaging blow of the entire undercover war. The Cairo Gang had had one instruction, to locate and destroy Collins and his organisation. They had failed and the implications of that failure were well understood. [60]

Finally, a special British Court of Inquiry was set up to look into the Sunday afternoon Croke Park affair. Of it Ryle Dwyer said:

The auxiliaries fired a total of 228 rounds of small arms fire, in addition to the fifty rounds fired from the armoured car. The court of inquiry found that the shooting was unauthorised and excessive, even if some member of the crowd fired on the auxiliaries first. [This claim had been authored as justification for the British opening fire at Croke Park.] Following the inquiry Major-General G. F. Boyd, commanding officer of the British soldiers in Dublin, concluded that the firing on the crowd, which began without orders, was both indiscriminate and unjustifiable.

Brigadier General Frank Crozier [C/O of the Auxiliary Cadet Division], who would shortly resign in protest against what he believed was the condoning of the misconduct of his men, publicly stated that one of his officers told him that the auxiliaries started the shooting. 'It was the most disgraceful show I have ever seen' one of his officers told him. 'Black and Tans fired into the crowd without any provocation whatever.' [61]

※

A week after 'Bloody Sunday' the tenor surrounding Ireland's struggle for independence was retched up even further. On 26 November, Arthur Griffith was arrested, likely in retaliation for Collins's raids. While he was held, Mick became acting president of the Dáil…an appointment that only increased the stress he was living and working under.

On the night of 27-28 November, the IRA expanded the war by burning seventeen warehouses along the docklands in Liverpool, England. The effect was dramatic, but in the end, many members of the raiding party were arrested.

At about the same time, Cathal Brugha's crazy efforts to assassinate members of Britain's ruling government were thwarted. The public gallery in the House of Commons was closed and Downing Street was barricaded to unauthorised traffic.

On the 28th, Tom Barry, a twenty-three-year-old guerrilla fighter and IRA commander, led a flying column of Irish freedom fighters in an ambush. Near Kilmichael in Co. Cork, they attacked a convoy of Auxiliaries coming from their barracks located in Macroom Castle. The fire-fight along this isolated stretch of road in West Cork was short-lived. Seventeen Auxies, almost an entire platoon, were killed while Barry lost just three of his men.

On 1 December, PM Lloyd George, who'd previously made some low-level, behind-the-scenes peace overtures, opened a new avenue aimed at formally beginning negotiations leading to a possible ceasefire with the IRA and Ireland's new government. Ironically, the man he chose was Australian Archbishop Patrick Joseph Clune, the uncle of Conor Clune, the innocent young man murdered in Dublin Castle on 'Bloody Sunday' evening. At the time the Catholic religious leader was travelling through Ireland on his way to Rome.

Doubtful of the PM's true motives, Michael gave the archbishop a list of conditions proposed by him and approved by the Dáil.

Upon delivering the list to Lloyd George, the PM said to Clune that holding actual talks would have to wait and as a show of good faith, the IRA must go underground and refrain from any aggressive actions for a month. Additionally, both Collins and Richard Mulcahy should leave Ireland for an extended period of time. With peace apparently on the prime minister's mind, the Welsh Wizard did an absolute about face and proclaimed martial law throughout most of Leinster and Munster.

Lloyd George's outlandish terms were followed two days later, 11 December, by the Tans looting and then burning much of central Cork City. Proudly, the British hoors stuck 'burnt corks' on the ends of their bayonets as they paraded around the town, terrifying the local inhabitants.

Then, on 17 December, the Squad was back in action. This time their target was an RIC officer, DI Philip J. O'Sullivan who'd served with honours in the British navy during the European war. He was shot on Henry Street as he walked along the footpath with his girlfriend.

O'Sullivan's fiancée had been warned that she was stepping out with a 'Black and Tan.' He chose to ignore the warning passed on from her and continued his association with his unsavoury mates. Additionally, Michael and the Crow Street Three feared the man was hot on the trail of locating one of Mick's finance offices, #45 Henry Street.

Tom Cullen, Frank Saurin and others had taken turns trailing the man for a week. When his daily pattern of travel was fixed, Joe Byrne, Ned Kelliher and two others were assigned to do the job.

❧

The tenor of Republican Dublin changed rather abruptly on 23 December. Éamon de Valera, Ireland's popularly recognised political leader and long-absent ambassador returned home from America. Tom Cullen and Batt O'Connor were sent by Michael to meet his ship at the Custom House Quay.

His eighteen-month sojourn had met with mixed results. He had raised a large sum of money in support of the Dáil Éireann. One estimate placed the amount in the five-million-dollar range. But in his time away he'd failed to secure either the American Democratic or Republican parties' support for Ireland's Republican cause. In addition to that disappointment, he'd managed to alienate much of Irish-America's leadership. On balance, his political scorecard was not an impressive one.

As the 'Long Hoor,' Michael's nickname for Dev, stepped ashore, his first words to Tom and Batt were likely – How are things going?

The ever ebullient but not very politically savvy Tom Cullen replied, "'Great! The Big Fellow is leading us and everything is marvellous,' said Cullen with a broad grin, which vanished at de Valera's reaction." [62]

"'Big Fellow! Big Fellow!' He pounded the guard-rail with his clenched fist and spat out, 'We'll see who's the Big Fellow...'" [63]

The Scottish historian and writer James Mackay continued:

> Michael himself had been up since five o'clock after a night of sleepless anticipation. He made sure that everything was ready for de Valera's reception at the home of the eminent gynaecologist Dr. Robert Farnan in [#5] Merrion Square (where the talks with Archbishop Clune had been held), but for some unaccountable reason he did not see the Long Fellow till early on the morning of Christmas Eve. The first Cabinet minister to confer with the Chief [Dev], therefore, was Cathal Brugha, who lost no time in shoving his oar in. Brugha complained that Michael Collins and his IRB group had got a stranglehold on power. Cathal weakened his case, however, by saying that he had been offered the Acting Presidency but had not taken it. 'And why did you not?' asked de Valera sharply. 'It was only at your refusal that the others came in.' [64]

While in America, de Valera was toasted, honoured and given the royal treatment, while back in Ireland Collins was a wanted man, 'on the run' with a price on his head, Britain's much publicised public enemy #1. It was Collins who had stayed home, made the difficult choices...the life and death choices required of a military man fighting a dirty little guerrilla war against the world's mightiest empire. A war Dev had helped start, but had walked out on in pursuit of 'higher ideals.' Yes, the Long Hoor was back, flexing his muscles and almost immediately ruffling feathers. His high-minded, romantic, idealistic views seemed unaffected by the violent, bloody conflict that had been raging in Ireland since the eve of his departure.

There, sitting across from him, was the Big Fella, the man Tom Cullen had been so quick to praise. Yes, it was Collins, who's tough-minded, pragmatic and no-nonsense approach had earned him a reputation Dev secretly begrudged.

In a short time, the two men would be vying for the reins of power and control.

❧

During the fallout from 'Bloody Sunday' and its political aftermath, Tom Cullen and Delia Considine became 'officially' engaged. Tom proudly told his Dublin friends that they would be married soon...on January 4th next.

The Wicklow man had thought long and hard about this decision. As happy as the hours were that he'd spent with Delia, something else had helped him make up his mind to marry. The war was wearing on him. The constant danger; the terrible violence; the ever-present feeling of standing on death's doorstep were taking their toll. The more Tom thought about them, the more he longed for the sanctuary of Delia's love and for her welcomed companionship. He dreamt of the day when they could live their lives together in quiet tranquillity, sharing the bounties of an Ireland at peace. Soon, maybe soon, his dream could become reality.

❧

With the military successes of November, the possibilities the British might be serious about treating with the IRA and now, with the announcement of Tom's pending marriage, Michael, in a moment of celebratory enthusiasm, invited Tom Cullen, Liam Tobin, Gearóid O'Sullivan and Rory O'Connor, a Dublin man who was currently the IRA's Director of Engineering, to a Christmas Eve dinner at the Gresham Hotel in Sackville Street [later renamed O'Connell Street].

In a carelessly festive mood, the men sat in the public dining room of the landmark hotel eating and drinking [likely to excess]. With their guard down and filled with the Christmas spirit, the five revolutionaries were thoroughly enjoying the moment when a group of Auxiliaries raided the building. As Tim Pat Coogan wrote: "…Dublin Castle could not have imagined a more welcome Christmas present…[one that] was very nearly delivered." [65]

The great Irish historian continued:

> …Collins was searched and a bottle of whiskey discovered in his hip pocket. 'For the landlady,' he said. Less convincing was his explanation for one of the entries in a notebook which was also discovered. 'Rifles,' said the Auxiliary. 'Refills,' said Collins. Understandably, after that exchange he felt a need to relieve himself and was taken to the lavatory under escort. When he didn't return Tobin became alarmed and went looking for him. He found him held under one of the bright hand-basin lights while an Auxiliary officer tousled his hair and compared his likeness with a photograph of Collins he held in his other hand. Collins had despairingly made up his mind to make a grab for the officer's revolver when suddenly he was released and he and Tobin were allowed to return to the table. It was still touch and go. Collins whispered to Tobin to 'be ready to make a rush for it.' But in his absence his whiskey bottle had helped to ease the atmosphere. O'Connor had offered the auxiliaries a drink and a second bottle of whiskey was ordered into the bargain. John Jameson spread a benign glow over the Auxiliaries and they departed without the Castle's five-man Christmas present. The Castle might have taken some small comfort from the episode had they known of the cosmic hangover the five proceeded to inflict on themselves. They finished the whiskey – and their wine – and then repaired to Vaughan's. Diarmuid O'Hegarty, who had not been at the Gresham either (sic), was horror-stricken at the prospect of a raid on Vaughan's and implored them to go home, with conspicuous lack of success. Delayed

reactions, and John Jameson's, had taken over and there were wrestling matches and tumblers of whiskey before the warriors were decanted into a car and poured into some of Mrs. O'Donovan's beds for the night. [66]

❧

[**Author's note**: Additional reading would include Joe Ambrose's *Seán Treacy and the Tan War*, (2007), Tom Barry's *Guerilla Days In Ireland*, (1993) & Peter Hart's *British Intelligence in Ireland 1920-1921: The Final Reports*, (2002).]

Tom Cullen, Michael Collins & Liam Tobin, Dublin, 1922

Front door, #15 Cadogan Gardens, London

Coy QM Sergeant Eamonn 'Ned' Cunningham, c. 1922

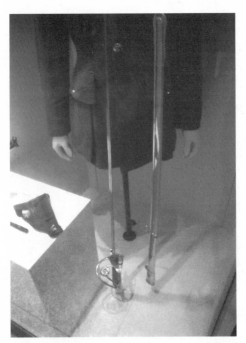

Michael Collins's sword given by Tom Cullen

Comdt.-Gen. Tom Cullen behind C-in-C Michael Collins, 1922

Rural road, Béalnabláth, West Cork

Ratra House, Phoenix Park, Dublin

Tom Cullen carrying Michael Collins's coffin, 1922

#27 Herbert Place, Dublin

Tom & Delia Cullen, Curragh Racecourse, Co. Kildare, c. 1925

Sand Finer Beach, Wicklow Town harbour

Lough Dan, Co. Wicklow

Maj.-Gen. Tom & Delia Cullen's grave, Rathnew, Co. Wicklow

Maj.-Gen. Liam Tobin's grave, Glasnevin Cemetery, Dublin

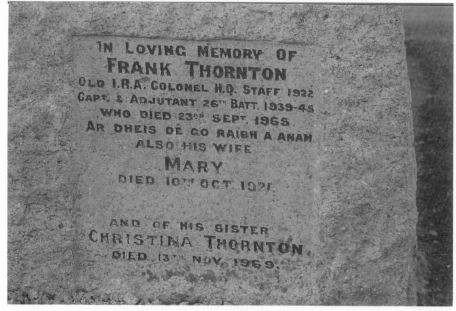

Col. Frank Thornton's grave, Glasnevin Cemetery, Dublin

9

"Something terrible has happened – I know
what you have come to tell me."

–Tom Cullen

The ever cheerful and resilient Tom Cullen came to the aid of Michael Collins and their friends.

With the departure of the Auxiliaries, Collins's Christmas Eve get-together shifted into high gear as the celebrants breathed a huge sigh of relief. Of that near tragic dinner party at the Gresham and afterwards, of the late-night frivolities at Vaughan's, historian and writer Margery Forester reported:

> For the first and last time in recorded history Collins proceeded to get drunk. Furthermore, he led his equally unsteady companions, the tremendous upsurge of relief gone to their heads as much as the gulps of neat whiskey, on to Vaughan's, then about the most dangerous spot in town even for men with their wits about them. Tom Cullen, fortunately, had kept some of his. Curfew was at hand. He herded them down Parnell [Sackville] Square to Devlin's and ran to find a car. Piaras Béaslaí turned up at this juncture to find Michael and Rory O'Connor 'sitting on the ground embracing one another and Gearóid half-lying on a chair.' [1]

Indeed, it was a night to remember...one that Tom Cullen and the others never forgot.

❧

On the eve of the New Year and his wedding to Delia, Tom had another real scare.

At midday on New Year's Eve, 1920, the Auxiliaries raided the flat of Eileen McGrane at #21 Dawson Street. Her home was only a stone's throw away from Mansion House, the official residence of Dublin's Lord Mayor since the early 1700s and the site of Dáil Éireann's inaugural meeting on 21 January 1919.

Eileen was one of Michael's secretaries. Collins, Tom Cullen, Ernie O'Malley and others occasionally met at her residence and Tom often stored intelligence files there. Leaving them at #21 was a huge mistake and gross oversight on Tom's part.

Whether the Wicklow man knew it or not [and he should have], Miss McGrane, a member of Cumann na mBan, attended meetings at their secret headquarters just across the street. Obviously, the authorities knew of the meeting site and must have observed her comings and goings.

This tempting target was too much for the Peelers to resist. During their New Year's Eve raid, they arrested Eileen and discovered Tom's secreted documents.

After her perfunctory trial, Miss McGrane was incarcerated in Mountjoy Prison and later sent to Walton Prison in Liverpool, England. Later, she was returned to Mountjoy. She was finally released after the Truce. [2]

Of Tom's files, Michael Foy humorously noted: "There was so much information that a van was required to convey it to the Castle." [3]

Though Michael and Tom were not personally endangered by the discovery, Ned Broy was. Copies of his G Division reports, ones that were months old and should have been burned, were uncovered.

Broy, one of Mick's chief undercover operatives at police HQ in Great Brunswick Street and the man who'd smuggled him inside to read files back in April, 1919, was compromised. Michael warned him but it was no use. Ned's chief was finally on to him.

Fearing for his life, but determined not to panic and run, Broy bluffed his superiors and sweated things out until he was tried in April, 1921. Rather than executed, he was sentenced to prison at

Arbour Hill Military Detention barracks.

Fortunately for Ned, Michael was finally able to arrange for his release after the Truce. Three months later, he was one of Mick's private secretaries during the two-month-long London Treaty negotiations in the autumn of 1921.

[**Author's note**: One of the reasons Broy didn't flee Dublin was his fear of exposing his friend and fellow undercover operative Detective Sergeant Jim McNamara. Unfortunately, McNamara's duplicity was discovered too. As a result, he went on the run and assisted members of the Squad with their work.

Of Collins's G Division informants, Foy noted they'd become 'wasted assets.'

> Joe Kavanagh had died in September [of a blood clot] after an appendix operation, by which time most political work was already concentrated in the Castle. Left behind at Great Brunswick Street in charge of office duties, Broy provided increasingly meagre information even before his world fell apart, literally overnight. [4]

This left Dave Neligan as Michael's main source of undercover intelligence information inside Dublin Castle as he'd been transferred from the DMP to British intelligence sometime earlier.]

※

As far back as September last, but more recently in mid-December, Mick and company hatched a scheme to import arms from Italy. Plans were finalised at a 16 December meeting at Barry's Hotel [1-2 Great Denmark Street, north of the Liffey] and Mick Leahy, Vice O/C of Cork No. 1 Brigade was chosen as the point man for the operation. Elaborate plans were undertaken to transfer the prospective 'Italian furniture,' a code description for the anticipated weapons, from the arriving ship to small boats near Rabbit Island in West Cork.

Leahy's O/C, Seán O'Hegarty, sent the man off to Dublin to arrange for a passport with Michael Collins. There he met with Gearóid O'Sullivan, another Cork man on 3 January 1921.

Making sure they weren't being followed, O'Sullivan drove him back and forth through the streets of Dublin before finally depositing him at Devlin's pub, which, as it turned out, was only a few blocks from where he was actually staying.

Annoyed by the obvious deception, Leahy assumed it had been done to impress him and to make sure they weren't being followed. He also speculated the obvious deception was undertaken to demonstrate the strict security measures Dublin GHQ employed to cover their tracks.

Upon his arrival at Devlin's [Joint #2], however, he was even less impressed. Tim Pat Coogan described what happened to the envoy in Leahy's own words.

> When we entered Devlin's pub, I was surprised to find nearly all the GHQ Staff assembled and a merry party in progress, this despite Gearóid's protestations that Dublin was a dangerous place for the likes of him. My choice of lemonade when whiskey was being pressed did not go down too well with Michael Collins who seemed to be master of the revels. Dick Mulcahy was in Devlin's, but was quiet in comparison to a number of them and left early... [5]

The gala festivities at Devlin's just happened to be Tom Cullen's stag party. The visiting Corkman was annoyed that no one paid him or his mission much attention until after the wedding breakfast the next day.

[**Author's note:** Through a series of misunderstandings, Leahy was forced to make his own way to Italy in March, but the Dublin money required for the arms purchase never arrived. Apparently the monetary transfer process proved faulty, a most understandable circumstance considering the state of affairs in Ireland at the time. Finally, in April, with no prospects of concluding the transaction in any satisfactory way and with Leahy running out of his 'own' money, Michael called off the arms transaction. Coogan speculated that because of Collins's inability to consummate the deal and "...combined with his flamboyance at the Cullen party, (it) injured his (Collins's) reputation in some circles for many years." [6]

As can be imagined, Tom was thrilled and chuffed at the party's turnout. Realising full well the danger everyone in the room risked to attend and honour him pleased the Wicklow man to the quick. The security pressures of the last three years weighed heavily on everyone's mind. One careless slip and the entire War for Independence could collapse in a heartbeat. Yet those present, his working friends and close colleagues, chose to risk it in order to wish their comrade well. Their presence was a clear indication of the high esteem and lofty regard the Dublin IRA men held for Tom Cullen. It was certainly a tribute they paid him for all the hard work and personal risk the Wicklow man had undergone for them.

What Tom didn't realise, but should have known, was that Michael had personally undertaken to organise security for the party. Members of the Squad and the Dublin Brigade formed a tight but discreet defensive ring, several blocks in circumference, around Devlin's. The British military and intelligence would've had a difficult time penetrating Mick's defences, giving the merrymakers ample time to seek safety.

No, Collins had no intention of compromising his hard earned advantage, but on the other hand, he wasn't going to deny his close friend Tom Cullen a memorable wedding send off.

The following day, many of Tom and Delia's closest friends gathered at St. Nicholas of Myra *'without'* Parish Church on Francis Street, in the heart of the Liberties, for the wedding.

[**Author's note**: The selection of St. Nicholas is somewhat curious. St. Patrick's Church in Wicklow Town would have been the logical choice for the wedding, considering the Considines' close affiliation with it. But to ask Dublin's IRA leadership to travel there during wartime would have been out of the question. The Republicans were much more at home and secure within the confines of Dublin Town.

So why did they pick that particular church on Francis Street? Was it Tom's choice after having attended Mass there while a resident at #26 Landerdale Terrace, New Row South, his parish church? Was it because of the church's somewhat secluded location, set back from the busy Francis Street? Or was it Delia's pick for whatever reason? Why not St. Kevin's Church on Harrington Street, just a couple of blocks from #58 South Circular Road, where Tom had lived and worked for Pat Dowling? Certainly he'd attended Mass there often. Or was St. Nicholas the only church to welcome Fr. Cogan, from Wicklow, to perform the marriage? Maybe the Wicklow priest was a close personal friend of St. Nicholas's parish priest? Unfortunately, we'll never know the answer.

The church itself, with its rather simple exterior and ornate interior was built between 1829 and 1834. Its portico and bell tower were added in 1860. The word *'without'* was part of its original name to distinguish it from the other St. Nicholas of Myra church originally built *'within'* Dublin Town's old walls. (The church was named for St. Nicholas, the 4th-century Bishop of Myra, a city located along the mountainous southwestern coast of Asia Minor.)

The name 'Francis Street' originated from a Franciscan Friary, founded in 1285, once located nearby. (The Dublin Franciscans were part of the Order of St. Francis of Assisi founded in 1209.)

Also shrouded in mystery are the names of those who attended the service. The wedding cert states that Thomas Cullen, a Dublin bachelor, married Mary Brigid Considine, a Wicklow spinster. Tom's occupation was listed as 'clerk.' Delia's profession, if any, was unlisted.

William (Liam) Tobin was Tom's best man and Tom's eighteen-year-old sister Annie was Delia's maid of honour. The Reverend Michael J. Cogan, C.C. from St. Patrick's in Wicklow performed the marriage.

I often wondered why Delia didn't choose one of her sisters or one of her Wicklow friends as maid of honour. Didn't they attend the ceremony? Was Dublin perceived to be too dangerous for the Considines to travel up for the occasion? Didn't they approve of the marriage? Had Delia, now twenty-nine, become friends with Tom's youngest sister or was it a matter of convenience? Again, we'll never know.

So who did attend? I'm quite certain both Michael Collins and Frank Thornton would have been there as would have Andy and

James Cullen. I'd also like to think that some of Tom and Delia's families were there, as well as some of Tom's IRA comrades. But maybe, for security reasons, no one other than the immediate wedding party attended: Tom, Delia, Liam Tobin and Annie Cullen.

As for the wedding breakfast Tim Pat mentioned in his Collins biography, I'd guess it was held back at Devlin's and that Michael's careful security measures were again in place.

Finally, with life being what it was at the time, I somehow doubt the newlyweds enjoyed much of a honeymoon. Maybe they slipped out of town, seeking the peace and tranquillity of the Irish countryside. But with the Tans and Auxies operating without restraint, it was more likely the two spent the night or so in a nearby hotel before Delia returned home to wait for the War for Independence to end.]

❧

Now, with his wife back in Wicklow Town and the revelry of the wedding over, Tom was filled with mixed emotions. Despite looking forward to his new life with Delia, he knew everything must be put on hold. There was much unfinished business demanding his attention. Despite his desire to see the War for Independence successfully concluded, Tom felt angry at the British for imposing their fecken' selves on the Irish...not just today but over the centuries. Why couldn't they live and let live? Why did they have to impose their egotistical, authoritarian ways upon Ireland...on Delia and himself? All he wanted was to live in peace, share his life with Delia and raise a few horses. But Tom knew the answers to his queries. It was all about greed, power, control, political advantage and money. The English viewed Ireland, its people and its economic resources as chattel to be possessed and exploited. It was the old story of 'if you can't have what you want, then you take it...if you can.' The Irish were in a bitter struggle to retain what was rightfully theirs and to prevent the Sassenach from keeping it. It was going to be a struggle to the death or until one side cried surrender. His dream of a life with Delia must simply wait...at least a while longer. His love for her and their life together was now another motivating force driving him on to see the dream of 'Ireland free' become reality. He knew Delia shared his views and was willing to wait...for him, for a new Ireland and for their life together.

⁂

With the New Year's Eve scare and the wedding in the past, life in Dublin returned to normal, if you can call living in a perpetual state of war usual.

On this particular evening, Tom and Michael occupied a snug in Kirwan's pub at #49 Great Britain Street, just a few doors down from Devlin's. Jim Kirwan was a Tipperary man who'd been a great friend of Seán MacDiarmada prior to Easter, 1916.

More recently, Kirwan had become fast friends with fellow Tipp men Dan Breen and Seán Treacy. Over the past year or so, Jim boasted to Michael that the two often slept upstairs in his most commodious 'home away from home.' Now, two months after Treacy's death, the mirror behind the bar was still draped with black bunting in remembrance of the fallen Tipperary freedom fighter.

On this 'soft' evening, Mick and Tom were having their evening tea while waiting for Dan to appear. After Breen's narrow escape with death in October, he'd been home recuperating. Now, at least according to his letter, he was fit again and hungry to return to action in Dublin. His last communiqué indicated Collins should expect him sometime about eight o'clock.

While the two comrades waited and dined, they had a chance to look back on recent political developments.

Lloyd George's peace talks had amounted to nothing...nil. Martial law was proving equally unsuccessful. Rule by the Tans and Auxies continued unabated while the Irish people and the IRA refused to knuckle under.

Realising that, the British prime minister tried a new tack. He hoped the legislative approach might bring Ireland's 'troubles' to an end.

Margery Forester explained:

On 23 December 1920 the government of Ireland Act was passed. Ireland was to be sawn in two against the will of the majority of her people, with two half-powered parliaments, one in Belfast grudgingly accepted by the minority whose interests it was designed to protect, and one in Dublin where a duly elected assembly was already functioning as best it could under impossible conditions. The most that could be said for the Act was that it partially repealed the Act of Union [1800], which the Southern Irish had always regarded as unconstitutional in any case.

Lloyd George himself, unsuspected by the Irish, hoped that Partition would provide an ultimate solution. Those able to regard it dispassionately admitted that it cleared one major obstacle from the path to settlement, since without it the Ulstermen would have remained irreconcilable to any recognition of a Dublin legislature. Sinn Féin, however, could hardly be expected to see Partition in this light. 'This plunderous and impossible Act,' Collins termed it. [7]

❧

With the partitioning of Ireland and the continued assault of Britain's special police on the citizens of Dublin dominating the local newspapers, the end of January saw the Squad back in action with the death of William 'Willie' Doran, a night porter at the Wicklow Hotel, located just two doors down from Grafton Street.

Ryle Dwyer noted, "Collins had [inside] information...that Doran was giving information about guests of the hotel to the British. People like Collins [himself], Tobin, Cullen, Gearóid O'Sullivan and Diarmuid O'Hegarty often used the hotel. Despite a number of warnings Doran persisted, and the Squad was sent to kill him." [8]

Tim Pat Coogan embellished Doran's death a bit by quoting Joe Dolan's Witness Statement.

The Squad made several attempts to get him but were unsuccessful. At last Mick Collins sent a dispatch to Liam Tobin to hurry it up, as he was doing a lot of damage. Tobin asked me to do it as I knew him [Doran]. Dan McDonnell and myself entered the Wicklow Hotel one morning [29 January] about nine o'clock, shot him dead in the hall, and walked away. I was back there at 1 pm having my lunch. [9]

Coogan, ever the thorough historian, further noted: "Not knowing who had had him shot, his destitute widow applied to the Sinn Féin for a pension. For the sake of the children, Collins directed that she should be paid." [10]

Apparently, Doran, forty-five and the father of three, had helped Michael and his intelligence triad in the past but recently had decided to 'take the King's shillin' instead. Knowing something of her husband's past Republican leanings, Mrs. Doran just assumed the Auxies had shot him for whatever reason. Not wishing to upset the widow any further, Michael ordered that she was not to be told of the circumstances surrounding his death.

※

At about that same time in January, Michael learned that a Corporal John Ryan of the British military police had played a key role in the McKee-Clancy arrests during the early hours of 21 November last. In contradiction to his own policy of 'no revenge killings,' the Big Fellow ordered the man's death.

T. Ryle Dwyer described what happened and quoted from Bill Stapleton's Witness Statement:

Paddy Kennedy was the intelligence officer selected to identify him. 'Before the two men were detailed to carry out the execution, I asked to be allowed to take part in it as I felt very keenly about the murder of Dick McKee,' Bill Stapleton explained. 'I fought in 1916 and served subsequently with him in the second [Dublin] battalion. My request was granted and the second man instructed to accompany me was Eddie Ryan.'

Kennedy located Ryan at about 10.30 a.m. on 5 February in Hynes' public house at the corner of Old Glouchester Place and Corporation Street [very near the north Dublin house where McKee and Clancy were arrested]. He [Kennedy] went into the bar along with Stapleton and Byrne, while Jimmy Conroy remained on guard. 'I saw Ryan standing facing the counter reading a newspaper and he was identified by the Intelligence Officer [Kennedy],' related Stapleton. 'Before doing the job we held him up and searched him but he had no guns or papers on him.'

'You are Ryan?' they asked.

'Yes, and what about it?'

'With that we shot him....' [11]

�֍

With de Valera's return, the political dynamics within the Republican leadership began changing. The British government, anticipating his arrival back in Ireland, considered Dev a political problem not a military one. As a result, he was not to be harassed or arrested.

> De Valera interviewed his Cabinet one by one. It soon became apparent that he was not concerned with getting their views of the situation so much as imposing his will on them and reasserting his ascendancy. In particular, this entailed putting Michael Collins firmly in his place. [12]

Gone was the rosy-cheeked greeting and naive welcome Tom Cullen showered upon Dev at the quayside back at the end of December. Now, the Long Fellow spent most of his time and energy criticising the military tactics the Big Fella had opted for during his absence. He had no interest in 'Flying Columns,' roadblocks or assassination squads. Unwilling to take a lesson from Ireland's historic 1916 page, de Valera ignored the lethal impact small, but well-chosen, guerrilla manoeuvres were having on the Sassenach. In their place, he began touting large-scale, static, military operations that would see the IRA attack and try to hold a key objective. The Custom House and Beggar's Bush Barracks were two targets that caught his fancy. The media and propaganda potential of such a tactic would be immense in Dev's eyes.

Despite their personal doubts that such a manoeuvre would succeed, Michael and Dick Mulcahy offered no objections to such talk despite the fact that taking on the enemy with its commanding manpower and superior weaponry was patently absurd in their unspoken opinions. The two men imagined the results of such a ploy would lead to a disastrous conclusion. Despite de Valera's obvious disdain for all Mick had achieved, the Big Fella still retained a modicum of respect and admiration for Dev and his contributions to Ireland's 1916 thrust for freedom.

What Michael was slow to realise was that de Valera didn't hold him in an equally flattering light. The Long Hoor was operating under no illusions. As Mackay wrote: "He [de Valera] viewed Collins as a dangerous rival. He alone had the skill and the ability to get things done, and for that reason he had become a powerful adversary." [13]

> [Despite Dev's frequent urgings,] Collins firmly refused to leave Ireland or to allow political possibilities to outweigh military realities. The British claimed to be putting down disaffection rather than waging a war in Ireland; yet, in the areas where there was little disaffection, the Crown forces acted no less repressively than in those where force answered force. The outcome of the [Archbishop] Clune talks had given Collins all the proof necessary that to slacken the I.R.A. campaign now might indeed lead to speedy peace talks – on British terms. [14]

※

Dev seemed to adopt two approaches to his 'Collins problem.' At first he did his utmost to convince the Corkman that it was in Mick's and Ireland's best interests to go to America. The status he'd gained in the eyes of Irish-America for his war efforts against the British and his orchestration of the 'Bloody Sunday' business would assure him a heroic welcome. Maybe Michael could even repair the divisions Dev had left behind, as well as increase the Dáil's coffers with more monetary pledges.

Mick would have no part of this tactic.

Dev then resorted to driving a wedge between Collins and several of his cabinet members, a division that was already fermenting. Michael understood his differences with Cathal Brugha, Minister for Defence, and Austin Stack, Minister for Home Affairs, were based largely on personal jealously. Brugha, in particular, took delight in quibbling over sums Collins, as Minister for Finance, had approved for the war effort.

During the early months of 1921, Michael took Tom Cullen into his confidence and poured out his heart over the disillusionment he felt regarding de Valera's tactics and the growing animosity percolating throughout the administrative workings of Dublin's nascent government.

With Griffith out of prison and de Valera back in saddle, Michael felt his authority gradually being questioned and diminished. But regardless of Dublin's political intrigue, Michael, Tom Cullen, Liam Tobin and the other intelligence men still had a war to prosecute. The daily dangers of living and working in Dublin had not lessened. In fact, they only increased.

Piaras Béaslaí, who lived through those perilous days, aptly described the state of Ireland in early 1921 as the war escalated. More well-armed and better-trained English troopers were arriving in Ireland while British intelligence was becoming wise to Collins's ways.

> As in Dublin, so in the country, the intensified campaign of the English Terrorists was met by greatly increased activity on the part of the Volunteers. This warlike activity was not spread equally over the country. In a large portion of the South of Ireland, and in some counties

in the other provinces, a condition of incessant guerrilla warfare prevailed from this time to the Truce [July,
1921], and encounters between the "I.R.A." and "forces
of the Crown" were of daily occurrence, but there were
some districts where hardly a shot was fired, and conditions were not very far removed from normal.

The ambushes of "Crown Forces," which were
now occurring daily in the country, were very unlike
what British propaganda depicted them as   a skulking
band firing from behind a hedge and retreating. They
were usually pitched battles, often lasting for hours, in
which a small handful of Volunteers, with a very limited
supply of ammunition, engaged strong bodies of well
equipped troops, armed with rifles and machine guns.
Losses by killing, wounding, or capture frequently befell
the columns; and practically all attackers captured by
"Crown forces" were either killed on the spot or court-
martialled and executed. But their [IRA] efforts were
effective in making transport and communications
difficult for the enemy. [15]

Frank Thornton, close friend and intelligence partner of both
Liam Tobin and Tom Cullen, had his own slant on things.

The war was now at its full height. Barracks were being
attacked and captured all over the country. Military
patrols were being ambushed and generally the enemy
was bewildered as the Army of the city and towns hit
hard and then suddenly disappeared. In the country they
formed themselves into flying columns which were so
elusive that they could never be contacted by the strong
enemy forces which tried to track them down. Intelligence was intensified everywhere and practically every
move of the British was known in advance. [16]

It's interesting to note that while Piaras's remarks were certainly pro-Irish, he did inject a note of sombre reality about what
was transpiring down the country. Frank's statement, on the other

hand, is full of enthusiasm and exudes a sense of confidence that the IRA was winning the war.

Of the three friends directing intelligence activities from Crow Street, Frank Thornton had this to say:

> ...Mick Collins left his headquarters practically every night bordering on curfew on his old Raleigh bicycle and on many an occasion Tom Cullen, Liam Tobin and myself left about the same time and started on our journey across town to Rathmines where we had a flat in Grosvenor Road, but on numerous occasions it was found necessary to stay the night, sometimes because of enemy activity in the immediate vicinity or because it was necessary to remain in town for an early morning operation the following day. [17]

In Dublin, the intelligence wars, far from abating after 'Bloody Sunday,' only accelerated. Colonel Ormonde Winter "...relied for intelligence on raids and searches. He believed that the Irish 'had an irresistible habit of keeping documents. They would hide them in the most unexpected places, but they seldom evaded discovery by the trained sleuths: and by this time the Dublin District Intelligence Service men had become outstanding experts.'" [18]

The raid on Mulcahy's office at Professor Hayes's home in November netted Winter's crowd invaluable information. Now, 'O' no longer shared his findings with DMP officials. They had proven to be too untrustworthy and ineffective. Instead, he kept things to himself and his own inner circle as they planned and executed their raids and arrests. For example, British agents combed through the names and addresses of the two hundred or so Volunteers that the Chief of Staff had left behind. One raid led to arrests which led to other important discoveries and further arrests and so on.

To counter the successes Winter's British intelligence agents were having, Collins's men tried luring raiding parties into IRA ambushes. In early February, Tom Cullen and Frank Thornton attempted such a ploy.

...a Volunteer GHQ intelligence officer spotted an enemy agent conducting surveillance in Seville Place, close to the O'Toole Gaelic Football Club whose rooms were used by many nationalist societies. After Crow Street had got the Club to organise a continuous flow of visitors to attract the British spy's attention, the Squad and the ASU positioned themselves in Amiens Street and Portland Row. Tom Cullen and Frank Thornton then detained the British agent, forcing him to reveal both his name and the telephone number of his Dublin Castle controller. Cullen then rang the controller, mimicking the spy's voice, with urgent news of a major republican gathering at the Club. As Cullen and Thornton walked down Talbot Street soon afterwards, a convoy of ten lorries passed them, but when they reached Seville Place there was no sign of the soldiers. Thornton speculated that a suspicious controller had tried unsuccessfully to contact his agent and then put out an alert. [19]

❧

The early spring of 1921 also saw increased violence in Dublin. Not only were the two intelligence networks progressively more active, but so too were the IRA and British military. With British manpower having the distinct advantage, the Dublin brigade refused to be cowed. At first, the Irish Republicans would lob hand grenades into passing lorries. To counter this, the Sassenach had wire-mesh screens installed over the open bays of their lorries. When the Dublin men found other ways of disabling their vehicles, the British resorted to lashing a kidnapped member of Dáil Éireann to a post positioned in the back of their military conveyances.

GHQ decided to retaliate. The Intelligence HQ in Crow Street was given the task of devising an appropriate plan. Frank Thornton and two others were dispatched to London with the intent of kidnapping members of the British parliament. Crow

Street developed a list of some twenty-five individuals to snatch and with the help of London's IRA were prepared to act. But the job was called off when the British stopped using Dáil deputies as hostages.

The bitterness on both sides became infectious. Ryle Dwyer wrote:

> [Cathal] Brugha wanted to resurrect his old scheme to kill members of the British cabinet. This was abandoned after Tobin concluded it would be suicidal. Collins realised this would be the same mistake that the British had made in Ireland. The IRA was not beating the British despite successful ambushes…which undermined Lloyd George's contention that he had 'murder by the throat.' But more and more British people began to question the democracy of a kind of paramilitary chaos in which the rule of law was being ignored. The reprisal policy was not intimidating the Irish but it was embarrassing the British and forcing more and more people to question both the morality and the efficacy of a policy of reprisals in which the crown forces were engaging in counter murder, arson and looting without regard to any law. [20]

Michael saw the futility of Britain's counter-reprisal policy and knew its failures were simply playing into his hands. As proof that Britain's strategy was beginning to give way, Brigadier General Frank Percy Crozier suddenly resigned his position as head of the Auxiliary Cadet Division. He left in disgust after General Hugh Tudor, the self-appointed Dublin Chief of Police, and he disagreed over Crozier's attempt to discipline some of his men for their disgraceful behaviour toward innocent Irish civilians.

❧

Near the end of March, the British assigned Captain Cecil Lees to active duty in Dublin. The man had a reputation for torturing his captives until they revealed what they knew. As a consequence,

Michael felt it necessary to eliminate the man as quickly as possible before he could inflict his own brand of violence on the IRA.

A tall man, standing six feet, three inches, Lees wouldn't be difficult to spot on the street. Rumour had it that he was staying in a hotel on Wicklow Street. Two members of the Squad were immediately assigned to watch for him, but their efforts netted no results until Tom Keogh and Ben Byrne were in the La Scala Theatre [a cinema] on North Prince Street when by a stroke of luck they spotted a man fitting Lees's description.

Unsure, they followed him, and sure enough, he led them back to the St. Andrew's Hotel on Wicklow Street.

Ryle Dwyer described what happened with the help of Ben Byrnes's Witness Statement.

> Next morning, 29 March [1921], Keogh succeeded in rounding up Noel Bolster and Mick O'Reilly to join Byrne and himself to wait for Lees, because they knew if it was him, he would be heading for Dublin Castle about 9.30. 'Bolster and myself were detailed to do the actual shooting,' related Byrne. 'Lees appeared without any undue delay, and, as he was already known to me, there was no need for any further identification. He was accompanied by a lady, but we had no interest in her. We opened fire on Lees, and he fell mortally wounded.' [21]

Two days later, on April 1st, Tom Cullen again came to his friend Michael Collins's aid.

Piaras Béaslaí gave a full accounting of the incident, but to summarise, Michael often used the house of Miss Patricia Hoey and her mother at #5 Mespil Road, along the Grand Canal near the Baggot Street Bridge, for his intelligence planning. Shortly after the nine o'clock evening curfew, the house was raided. The intruding Auxiliaries discovered two of Mick's revolvers and some of his papers.

Upon questioning, Miss Hoey explained the rooms were used by a day-lodger named Mr. O'Brien. When asked to describe the man, she replied he was a 'bald-headed, elderly gentleman.'

With their suspicions still aroused, the woman was taken to Dublin Castle for interrogation.

Managing to retain her composure after an hour of questioning, Miss Hoey demanded to be returned home to care for her ailing mother.

After verifying her story that her brother-in-law was an officer at Colonial Headquarters, she was taken back home. Still uncertain, the Auxiliaries organised an ambush for 'Mr. O'Brien' who they'd been told was scheduled to return to the house the following morning.

Nearly panicked that Michael would be killed as he approached the dwelling, she murmured to her mother to feign serious illness.

With her mother suddenly wailing in mock distress, her daughter was permitted to seek medical help, accompanied by an Auxies of course, at the home of a nearby physician.

With the doctor preparing to accompany the woman and intelligence officer back to #5 Mespil Road, Miss Hoey was able to whisper to the doctor that he must alert Colonel Joe O'Reilly or any Volunteer that Michael Collins would be killed in the morning, if he even so much as approached her house.

The good doctor did as asked, but Joe's problem was he didn't know where the Big Fellow was sleeping that night. His only choice was to station key people at every possible approach to the Mespil Road dwelling.

O'Reilly called on Tom Cullen to help head up the operation and he, Tom and others successfully alerted Mick as he pedalled his bicycle toward certain danger the following day.

Béaslaí concluded the lengthy story with these words: "The Auxiliaries remained in wait in the house from Friday night until Sunday, keeping Miss Hoey and her mother prisoners. Miss Hoey was afterwards arrested and subjected to shocking ill-treatment." [22]

❧

A month later, Tom had another scare. That is not to say he didn't live daily on the narrow edge between life and death. Sure he willingly understood that taking risks was his responsibility as an undercover revolutionary, intelligence officer and Irish patriot.

This time, though, there were greater risks than usual. The matter at hand involved trusting an Auxiliary informer, a chancy proposition at best. Cadet McCarthy, a newly arrived Auxiliary assigned to F Company, was based in Dublin Castle. Wishing to earn some extra 'tea money' and unafraid of the possible consequences, he was recruited and began selling Castle documents to the IRA.

Liam Tobin, Tom Cullen or Dan McDonnell would slip him an envelope in exchange for his printed information while they dined at La Scala, located adjacent to the La Scala Theatre on Prince Street hard by the GPO.

Dwyer's book, *The Squad*, provided a detailed accounting of what transpired on one fateful day in early May, 1921. The historian included selected quotes from Dan McDonnell's Witness Statement.

> Tobin, Cullen and McDonnell had been having lunch regularly in La Scala restaurant…. 'We were there for lunch every day [rather unlikely as repetitive behaviours often led to arrests] and we went to the one waitress,' McDonnell explained. One Friday Tobin was wearing a new brown suit. 'Sitting across the room from us was McCarthy, the auxiliary, with two other fellows whom we didn't know. McCarthy made no attempt to recognise us, which didn't create any suspicion in our minds at the time.' Next day the three of them [Tobin, Cullen and McDonnell] were discussing operations in their Crow Street headquarters, along with Frank Saurin and Charlie Dalton, when Tobin was called away for a meeting with Collins. Cullen then went somewhere else and McDonnell headed off for lunch at La Scala with Saurin.
>
> Crossing the Halfpenny Bridge he [McDonnell] noticed a convoy of army and auxiliaries crossing O'Connell Bridge, headed north, but he did not take much notice as it was by then a regular occurrence. 'I went on towards the La Scala, crossed over towards the

old Independent office and went up on the left-hand side of Middle Abbey Street going towards O'Connell Street,' McDonnell said. 'When I reached the narrow laneway running between Middle Abbey Street and Princes' Street two auxiliaries stepped out and held me up, demanding to know where I was going. I was searched, and on informing them that I was on my way home, was propelled by their boots.' He found O'Connell Street occupied by solders and auxiliaries. Later he learned that they had raided the La Scala restaurant and detained the patrons there for up to two hours.

'When the raiding party entered the restaurant they immediately went to the table that we had been at for the previous week and demanded of the waitress the names of the three men, giving a very accurate description of the three of us, and particularly describing the tall thin man wearing a new brown suit,' McDonnell noted. 'They insisted that we must have come into the building and that we must be hiding somewhere. However, they ransacked the place from cellar to garret, but needless to remark they didn't get us because we weren't there.' [23]

Later in his witness statement, McDonnell stated quite philosophically: "These, however, were the chances which had to be taken when dealing with men of the McCarthy type, who after all were only working for the pay they received." [24]

❦

In mid-April, with a ceasefire again on Lloyd George's mind, he sent Lord Derby to Dublin. [**Author's note**: Derby, born Edward George Villiers Stanley was the 17th Earl of Derby and had served as the British government's Minister of War from 1916-1918.]

Initially, the PM thought it was Collins who should be consulted but the conservative element in his party including Derby, thought otherwise. They felt it was de Valera who was the one to approach.

With the proper contacts made, Derby, travelling under the assumed name of Mr. Edwards, checked into the Gresham Hotel which faced out onto O'Connell Street, not far from the GPO. Michael assigned Tom Cullen and Liam Tobin the task of squiring the Englishman to and from his appointment with Dev. The meeting was scheduled for one of the Long Fellow's favourite rendezvous: the home of James O'Mara at #43 Fitzwilliam Place, just off of Leeson Street.

Joe Hyland, one of the Big Fella's usual drivers, was behind the wheel when the hackney motor pulled up in front of the Gresham. [**Author's note**: Joe and his brother Batty had an automotive garage in Denzille Lane, near Merrion Square, and often drove for Michael.]

In his Witness Statement given to the Bureau of Military History in 1952, Joe clearly remembered the Derby incident.

> One night Joe O'Reilly instructed me to go to the Gresham Hotel and pick up a Mr. Edwards there and I would be instructed to take him to a certain place. When I reached the Gresham Hotel I saw Tom Cullen and Bill [Liam] Tobin standing on the footpath. Tom Cullen told me I was to take this old fellow to O'Meara's (sic) at Fitzwilliam Place. He [Cullen] said, "He is not to be told his destination and you are to travel on a round-about route." With that Tom Cullen brought this gentleman to my car. He [Cullen] got in beside him and Liam Tobin got in front with me.
>
> I drove him for a considerable time through streets and side streets in Dublin and over several canal bridges. After a considerable time we reached O'Meara's. I left him there and Tom Cullen and Liam Tobin came back with me to the garage.
>
> After an hour we went back and picked up the old gentleman at O'Meara's and brought him direct, this time to the Gresham Hotel. By this time I knew who my passenger was – Lord Derby. He must have been surprised that it took such a long time to get to O'Meara's and such a short time to get to the Gresham. [25]

Later, though nothing concrete came of the man's visit to Ireland, Dev was heard to remark, "My time with Lord Derby was the first important contact between the British and ourselves."

❧

Joe Hyland recalled another adventure he shared with Tom Cullen and Joe O'Reilly. This time, however, the three men narrowly escaped capture.

[**Author's note**: As I've mention before, Tom and his fellow Republicans were constantly faced with the possibility of arrest. If you were an ordinary citizen, you might expect a night in jail and/ or a good beating just for 'luck.' If you were a 'wanted' person, as Tom was, you could expect more…jail, a beating, a trial and likely deportation. On the other hand, the authorities might just forego all the legal niceties and shoot you in the back of the head…'while trying to escape,' of course.]

In Joe Hyland's own words, he described the harrowing episode.

> I remember [the] many occasions I took Joe O'Reilly and the late Tom Cullen [then doubling as Dublin Brigade Quartermaster General] down to the South quays to take ammunition off Cross-Channel boats. I can vividly recall one incident. A consignment of ammunition was packed in soldiers kit bags.
>
> [The]…three of us loaded up my car with this ammunition and conveyed it to Pembroke Lane where some local battalion had a dump. On the way up from the boat, I turned into Clanwilliam Place and into Northumberland Road. There I was intercepted by a British patrol which had left Beggar's Bush Barracks. These patrols were sent out by the British unexpectedly as surprise tactics. At this particular time you were liable to meet them any place. [26]

Luckily, the British sergeant in charge, though not entirely satisfied with Joe's photograph on his vehicle permit, accepted his cover story about delivering the soldiers' baggage to Kingstown for shipment back to England. If the NCO had taken the time to examine the contents of the kit bags, the three IRA men, with little chance of escape, would have been hanged.

Joe concluded this episode with an obvious understatement, "I may say that both (sic) Tom Cullen, Joe O'Reilly and myself had a few unhappy moments while the [sergeant's] questioning was going on." [27]

*

As spring became summer, the tension between Mick and Dev turned palpable particularly over the Long Fellow's desire to stage a major military confrontation. Tom Cullen thought at the time that Dev was trying to exorcise the 1916 demons from his head by staging a successful, not a failed, attack on an important British holding in Dublin Town. Michael concurred with the Wicklow man.

Oscar Traynor, who'd replaced Dick McKee as O/C of the Dublin Brigade agreed with both Tom and Michael. The three men didn't think the IRA was in a position to challenge the British on such terms. The Brigade didn't have the manpower or military capability to match the Sassenach's. They feared only disaster would result. But regardless of their feelings, Traynor was ordered to investigate the possibilities of successfully pulling off such a confrontation.

Ryle Dwyer described de Valera's determination to have his way, reasoning which seemed largely based on wishful thinking.

> 'Something in the nature of a big action in Dublin was necessary in order to bring public opinion abroad to bear on the question of Ireland's case,' de Valera argued according to Traynor. 'He [Dev] felt that such an action in the capital city, which was as well known abroad as London or Paris, would be certain to succeed....' [28]

Two targets were immediately placed on the table for consideration: Beggar's Bush Barracks and the Custom House.

Beggar's Bush was a prime target because it was the HQ of the Black and Tans.

– It would be the popular choice because of all the hated violence those blighters have dished out, said Tom at the group's next meeting.

– Seizing the barracks would also be a major blow in limiting their activities here in town, added Tobin.

– On the other hand, the Custom House is a vital British administrative centre in Ireland, offered Frank Saurin.

T. Ryle Dwyer wrote: "It [the Custom House] was the headquarters of the Inland Revenue and various tax offices, the assay office, local government and the Companies Registration office." [29]

❧

Oscar Traynor, O/C of the Dublin Brigade, took responsibility for evaluating the merits of an attack on either site.

After careful consideration, the Custom House received the top nod. Beggar's Bush was walled and well reinforced with British military, while the Custom House lay virtually unprotected having no surrounding walls or military troops to initially ward off an attack.

Michael Foy noted:

> Since the Custom House was in [the] 2nd Battalion's area, Traynor gave operational control to its commandant, Tom Ennis. He intended using only his own men and 2nd Battalion members of the Squad until Paddy [O'] Daly protested to Collins that this would divide the Squad. Ennis grudgingly backed down but got his own back by giving the Squad a roving commission on the Custom House's periphery, neutralising guards, acting as look-outs and rounding up civilian visitors. [30]

It was decided by the IRA's leadership to burn the huge building rather than capturing and trying to hold it as a trophy of IRA defiance and resistance.

As a result, according to Dwyer, "The first battalion was to protect the outside of the building in the event of a surprise attack by the enemy, as well as deal with any fire station in their area. The third and fourth battalions were likewise to ensure that the fire brigades in their areas were blocked. The fifth was to cut communications between the Custom House and Dublin Castle." [31]

The men of the 2nd Battalion were responsible for entering and firing the building. The biggest Dublin Brigade operation since Easter, 1916 was planned to begin at 12.45 pm on May 25th.

In Paddy O'Daly's Witness Statement, he said:

> The Squad was to take charge of all the entrance doors of the Custom House. I posted my twenty men at the various doors. Their instructions were to allow nobody to leave the building once they went into position, but any civilian entering the building on business was to be admitted and then held prisoner so that the outside public would not be given the information that the building was held by the Volunteers. [32]

As for Cullen, Tobin, Thornton and the other Crow Street intelligence men, Collins gave strict orders that they were to stay away from the eastern end of the Quays. He didn't want everyone involved in the operation just in case something went wrong. Disappointed at not playing a part in the forthcoming battle, they reluctantly obeyed.

Initially opposed to the Custom House affair, Michael relented at the last minute. Taking his usual risk, the Big Fella cycled down to the Quays and wished the men 'good luck' on the morning of the attack.

But as carefully planned as things were, the attack was only a partial success. In their effort to protect civilians, the initial fire lighting was delayed. Then the Tans unexpectedly arrived at quayside…at first a single lorry load of them happened by, but almost immediately they were followed by more lorries and an armoured car.

Rifle fire and machine gun burst became general. A mass detainment of all persons, including some of Collins and Traynor's men, began under the direction of Auxiliary Cadets. To add to the debacle, many Volunteers and Squad members were wounded and five IRA men were killed.

Squad member Jimmy Slattery's hand was shattered by a bullet and Seán Doyle, wounded in the fray, managed to evade capture but died two days later. [**Author's note**: Slattery's right hand was badly injured, and soon after had to be amputated. Later, upon returning to active duty, he joked he was now 'a left-handed gunfighter.']

Vinnie Byrne received a terrible beating at the hands of two Auxies but escaped capture. Luckily, Paddy O'Daly and Joe Leonard successfully melted into the throng of people massing in Beresford Place, but most of the Squad were taken into custody by the Sassenach. Of the one hundred plus Volunteers and Squad members involved in the operation, over eighty were captured.

In summary, Michael Foy wrote: "IRA losses at the Custom House were severe, with five Volunteers dead and eighty-three captured. [The] 2nd Battalion, the operation's spearhead, had lost three men and almost sixty had been taken prisoner." [33]

[**Author's note**: Today, a Custom House Memorial plaque in the front garden of the building remembers those Irishmen who fought and died that day. It reads: "They gave their all; may they rest in peace. Edward Dorrens, Seán Doyle, Daniel Head, the brothers Patrick & Stephen O'Reilly who died in battle 25 May 1921 and officers & men of the 2nd Battalion, Dublin Brigade and other units of Dublin Brigade IRA who gave their lives for Irish freedom."]

On the other hand, the building was set alight and burned for nearly twenty-four hours. An unknown number of the enemy were killed or wounded. Additionally, British civil service operations were drastically disrupted.

> In reality the attack on the Custom House was a military disaster, but de Valera was interested in its propaganda value. It turned out to be a propaganda success and a political victory, because the British government came under intense international pressure to try to negotiate a settlement. [34]

※

From that day forward, though the air of mystery and the aura of secrecy that surrounded Michael Collins continued to grow, effectively he lost control of the Squad and his influence within the IRA began to ebb. Despite retaining his role as Director of Intelligence, his Crow Street operation was almost totally shut down. Michael's undercover operatives within the ranks of the Dublin police had been exposed with the exception of Dave Neligan. With all these sudden and dramatic changes, needless to say, Tobin, Cullen and Thornton were devastated.

In retrospect, Michael Collins had created his IRA intelligence network in Crow Street and formed his 'twelve apostles' to defeat Dublin Castle's network of spies and agents. He knew that if he could eliminate its key offensive cast, the Castle would be impotent.

Of Collins's tactics, Michael Foy further noted:

Without their police throughout the country how could they find the men they 'wanted'? Without their criminal agents in the capital how could they carry out that 'removal' of the [Irish] leaders that they considered essential to their [British] victory? Spies are not so ready to step into the shoes of their departed confederates as are soldiers to fill up the front in honourable battle. And even when the new spy stepped into the shoes of the old one, he could not step into the old one's knowledge. [35]

※

Other adjustments followed almost immediately. With IRA losses from the Custom House operation taking their toll, Traynor was forced to reorganise the Dublin Brigade. He joined the Brigade Volunteer ASU, the Squad and Michael's Crow Street intelligence corps into a single unit called the Dublin Guard with Paddy O'Daly as OC.

Though English intelligence failed them again, the British forces in Dublin, without their even realising it, had gained the lion's share of control in the city. The IRA, critically short of weapons and ammunition, had to curtail most of its operations. The newly organised Dublin Guard, however, did try to keep up offensive appearances by attacking soft targets: mostly off-duty Auxiliaries.

On 26 June, the Guard shot two British officers who were staying with their wives at the Mayfair Hotel. The two men were attacked in the hotel's dining room while having tea. One was shot in the chest and died immediately while the other was shot in the face but survived.

Despite its months and months of successes, Foy noted:

> But overall the IRA was effectively beaten in Dublin by late June 1921. Traynor's health had collapsed and his doctor sent him to convalesce in Wales, by which time the republican leadership was receptive to a truce. Thornton conceded that had one 'not taken place we would have found ourselves very hard set to continue the fight with any degree of intensity.' [36]

❧

The day after the Custom House affair, Michael had another close call. He was expected back at his Mary Street office after lunch. Fortunately, he didn't return. Instead of the Big Fella arriving, it was the Auxies who came.

Relying on a sudden hunch, Mick and Gearóid O'Sullivan stopped off at a pub and then went on to Gearóid's office.

Joe O'Reilly happened to see the British raid in Mary Street and cycled off in search of his boss. Finding him, Joe told the Big Fella what had just happened.

With a second raid on the place in a week, Michael was convinced there was a 'quisling' in his midst. Dejectedly, he told O'Reilly, – It's over! The game is up!

Sadly, James Mackay wrote:

O'Reilly was startled to see Michael in such deep despair. He had never seen him in such a black mood before, one moment deathly pale, the next extremely agitated. Normally Michael was a man of few words, but now he paced up and down speaking rapidly for over an hour. Later, in Devlin's, he broke down completely and wept bitterly, repeating over and over again, 'There's a traitor in the camp.'

Michael was also unduly upset at the loss of a favourite fountain pen; again his comrades were taken aback at the way such a trifle got to him. In fact, Michael, who had been working twenty hours a day and whose nerves were taut as a drawn bowstring, was on the verge of a complete mental breakdown. Then, suddenly, he stopped his ranting and raving and by some fantastic effort of will pulled himself together. [37]

❧

Understandingly, the impact of Ireland's general election on May 24th took a back seat to the Custom House affair. The vote in the North produced no surprises as unionists filled all the vacant seats for the British House of Commons. In the South, no polling took place as all sitting TDs were returned unopposed.

Sinn Féin, in fact, took all 124 seats in southern Ireland, plus the four seats allocated to the National University [UCD]. The only seats held by the southern Unionists were, in fact, the four seats allocated at Trinity College. As a result of this election the Six Counties officially became Northern Ireland, and Sir James Craig prime minister at Stormont, the Northern Irish parliament. Ireland was now effectively partitioned and the political situation sharply polarised. [38]

❧

[**Author's note**: Sometime in the early summer of 1921, Michael organised a Criminal Investigation Department (CID) that quickly became identified with the building at #36 Westland Row used as its headquarters, Oriel House. First headed by Liam Tobin, he was assisted by Tom Cullen and other associates of the Big Fella's now largely dismantled Crow Street intelligence operation as well as former detectives Dave Neligan, Ned Broy and Jim McNamara. Also joining were men of the Dublin Brigade's military intelligence corps plus former members of Mick's IRA assassination team, the Squad.

The exact date of its founding is cloaked in obscurity as are its often sinister, clandestine activities. But with the advent of the Truce, Oriel House became more active. Wearing plainclothes, its well-armed membership was *not* to be confused with being a 'civilian' police force.

Eunan O'Halpin, in his chapter entitled "Collins and Intelligence 1919-1923: From Brotherhood to Bureaucracy" which was included the book *Michael Collins and the Making of the Irish State* stated:

> When the Truce came into operation Collins' immediate concern appears to have been that the British might seek to steal a march by reorganising their intelligence services in Ireland in preparation for a resumption of hostilities, and the maintenance of vigilance against the British in the twenty-six counties remained his first intelligence priority until the Treaty was signed and ratified by the Dáil. His second priority was intelligence on political and military affairs in Northern Ireland, where nationalists were already suffering under the new Stormont regime and where there appeared to be possibilities for eventual action. [39]

O'Halpin further described Oriel House's primary mission.

> Its initial functions were to provide protection for key figures in the independence movement, to monitor the covert intelligence activities of British military and civilian agencies, and to tackle armed crime in Dublin. Its activi-

ties subsequently expanded to include intelligence work against opponents of the Treaty and, notoriously, the suppression of the IRA in Dublin during the Civil War. [40]

Michael sent a memo to W. T. Cosgrave who'd become the Chairman of the Provisional Government when Mick stepped down on 12 July 1922 to become the Free State's military Commander-in-Chief.

> The Government is aware of plots to murder the members of the Government who are carrying out the people's mandate to restore order to the country. They are further aware that certain Officers in the Army whose military services are well known are marked down similarly. [41]

Collins went on to say that anyone identified or apprehended carrying out such a plan would 'be held responsible and brought to account.'

Tim Pat later wondered:

> What part Collins himself played in the 'bringing to account' process as practiced by certain members of the Squad and ASU who found themselves in a Special Branch capacity in the CID HQ in Oriel House can only be speculated on. But certainly the Squad's Tan war policy of shoot-to-kill was often indistinguishable from its [Oriel House's] activities during the civil war. [42]

On 31 July 1922, with the Irish Civil War entering its second month, the leadership of Oriel House changed. Its oversight was added to the brief of TD Joe McGrath [Minister for Labour]. Possibly due to political conniving or Liam Tobin's ill health, day-to-day control of CID operations passed to Captain Pat Moynihan.

I also guess that with his friend and comrade Liam Tobin's departure, Tom Cullen also left knowing that a new position awaited them both...one secured by Michael in advance of his death. Liam and Tom were soon to become ADCs to Ireland's yet-to-be-appointed, new Governor-General.

With the death of Michael and Tobin's steady hand missing

from the tiller of Oriel House, its growing reputation of extra-legal political and policing activities escalated.

In his *Defending Ireland: The Irish State and its Enemies since 1922*, Eunan O'Halpin noted: "Oriel House succeeded in its task of suppressing small scale (IRA) republican activities in the Dublin area, not by the sophistication and efficiency of its intelligence work...but by the more direct method of striking terror into its opponents." [43]

In a self-published booklet entitled *Wolfe Tone Annual, 1962: Salute to the Soldiers of 1922*, author Brian O'Higgins documented "...at least twenty-five murders of (IRA) Republicans in the Dublin area alone." [44]

This supports C. S. Andrews's contention in his *Dublin Made Me that*, "It would, of course, be possible to suggest names but it would be undesirable to do so for the same reason that the names of the men responsible for the 153 'unauthorised murders' are better left unrecorded. They were Irishmen like us; I am sure that many of them regretted their activities." [45]

As can be inferred, the men and 'jobs' associated with Oriel House are shrouded in mystery. What role Tom Cullen played is unknown, but he certainly was not someone to treat intimidation and murder lightly. I feel that as the role of Oriel House expanded, Tom would have rejected any mindless use of violence based solely on one's own prejudice and Treaty beliefs. Tom Cullen was too skilled an intelligence officer and too familiar with recent War for Independence violence to treat such actions lightly.

With Michael immersed in bringing the Civil War to a rapid conclusion coupled with Liam Tobin's replacement as head of Oriel House, either for health, political or ethical reasons, I believe Tom left to devote his full energies in support of Collins's work.

During its short existence, several Oriel House men were killed 'in the line of duty' and the building became such a symbol of revulsion on the part of some that a number of attempts were made to blow it up.

At the end of October, 1923, the activities emanating from Oriel House ceased. The Civil War fighting had ended, but thousands of anti-Treaty IRA men were still being held in internment camps. They would be held well into 1924. But what wouldn't end was the bitterness, the hatred and the divisions the Treaty split and the war caused Ireland, not to mention all the illicit activities associated with Oriel House.]

❧

During the spring of 1921, the British government was pressurised by both local and international groups for its harsh policies toward and its callous treatment of the Irish people.

Irish and British leaders began holding meetings. Peace was in the air.

In early July, the bulldog General Macready and other top British brass met with Ireland's Éamonn Duggan and Robert Barton at Mansion House. A Truce was negotiated.

On the morning on Monday, 11 July 1921, British lorries, armoured cars and sundry military vehicles, all filled with troopers, began returning to their barracks across Ireland.

At twelve noon, on a beautiful, warm, sunny afternoon, church bells in Dublin and throughout the countryside began ringing, letting all know that the War for Independence was over.

That evening, Irishmen, women and children took to the streets. Hardly able to believe peace had returned, they celebrated, lit bonfires, danced, sang and celebrated as never before.

Tom Cullen packed his case and took the last evening train to Wicklow Town. He'd seen a lifetime of trouble…more than enough to satisfy any three men. His new life with Delia waited just an hour's ride south.

Michael Collins, still at work, looked up from his desk at #17 Harcourt Street. The sound of music and laughter drifted into the room on a warm summer's breeze. Rising, he walked over to the open window and looked down. A group of young people were walking arm in arm up the street…talking excitedly and laughing. The Big Fella watched as they disappeared up toward Stephen's Green. Smiling, he returned to his desk stacked high with papers.

Peace had finally returned to Ireland, and, please God, the shadow of the gunman was gone.

※

[**Author's note**: Discovering Tom's whereabouts or his activities after the Truce was declared proved difficult. I uncovered little information and very few references to him.

Where he lived is but an educated guess, but I imagine he and Delia moved in with her mother, as least initially. I believe she'd been residing with her step-brother J. J. and his wife Lil above their Wicklow shop in Abbey Street for the time prior to the war's end.

But I imagine it would have been difficult for Tom to stay away from Dublin. His close friendship with Michael Collins and the others would have drawn him back. Delia probably remained in Wicklow Town with her family when her husband went up north.

Knowing Collins, I believe Tom and Delia wouldn't have been destitute. They likely wouldn't have had to depend on family for a place to live or food for the table. During his time in Dublin, money was never a problem for Tom yet he wasn't a wealthy man. Surely, Mick would have seen to it that Tom always had a quid or two in his pocket over and above his Crow Street salary.

My guess is that Tom, Liam Tobin and Frank Thornton kept their flat in Grosvenor Road, at least for awhile. The Truce, though holding, was frequently violated and Michael certainly would've wanted his faithful troika close at hand, just in case.]

Tom and Delia were both in Dublin around August 22nd. In both Tim Pat Coogan's biography of Michael Collins and in Meda Ryan's book about Tom Barry, the couple was pictured at Tom Barry and Leslie Price's wedding reception in the back garden of Vaughan's Hotel.

Photographed among the assembled guests is Tom Cullen. He's likely standing on his tip toes, craning his neck to see the camera over Marie O'Reilly's hat.

[**Author's note**: Maybe Tom found himself standing in a dip in the lawn, necessitating his raised chin and upturned face. He obviously wanted to be in the shot, but not Michael. There's the Big Fella, in the back row with his head down, trying to avoid the camera's probing eye. For the Corkman, the need for caution and secrecy was obviously still an issue.

Delia, standing to Tom's right, looks very stylish wearing the latest millinery fashion as she peeks over the left shoulder of the taller Eoin O'Duffy.

Approximately forty men and a dozen or so women were grouped around the sober-faced couple. The only anomaly in the photograph is the egoist, Éamon de Valera...he's sitting *between* the two newly weds. (Why the cheek of the man!)]

Comfortably assembled behind 'Joint #1' were some of Ireland's finest revolutionaries, patriots and freedom fighters of the day. Beside Tom Barry, some of those present, and in no particular order, were: Dev, Gearóid O'Sullivan, Harry Boland, Liam Deasy, Countess Connie Markievicz, Michael Collins, Dick Mulcahy, Eoin O'Duffy, Liam Tobin, Emmet Dalton, Rory O'Connor, Liam Devlin, Joe O'Reilly and, of course, Tom Cullen.

Looking at the snap, I'm positive Tom, amid all the festivities of the day, would've paused to remember the many nights of comradery he and the others had spent in that hotel. Also on his mind would've been the many adventures he'd endured, escaping the long arm of British injustice, as he and others fled that legendary hostelry.

I also imagine both Tom and Delia likely recalled their own wedding, just eight months earlier and held under very different circumstances. Their vows were celebrated under tight security and in deathly fear of being interrupted by a police raid. But on that August day, everyone was relaxed, swapping 'war' stories and looking forward to an Ireland marked by peace and tranquillity.

❧

The next time Tom surfaces, he's in London with Mick as the Treaty negotiation talks are on the cusp of beginning in mid-October.

With hostilities on hold, the Big Fella had kept busy. His Minister for Finance duties and preparation for the peace talks would've occupied many of his waking hours. He also spent considerable time travelling the country on military inspection tours.

As summer 1921 came to an end, Michael was certain that Britain would never concede complete independence to her island neighbour and the Big Fella wanted Ireland's IRA to be ready in case hostilities reignited.

On 16 August, de Valera finally was formally elected President of the Irish Republic, a title he'd so boldly assumed two years earlier. In justification, Dev said it was necessary for its propaganda purposes while he was in America. Others knew the likely truth. The title was more ego enhancing than a political necessity.

❧

After a volley of letters between Lloyd George and de Valera, terms were agreed to for commencing formal peace talks. Arthur Griffith was chosen to lead Ireland's delegation. Michael would be its Vice-Chairman. Joining them were Robert Barton, Éamonn Duggan and George Gavin Duffy. A dozen secretaries and ancillary staff were selected to accompany the Irish plenipotentiaries.

James Mackay succinctly described the task the Irish delegates faced on the eve of the talks.

> At this juncture the long shadow of the Declaration of Independence published in January, 1919, lay across them. It was inevitable that, following the Truce, there would have to be some sort of compromise. De Valera realised this, and reminded the Dáil that he was no doctrinaire Republican. He refused to [publicly] let the Dáil place restrictions on the delegates, and would not even permit the Dáil to debate beforehand the sort of terms which Lloyd George might offer, and whether they would be acceptable or not. In fairness to de Valera, he was concerned lest word of such wrangling got back to Westminster, and thereby weakened the Irish bargaining position. On the other hand, no limit was ever laid down beyond which Collins and Griffith must not go in accepting an agreement. It was never defined – until Collins and Griffith returned from London with less than expected. But in October 1921 de Valera was

imploring Michael 'not to mention the word Republic'.
To Griffith, the President likewise besought some way
to 'get him out of this strait waistcoat of a Republic.' [46]

The main body of negotiators stayed at #22 Hans Place, leaving Dublin together on Saturday, 8 October.

One the other hand, Michael and his party departed from
Kingstown [later renamed Dun Laoghaire] the following day,
Sunday, 9 October.

Besides Tom Cullen, Mick's London party included Liam
Tobin, Emmet Dalton, Ned Broy, Joe Guilfoyle, Joe Dolan and
the seventeen-year-old Seán McBride, son of Maude Gonne, Irish
revolutionary, feminist and actress, and the executed 1916 leader
Major John McBride.

The Big Fella's party of intelligence men and personal bodyguards resided several blocks away from Griffith's group at #15
Cadogan Gardens in the fashionable suburb of South Kensington,
London.

[**Author's note**: With Mick's emergence from his self-imposed
War for Independence isolation, any chance of his remaining an
anonymous warrior, if hostilities were to resume, was gone. The
same can be said for his Crow Street intelligence lieutenants, Tom
Cullen and Liam Tobin.

On the surface, Michael's operatives, living at Cadogan
Gardens, could come and go away from the limelight, but that
was only in theory. Also staying at #15 were the delegation's
pressmen, headed up by Mick's good friend Diarmuid O'Hegarty.
Assisting him were Joe McGrath, Dan MacCarthy, Seán Milroy
and others. Their presence only helped bring the full glare of the
public spotlight to focus on the assembled Irishmen. There was
no hope of hiding Collins and his men from notoriety.]

Though the house in Cadogan Gardens was not a sumptuous
accommodation, it was certainly comfortable for men who "…like
Collins and [his] associates like Tobin and Cullen knew what it was
to spend nights in the open, literally within seconds of death." [47]

Tim Pat Coogan, later in his Collins biography, stated:

> The houses where the delegates stayed were not especially grand by London standards but consider the

effects of the following description of a party at Hans Place (on 10 November 1921) on the imaginations of flying-column men who slept fifteen or twenty to a room in wet clothes– and made sure they broke nothing and, if they could, paid for everything before they left.

When [Coogan, quoting from Napoli MacKenna's memoir] the feast was at its height Mick with Liam Tobin, Tom Cullen, Emmet Dalton, Joe Guilfoyle and Joe Dolan joined us [Griffith and the other delegates at #22 Hans Place]. They were jovial boisterous men who preferred horseplay to formalities. It was not long before they began throwing cushions at one another, then tangerine oranges, apples, and nuts from the table, and finally coal from the coal-scuttles! [48]

※

[**Author's note**: Reluctant to detour too far down the road of Michael's love life, a short discussion at this point seems appropriate. Much as been written of it and even more speculated about it.

As Meda Ryan described in her book *Michael Collins and the Women Who Spied for Ireland* (2006), "To the young ladies who knew him, Mick Collins was a tall, dark, handsome man with sharp intellect and a mysterious aura. He had no difficulty in getting them to do intelligence work for him." [49]

During the height of the War for Independence [1919-1920], Mick's girlfriend was twenty-year-old Madeline 'Dilly' Dicker.

Meda Ryan described her as "… light-hearted, musical, beautiful and full of bounce. Her personality appealed to Mick and she accepted that he had to duck in and out of her life as the occasion demanded." [50]

Ryan, a gifted author, went on to add more detail.

In the early days (of the War for Independence) Dilly took messages to Liam Tobin and Tom Cullen about meeting times and places but as time progressed a romance (with Collins) blossomed.And just as Susan Killeen (an earlier Collins flame from his London post office days) had entertained him with poetry, Dilly played the piano to ease his tired mind. She would also play the harp and zither in the background while Mick scribbled on his spiral notepad.

Many a night Mick would arrive (into Dilly's house on Mountjoy Street) with a paper-fist of bull's-eyes (boiled hard sweets), which they would savour on the tram to Dalkey as he headed out to meet Liam Tobin and Tom Cullen. The pair would sit at the front after Mick had a brief word with the driver, who always seemed to be 'one of ours.'[51]

In May, 1919, during the by-election campaign in South Longford for Joe McGuinness, Michael, accompanied by his friend Harry Boland, stayed at the Grenville Arms, run by the Kiernan family. There the two men met the four Kiernan sisters. Harry soon fancied Catherine Brigid 'Kitty' Kiernan while Michael was attracted to her sister Helen.

A month later, Harry departed for America to join de Valera, leaving the love of his life in the care of his best friend Michael.

Between June, 1919 and the eve of the London Treaty negotiations, Michael and Kitty gradually saw more and more of each other. Contrary to popular myth, Harry's frequent absences did not make Kitty's heart grow fonder.

With Collins supporting the Anglo-Irish Treaty and, in due course, his formal engagement to Kitty at Christmas, 1921, Harry and Mick's friendship collapsed. Eventually in the spring of 1922, Collins, a supporter of the Treaty, and Boland, who sided with de Valera's anti-Treaty position, became political and personal rivals.

On the evening of 30 July, as events sadly played out, Harry Boland, who'd been staying at the Grand Hotel in Skerries, was wounded in a Free State army raid. At first, he was taken to Skerries (Free State) military barracks. Four hours later, the seriously wounded man was transferred to Portobello Barracks in Dublin then on to St. Vincent's Hospital in Stephen's Green.

Harry died on Wednesday, 2 August. Not surprisingly, Collins was crushed by his death. In a letter to Kitty, written on August 3rd, Michael wrote in part:

Last night I passed Vincent's Hospital and saw a small crowd outside. My mind went into him lying dead there and I thought of the times together, and whatever good there is in any wish of mine, he certainly had it. Although the gap of 8 or 9 months was not forgotten – of course no one can ever forget it – I only thought of him with the friendship of the days of 1918 and 1919. They tell me that the last thing he said to his sister Kathleen, before he was operated on, was 'Have they got Mick Collins yet?' I don't believe it so far as I'm concerned and, if he did say it, there is no necessity to believe it. I'd send a wreath but I suppose they'd return it torn up. [52]

As fate would have it, Collins too was killed three weeks later. Kitty eventually married Felix Cronin, the Quartermaster of the new Irish army. They would have two sons, the second she named Michael Collins Cronin.

Many inches of newspaper column have been devoted to Michael's 'supposed affairs' with the married Lady Hazel Lavery and Moya Llewelyn Davies. Talk of 'a child' occasionally surfaces. Regardless of all the gossip, the myth that was Michael Collins and the women in his life continues and endures.]

❧

Piaras Béaslaí commented on Michael's time in London.

Collins, had, indeed, little leisure during these days in London. [He]…was present at almost every meeting of the Peace Conference and its [many] sub-committees. Besides that he had a series of interviews daily with various persons in connection with Irish affairs. Tobin, who acted as Director of Intelligence in his absence, and Tom Cullen visited him in London, and he still kept in touch with the Intelligence Department and the business of the Ministry of Finance. [53]

Tom Cullen spent the next two months going back and forth between Dublin and London with Michael. Sometimes he'd remain in Dublin looking after Mick's interests there.

On one particular occasion, toward the end of November, Collins had spent a frustrating weekend keeping the Irish cabinet informed of the London delegation's progress. On the way to catch the mail boat to Holyhead, Michael complained to Tom, "I've been there all day and I can't get them to say Yes or No, whether we should sign or not." [54]

During Collins's London stay, Margery Forester wrote of the strain the Big Fellow was under. To ease his mind, Michael called on his closest friends for help. "Pressure of work occupied time he [Mick] would otherwise have spent with Kitty. He had, indeed warned her so, and delegated Tom Cullen and Gearóid O'Sullivan to look after her, a thoughtful gesture which she could hardly appreciate." [55]

❧

About two o'clock in the morning of 6 December 1921, the two delegations returned to the #10 Downing Street's conference room. After several minor alterations, the Irish and British negotiators signed the Anglo-Irish Treaty.

"When [Lord] Birkenhead appended his signature to the articles of agreement, he turned to Michael and said, 'I may have signed my political death-warrant tonight.'

The Big Fellow replied, 'I may have signed my actual death-warrant.'" [56]

❧

Michael and Arthur Griffith returned to Dublin on Thursday morning, 8 December. Tom Cullen was waiting for them as they arrived at the North Wall.

At the bottom of the gangway, the Big Fella seized Tom by the shoulder.

– Tom, what are our own [IRB] fellows saying?

– They're saying what's good enough for you, Mick, is good enough for them.

The full truth would soon become readily apparent.

❧

The London Irish were ecstatic. The Dublin Irish were less so.

He [Michael] knew in his heart of hearts that de Valera would not accept the Treaty, if only for selfish reasons. It was a compromise, the best possible in the circumstances, but it was not de Valera's compromise. Now, too late, it dawned on Michael that de Valera had anticipated as much, and that was the [real] reason why he had refused to lead the delegation. [57]

Michael had every right to be disheartened. The seven-person Irish Cabinet split over the document, finally endorsing its ratification by a four to three vote. [Collins, Griffith, W. T. Cosgrave & Robert Barton voted for its approval while Dev, Cathal Brugha & Austin Stack voted against it.] Thus, despite the divide, the Treaty was forwarded to the Dáil for debate and possible approval.

[**Author's note**: On 10 December, the Treaty received another important endorsement. The Supreme Council of the IRB, of which Michael was head, affirmed its support for the document, voting eleven in favour with four members opposed.]

On Wednesday, 14 December, the Dáil Éireann Treaty Debates began at University College Dublin on Earlsfort Terrace.

After two weeks of contentious and bitter exchanges sandwiched around the Christmas and New Year's break, the Dáil ratified the Anglo-Irish Treaty by a sixty-four to fifty-seven vote on Saturday, 7 January 1922.

Three days later, a vote to re-elect President Éamon de Valera was defeated fifty-eight to sixty. Dramatically, de Valera and many of his TD supporters walked out as Arthur Griffith was elected Ireland's second president. Soon after, Michael Collins was chosen to head Ireland's one-year Provisional 'caretaker' government while the various terms of the Treaty were gradually implemented. Of critical importance would be drafting a constitution and staging an election for the Irish people to express their approval or disapproval of the agreement.

❧

During the next six months, Ireland experienced many seismic upheavals as the government, the IRA and the Irish people split over the terms of the Anglo-Irish Treaty.

Michael and his followers supported the document and became known as pro-Treatyites or Free-Staters, the Treaty's name for Ireland's new twenty-six-country unit [Soarstát na hÉireann]. A new Irish National army was formed, and with British help, it was equipped and training begun. Gradually, the country started returning to a modicum of normalcy.

Dev and his followers opposed the Treaty and became known as anti-Treatyites or IRA Republicans, named for their uncompromising stance that refused to accept anything but a thirty-two-county Irish 'Republic.' Their alternative to the Treaty was going back to war with England with the intent of winning the 'complete victory' Ireland had been unable to win during the previous three years.

In April, IRA Republicans, led by Rory O'Connor, Liam Lynch, Liam Mellowes and others occupied key buildings in Dublin as a visible protest to the pro-Treatyites and as an affirmation of their determined resistance to the agreement with Britain. The structures occupied by the IRA included the Four Courts [on the Quays], the Masonic Hall [Rutland Square], the Ballast Office [corner of Aston Quay & O'Connell's Bridge], Moran's Hotel [Talbot Street] and Kilmainham Gaol [west of town].

During the past months since the Dáil ratified the Treaty, the British government had been exerting great pressure on Michael Collins's Provisional government. It wanted an orderly implementation of all the Treaty's terms. No quarter to the anti-Treaty followers was offered or given.

With Michael in charge of the Provisional government, the great majority of British army personnel left Ireland and returned home. Most of their former British barracks were taken over by Free State forces, but selected barracks were contested and a few fell into IRA Republican hands.

On 16 January 1922, Collins accepted the British handoff of Dublin Castle along with its administrative personnel who were prepared to work for Ireland's cause. Additionally, a new Free State police force was formed. Branded the Civic Guard, it was first headed by Michael Staines, then seven months later by Eoin O'Duffy.

But the obvious thorn in everyone's side was the growing realisation that Ireland was steadily marching down the road toward Civil War. Old friends and War for Independence allies were choosing sides and preparing to face off. Michael Collins, Tom Cullen and their followers, filled with frustration, anger and disillusionment over the prospects of having to line up against their old comrades, did their best to find a way out of the predicament.

> The opposing sides called each other names and one cast doubts on the other's republican parentage. Neither side paid any attention to what the other was saying. The British for their part made little or no distinction between them even when handing over posts and equipment: they were all 'Shinners' to them. Many who took opposing sides afterwards admitted that they could as easily have gone one way as the other. It was force of circumstances at the time, a flick of a coin. [58]

Two other dynamics emerged as winter turned to spring. With his resignation from active participation in the Irish government, de Valera's influence in the politics of the country diminished. On the pro-Treaty side, while Michael tried walking the narrow line between the two opposing forces of former comrades, Arthur Griffith's views hardened in favour of the pro-Treatyites.

Mackay astutely observed:

> It was at this time that the close comradeship that had grown up between Michael and Griffith during the negotiations began to flounder. Griffith saw all too clearly that civil war was imminent and probably unavoidable. It was imperative that the campaign should be as short, sharp and decisive as possible. [59]

[**Author's note**: Though I could find no written record of exactly when Tom Cullen 'formally' enlisted in the nascent Irish national army, I imagine it was in June or July of 1922, on the cusp of the Civil War or immediately after its outbreak. It would've been then that Michael Collins rewarded his loyal friend with the rank of commandant-general. (Also Tobin and Thornton were likely inducted at the same time as well. Liam was awarded the rank of major-general while Frank was confirmed a colonel.)

Later in August, 1922, at both Arthur Griffith and Michael's funerals, Tom wore the uniform of a commandant-general. But a month earlier, when Tom most likely presented Michael with the gift of an officer's sword, he referred to himself as a 'major-general.'

I believe the 'Cullen-Collins sword ceremony' occurred in July to mark the advent of Michael's short-lived military career.

According to John Duggan in his book, *A History of the Irish Army*, "Collins, who was head of the Provisional Government established by the Treaty, did not enter the Regular Army until the start of the Civil War. He then became Commander-in-Chief with full General's rank and had his office in Portobello Barracks." [60]

Finally, again concerning Tom's military rank, his cemetery marker denotes 'Major-General' and from 1922 on, the literature credits Tom with that rank.]

In the spring of 1922, as Ireland struggled to resolve its pro- and anti-Treaty differences, a 'possible' acquaintance of Tom Cullen's, a member of the newly formed Irish Guard, recalled some of his thoughts and experiences in an unpublished memoir written in 1952. Much like the 1913-1921 Witness Statements recorded by the staff of the National Archives, begun in 1947, Eamonn Cunningham authored a personal accounting of events that took place in 1922 Dublin. They would've been ones very familiar to Tom.

Edward Francis 'Ned' Cunningham, usually referred to as Eamonn Cunningham, was born on 12 August 1900. His Óglaig na hÉireann Statement of Service in the Defence Forces listed his period of enlistment extending from 10 April 1922 to 14 June 1957...a period of thirty-five years and sixty-six days. He retired as a Company Quartermaster Sergeant with an 'exemplary' service record...a fine and dedicated Irishman there is no doubt.

Eamonn commenced his chronicle with a personal comment explaining his reason for writing.

> During my 30 years of service with the Irish Army (it goes back to March 1922), it has often occurred to me to write an article on the Army from the setting up of the Irish Free State and the "coming into Barracks" of the Irish Republican Army (or that part of the I.R.A. who agreed with the Treaty.) I have always expected that some more worthy writer would tackle the job, but to date (June 1952) no writer that I know of has taken on the task. If my effort proves unworthy of publication, well, I hope it will be a help, at least, to some more worthy writer.
>
> Many of my old comrades will, I feel sure, enjoy such an article, and it should be interesting and instructive historically, to the younger generation. [61]

He next briefly recalled his early years spent living in England before returning to Ireland in the spring of 1922.

> I was President of the Huddersfield branch [located in West Yorkshire about two hundred miles north of London] of the Irish Self-Determination League (I. S. D. L.) in England and a member of the Sheffield [South Yorkshire] District Council I. S. D. L., 1920-1921. [The I.S.D.L. was established in Britain in 1919 to rally the support of Irish, then living in Britain, for Ireland's quest for independence. Attendance reached approximately 20,000 and was limited to Irish citizens or their direct descendants.]

Those political affiliations gave me the right to enter Marlboro Hall (now Coláiste Caoimhín in Dublin) Glasnevin in March 1922, as a Free State soldier. The O.C. of Marlboro Hall at that time was Comdt. P. [likely Patrick] O'Connor (later Col. O'Connor), and Capt. Ned Breslin [a former member of Collins's Squad] was, I believe, 2nd I/C [in charge]. It was necessary at that time to show proof of membership of the IRA, Sinn Féin, or kindred association to become a member of the Free State Army.

Uniforms were only in the course of manufacture, and very few of our garrison were uniformed. My first guard duty was performed in civilian attire. However, I was one of the lucky ones and soon received my full uniform issue, of which I was very proud. I recall the people of Dublin standing to look at us, as the uniform was then a novelty. Some of the boys were so anxious to be uniformed that they wore semi mufti, and it was not uncommon to see an IRA man (as we all termed ourselves then) parading O'Connell Street with civilian trousers, army tunic and cap or vice versa, etc.

However tranquillity was not to reign. The Smith-field meeting of the IRA made a split in the I.R.A. complete and the I.R.A. broke into two sections: one section the Free State Army or Regulars. The other section, we termed Irregulars. Let me comment on this, that in my humble opinion, it was a sad happening and a very bad climax to the great era of unity, for the fight for Ireland's freedom.

As one who was serving with the Regulars, I can vouch for the sincerity of purpose that existed among us. We were men who sincerely believed that The Treaty gave us a great help towards achieving complete inde-pendence for all Ireland. The chance to get the British Military out of our country, to secure arms, equipment, etc., a Police Force, in fact we could not understand how such a great opportunity should be scorned by anyone, but then, of course, we were young, and had not the political knowledge of the older leaders, so if history proves us wrong, let this explanation excuse us. When the Irregulars took over public buildings, as they did the Four Courts, the Ballast Office, and several others in Dublin, I could see we were heading into Civil War, and when we discussed it among ourselves, none of us wished for such a thing to happen.

In April 1922 I was with a Detachment which went from Marlboro Hall to (Wellington Barracks) now Griffith Bks. And there The Dublin Guards were being formed. The minimum height for The Dublin Guards was then 5'8". I became a Dublin Guard (not Civic Guard or Garda Siochána) as younger readers might misinterpret. [62]

[**Author's note**: Wellington Barracks was taken over as a Free State military installation on 22 April 1922.]

John Duggan commented on the public's response to the army's call for recruits in both the Guard and National army.

"By April 1922, 3,500 had enlisted (in the Dublin Guard). The expansion of the active service unit (ASU) was well under way. The (Dublin) Guards went into the 'Bush' (Beggar's Bush Barracks was first occupied by the Free State army on 29 January 1922) as a company in February. In March they were a battalion with (Paddy) O'Daly still in command; in May they became a brigade...." [63]

The Free State army also rapidly expanded in size during the early months of 1922.

About this, Duggan noted: "The government now got an overwhelming response to its well-timed 'Call to Arms'. Recruitment proceeded at the rate of 1,000 a day until a strength of 60,000 was reached." [64]

As a result of this unprecedented enrolment, the Dublin Guard and National army experienced general disorganisation coupled with some personal inconveniences. Besides lack of proper uniforms and military equipment, many were forced to endure payless paydays. In that vein, Eamonn mildly complained, "Up to this, tho, 6 or 7 weeks had elapsed [and] many of us had received no pay." [65]

Another issue quickly surfaced, causing resentment. The new Irish army lacked an adequate cadre of training NCOs. As a consequence, former British soldiers with military and combat experience were recruited to train Irish enlistees; some of these soldiers had seen active duty in Ireland, facing off against the IRA! Needless to say, this didn't go down well with Irish Republicans and nationalists who justifiably resented their presence.

Further along in his memoir, the then Corporal Cunningham described his first combat experience.

> We were to form the Ceremonial Unit of the Army. I was posted to "B" Coy. (Comdt. J. [Joe] Leonard was our O.C.) and we were not long formed when "B" Coy. proceeded to Kilkenny where the Irregulars were in occupation of Ormonde Castle and a Police Barracks. [It was there that]…we got our first shooting experience in the [approaching] Civil War. [66]

[**Author's note**: The events Eamonn described occurred in May, 1922, just prior to the official outbreak of the Civil War. IRA Republicans had taken over some buildings in Kilkenny Town and the Dublin Guard was sent to recapture them.]

> The fighting was not bitter as neither side were anxious to cause casualties, and on all sides one could hear such remarks as "fire into the air," "hit near the window, not through it," etc. and indeed, we actually ceased fire for meals and sleep, as no firing was heard by night.
>
> We had some excitement such as our armoured car crashing in through the gates at Ormonde Castle and the ultimate surrender of the Irregular garrison and their being placed in the barbed wire compound in Kilkenny Barracks.
>
> Another amusing incident occurred which is worth relating. I was appointed Acting Sergt of a guard which took over Kilkenny Prison [likely a jail]. On the first

night of my guard duties, I noticed that my sentries showed signs of alcoholic intoxication. I was puzzled at this, and made investigations to discover that the members of my guard had located some casks of port wine in the prison and were freely partaking of it.

The casks contained seized wine which the British had left after them when they vacated the prison and seemingly had not handed [it] over.

When the Kilkenny incident concluded we came back to Dublin for one of the proudest moments in my life, the taking over of Portobello Barracks from the British Forces. [67]

[**Author's note:** Of that Kilkenny episode, John Duggan wrote:

Early in May there were clashes again in Kilkenny but, though there was fierce fighting for Ormond Castle and a profligate expenditure of ammunition, causalities were minimal. Old comrades were loath to kill each other. A detachment of the Dublin Guards (the ASU) was again hurried there to restore order, which they did.] [68]

Back in Dublin, Eamonn personally described the events of 17 May. At 3 p.m., Commandant-General Tom Ennis, O/C of the 2nd Eastern Division, led Irish National army troops into Portobello Barracks to take possession of that military compound from Major Clarke, 5th Battalion, Worcestershire Regiment.

Tom Cullen could well have been present when Eamonn marched in. Soon, Portobello Barracks would become National army GHQ under the command of General Michael Collins.

Crowds of Dubliners lined the Route, particularly around Portobello, in windows, on roofs, walls, every vantage point was taken up and when the Union Jack came down, and the Irish Tricolour went up the flag pole, to the cheering of the vast crowd, it was indeed a day to remember and a proud moment for us taking part. Companies of British soldiers were formed up on the square and companies of the Irish Army [were too].

One thing struck me very much, that was the cleanliness of the Barracks in general. It was indeed a credit to the British Army everything was copiously clean. [69]

[**Author's note:** I found Eamonn's account of 'coming into barracks' interesting. I've often been told that when the British army handed over a barracks, the sergeant-major made sure the base of the flagpole was sawed almost completely through. Then, as the last Tommy exited, a top NCO would give it a good kick with his boot and the flagstaff would ceremoniously topple to the ground.

If this had happened in Eamonn's presence, surely he would have commented.]

❧

The pro-/anti-Treaty jousting greatly disturbed London. Annoyed and concerned that Collins wasn't able or willing to implement the full terms of his Treaty obligations, and that he was currying favour with his old IRA comrades, Lloyd George and Winston Churchill stepped up the pressure on Michael.

Duggan stated:

The British grew increasingly uneasy at the way the situation was developing. Apart from the occupation of the Four Courts, large areas in the south and west appeared to be occupied by anti-treaty forces, and there were even clashes between pro-treaty forces and British troops in the Belleek and Pettigo areas. Contingency plans for reoccupation were drawn up. [70]

On 16 June, the ratification or not of the Anglo-Irish Treaty was put to a vote by the Irish people on the same day the new constitution was published. Seventy-two percent of the voting public whole-heartedly approved of the agreement. With the polling ended, eighty-nine pro-Treaty TDs were elected while only thirty-six anti-Treatyite TDs were affirmed.

Now, with the war drums beating louder and louder, the Big Fella finally "…made up his mind that the public would not support 'going another round with Britain.'" [71]

Tim Pat Coogan described Michael's determined mood to now stand up for Ireland in its time of crisis.

The worst fate that can befall a nation was about to strike Ireland: civil war. [Quoting Collins's words from the Irish Independent 29/6/1922, the historian continued] 'The safety of the Nation is the first law and henceforth we shall not rest until we have established the authority of the people of Ireland in every square mile under their jurisdiction.' With these words Michael Collins took off the gloves and went to war with his former friends. Even though the new National Army was in a chaotic, disorganised condition, once he made up his mind to fight the result was practically a foregone conclusion. [72]

※

On 22 June, Field Marshal General Sir Henry Wilson, a bitterly hated opponent of Irish nationalists and Republicans, was shot and killed in front of his home by two Irishmen, Reggie Dunne, the O/C of the London IRA and Joe O'Sullivan, one of his trusted men. The retired general lived in a Victorian home on a residential street at the corner of Eaton and Belgrave Place, not far from Victoria rail station.

Both men were captured as they made their escape. O'Sullivan, who'd lost a leg in the World War, had difficulty controlling his bicycle after the attack. Dunne, having made his getaway returned to help his fallen companion. It was then that the two were arrested.

Michael, thinking it was a repeat of the McKee and Clancy incident, dispatched his trusted intelligence officer Tom Cullen to London to try and arrange for their escape. But for once in his life, Tom failed Michael. Try as he might, even with the help of the local IRB and IRA, the two Irish revolutionaries were tried, convicted and on 10 August, they were hanged in London's Wandsworth Gaol.

✻

Tragically, Civil War fighting abruptly broke out in the early morning hours of 28 June when Michael ordered the Four Courts attacked by his Free State army.

In just over a week, fighting was reported in other parts of the country as Free State soldiers took the offensive.

Eamonn Cunningham remembered that fateful day. Early on the morning of June 28th, he and his fellow Dublin Guard were back in action.

> When the siege of the Four Courts began, again, it was the Dublin Guard that got the job. I recall moving out about midnight with 20 rounds of ammunition each. Down Rathmines Rd. into Harcourt St., Grafton St., O'Connell St., Henry St., Mary St., across Capel St. and into the back streets my section took up position in the Medical Mission Hall [most likely in Chancery Street, immediately behind the Four Courts] from where we could hear the Four Courts garrison (Irregulars) conversing among themselves.
>
> The start of the attack was to be signalled by the explosion of 2 grenades. Our orders were to open rifle fire when the explosion was heard. We had not long to wait, and when the grenades were exploded, the rattle of rifle fire broke out as the Four Courts garrison were also ready. Their bullets ripped the ceiling of the room we occupied in the Medical Mission Hall. Women and children, who were living in the vicinity added to the din by screaming and crying. An early casualty in our room added to our difficulties, but it turned out to be only a flesh wound on the back of the neck.
>
> None of us relished the idea of firing at our brother Irishmen and I had several proofs that our opponents in the Four Courts were not anxious to inflict casualties either. I will relate one of them.

One evening I took the chance of looking into the Four Courts yard from a window of a room we were occupying in the Four Courts Hotel. [Apparently, Eamonn and the others had relocated from the Medical Mission around to the southwest corner of the Four Courts complex where the Four Courts Hotel was located.] I had been looking into the yard [of the Four Courts] for some minutes and nothing happened. Consequently, I felt secure, and actually leaned out the window. (My barricade was a mattress.) Then a burst of machine gun fire ripped through the top of the window. When the burst of fire ceased, a voice which was very near said, "It's a good job I know you Cunningham, or I would not have fired high. Get back from the windows well." I did! [73]

On 4 July 1922, the *New York Times* reported:

Dublin, July 3. – The Dublin Guards, many of whom were on active service in the World War and were trained in street fighting, are playing a prominent part in the attack on the remaining rebel posts. They are using rifles, grenades, bombs and machine gun barrages, and under this hail of varied fire the small garrisons holding the different fortified posts are retiring. Tunnels have been discovered through which some of the irregulars have managed to escape. [74]

❦

By July 5th, street fighting in Dublin had ended as the thrust of the fighting now shifted to the countryside, principally to the southeast and then the southwest.

On 12 July, the Council of War of the Provisional government met and Michael Collins was appointed Commander-in-Chief of the Free State national army. He dutifully handed over the reins of the Provisional Government to his respected associate W. T.

Cosgrave and Mick took up the mantle of leading the army, in what he hoped was to be a short, straightforward and relatively painless tour of duty.

It was on the 15th or soon after that Tom Cullen presented Michael with the gift of his specially engraved officer's sword.

One month later to the day, Arthur Griffith, exhausted by events of the last twelve months and suffering from an acute case of tonsillitis, died unexpectedly of 'heart failure' in St. Vincent's Nursing Home in Dublin.

Arthur, only fifty-one, had been in poor health for some time. The stress of the war, his imprisonments, the difficult negotiations with the British over the terms of a peace agreement, the frequent journeys back and forth to London, and finally, the recent national bitterness over the Treaty split had broken his health. On the advice of his doctor, Griffith had been admitted to the nursing home for rest and recovery.

Michael, who was on a tour of military installations in the west of Ireland at the time of Griffith's death, returned to Dublin for his old friend and mentor's funeral on August 16th.

It was on that day that Michael Collins and Tom Cullen were last pictured together with other members of the GHQ general staff as they marched in Griffith's funeral procession behind his coffin. It was the first time the Big Fella had appeared in public in his military uniform.

Since Portobello Barracks had become Michael's GHQ, moving over from Beggar's Bush Barracks, Tom and Joe O'Reilly had been living in its officers' quarters near the house Michael now occupied.

The next evening, Thursday, 17 August, Mick attended an evening dinner party at the home of Moya and Crompton Llewelyn Davies in Furry Park. Moya was a dyed-in-the-wool Republican and had carried messages for the Big Fella during the War for Independence. Her husband of twelve years was a successful lawyer and confidant of PM Lloyd George. Also sitting around the elegantly set table were Sir John and Lady Lavery, Sir Horace and Lady Plunkett, Piaras Béaslaí and Joe O'Reilly.

Just prior to dining, Joe informed Michael a sniper was rumoured to be on the estate.

Michael instructed his body guards, of which Tom Cullen was mostly likely one, to search the property. They spotted a former Connaught Ranger, a man named Dixon, holding a high-powered rifle, in a tree overlooking the house. Collins's men marched the hapless man away from the house and shot him.

On Saturday, 19 August, Dick Mulcahy had breakfast with Michael, who was suffering from a severe cold and stomach pains. [Throughout the summer of 1922, Collins had endured a painful case of gastric ulcers.] I wouldn't be surprised if Tom Cullen and Liam Tobin had sat in on the meal. It likely was the last time the three good friends saw Michael alive.

Michael left early on Saturday morning to continue his tour of the southwest that had been interrupted by Griffith's death. Besides a military inspection of Free State barracks that he felt would be a morale-booster for National army soldiers, he planned to visit some of his old boyhood haunts and visit family. Michael also hoped to continue peace talks with some of his former IRA associates who'd declared their neutrality in the present conflict and were acting as intermediaries with their Republican comrades. Finally, the Big Fella wanted to commandeer a large amount of money the IRA had taken from a special banking tax account in Cork.

Tim Pat described Michael's departure.

> Mulcahy says that before he [Collins] left Portobello on his last journey he was 'writhing with pain.' He roused a friend to say goodbye and joined him in a farewell drink. Told by Joe Sweeney he was a fool to go he replied, 'Ah, whatever happens, my own fellow countrymen won't kill me.' As he [Michael] walked down the stairs to wait for his armoured car he tripped and his gun went off, an ill-omen. Roused by the shot, Joe O'Reilly rushed to his window. He saw Collins outside, a small green kitbag on his back, his head bent in depression. O'Reilly pulled on his trousers and rushed downstairs. Too late; the Big Fellow was gone. [75]

❧

As the Civil War ferocity continued to mount, Tom Cullen and Joe O'Reilly waited in Dublin Town for Michael's return.

Delia Cullen remained in Wicklow Town, living with her mother.

Kitty Kiernan, home in Granard, came to the realisation that one of the dates she and Michael had chosen for their wedding, 22 August, seemed unlikely now with him heading off for West Cork.

Colonel Frank Thornton had been sent by Michael to affirm that the area around Clonmel was free of IRA Republicans. The anti-Treatyites had recently abandoned their position in Tipperary Town and had moved on Clonmel, which was now under the command of Paddy O'Connor and the National army. But while on tour, Frank and his men were ambushed and he was badly wounded in an IRA gun battle.

Major-General Liam Tobin accompanied Major-General Emmet Dalton on his Free State seaborne landing and capture of Cork City. On 9 August, Dalton's forces landed at Passage West with other soldiers coming ashore at Youghal and Glendore. Liam took part in the heavy fighting that was encountered at Rochestown, but the IRA was surprised and overwhelmed by the manoeuvre and its members retired, fleeing west. Two days later General Dalton victoriously marched into Cork City without further resistance.

Liam, suffering from scabies and mental exhaustion, returned to Dublin just prior to Mick's departure on 20 August.

❧

Early in the morning on 23 August, the word of Michael's death at Béalnabláth reached Portobello Barracks in Dublin. Adjutant Gearóid O'Sullivan was the first to receive the coded message. He immediately went and informed Emmet Dalton's brother Charlie. Tim Pat described what happened next.

> He [Gearóid] did not greet me as customarily, but stood rather bewildered-looking for a second or two

and then broke down weeping and spoke in a rather uncertain voice saying "Charlie, The Big Fella is dead." The first two they broke the news to were Joe O'Reilly and Tom Cullen. Cullen lit a candle as they entered his room and in its light looked at their faces and burst out, 'Something terrible has happened – I know what you have come to tell me – The Big Fella is dead! I've been dreaming about him.' They [Tom and Joe] then went to break the news to Batt O'Connor: even sixty years later the memory of the consternation and grief caused in her home by the news made Sister Margaret Mary fall silent as she spoke to me about the telling. Messengers were sent about the city and all through the night shocked men were ushered through the sandbags and barbed wire guarding Government buildings. The shock was so palpable that Cullen and O'Reilly burst into tears when they saw the grey, taut faces. With finger raised, Cosgrave stepped forward. 'This is a nice way for soldiers to behave...' Mulcahy slipped away to write a message to the Army directing how he thought soldiers should behave: "Stand calmly by your posts. Bend bravely and undaunted to your work. Let no cruel act of reprisal blemish your bright honour. Every dark hour that Michael Collins met since 1916 seemed but to steel that bright strength of his and temper his gay bravery. You are left each inheritors of that strength." [76]

Michael's body was returned to Dublin by cutter. His remains were taken to St. Vincent's Hospital on Stephen's Green. They occupied the same mortuary chapel where Harry Boland's lay earlier that month.

While there, the famed artist Sir John Lavery painted Michael in repose. He titled his work: *Michael Collins, Love of Ireland.*

Michael's friend Oliver St. John Gogarty, poet, author, politician and physician embalmed the body while Albert Power, famed

Irish sculptor, crafted his death-mask.

Tom Cullen, Liam Tobin, Joe O'Reilly, Kevin O'Higgins, Tom Ennis and Diarmuid O'Hegarty carried Michael's remains down the steps of St. Vincent's as the Big Fella's coffin was removed to City Hall where his open casket lay in state for three days. Thousands upon thousands of Irish passed by to pay their respect to their beloved fallen leader.

On the 28th, Michael was honoured by a Requiem Mass at St. Mary's Pro-Cathedral. His coffin was then placed on a gun carriage pulled by six black horses and transported the six miles to Glasnevin Cemetery. Richard Mulcahy and seven other Irish army generals, including Tom Cullen and Liam Tobin, marched alongside their fallen friend and commander. Somewhat ironically, the gun carriage that transported Michael's remains had been used to support one of the field guns employed in the shelling of the Four Courts that sparked the Civil War two months earlier. Over one-half-million mourners lined the streets as the funeral procession passed. A solitary white lily rested on the Irish Tricolour draping the coffin. The flower was a special remembrance from Kitty, his betrothed.

❊

Richard Mulcahy delivered the graveside oration as Michael was laid to rest along side other fallen Irish Volunteers.

> Tom Ashe, Tomás MacCurtain, Trolach MacSuibhne [Terence MacSwiney], Dick McKee, Micheál O'Coileáin, and all you who lie buried here, disciples of our great Chief, those of us you leave behind are all, too, grain from the same handful, scattered by the hand of the Great Sower over the fruitful soil of Ireland. We, too, will bring forth our own fruit.
>
> Men and women of Ireland, we are all mariners on the deep, bound for a port still seen only through storm and spray, sailing still on a sea full of dangers and hardships, and bitter toil. But the Great Sleeper lies smiling

in the stern of the boat, and we shall be filled with that spirit which will walk bravely upon the waters. [77]

Meda Ryan poignantly wrote:

On that August morning in Glasnevin Mick Collins' sisters, Hannie, Margaret, Mary and Katie, his brother Johnny and many of Collins' comrades in arms and in politics now stood at the graveside men like Dalton, Mulcahy, Dolan, O'Reilly, Cosgrave, O'Higgins, Blythe, Tobin, Cullen, O'Duffy, women like Jennie Wyse-Power, Min Ryan, Moya Llewelyn Davies. [78]

After Michael's death, Piaras Béaslaí said:

Michael Collins led a revolution, but he only destroyed to rebuild. His mind was essentially constructive, and to him the English evacuation embodied in the Treaty was only a clearing of the decks for fresh action. The fatal folly of some of his countrymen took him from us before he could "get on with the work." [79]

Of the consequences brought to bear by Michael's death, Ryle Dwyer observed:

Most of those closest to Collins were unable to make the adjustment to civilian authority. They were virtually leaderless without him. They tried to live up to his ideals, but as the Big Fellow was such a secretive individual, nobody was ever quite sure where he really stood. [80]

※

The British House of Commons had ratified the Anglo-Irish Treaty ten days after it was signed with little adversarial debate on 16 December 1921. The affirmative vote was 401-58. On the same day the House of Lords followed suit, 166-47. As remembered, the Irish parliament, Dáil Éireann, took a full month of contentious arguing and vindictive debating to approve the Treaty 64-57 on 7 January 1922.

The agreement also required the approval of one other body: the 'Southern' Irish parliament. With the passage of the Government of Ireland Act of 1920, Ireland had been divided into two territories with two self-governing parliaments, both North [Belfast] and South [Dublin].

Technically, the general election of May, 1921, returned 128 representatives to the Parliament of Southern Ireland including 124 Sinn Féin TDs who formed Ireland's legislative 2nd Dáil Éireann.

As a result, on 14 January 1922, Arthur Griffith had called to order Ireland's 'Southern' Parliament for its once and only meeting. As Chairman of the Irish Delegation of Plenipotentiaries under the terms of the Anglo-Irish Treaty, he presided. With its anti-Treaty representatives absent, the assembly unanimously ratified the Treaty and adjourned for the first and final time.

Finally, on 6 December 1922, the Anglo-Irish Treaty became law. The one-year, provisional Irish caretaker government, now under the guidance of Chairman W. T. Cosgrave, was dissolved. A thirty-two county Soarstát na hÉireann formally seceded from the United Kingdom and became a dominion of the British Commonwealth. Two days later, again according to terms of the Treaty, the six-county entity known as 'Northern Ireland' opted out of Soarstát na hÉireann and rejoined the United Kingdom, thus copper-fastening Ireland's partitioning. The remaining twenty-six county unit legally adopted the name of Soarstát na hÉireann or Irish Free State.

Also on 6 December 1922, again according to the terms of the Treaty, the Free State appointed Timothy Michael Healy as its first Governor-General. [Re: Article #3 of the Anglo-Irish Treaty stated: "The representative of the Crown in Ireland shall be appointed in like manner as the Governor-General of Canada, and in accordance with the practice observed in the making of such appointments."] [81]

[**Author's note**: Initially, the exact designation of the largely ceremonial position was not stated in the Treaty, but with the drawing up of the Irish constitution, Michael Collins had decided on the title of Governor-General in accordance with the practices in other dominions. Michael felt it would help guarantee that if the

British government tried having the Irish governor-general inter-fere with the functioning of the Free State, the other dominions, fearing British interference themselves, would strongly object and intercede on Ireland's behalf.]

Soon after Healy was installed, Tom moved from his officer's quarters in Portobello Barracks, and with Delia by his side, they moved into Ratra House, nicknamed 'the Little Lodge,' in Phoenix Park. Soon joining them would be the two other ADCs, Liam Tobin and Seán O'Connell.

Ratra House was situated close to the Vice Regal Lodge. The grand lodge, Healy's new residence, had been the home to Britain's Lord Lieutenant or Viceroy to Ireland for almost one hundred fifty years.

As for Tom and Delia, their new home was certainly a grand accommodation as compared to their humble upbringing and recent housing.

Padraic O'Farrell in his book Down Ratra Road: Fifty Years of Civil Defence in Ireland, described the building:

> Built c. 1786, the residence was of two storeys. Down-stairs there was a porch and cloakroom, two dining rooms, two drawing rooms, two breakfast rooms, pantry, kitchen, larder and maids' room. There were nine bedrooms and two bathrooms upstairs. A large conservatory and extensive verandah stretched along an external wall. The roof covered a quarter of an acre. [82]]

[**Author's note:** Of note, Lord Randolph Churchill, his American wife Jennie and their son Winston lived in Ratra House from 1876 until 1880. Winston, Britain's future PM, was two in 1876. His brother John was born there in 1880, just prior to the family returning to England to live. The Cullens and other residents must have had to lay in a large supply of candles and oil lamps as the home was not finally connected to the Electric Supply Board mains until December, 1937.

From 1951 to the present, Ratra House has been used as the Civil Defence School and training centre.]

With such a large home, staffed with household help, Tom,

Delia, Liam and Seán would've had no trouble sharing space.

The three men remained as ADCs for the Governor-General until they were terminated in March, 1924 over a political upheaval in the Irish army. No salary is listed for the three, but their successor received an annual pay of £300. An educated guess would place their remuneration at c. £250 per annum.

Though no record exists of Tom's ADC responsibilities with the exception of knowing he was paid to look after Tim Healy. I imagine he acted as the man's personal assistant, secretary, driver, body guard and travelling companion. I only hope Healy appreciated Tom's effervescent personality, quick wit and loyalty to Ireland.

This new position was certainly a change from his previous one as Assistant Director of Intelligence for Michael Collins. Clearly less dangerous and exciting, I think Tom would have bent his back and done the best job he could, though I'm sure he may have suffered feelings of withdrawal, missing the Big Fella as he did. Absent too was the sense of responsibility and dedication he'd felt earlier for helping Ireland in its struggle for independence.

But despite the feeling of satisfaction Tom must have felt with the recent achievements won on the 'battlefield' and in the political arena, Tom's desire to see Ireland completely independent of England's encumbrances would have still dominated his thoughts and actions.

❧

Not unexpectedly, the three men were forced from their ADC positions and comfortable lodgings in March of 1924 for their parts in the Army Mutiny. Often referred to as the Tobian Mutiny, it reached its climax that March, but its origins began percolating during the pervious year, if not long before.

Maryann Valiulis in her *Portrait of a Revolutionary: General Richard Mulcahy and the Founding of the Irish Free State* set the stage.

The civil war had left the country weary and disillusioned. De Valera's proclamation and Frank Aiken's

order to dump arms [May, 1923] did not restore peace
to Ireland [but it did bring the Irish Civil War to an 'unofficial' end]. The main Irregular organisation had been
broken, but numerous groups of three or four soldiers,
bent on avoiding capture and arrest, continued to fight
against the Free State army. Too many guns had fallen
into private hands and violence had become too much
a part of daily life. The army was thus still involved in
putting down lawlessness and trying to impose the rule
of law. [83]

At about this time, the government began a huge demobilisation of its military men. With the army's rolls approaching 100,000
soldiers, the Free State government, on the cusp of peace, had
to reduce those numbers immediately. The country's financial
system was in tatters after nearly four years of continuous warfare.
The Irish government was having a difficult time rebuilding its
economy and simply couldn't afford to meet its swollen army
payroll.

Valiulis wrote:

The efforts to professionalize and demobilize the army
would trigger the events of the army mutiny of 1924.
At issue were questions of power and prestige within
the army. [Richard] Mulcahy and his staff would be
the targets of the dissatisfaction and the victims of the
mutiny. In the end, the army would lose many of the
men who had guaranteed the very existence of the Irish
Free State.

Resistance to change was immediate. In January
1923, a group of pre-Truce officers founded the Irish
Republican Army Organisation or the "Old IRA." They
felt they were being treated in a manner inconsistent
with the sacrifices they had made for Ireland during the
struggle for independence and sought more power and
prestige within the army. Liam Tobin, Charles Dalton,
Frank Thornton and Tom Cullen – all former members
of Michael Collins' Intelligence Unit – were its founders.

The Old IRA held their first meetings in January
and February 1923. Tobin was appointed chairman
and Tom Cullen, organizer. Membership was available
only to those officers with the proper "past and present
outlook from a national point of view." Their objective
was clear: a "strong voice in Army Policy, with a view
of securing complete Independence when a suitable
occasion arose." They urged their members to take
"control of the vital sections of the Army and oust those
undesirable persons who were and are holding those
positions." [84]

During these initial days, Mulcahy, Minister for Defence, was
opposed to the efforts of the disaffected men and their attempts
to organise.

But Joe McGrath, Minister for Industry and Commerce
[Labour], sided with the men of the Old IRA and convinced
Dick Mulcahy to continue meeting with them. [This is the same
Joe McGrath who'd been involved with Oriel House several years
earlier.]

In dealing with the estrangement of Tobin, Cullen and the
others, two events continued to play themselves back in Mulcahy's
mind: the Treaty split and bitter lessons of the Irish Civil War.
Not wanting the army to divide as the country had done over the
terms of the Anglo-Irish Treaty, he continued meeting with the
Old IRA men who'd made such sacrifices for the cause of Ireland.

On the other hand, the Civil War with all its atrocities and
executions had toughened this thinking. He resented the 'selfish'
actions of the men who'd fought for the Treaty and the establishment of the Free State, but were now trying to divide the country.
He saw them using the military as a political ramrod to resist
change and impose their thinking on the government.

Things continued to fester for the remainder of 1923 and into
the beginning of 1924. On 7 March, Minister McGrath resigned
his position. Two days later, records show that over nine hundred
officers had been demobbed and a further number of officer
demotions had been made.

Uinseann Ó Rathaille Mac Eoin, in his book *The I.R.A. in the Twilight Years 1923-1948*, summarised the events leading up to mid-March.

> Major-General Liam Tobin and Colonel Charles Dalton had demanded the removal of the Army Council and the suspension of demobilisation; at the same time charging the government with pursuing a policy 'not reconcilable with the Irish people's acceptance of the Treaty.' Orders were issued at once for their arrest, and several houses were searched for them. In the provinces, members of the Army absconded with some arms, ammunition and equipment.
>
> On March 17, a statement was issued that arms carried from military barracks must be returned by March 22, and the persons concerned should surrender at the same time. On March 19, a serious incident took place at Devlin's public house, 68 Parnell Street. [85]

The National army surrounded the pub. Inside the recalcitrant officers refused to surrender. Both sides were reluctant to fire on the other. The stand-off lasted for much of the day.

To the men inside, visions of 1919-1921 must have flashed through their heads. Instead of being hunted and surrounded by the Tans or Auxies, it was *their* own lot, members of *their* own National army that were trying to apprehend them.

Finally, the military entered Devlin's and a number of officers were arrested, but not Tobin, Cullen and Thornton. Using the cunning and 'daring-do' they'd learned during the War for Independence, the three old friends slipped out the back and escaped over the rooftops.

In his chronology of 1924, Uinseann Mac Eoin quotes an account written by John Regan for the *Irish Times* newspaper that appeared in its 7 March 1994 edition. In Regan's story, he stated:

> ...shortly after 10 o'clock on the night of Thursday, March 6 [1924], an ultimatum was presented to W. T. Cosgrave, President of the Executive Council [of

the Free State government], signed by Liam Tobin and Charlie Dalton, acting on behalf of the secret body within the Free State Army styling itself the Irish Republican Army Organisation. The two, with Tom Cullen, Frank Thornton, Joe O'Reilly, Joe Leonard, Joe Dolan, Pat Mc Crae, Bill Stapleton, [Ned] Kelleher and [Jimmy] Slattery, were the core of the Collins Squad....

The ultimatum demanded the removal of the senior general staff known as the Army Council, comprising Richard Mulcahy, Minister for Defence, Gen. Seán McMahon, Chief of Staff, Gen. Gearóid O'Sullivan, Adjutant-General, and Gen. Seán Ó Muirthile, Quartermaster-General.

Furthermore, they wanted the drastic demobilisation then taking place to cease; and finally, they sought that a conference be called to discuss their aspirations towards 'achieving a Republic.' This latter is incomprehensible in view of their [pro-Treaty] actions throughout the Civil War suppressing the Republic. ...the core of their complaint lay in the restricted prospects in an army shrinking to one fifth of its then size; and also the tedium of coming under the thumb of nine-to-five civil servants at Parkgate Street [Irish army HQ], Dublin. [86]

The upshot of the 'bloodless' army mutiny saw the men who had been arrested inside Devlin's released. The officers comprising the Army Council resigned their positions by order of Cosgrave's government. Tom Cullen and Liam Tobin lost their appointments as ADCs and were forced to vacate Ratra House. The two submitted their resignations from the army and retired as major-generals. In grateful recognition for their years of service to Ireland, they were permitted to retain their military pensions. Tom Cullen, a man of determined action throughout his life, ended his exceptional military career on a displeasing note. By taking the political stance that he did, he was standing up for his friends and fellow officers who'd gone to war for Ireland.

Of Tom's military retirement, *The Wicklow People* later reported:

When he went to the city [Dublin after the Wicklow Town riot of April, 1918], ...[Tom Cullen] joined up with the Dublin Brigade, became attached to the late Gen. Michael Collins' bodyguard, and [became] his most trusted officer and friend. He [Tom] fought with distinction all through the warfare, so much so that he was one of the most "wanted" men by the British, but he came through his exploits unscratched. He had two brothers [Andy and James] serving with the I.R.A. at the same time. In the events following the declaration of peace between England and Ireland, he remained loyal to his hero, Gen. Collins, and supported the Treaty campaign, and when the Free State Government was established, he was appointed aide-de-camp to the Governor-General [Healy]. This position he maintained until in 1924, at the time a number of officers demonstrated against the government [the Tobian Mutiny], when he relinquished his position and rank in union with them, and since then he has been following a civil occupation. [87]

Maryann Valiulis concluded the army mutiny affair by stating:

The army mutiny of 1924 was the final echo of the civil war, the last vestige of the Volunteer mentality of an independent, political army. The mutiny precipitated a cabinet crisis during which two ministers resigned and the army council was dismissed. Moreover, it brought to a climax the conflict between Kevin O'Higgins [Minister for Home Affairs] and the new breed of leaders and Richard Mulcahy [Minister for Defence] and the veteran officers [Tobin, Cullen, Thornton, etc.]. The antagonism between the two men and two groups was not personal, but rather the result of differences in strategy, technique and philosophy.

By resigning on the command of the government – regardless of the validity of the government's decision – the army council upheld the right of the government to control the army. Despite the excuses and disclaimers, the fact remained that the Cosgrave government was willing to come to terms with men who had threatened the stability of the state. It was the leaders of the army who refused to condone mutiny. The [Cosgrave] cabinet gambled on the loyalty of the army council – and won. [88]

❧

Humbled but not broken, Tom and Delia Cullen took up residence at #27 Herbert Place in Dublin. The attractive, Georgian brick building looked down on the tranquil Grand Canal not far from Portobello Barracks where he'd so faithfully served Michael Collins.

I imagine Tom, Liam Tobin and the others continued to meet with their fellow Old IRA friends over a pint to discuss the politics of the day. I'm sure the thought of seeing Ireland become a united, thirty-two county, sovereign nation was never far from their thinking.

[**Author's note**: On 6 November 1924, ex-Major-General Tom Cullen with former comrades ex-Major-General Liam Tobin and ex-Major-General Piaras Béaslaí, among others, paid tribute to their friend Colonel-Commandant Tom Kehoe (Keogh) at the unveiling of a large marble Celtic cross at his grave site in Knockananna, Co. Wicklow. The memorial (£600) was paid for by Kehoe's former comrades-in-arms who were founding members (1923) of the Old IRA Organisation/Association.

Both Tobin and Béaslaí spoke to a gathering of some three thousand onlookers. The honoured Co. Wicklow man, a member of the National army GHQ, was killed, along with six others, during Civil War action on 16 September 1922 when a Republican road mine exploded at Carrigaphooca Bridge near Macroom, Co. Cork.

British Pathe News recorded the tribute (www.britishpathe. com and search under 'comrades tribute'). Both Liam and Piaras were filmed speaking. Tom Cullen, wearing an overcoat, white shirt and necktie, is seen to the left of the high cross without hat. Later in the film clip, he's shown wearing his hat while standing beside a 'weeping' woman who is next to Béaslaí, who's wearing an Irish cap.]

I firmly believe Tom kept alive Michael Collins's belief that the Anglo-Irish Treaty was but a 'stepping stone' to Ireland's full independence, but unfortunately, Tom and Delia's lives faded into the background as Ireland became more comfortable with its partial freedom.

Besides maintaining the contacts with his old comrades, Tom continued enjoying the odd day of racing. The wonderful photograph of the couple, posing for a snap at The Curragh Racecourse in the mid-1920s, is testament to that.

Tragically, the next accounting of the Wicklow revolutionary come to light in the summer of 1926, two years after the ill-fated Army Mutiny. On June 20th, Tom and three of his good friends decided to met and spend the afternoon swimming in Lough Dan up in the Wicklow Mountains.

On that day, the angel of death fluttered its wings over Tom and took him away.

※

[**Author's note**: Additional reading would include: Frank Pakenham's *Peace by Ordeal: The Negotiation of the Anglo-Irish Treaty 1921*, (1992), T. Ryle Dwyer's *Big Fellow, Long Fellow: A Joint Biography of Collins & de Valera*, (1998) and Meda Ryan's *Michael Collins and the Women Who Spied for Ireland*, (1996).

IO

T he headlines of *The Wicklow News-Letter* [26 June 1926] told
the sad story:

"EX-MAJOR-GENERAL DROWNED."

The lengthy newspaper article began by stating, "A very sad
fatality occurred on Sunday last [20 June] at Lough Dan, the
victim being ex-Major General Thomas Cullen, a Co. Wicklow
native and a former A.D.C. to the Governor General [Timothy
Michael Healy]." [1]

The piece mentioned Delia, as well as her mother and step-
brother's names. It stated Tom had come to Wicklow Town [1917]
to work for Mr. L. [Larry] Byrne as a shop assistant and that
he'd been involved with the Irish Volunteers. Of course, it went
into detail describing the events of his arrest, trial and his forced
removal from Wicklow to Dublin in April, 1918.

It stated that after Tom's release from prison, he'd become a
member of the old Dublin Brigade of the I.R.A. and that for 'a long
period' he played a prominent part in the 'Anglo-Irish warfare,'
but through all his activities 'he escaped unnoticed.'

In describing the events of the day leading up to his death,
the newspaper mentioned Tom had gone 'fowling' [bird hunting]
with friends earlier in the day and as it was 'intensely hot for this
time of the year,' he 'went for a swim.'

The extended coverage also linked Tom with Michael Collins.

He was the principal bodyguard and trusted friend of the late General Michael Collins. After the declaration of peace, he became an adherent of the Free State Government, and shortly after the death of General Collins was appointed A.D.C. to the Governor-General. He remained in this position until 1924, when he resigned and joined with other officers in the demonstration against the government [the Army or Tobian Mutiny].

Aged 35 years, he was married 5 ½ years in Dublin by the Rev. M. Cogan, C.C., Wicklow. After the ceremony, in a secret retreat in the city, despite the terrors and dangers of the period, a distinguished company of the officers of the I.R.A., including General Collins, assembled to honour the deceased and his bride, who was herself a prominent member of the Cumann mBan.

On Sunday night news of the drowning accident reached Wicklow [Town] from the Roundwood Barrack, and the local Civic Guard had the news conveyed to Mrs. Cullen and her mother. After the inquest on Monday the remains were removed to Wicklow, and outside the town the hearse was met by a large number of people, who accompanied it to the residence of Mrs. Considine. At 9.30 p.m. a large crowd of sympathisers followed the remains to St. Patrick's Church and joined in the prayers, which were recited by Rev. M. Cogan and Rev. D. Gallagher. [2]

✀

An inquest was held the day following Tom's death [21 June] at Mrs. Keenan's Hotel in Roundwood. Coroner [James] Murray [of Arklow, Co. Wicklow] conducted the inquiry into his death.

Mr. J. Keenan was the foreman of the jury. James Joseph [J. J.] Fallon, Wicklow, said deceased was his brother-in-law, and witness [J. J.] last saw him alive about 1.15 p.m. on Sunday in witness's home at Wicklow. [**Author's**

note: I also recall reading that J. J. reportedly stated that "Tom was in good health and strong."]

Dr. T. C. Harte deposed that death was due to shock caused by sudden immersion in very cold water. The water in Lough Dan was very cold, as there was a rocky bottom. [**Author's note:** Dr. Harte made a superficial examination of Tom's body. He ascertained that death was due to shock by "sudden immersion in very cold water." He also commented that it was a "common cause of death at that time of year while bathing on the first or second hot day of the summer season."]

Mr. Michael Fitzgerald [#55] Landsdowne Road, Dublin, said he was living temporarily [while on holidays] at Mrs. Doyle's Hotel, near Lough Dan. On Sunday himself and [his brother] Joe [Joseph G.] Fitzgerald, Fred [Frederick 'Freddy' Henry] Boland [of #25 Earlsfort Terrace, Dublin] and the deceased [Tom] took out a boat on the lake at 4.30 [p.m.] to go for a swim, with the exception of Mr. Cullen, who, however, brought his bathing togs with him in case he would decide to bathe. They also brought a fishing rod and a gramaphone and rowed to Mr. [Blaney] Hamilton's side [another man in a boat on the lough], nearly a mile across. They went ashore for about 20 minutes, when Mr. Boland and witness's brother [Joe] went out swimming. Witness brought the two men – his brother and Fred Boland – out in the boat and they bathed around, going in and out for about 20 minutes. Mr. Cullen, who was in a jocular mood, got out to swim and said he would swim out to the boat. Deceased told Joe Fitzgerald to swim with him in case anything happened.

Supt. [Garda Superintendent Casserly] – Was Mr. Cullen a good swimmer?

Witness [Michael] – No, but he swam strongly to the boat. When within two yards of the boat he seemed to be in difficulties, made a grab at it, and witness jumped up in the boat when one of the oars fell out.

Joe Fitzgerald came from the shore to his assistance. He got a hold of the deceased and then witness, who could not swim [because he was recovering from a recent surgery], flung the other oar towards the struggling men and shouted to his brother, who did not seem to hear him. The oar fell within a foot of his brother and the boat was then only about two or three yards from him.

Supt. – Your brother did not grasp the oar?

Witness – No, he didn't hear me. I had no control of the boat then as the two oars were gone and I could not swim. Then I shouted for help to Mr. Blaney Hamilton, who was out in a boat some distance away. My brother caught hold of deceased, who afterwards sank. Mr. Hamilton came up and witness got his oars and rowed off for assistance. When I looked again, Mr. Cullen had disappeared.

Joseph G. Fitzgerald said deceased told them he was not a very good swimmer and was nervous of deep water. At first deceased swam out to the boat and came back some distance. Witness [Joe] was standing in shallow water looking about him. The shore shelved steeply, so that about 4 feet out there would be a depth of about 20 feet. Suddenly witness saw deceased sinking.

"I immediately leaped into the water," continued witness, "and swam towards him. He [Tom] was three feet away from the boat at this time. He was in about 30 feet of water, and I can't say if he was over the water when I reached him or not. I grabbed him." He clutched at me and ripped my bathing togs down the breast and I pulled away from him. Then I got a breather and made anther go for him. I grabbed him the second time and he clutched me again. I was not able to keep him up and he was pulling me down. He was not making any attempt to swim and he did not shout or speak. I was getting suffocated under the water. I can't say how I got free. Mr. Blarney Hamilton came over and dragging operations started.

Frederick H. Boland, 25 Earlsfort Terrace, said he was staying at the hotel with the other witnesses. Witness [Freddy, then twenty-two years old] was only learning to swim. He was on the shore when Mr. Cullen entered the water, and as it reached above his ankles, Mr. Cullen said jocosely that he had a cramp. Witness said 'You should not stay in long because you have been already in this morning.' Mr. Cullen said, "I'll swim out to the boat." The boat was then 25 yards out. Deceased, who was nervous in deep water, said to Joe Fitzgerald – "Be ready to grab me if I sink."

Then he swam out strongly, and when he reached his hand up to grab at the boat he missed it and his effort seemed to have carried him under the water and he disappeared completely. Apparently he made no further effort to swim. The drift was carrying the boat down and it was carried beyond the spot where deceased went down. His hands and wrist only appeared. His hands came up rapidly. Sometimes I could see the white gleam through the water of an arm while Mr. [Joe] Fitzgerald was trying to rescue him.

To the Coroner – The two men went under the water for five or six seconds, and the witness thought both were drowned, but Mr. [Joe] Fitzgerald's head appeared and he said "Oh God! Tom is gone!"

Supt. Casserly stated he received word of the drowning about 7.30 p.m. He obtained grappling hooks and went to Lough Dan about 8.40 and supervised dragging operations carried out by the Roundwood Gardai. The body of the deceased was recovered at a depth of 40 feet. They tried artificial respiration without avail.

The Coroner said there was no blame to be attached to any of the comrades, who appeared to have done their best. They were not proficient swimmers. It was not easy for one to have the right presence of mind when such a calamity occurred. Everyone sympathised with the relatives of deceased, who was allied to one of the most respectable families in Co. Wicklow. The jury would join with him in expressing deep sympathy to the relatives in the great sorrow which it pleased Providence to send them.

Mr. L. [Laurence] Murphy [member of the jury] – Mr. [Joe] Fitzgerald had a very narrow escape in diving to the rescue.

Coroner – Yes, they did their best, especially Mr. [Joe] Fitzgerald.

On behalf of the Gardai, Supt. Casserly joined in the expression of sympathy.

Mr. [J. J.] Fallon returned thanks on behalf of the relatives, and paid a tribute to the Guards [Gardai] for their prompt assistance.

The Coroner said Supt. Casserly and his men acted with great promptitude.

The verdict of the jury was to the effect that death was due to accidental drowning. They attached no blame to anyone, and commended the prompt action of the Civic Guards. They expressed deep sympathy to the relatives in their great affliction.

At the conclusion of the inquest the remains were conveyed to Wicklow [Town]. [3]

[**Author's note**: *The Wicklow People*, also a county weekly, ran a comparable story on 26 June 1926. It reported Tom's death with much the same detail as that carried in *The Wicklow News-Letter*'s account of the same date.]

The *Dublin Evening Herald*, dated June 21, 1926, repeated a similar story under the headlines:

EX-OFFICER'S FATE

Gallant Rescue Efforts in Lake

WICKLOW TRAGEDY

A verdict of accidental drowning was returned at an inquest held at Roundwood today by the Coroner, Mr.

James Murray, Arklow, on the body of ex-Major-General Thos. Cullen, aged 35 of 27 Herbert Place, Dublin, who lost his life in tragic circumstances while bathing in Lough Dan yesterday.

Mr. Joseph G. Fitzgerald, of 55 Landsdowne Rd., Dublin, deposed that with his brother, Michael, the deceased, and Frederick H. Boland, 25 Earlsfort Ter., he proceeded by boat to the east shore of Lough Dan to bathe. Michael Fitzgerald, who was an invalid, recovering from the effects of a recent operation, did not enter the water, but witness and Boland undressed and went in. Boland remained in the water for a considerable time, but deponent retired early to the shore to wait for Mr. Cullen who was undressing.

Deceased eventually plunged in and had a few short swims. He was not a good swimmer in witness's opinion. When a short time in the water Mr. Cullen announced his intention of swimming out to the boat which was drifting about 20 yards from the shore.

He swam steadily to the spot, but just when he reached it, the boat, [he] suddenly sank.

Witness swam as quickly as possible to his rescue, and actually reached him when he was only partly submerged. As soon as deceased observed deponent, he clutched at him and dragged him under.

With difficulty Mr. Fitzgerald released himself and got a breather. He then gripped the deceased again and managed to prevent him from sinking entirely but the struggles and tight grasping of the deceased wore him down. Mr. Fitzgerald, feeling that he was drowning, shook himself free. The deceased did not come to the surface again, and with difficulty Mr. Fitzgerald was later able to reach the shore.

The jury expressed deep sympathy with the relatives, and attached no blame to anyone for the occurrence. The prompt action of the Civic Guard was commended.

The late Mr. Cullen was a native of Wicklow and the

funeral takes place from Wicklow Church [St. Patrick's] at 3 p.m. tomorrow for local burial. [4]

Two days later, the same (Dublin) *Evening Herald* ran the following story:

THEIR LAST TRIBUTE.

~~~

Funeral of Ex-Major-General T. Cullen.

Many of those who were prominent in the pro-Treaty fighting attended the funeral yesterday of ex-Major-Gen. T. Cullen which took place from Wicklow to Rathnew.

There were a large number of wreaths, including those sent by the members of the former Dublin Brigade, I.R.A. and the Irish Republican Army Organisation.

A guard of honour was formed by ex-Major-Gen. L. [Liam] Tobin, ex-Cols. [Frank] Thornton, [Charlie] Dalton, [Tom] O'Connell, P. [Pat] McCrea, J. [Joe] Slattery, Comdt. C. [Charlie] Byrne and deceased's brother, James.

[A listing of those in attendance followed.] [5]

❧

[**Author's note**: It is hard for me to convey the emotional upset I felt reading those newspaper accounts of Tom's death three years ago. Again, I experienced the same reactions while typing their words.

To think of all the harrowing events Tom Cullen lived through and survived in his short life and then to die in such a tragic, fool-hardy manner disturbed me. It absolutely turned my stomach. But, I suspect, going for a swim in Lough Dan with three of his friends was simply another escapade in a life-long series of adventures for Tom.

As you must know by now, he was a chancer. He lived his life to the fullest. He enjoyed the companionship of friends. He took pleasure in pushing the limits. He was a gambler. He did things few others would've had the courage to even attempt.

(I should further note that two of Tom's brothers, Andy and James, were members of the IRA and had fought in the Tan War too. According to *The Wicklow People*'s account of Tom's funeral, it mentioned James was a member of the Irish Republican Army Organisation.)

�σ

So it was that on that fateful Sunday afternoon, Tom jumped at the opportunity of tasting the joys of living...to feel the rush of diving into ice cold water...to test his ability to swim a distance that his rational mind might well have told him that he was stretching the boundaries of his ability. This time, however, the chance he took cost him his life.

How many times during the War for Independence had he risked all and survived? Maybe he'd developed an air of invincibility...a feeling that if he played his cards just right, he'd come through whatever without a scratch.

This time Fate didn't smile down on him. Instead it dealt him an unkind hand...the cruellest of all.]

�σ

I clearly remember that my suspicions and curiosities were aroused, back in 2005, when I first learned of Tom's death. Lough Dan is in a remote location, even today. Nestled in the Wicklow Mountains near Roundwood, the ribbon lough has a dual reputation of being a sporting paradise and a site for committing suicide. Fed by the cold waters of Lough Tay to the north, Lough Dan, occupying a glacial valley, is the source of the River Avonmore (Irish for big river) made famous in Thomas Moore's poem *The Meeting of the Waters*.

So, as a result and *prior* to reading the findings of the coroner's inquest, I wondered if Tom's death was actually a murder, suicide or just an accident. Did he simply drown in an unfortunate mishap or did he take his own life, depressed after Collins's death and

and disheartened over his army resignation? On the other hand, was Tom murdered by British agents or assassinated by some of Éamon de Valera's anti-Treaty followers? Clearly, human emotions in Ireland were still running raw only three years after the Civil War's end. Certainly, he'd made numerous enemies on both sides of the water with his clandestine anti-British intelligence actions and his pro-Treaty political liaisons.

Back in 2005, I pondered these possibilities. Could it be that Tom Cullen's unexpected death was tied to his close friendship with Michael Collins and their many wartime activities? Or was Tom's death linked to his pro-Treaty/Free State stance taken after the 'split'? Maybe it was his close association with the nascent Irish national army and the numerous atrocities it committed against former comrades who now formed the opposition...anti-Treaty, IRA Republicans? Could it be his post-War for Independence association with Oriel House and the Free State's newly established Criminal Investigations Department (CID) with its growing legacy of extra-legal political and policing activities that led to his death? Finally, what about his involvement in the foiled 'Tobian' Army mutiny of 1924? Did any of these lead to his death... murder...suicide or possible political assassination?

Certainly, Tom's involvement with Dublin's anti-British campaign during the Irish War for Independence would have given any embittered British agent ample reason for striking back. Some, even today, speculate that Michael Collins's death was a British conspiracy carried out by some undercover spy. If so, the killing of one of Collins's closest associates certainly wasn't beyond the realm of possibility.

Sure hadn't the embryonic Free State government, the one Tom pledged his allegiance to, executed seventy-seven Republican prisoners of war during the ten-month-long Irish Civil War.

Earlier in the autumn of 1922, as the intensity of the internecine conflict accelerated, reports surfaced that the newly formed Criminal Investigations Department, housed in Oriel House, of which Tom Cullen was a member, were abducting anti-Treaty Republicans in Dublin and executing them. The number of twenty-five killed was suggested, according to one British intelligence report. All the dead men where either shot, taken from the city and buried in remote locations or they were killed and their bodies dumped in public places around the city. One well-known case involved Noel Lemass, brother of Seán Lemass who later become Ireland's Taoiseach from 1959 to 1966. Noel was an anti-Treaty IRA officer. While in Dublin, he was kidnapped in June, 1923, supposedly by Free State CID men, and secretly held. The following October his body was discovered buried in a shallow grave, south of town up in the Dublin Mountains. He'd been severely beaten and many of his bones broken.

After the autumn of 1922, following Collins's death, the Irish Civil War took a tragic, abhorrent turn. For example, during just one embittered, hateful twenty-four-hour period in March, 1923, hadn't former Squad member, now Dublin Guard Commander Paddy O'Daly, taken nine Republican prisoners from Ballymullen Barracks in Tralee, tied them to a land mine at Ballyseedy Cross and attempted to kill them all in one go. Eight of the nine were blown up and their bodies later machine gunned while the ninth, Stephen Fuller, was blown free and luckily survived to tell the story.

Later the following day, five more Republican prisoners were purposefully killed by a land mine at Countess Bridge near Killarney while four other IRA men were executed near Cahersiveen...all in Co. Kerry. Finally, wasn't another Republican prisoner of war, Seamus Taylor, taken into Ballyseedy Wood and executed by Free State soldiers.

These are but a few of the many incidents of atrocities committed in Ireland during the Irish Civil War and the months that followed. The old wounds of the pro-Treaty/anti-Treaty divide, still enflamed and bleeding, dominated the feelings and memories of many in Ireland for years to come.

Of course, someone with a Republican bias or a personal grudge to settle could have killed Tom. Wasn't Kevin O'Higgins, Ireland's Free State Minister for Justice, gunned down in a Dublin street on his way to Mass just thirteen months later in July, 1927. Certainly, an unsuspecting Tom Cullen would have been an easy target for such a reprisal.

But *no*! Let me put the record straight. I don't think any of these suppositions or individuals from Tom's past had anything to do with his death. I sustain the ruling of the coroner's inquest: death by accidental drowning.

Sadly though, were there extenuating circumstances that *did* contribute to his death? Factors that weren't introduced or testified to at the inquiry.

I found the newspaper accounts of the inquest were devoid of one key element...the role alcohol might have played in the circumstances leading up to Tom's death. How much drink, if any, was taken by the four men that day?

Why would I suggest such a thought? *The Wicklow News-Letter* accounting mentioned the weather was 'intensely hot.' It was so hot on the 20th that before or more likely after Mass, Tom went swimming back in Wicklow Town.

He and Delia would have spent the previous night at either J. J.'s lodgings above his newsagents shop in Abbey Street or at Delia's mother's house in St. Patrick's Road.

After Mass and breakfast, with the heat of the day now reaching uncomfortable levels, I imagine Tom cycled down to Wicklow's harbour and went swimming at Sand Finer beach. It's a tiny strip of sand inside the protection of the harbour and its two sizeable piers. The calm, shallow water of the port would have been cool and refreshing, certainly not like the biting cold of Lough Dan.

In his statement at the coroner's inquest, J. J. Fallon testified he last saw Tom alive at about 1.15 p.m. at his abode in Abbey Street.

My best guess is that after his morning swim, Tom washed up, dressed and with Delia he had lunch at his brother-in-law's. With the day growing hotter and knowing his three friends were staying up at Lough Dan, he decided to cycle up and spend time with them. Certainly, it would be a few degrees cooler up in the Wicklow Mountains and the possibility of another swim was as appealing as was the companionship of friends. (Sure, maybe the rendezvous had been planned in advance, but in any event, Tom left Wicklow Town soon after 1.15 in the afternoon.)

The approximate fifteen-mile bicycle ride was almost entirely uphill. With the heat, the steady incline and the rough road, the journey would have taken about one-and-a-half hours, all testifying to Tom's fine level of physical fitness.

Arriving fatigued at Mrs. Doyle's Hotel (today, it's owned by the Wicklow County Council and is used as a scouting retreat), the first thing his friends would have offered him would've been something cool to drink. If it was water, I'm sure it would have been followed by a beer or two. Next, apparently the four lads went 'fowling' in the nearby fields or woods.

Returning a short time later, I imagine more drink was consumed prior to taking the row boat out onto the lake at about 4.30 p.m.

Back in 1926, the idea of an ice chest filled with beer was unheard of. So if they did take drink with them, it likely was a bottle or two of whiskey. Why would I think that? They were going out on the lough for a swim, maybe some fishing, but mainly to relax and socialise. Didn't they have a 'gramaphone' with them? I'm also confident they'd have arranged with Mrs. Doyle for some sandwiches to be included on their outing. Remember, it's the 20th of June, midsummer's eve, and it would remain light until after eleven o'clock in the evening. Surely, Tom had planned to spend the night at the hotel with his friends rather than cycle back to Wicklow in the dark. We know he'd taken his swim 'togs' with him and likely he'd have also brought along a change of clothing, maybe even a toothbrush, in some sort of small rucksack or carry-all.

I also question the timeline testified to at the inquest. The Irish have never been great ones for punctuality and back in 1926 wrist-watches weren't the fad, pocket-watches were. I find it hard to believe four men, out on a spree, would have carried one with them while out on the lough. Why would they? They were facing no time constraints whatsoever.

Now, according to their own testimony, Michael 'jumped up in the boat when one of the oars fell out.' It well could have been an accident, a reaction to a panicked move after seeing Tom struggling in the water, or possibly Michael wasn't in full control of his faculties. Remember, the three men had been at the hotel until Tom's arrival around three o'clock. Surely, they'd had some lunch at Mrs. Doyle's and it is hard to imagine they didn't have a pint or two with their meal. Remember, they're there on a bit of a 'mini' holiday and sure why wouldn't an Irishman have 'a tipple' or two with his midday meal?

The next thing we know is that in all the excitement to help save Tom, Michael panics and throws the second oar into the water instead of using it to propel the boat the two or three yards to where Tom is floundering. But in this case, logic takes a back seat to panic.

Now, what kind of condition is Tom in at this point, 4.30 or 5.00 in the afternoon? Most likely he spent a restless night sleeping in a strange bed on an 'unusually warm' night. He and Delia may have had a late Saturday night with friends and Tom's brother Andy. Certainly drink would have been taken that evening. During a relaxing weekend in Wicklow, Tom customarily wouldn't have declined a drink or two. Up early Sunday morning, tired and possibly with a sore head, he likely went to eight o'clock Mass. It would've been followed by breakfast and his swim in the harbour. Back for a wash up and lunch, Tom then undertook a difficult fifteen-mile, uphill bicycle ride on dirt-packed roads to Lough Dan. Likely dehydrated, physically tired from the exercise and suffering from lack of sleep, Tom was a likely subject for muscular cramp...especially, after diving into the icy-cold water of the lough.

You know the rest. Four young men, possibly experiencing some degree of inebriation, have a swimming accident. Michael, unable to swim because of a recent surgery and possibly not at all because he didn't know how; Freddy just learning to swim; Tom, supposedly 'not a good swimmer' and Joe, who seemingly was the only capable swimmer, all out together on a extremely cold, deep-water lough...it was a formula that spelled out 'trouble.'

This brings into question Tom's swimming abilities. First of all, he was a talented athlete, but being an athlete doesn't mean he was a swimmer. Next, he did go 'swimming' earlier in the day back in Wicklow Town, but was he truly swimming or merely just splashing around to refresh himself...no one knows. Certainly, he wasn't afraid of water. If he was, I doubt he'd have gone alone to Sandy Finer beach that morning or taken his swim togs along with him to Roundwood. But, for whatever reason, he was unsure of himself in the lough. Was it his lack of swimming skills, his early onset of cramping or the fact he felt some level of intoxication?

Didn't Michael Fitzgerald state to the coroner that Tom 'was in a jocular mood'?' What did he mean by that comment? Was he simply pleased to be with his friends or was alcohol alternatheightening his disposition?

Freddy testified, "Mr. Cullen said jocosely that he had a cramp." Was Tom trying to save face in front of his friends about his lack of swimming abilities and offered the excuse of 'having a cramp' to cover-up that weakness or did he actually have a cramp? Again we will never know. (A friend of mine has stated he knows a man who believed Tom *was* a good swimmer.) Certainly, as I've stated above, on the day of his death, Tom was a likely candidate for having a cramp for several reasons.

In conclusion, a logical set of circumstances came together on June 20th, all contributing to the unfortunate death of a lovely man, a stalwart Republican and a dedicated Irish patriot.

❧

The Wicklow News-Letter continued its extensive tribute to Tom Cullen.

At the Co. Council meeting on Monday, Mr. Everett [likely a county commissioner] proposed a vote of condolence with the widow of the late General Cullen. As one who was associated with deceased both in Wicklow and Dublin, and, he was sure, every member of the Soarstát regretted his untimely end. He was a great soldier and patriot. It was very sad to see that his life should be taken away at such short notice, but it was all God's will, and they could only extend to his widow and the people of Ireland and his relatives, her mother and brother, their sincerest condolence. He said all this in the absence of Deputy Byrne, who was very intimate with deceased.

Mr. Fleming seconded.

Passed in silence, the members standing.[6]

Finally, *The Wicklow News-Letter* concluded its homage to Tom.

At the request of the choir – solemn Requim (sic) Mass was celebrated on Tuesday morning by the Rev. M. Cogan, and was attended by a large number.

The funeral took place on Tuesday afternoon at 3 o'clock to the New Cemetery, Rathnew. Prayers were recited in the church by Rev. M. Hoey, P.P., Rev. M. Cogan, C.C., and Rev. D. Gallagher, C.C., after which, surrounded by floral wreaths and draped in the tricolour, the coffin was borne from the church to the hearse by his comrades of the old Dublin Brigade. The following formed a Guard of Honour around the hearse Ex-General Liam Tobin, ex-Colonels [Frank] Thornton, [Emmet] Dalton, [Tom] O'Connell, P. [Pat] McCrea, J. [Jim] Slattery, ex-Commandant C. [Charlie] Byrne, and his own brother James Cullen. Immediately following the hearse were a large number of the old Dublin Brigade, and these were followed by many of the Volunteers drawn from Dublin and County Wicklow.

The chief mourners were: Mrs. Cullen, widow; Andrew Cullen, father; Andrew, James and Patrick Cullen, brothers; Miss [Annie?] Cullen, sister; Mrs. Considine [Delia's mother & Tom's mother-in-law], and Mr. J. J. Fallon [Delia's half-brother & Tom's] brother-in-law.]

More than one thousand people, drawn from all over the country, formed one of the most impressive corteges ever seen leaving the town. At the Cemetery the Guard of Honour carried the coffin to the graveside, where a cordon of his old comrades was drawn up. The last prayers were said by the three clergymen and the remains were laid to rest. The wreaths and crosses were laid on the grave.[7]

One of the most striking tributes the newspaper accolade made were its comments about the times, the mourners present and its extensive listing of attendees at Tom's funeral. Their presence marked the profound respect so many in Ireland had for Tom... for the man as a person and for all the many contributions he made for Ireland's quest for freedom and self-governance. Sadly, it took his death and its observance for Tom Cullen to be publically recognised as one of the country's true patriots and revered revolutionaries.

> What was particularly striking about the funeral cortege was the large number of I.R.A. men, not only from Dublin and Co. Wicklow, but from such far away places as Cork, Tipperary, Roscommon and Meath, names which to the majority of the people are reminiscent of those by-gone days of warfare and trouble, of heroism and sacrifice, names that will ring in history through the ages. They may nowadays be divided into groups, supporting the Free State Government [pro-Treaty], actively or passively, neutral or in opposition [anti-Treaty Republicans] to the principles of an autonomous State within the British Empire, but on this sad occasion they comingled with one another [as in days gone by], united in the one regret for a brave comrade, an unselfish patriot of those recent days of general strife [the Civil War] and national unity [the War for Independence]. In this spontaneous tribute to the memory of their comrade, there had gathered together an unique and historical array of fighting men, and of men whose sympathy and support in other directions than by force of arms was on their side through the Anglo-Irish warfare and the Sinn Féin agitation, making the day one worthy of note. [8]

The same newspaper listed the names of some two hundred Irishmen who'd served with and fought for many of the same principles and ideals that Tom did. The list included the following persons but it should not be considered complete: President William T. 'Willie' Cosgrave, President of Ireland's Executive Council and his former O/C at SDU during Easter Week, 1916; Seán Collins, Michael's brother Johnny; General Seán McKeon, nicknamed The

Blacksmith of Ballinalee, Co. Longford; Ex-Major-General Liam Tobin; the brothers Frank & Charles Saurin; Joseph 'Joe' McGraw; Batt O'Connor, T.D.; Seán McGarry; Joseph 'Joe' Dolan; Colonel David Neligan; former Major-General Emmet Dalton; Liam Devlin, owner of Devlin's Public House, Dublin; Major-General Gearóid O'Sullivan; Commandant P. S. O'Hegarty; famed writer and Republican Piaras Béaslaí; Colonel Ned Broy; F. X. Coghlan, President, old Dublin Brigade; F. Cronin, Q.M.G. [Felix Cronin married Kitty Kiernan, Michael Collins's former fiancée]; Sam Maguire, of IRB & Gaelic football fame; Colonel Joe Vize [later buried in New Cemetery, Rathnew]; Major Joe Furlong [also buried in New Cemetery, Rathnew along with Tom, Joe Vize & William O'Grady]; Ex-Commandant A. Fitzpatrick, Tom Cullen's first Wicklow recruit in the Irish Volunteers in 1917; William O'Grady, of Wicklow riot fame described in Chapter #4; as well as Mrs. Ned Broy and Mrs. Markan, close friends of Mrs. Delia Cullen. [9]

[Author's note: On 24 June, President W. T. Cosgrave sent Delia a short note, again expressing his condolences and giving the reasons why Minister for Justice Kevin O'Higgins and Colonel Joe O'Reilly, Michael Collins's loyal friend and aide-de-camp had been unable to attend Tom's funeral. The reasons were not stated.] [10]

❧

On 10 July, three weeks after Tom's death, *The Wicklow News-Letter* carried a short piece written by an unnamed 'contemporary':

The late Mr. Thos. Cullen, who was drowned in Lough Dan recently, was a brother of Mr. Andy Cullen, Mountmellick, Co. Leix. At the time of the Rising he was employed as bookkeeper and shop assistant at the "South Pole" Hotel, in Wicklow, owned by Mr. L. Byrne. He subsequently joined the army and rose to the rank of Major General. He was a fine [Gaelic] footballer, a good hundred yards man, and all round an excellent athlete. A few years ago he married a Miss Considine, of Wicklow. Much regret is expressed at his sad and sudden demise, at a time when life seemed to him but a garden of roses. [11]

❉

[**Author's note:** Of his three friends Tom met at Lough Dan on that fateful day, I don't know what became of the two Fitzgerald brothers, but Freddy Boland went on to lead a distinguished life. After receiving his B.A. and LL.B. degrees in Dublin, he did graduate work at Harvard, the University of Chicago and the University of North Carolina between 1926 and 1928. He became Ireland's Assistant Secretary of the Department of External Affairs from 1939 to 1946 and its Secretary between the years 1946-1950.

In 1950, he was chosen Ireland's ambassador to Britain. In 1956, he was appointed his country's representative to the United Nations.

As a point of interest, Freddie was president of the U.N.'s General Assembly on 12 October 1960 when the Soviet Union's President Nikita Khrushchev, responding to a charge of 'employing a double standard by decrying colonialism while dominating Eastern Europe,' took off his shoe and began pounding it on his desk. The Irishman, outraged at the delegate's behaviour and, in an effort to restore order, broke his own president's gavel while hammering it on the podium. That entire episode certainly proved an historical oddity in the UN's history.

Toward the end of his illustrious career, he became the twenty-first Chancellor of Trinity College (1963-1982).

Freddie died in 1985 and was honoured by the Irish Republic with a postage stamp issued in 2005.]

❉

After Tom's death, Delia closed their Dublin flat at #27 Herbert Place. She may have moved back in with her mother, but eventually Delia resided with J. J. and his new wife Elizabeth 'Lil' [married c. July, 1927]. Initially, I believe, she spent part of her time working in her step-brother's newsagentss shop on

Abbey Street, across the road from where she'd first noticed Tom working in Fitzpatrick's.

Her life was not an easy one. She suffered from epilepsy and was subject to seizures. This affliction may have been a contributing factor in Tom and Delia not having children.

Economically, she struggled. In fact, out of desperation, she wrote to Tom's old friend and SDU comrade, then Ireland's President, W. T. Cosgrave in Dublin. She asked for his help in finding employment. But the first record of correspondence between Delia and Willie Cosgrave occurred a month after Tom's death. On 17 July 1926, Delia wrote to President Cosgrave regarding Tom's resignation from the National army.

> Letter to the President from Delia Cullen, 17 July 1926, thanking him for his kindness [in attending Tom's funeral, I suppose.] 'It was on my mind to tell you the real reason for Toms [sic] resignation, but again I have failed, however if you would care to hear it perhaps I could see you some time I am in town.' [12]

Two days later, on 19 July, President Cosgrave answered Delia's letter. He stated, 'that he would be please to see her when she is in town' plus he gave her some details about his wife's recent illness.

Soon after, Delia must have communicated with Cosgrave about meeting him in Dublin for on 30 July, the President writes with details regarding their forthcoming meeting. [**Author's note:** Their meeting must have been a private one as there is no public record of it to be found. It likely would have been a fascinating conversation to learn, from Tom's point of view, why he resigned his position from the Free State army back in March, 1924.]

Seven months later, the President did receive correspondence, from an unknown party, quite possibly Rev. Michael J. Cogan C.C., concerning a fitting memorial for Tom in the Rathnew Cemetery. It was answered by Cosgrave's secretary, Mr. E. Lyons.

The following dispatch from the 'Department of the Taoiseach,' dated 26 January 1927 and filed under the heading 'Mr. Thomas Cullen, Grant from Dáil Special Fund' stated:

> Notes relating to the Tom Cullen Memorial, signed

E. Lyons, 26 January 1927. The first note states that the President thinks that the best Memorial that could be offered to the late General Cullen would be to do something for his widow. [13]

On 28 March 1927, two months later, a confusing piece of correspondence was sent from MJ [Michael J.] Cogan, CC to the 'Department of the Taoiseach' which was filed under 'Mr. Thomas Cullen, Grant from Dáil Special Fund.

The letter in question was not sent to President Cosgrave but to [Minister for Justice] Mr. K. [Kevin] O Higgins (sic). Cogan is writing on behalf of the widow of the late Tom Higgins (sic). [The Rev. Cogan must have confused the last names and wrote Tom Higgins instead of Tom Cullen.] His letter stated:

> To Mr. O Higgins from MJ Cogan, CC, Wicklow, 28 March 1927, writing on behalf of the widow of the late Tom Higgins, who is, he declares, penniless. 'She lives with her brother, who is to be married and does not want the sister; she has no claim on him.' [14]

Tragically, Delia's half-brother J. J. no longer wished to have her living in his home despite the fact that she is 'penniless.' The next entry attached to Tom's file was dated Good Friday, 14 April 1927. It read:

> Copy minute to the Private Secretary, Minister for Justice, 14 April 1927, stating that the President [Cosgrave], in response to a letter from [Rev.] MJ Cogan, CC, has started enquires as to the possibility of assisting Mrs. Tom Cullen to a suitable position. In the meantime a grant of £50 is to be paid to her out of the Dáil Special Fund. [15]

On the same date, four days prior to the 11th anniversary of the 1916 Easter Uprising, the following was added to Tom's file:

> Unsigned note [from Cosgrave] to Diarmuid O'Hegarty, 14 April 1927, authorising him to pay £50 out of the Dáil Special Fund to Mrs. Tom Cullen. [16]

In addition to the foregoing, same date, the following posting was included in the file:

> Copy minute to the Private Secretary, Minister for Posts and Telegraphs, 14 April 1927, relating to the case of Mrs. Tom Cullen, who is 'in very necessitous circumstances and it is the desire of the President that an early effort should be made to assist her to some suitable employment.' The Minister for Posts and Telegraphs is asked to interest himself in the case. [17]

Again from the 'Department of the Taoiseach' another missive was sent.

> Copy minute to the Private Secretary, Minister for Local Government and Public Health, 14 April 1927, relating to the case of Mrs. Tom Cullen, who is 'in very necessitous circumstances and it is the desire of the President that an early effort should be made to assist her to some suitable employment.' The Minister for Local Government and Public Health is asked to interest himself in the case. [18]

Also on the same date, 14 April 1927, President W. T. Cosgrave, who seemed to be making an effort to help Delia, sent a duplicate minute to the Private Secretaries of the Minister for Finance and the Minister for Education. [19]

Seven days later, on Easter Thursday, April 20th, President Cosgrave received a note from Delia, thanking him for organising the ex-gratia grant of £50 from of the Dáil Special Fund. [20]

On the same day, Cosgrave was in receipt of a reply from the Minister of Posts and Telegraphs, Mr. James J. Walsh, which read:

> Minute to Paul Banim, President's Office, from the Secretary to the Minister for Posts and Telegraphs, 20 April 1927, stating in regard to Mrs. Thomas Cullen that the only vacancy likely to be available in the Department would be a City Sub-Post Office. He enquires whether Mrs. Cullen would desire to be considered for the post of Sub-Postmistresses if it became available. [21]

Another reply concerning the President's request was received that same day.

> Minute to Paul Banim from the Secretary to the Minister for Local Government and Public Health, 20 April 1927, stating that there is no suitable post in the Department for Mrs. Tom Cullen. [22]

[**Author's note**: Oh, how quickly some people forget!]

⁂

Unfortunately, the Sub-Postmistresses position didn't materialise and apparently none of the other ministerial requests bore fruit. Then on 13 June 1927, a week before Tom's the first anniversary of Tom's death, Rev. MJ Cogan, CC, of St. Patrick's Church in Wicklow wrote to President Cosgrave on behalf of Delia.

> Letter to Cosgrave from Rev. MJ Cogan, CC, 13 June 1927, writing with reference to the case of Mrs. Tom Cullen. She lives with her brother 'who is about to be married and naturally she feels in the way and is very anxious to get something to do.' [23]

Six days later, the President Cosgrave responded to Rev. Cogan's request:

> Copy letter to Rev. MJ Cogan, CC, from the President's Office, 19 June 1928 [likely a typographical error, but maybe not], stating that everything possible has been done to secure employment for Mrs. Cullen. The Post Office have promised that they will give her the first sub-office vacant provided she found her own premises [for the sub-office]. So far, however, no such vacancy has arisen. [24]

Another point of confusion. It seems improbable that an entire year has passed since Cosgrave replied to Cogan, but it's possible. If it had been a year, the Irish government has been irresponsible and grossly negligent in not responding more promptly.

> Copy letter to Rev. MJ Cogan from the President's
> Office, 23 June 1928, stating, with reference to the
> case of Mrs. Cullen, that the Commissioners of the
> Dublin Union will make an appointment of a Visitor
> [inspector] under the Children's Act 1908. A copy of the
> advertisement is enclosed. A letter has been addressed
> to the Commissioners asking them to deal with the
> application of Mrs. Cullen 'most sympathetically when
> the appointment is being made.' [25]

Again, another confusing date crops up. This leads me to
believe that the above correspondence was actually 1927 and not
1928 as stated.

> Copy letter to Mr. Commissioner MacLysaght from
> the President's Office, 23 June 1927, asking, on be-
> half of the President, that the application from Mrs.
> Tom Cullen for the post of Visitor [school inspector]
> under the Children's Act, 1908, receive every possible
> consideration. The President desires it to be 'treated as
> a special case.' Mrs. Cullen, the letter states, is 'nicely
> educated. Being a teacher by profession, and has a good
> knowledge of children. Her appearance and address are
> all that are to be desired.' [26]

The issue of dates continues to confound.

> Letter to Cosgrave from Michael Colgan (sic), CC,
> 25 June 1928. He feels confident that the position of
> Visitor under the Children's Act, 1908, is as 'good as
> secured' for Mrs. Cullen. [27]

The following day, Delia wrote to W. T.

> Letter to President Cosgrave from Delia Cullen, 26
> June 1928, thanking him for his interest in her affairs.
> The appointment in Dublin Union, she states, 'seems
> heaven sent.' [28]

At last, it appears as if W. T. has succeeded in helping Delia
find a job.

Three days later, a letter from the Taoiseach's office was sent to Delia. It stated:

> Copy letter to Mrs. Delia Cullen from the President's Office, 29 June 1928, asking her to meet the President the next time she is in Dublin to discuss the question of an appointment for her under the Dublin Union Commissions. It is expected to be possible to provide a post for her within the next fortnight. [29]

But a little over a month later, things took a turn for the worst.

> Minute to the President from the Department of Local Government and Public Health, 2 August 1928, returning papers with regard to Mrs. Tom Cullen. 'The position in this case is that in early 1923 Mrs. Rose Clancy was appointed...to the position of Visitor under the Children's Act 1908 in a temporary capacity. She has been so employed ever since and gave the most satisfactory service. It is clear to the Commissioners that this position would be permanently required and they got the permission of the Department to make it permanent. It was necessary to issue an advertisement before permanently filling the vacancy which was filled by the Commissioners themselves and Mrs. Clancy was appointed on her own merits and on the merits of the case. She has three children; she was married a second time; her second husband is an idler, and won't work, and is not living with her – in this matter I am told, the reflection is entirely on the husband.' [30]

But to Cosgrave and MacLysaght's credit, they refused to give up trying to help Delia.

> Note relating to the case of Mrs. Cullen, 15 August [1928]. The first states that MacLysaght will approach General [Richard] Mulcahy with a 'view to engaging his good offices for Mrs. Cullen.' A further note states that MacLysaght says he has good news to impart. [31]

MacLysaght, presumably pressurised by Cosgrave himself, now corresponded with Mr. Banim in Cosgrave's office.

Minute to Banim from MacLysaght, 9 August 1928, relating to the case of Mrs. Cullen. The chief difficulties of the Commissioners in offering Mrs. Cullen a post is the lack of suitable positions 'since the female staff is mainly composed of ward-mistress' and this is a very menial post. He states that the City Commissioners would be in a better position to offer Mrs. Cullen a post. [32]

[**Author's note**: The paradox of Delia possibly finding work at South Dublin Union doesn't escape me. It was there at SDU that her husband Tom and Ireland's President W. T. Cosgrave fought for Irish freedom during Easter Week, 1916.]

W. T. Cosgrave is unrelenting. Additionally, he has graduated from referring to Delia as Mrs. Tom Cullen to Mrs. Delia Cullen.

Minute to the Private Secretary, Minister for Local Government and Public Health, from the President's Office, 22 August 1928, asking the Minister to assist in finding suitable employment for Mrs. Delia Cullen. [33]

Besides Willie Cosgrave, Delia still had Rev. Cogan on her side.

Letter to the President from Rev. MJ Colgan (sic), 20 August 1928, reminding him of his promise relating to Mrs. Cullen [to assist her to find suitable employment]. [34]

Finally, the last piece of correspondence I've uncovered regarding the efforts of others to find Delia employment.

Copy letter to Rev. MJ Colgan (sic) from the President's Office, 22 August 1928, acknowledging his letter and stating that the President has not lost sight of Mrs. Cullen's case. [35]

Sadly, it appeared Delia's hopes for finding a government position were dashed. Apparently, the President was unsuccessful in helping her secure employment, but we'll never know what private avenues the Taoiseach or other individuals may have explored on Delia's behalf. I also wonder about what efforts Delia undertook herself to find work.

[**Author's note**: Curiously, on Delia's death certificate, it lists her profession or occupation as 'Inspector' under the Children's Act & Widow of General Thomas Cullen, N.A. (National Army). When she began her career as an 'inspector' is unknown. So, in the end, it does appear that President Cosgrave's efforts to help Delia were not all in vain.]

What work did Delia undertake between Tom's death and her own? The picture is unclear. Besides working part-time in J. J.'s shop on Abbey Street, she likely helped her mother, Marianne Considine, who began operating a 'well-respected' girl's' school across from the courthouse in Wicklow's Market Square. Most probably, Delia later divided her time between teaching in her mother's school and carrying out her own responsibilities as an inspector.

[**Author's note**: In February, 2007, I received an email from Mrs. Irene Parsons who lives near Wicklow Town. She commented that '(she) grew up with (her) mother talking a lot about (Tom Cullen) but (notes), as with a lot of young people growing up, (she) did not listen or pay too much attention to the details of what (her mother) had to say about Tom Cullen.'

Mrs. Parsons went on to write that 'Mrs. (Marianne) Considine ran a private school in premises now known as The Steak House in the Market Square, Wicklow Town. A relative of mine was a pupil there.' She adds, '(It was) always a bone of contention with (her) mother that she did not get private education, a luxury few could afford in those times!'

Irene's kind missive continued, 'I have a recollection of my mother always saying that my father, Tom Kilcoyne, had Tom Cullen's uniform. My father got a tip-off that his house was to be raided (presumably by the Black and Tans), so the uniform was burnt and all that remains of it is one button, which I have in my possession. I have some photos of my late father in uniform but cannot verify if this is the one worn by Tom Cullen.' (See photographs)

Today, the building that housed Marianne's school, which Mrs. Parsons referred to above, is fittingly painted red and remains the site of The Square Steak House.]

❄

Tragically and unexpectedly, Delia Cullen died in J. J.'s home, above his newsagent shop, on Sunday, 27 August 1933. Elizabeth Fallon, her sister-in-law, was present at the time Delia suffered a fatal epileptic seizure(s), but was unable to save her. Delia died of asphyxia.

Again, *The Wicklow People* published her obituary.

MRS. DELIA CULLEN, ABBEY ST., WICKLOW.

The death took place on Sunday morning last at Abbey St., Wicklow, of Mrs. Delia Cullen, daughter of Mrs. Considine, Abbey St., and the late Mr. Jas. Considine, and the widow of the late Gen. Tom Cullen, who was drowned while bathing in Lough Dan in June, 1926. The news of her death, which was totally unexpected, was learned with deep regret in her native town amongst the people of which she enjoyed a high popularity and also by the many friends she had made in the city [Dublin] and adjoining counties, and the most sincere sympathy in their sad bereavement.

The remains were brought to St. Patrick's Church on Monday night and were received by Rev. P. Fahey, C.C.

On Tuesday morning, Requiem Mass for the repose of the soul of the deceased was celebrated by Very Rev. Canon Hoey, P.P. The Mass was sung by the choir of which deceased's mother was director and organist.

The funeral took place in the afternoon from the Church to Rathnew Cemetery. The cortege was an impressive one and a beautiful tribute to the memory of the deceased. A long line of cars followed the large body of people who walked behind the hearse, amongst whom were numbered many who were prominent in the struggle for National independence and comrades of the late General Cullen.

The last prayers were said by Very Rev. Canon Hoey, assisted by Rev. P. Fahey, C.C., and Rev. M. Clarke,

C.C., Dalkey [Co. Dublin].

The chief mourners were Mrs. Considine (mother); J. J. Fallon (brother); William Considine (uncle); Mrs. [Elizabeth 'Lil'] Fallon, Miss May Cullen [possibly a nickname for Tom's sister Margaret]; Mrs. Magee and Mrs. O'Neill (sisters-in-law); Jas. Cullen (brother-in-law); and Mrs. Cullen [likely Tom's step-mother]; P. O'Dowd, William, Patrick, Gertie, and Mrs. Egan, R. S. Henchy, Mrs. Giffney and Hannah Bergin (cousins).

[A listing of some fifty others who sent Mass Cards followed.]

A number of beautiful floral tributes were laid on the grave, amongst others from the following Mother, Joe [J. J.] and Lil [Elizabeth]; Joe and Eileen McGrath; Charlie Dalton and Frank Saurin; Liam and Mrs. Tobin; Miss McDermot, Co. Hotel, Harcourt St. [Dublin]; Mr. and Mrs. Markan and Mary Cullen [likely Tom's sister Maria Anna]. R.I.P. [36]

❧

Most likely, sometime in the early 1930s and prior to Delia's death, an unembellished, ten-foot high Celtic cross, carved from granite was erected over Tom's and, what soon would be, Delia's grave. I believe Liam Tobin was the principale organiser of this tribute.

The inscription on the cross's pedestal states in Irish:

"GUIOID AR SON ANINA TOMÁIS UI CUILINN SAIGDIUR CRÓGA INARM NA HEIREANN" [In English: "Pray on behalf of the soul of Thomas Cullen, a brave/valiant soldier of the Army of Ireland"]

Also in English are the words:

"PRAY FOR THE SOUL OF MAJOR GENERAL THOMAS J. CULLEN WHO SERVED UNDER MICHAEL COLLINS IN THE ANGLO-IRISH WAR

AND WAS ACCIDENTLY DROWNED JUNE 20TH 1926. MAY HE REST IN PEACE."

Near the cross's base are carved the words:

"ERECTED BY HIS FRIENDS & COMRADES IN ARMS" and "GO NOCINIO DIA TROCAIRE AR A ANAIN" [In English: "May God have mercy on his soul"].

Today, along the base of the monument the following words are carved in the stone:

"PRAY FOR HIS WIFE DELIA CULLEN WHO DIED AUGUST 27TH 1933."

❧

[**Author's note**: If I were to guess, I suspect J. J. Fallon purchased two plots in the New Cemetery in Rathnew immediately following Tom's death in 1926. The first was the one Tom and later Delia were buried in and the other, next to it, was for his family. It too is adorned with a Celtic cross and the following inscriptions:

In loving memory
Marianne Considine,
Organist St. Patrick's Church
Wicklow.
Who died January 10th 1942,
Aged 86 years.

Also her grandson
Raphael Patrick Fallon.
Died April 23, 1943, aged 5 years
and her son
James Joe Fallon.
Died June 10th 1953
Elizabeth Fallon.

Died October 3rd 1973
Erected by her loving son.

Mercy + Jesus + Mercy.
R.I.P.

Of Elizabeth 'Lil' Fallon, I discovered one woman in Wicklow Town who remembered her. Her family had taken over the newsagent shop in 1975, two years after Lil's death. It was renamed Earls Newsagents and remains so today. Eileen Earls simply stated, "Lil was a lovely, white-haired, gentle woman who often worked behind the counter (of Fallon's newsagent shop)".]

Lil and J. J. had three sons. Joe became an accountant and remained a resident of Wicklow Town. Both he and his wife Joan are now dead; Seán chose the priesthood but was killed in an unfortunate automobile accident while a missionary in Africa; and William 'Billy' Fallon who grew up to be a solicitor and lived in nearby Arklow. He was eighteen years old when his father died. Billy married and had four children...two sons, Mark and Paul, and two daughters, one named Orla Coleman née Fallon.

※

I recently was sent an old newspaper clipping of a photograph of Tom's grave with its the high cross in place. The only inscription missing was the mention of Delia's death. After numerous inquiries, I've been unsuccessful in dating the picture. My best guess is that the snap was taken soon after the marker was installed and the men gathered around Tom's grave were honouring him and placement of the memorial. I think one of men standing behind the cross was Liam Tobin, but as his head is tilted down and I can't be certain.

As Delia's name is absent from the base, I'm thinking it was just before or soon after her death, but I am puzzled by the fact that no women are pictured.

In the last few months, I also received a clipping from the Winter, 1965 issue of *An Phoblacht* [*The Republic*], an Irish

Republican newspaper. I was pleased to read the following under the headline:

> "Cullen-Keogh Sunday"
> The Annual pilgrimage of the A.S.U. and friends to Rathnew and Knockananna was made on Sunday, 19th September. Survivors of the East Wicklow Brigade joined the A.S.U. and headed by St. Patrick's Pipe Band, Wicklow, marched to the grave of Maj. Genl. Tom Cullen in Rathnew. Comdt. Vinny Byrne [one of the original members of Collins's Squad] was in charge. A wreath was placed on the grave. A decade of the Rosary was recited by Mr. P. Cauldwell, and an oration delivered by Mr. A. Cullen [most likely Tom's brother Andy], State Solicitor, Wicklow. Bugle Cpl. O. Walsh, sounded the Last Post and Reveille, and the ceremony terminated. [37]

Needless to say, I was pleased Tom's memory and the memories of others of his generation are being honoured...at least they were back in 1965. Today, however, I doubt few such tributes are held. Except for the momentous dates of 1607, 1798, 1847, 1916, 1922, 1949, 1972 and 1998, I fear today's Irishmen and womaen have little desire to honour the past.

Certainly, there are the occasional remembrances of Ireland's struggle for freedom and independence, centred mainly on the people and events of the last few decades, particularly in Northern Ireland. But as times washes over the years, these commemorations will, no doubt, become fewer and fewer.

Sadly, with my heart filled with countless emotions, I bring to an end my tribute to the life and deeds of Thomas J. Cullen. He was a special man; a hero; a patriot; a brave Volunteer; an Irishman who fought for his beloved country and died far too young. For in the words of Sir Walter Scott, "One hour of life, crowded to the full with glorious action, and filled with noble risks, is worth whole years of those mean observances of paltry decorum, in which men steal through existence, like sluggish waters through a marsh, without either honour or observation."

❧

May the words and photographs in this book help others appreciate Tom's many exploits and know of his passionate commitment to the 'cause of Ireland.' May his life serve as an inspiration to a new generation of men and women who wish to see Ireland's dream of unity and full independence finally achieved.

"All That's Bright Must Fade"

All that's bright must fade,
The brightest still the fleetest;
All that's sweet was made
But to be lost when sweetest.
Stars that shine and fall;
The flower that drops in springing;
These, alas! Are types of all
To which our hearts are clinging,
All that's bright must fade,
The brightest still the fleetest;
All that's sweet was made
But to be lost when sweetest!

– Thomas Moore (1780-1852)

GLOSSARY

Amadán: Fool

An Taoiseach: Head of Ireland's government; The Prime Minister

Ard Fheis: Political convention

Anti-Treaty IRA: Irishmen & women who opposed the Treaty; an unpaid paramilitary force commonly known as Republicans, anti-Treatyites or anti-Treaty IRA & nicknamed by pro-Treatyites as 'irregulars' or simply 'bands'

Auxiliary Cadets: The Police Auxiliary Cadet Division, a paramilitary 'police' unit, sent to Ireland during 1920-1921 as a mobile strike & raiding force; composed of former British military officers, they helped reinforce the RIC's efforts to suppress revolution during Ireland's War for Independence [1919-1921]; though part of the RIC & under the overall command of General Hugh Tudor, they usually operated independently under the command of Brigadier-General Frank Crozier; nicknamed Auxiliaries or Auxies, they were paid £7/week plus room & board; the Auxies were noted for their cruelty and brutality, especially toward the civilian population, surpassing even the dreaded Black & Tans; usually carrying two side arms, they wore RIC or British army officer uniforms along with their signature piece of attire, a tam-o'-shanter cap; by the summer of 1921, there were c. 2,000 stationed in Ireland

Baccy: Tobacco

Billy can: A lightweight cooking pot often called a 'billy'

Black & Tans: Nickname for former British military enlisted men sent to Ireland during 1920-1921 to reinforce the RIC's efforts to suppress the growing revolution taking place known as the Irish War for Independence; their commanding officer, stationed in Dublin, was Major-General Sir Henry Hugh Tudor; paid 10s/day plus room & board, the Tans were noted for their cruelty and brutality, especially toward the civilian population; by the summer of 1921, there were c. 10,000-12,000 stationed in Ireland; wearing a combination of Irish RIC dark green & British army khaki uniform tunic & trousers, their attire [from a distance] resembled the coats of Irish hunting hounds who were originally nicknamed the 'black & tans'

Bob: Monetary nickname for one shilling or 1/20th of a pound

Bog-trotter: A country hick or simpleton

Boreen: A narrow country lane

By-election: A special election to fill a vacant political office that is held between regularly scheduled general elections

C.C.: Curate-in-Charge; a Catholic priest typically subordinate to the P.P., the parish priest

Ceann Comhairle: Chairman [of Dáil Éireann]

Céilidh: A traditional Irish social gathering that usually includes music & dancing

Chuffed: Delighted; pleased

Cairo Gang: A group of British intelligence agents sent to Dublin [c. autumn, 1920] to counter Irish intelligence network; besides their spying activities, they also engaged in political & revengeful assassinations

Corn: A generic term for any field-grown grain crop

Cronje Hat: A soft hat with brim & high crown; typically, the left brim is pinned to the crown; named after Boer General Piet Cronje

Cumann: Irish for an 'association' or the lowest/local branch of a political party

Cuppa: A cup of tea

Dáil: The lower house, but the principal chamber of Ireland's parliament or Oireachtas

Demesne: Land adjacent to an estate that's often walled

DI: Detective Inspector

DORA: Defence of the Realm Act passed by the British government on 8 August 1914 giving it wide-ranging powers during the war period; it also ushered in many authoritarian social control measures including censorship that were frequently imposed in Ireland as England attempted to control rebellion & anti-British behaviour

Dray: A low, heavy, sideless cart used for hauling

Dump: A secure place for hiding arms/ammunition

Eejit: An idiot or fool

Fenian Brotherhood: United States counterpart to the Irish IRB whose members were known as Fenians; later renamed Clan na Gael in the late 19th century

Fianna Fáil: Warriors/Soldiers of Destiny: major Irish political party founded 23 March 1926 by Éamon de Valera; its historic ties lie with the anti-Treaty wing of Sinn Féin

Fine Gael: Family of the Irish; major Irish political party founded 3 September 1933 from the consolidation of Cumann na nGaedheal, the Centre Party & the Army Comrades Association; its historic ties lie with the pro-Treaty wing of Sinn Féin

Flying Column: A military force capable of rapid deployment and independent movement; usually composed of 15-20 men dressed in mufti who would engage the enemy via a surprise attack & quickly withdraw, if necessary

Footpath: Walkway or sidewalk

Frogmarched: A method of carrying a resisting person; each limb is held by a different person & the victim is carried face down with body horizontal to the ground

GAA: Gaelic Athletic Association: An amateur Irish cultural & sporting organisation, founded in 1884, to promote Gaelic sports, music, dance & the Irish language

Gaelic League: A non-governmental organisation, founded in 1893, to promote the Irish language

Gaol: Jail or prison

Gelignite: Blasting gelatine invented by Alfred Nobel, who also invented dynamite; an inexpensive explosive material relatively safe to handle

Gardai: Garda Siochána [Guardians of the Peace]; Ireland's police force founded in 1922

Hoor: Whore

Husting: A platform/stage on which candidates make political speeches

IRA: Irish Republican Army [Óglaigh na hÉireann]; a revolutionary Irish Republican military organisation whose 20th-century origins spring from the renaming of the Irish Volunteers by James Connolly during the Easter 1916 Uprising

IRB: Irish Republican Brotherhood [originally the Irish Revolutionary Brotherhood]: A secret, oath-bound, revolutionary fraternal society, begun in Ireland in 1858, dedicated to the establishment of an independent, democratic Irish Republic

Jackeen: Little Jack [the Union Jack flag]; a pejorative name for a Dubliner; a Shoneen or West Brit

Jaunting car: An Irish sprung [spring] cart also called a sidecar; a light, single horse-drawn, two-wheeled, open vehicle with seating for 4-6 passengers; often the driver was called a jarvey

Kit bag: Knapsack; rucksack; duffle bag

Knocking-off time: End of the typical work day, c. 5-6 pm

Loyalist (Ulster): A person loyal to Ulster's independence from 'southern' Ireland & its union with Britain; traditionally Protestant & often working-class; believes in violence, if necessary, to achieve objectives

Martial Law: The usually temporary imposition of military rule by military authorities when a civilian government fails to function effectively; a draconian measure of last resort when a civil society collapses

Mufti: Civilian attire as opposed to military dress

Navvy: A labourer

Nationalist (Irish): A person motivated by a love for all things Irish, including its people, culture, history & language; politically [traditionally] supports a united, 32-county Ireland via constitutional pathways

Oireachtas: Ireland's national parliament & Ireland's legislature composed of the President of Ireland & its two houses: Dáil Éireann [lower house] & Seanad Éireann [upper house]

Orange Order: A Protestant fraternal organisation, founded in 1795 in Co. Armagh, and politically associated with 'unionism' & strongly anti-Catholic; named after the Dutch-born, British King William III who defeated Britain's King James II at the Battle of the Boyne in Co. Meath in 1790 which assured the continuation of a Protestant supremacy in Ireland

P.P.: Parish Priest; the head of a local parish church

Parabellum: Traditionally, a 7.63 mm Mauser C96 semi-automatic pistol that could be fitted with a hollow wooden stock; it was often referred to as a 'Peter-the-Painter,' named for the Latvian revolutionary leader Peter Piaktow who used the weapon in the 1911 Sidney Street Siege, London

Peeler: Slang for a policeman; nicknamed after British PM Sir Robert Peel who reorganised the Irish Constabulary in 1836
Penal Laws: A series of harsh, 18th-century British laws imposed on Ireland to limit or remove power from the majority Catholic population;

they took the form of social, political, economic & religious constraints; they were gradually relaxed toward the end of the 1700s & totally eliminated piecemeal in the 1800s

Plenipotentiary: A representative who has full, independent power of action; a diplomat with full powers to act & represent his/her government

Portmanteau: A suitcase or travelling bag

Pound (£): Monetary unit equal to 240 pence or twenty shillings

Pro-Treaty IRA: Irishmen & women who supported the Treaty & were known as Free-Staters, Staters, pro-Treatyites, pro-Treaty IRA; a paid military force commonly called the Provisional National army, the National army or Irish army

Quay: A ship's dock, wharf or pier for the loading/unloading of goods or passengers

Quid: Monetary nickname for a pound & equal to twenty shillings

Quisling: Traitor or collaborator

Rashers: Irish bacon also called streaky [marbled with fat] bacon or streaky rashers

Republican (Irish): A person who believes that Ireland deserves to be a united & independent republic, independent of outside [British] rule or interference; traditionally Catholic & often working class; believes in violence, if necessary, to achieve objectives

Rozzer: Slang for a policeman

Sassenach: Repugnant nickname for an English person; The Stranger

Shilling: A monetary unit; a coin equal to 1/20th of a pound

Shinner: A member of Sinn Féin

Shoneen: Unflattering nickname for an Irish person who imitates English ways; a traitor or collaborator

Sinn Féin: Translation: We ourselves/ourselves alone; Irish political party, founded in 1905 by Arthur Griffith, advocating Ireland's independence & self-sufficiency

Slag/slagging: To tease or make good-natured fun of

Snug: A small private room or booth in a pub

Soarstát na hÉireann: The Irish Free State which came into existence in 1922 with the Irish & British government's ratification of the 1921 Anglo-Irish Treaty

Soft day: A damp, drizzly, wet day

Snap election: An election called earlier than expected or scheduled, often to the advantage of the political party in office

Stone: A measure of weight equal to fourteen pounds

Tan War: A reference to the Black & Tans' time; Ireland's War for Independence, 1919-1921

Tans: Members of the Black & Tans

Tea: An evening meal or supper

Tea money: Extra money…sometimes kept in an empty tea tin; a bribe or under the table payment

The Stranger: The English; a Sassenach; The Foreigner

Tommy: Nickname for a British soldier

Trap: A light, two-wheeled, horse-drawn carriage

Trucileers: A contemptuous name given to some new members of the National army who'd enlisted after the Truce was declared in July, 1921; persons who never fought in the Irish War for Independence but were glad to take credit for its successes

Ulster: One of Ireland's four provinces composed of nine counties: Antrim, Armagh, Cavan, Derry, Donegal, Down, Fermanagh, Monaghan & Tyrone

Unionist (Irish): A person who believes in fostering & maintaining strong political, economic & cultural ties with Great Britain; traditionally Protestant & supporter of a six-county, Northern Ireland political unit separate from the Irish Republic via constitutional pathways

Warder: Jailer; a jail/prison officer or guard

Yob: A lout or thug; an uncouth individual

ENDNOTES

A Word To The Reader:

1 - Ernie O'Malley, *On Another Man's Wound*, (Anvil Books, Dublin, (1979), p. 108.
2 - Frank O'Connor, *The Big Fellow*, (Poolbeg Press Ltd, Dublin, 1991), p. 37-38.
3 - Jeannette Walls, *Half Broke Horses*, (Scribner, New York, 2009), p. 271.
4 - *Ibid.*, p. 272.
5 - *1916 Easter Rebellion Handbook*, (Mourne River Press, Dublin, 1998), p. 76.
6 - *Ibid.*, p. 93.
7 - Christopher M. Byrne, Witness Statement 1014.
8 - Letter dated 14 July 2006 from Paul O'Brien, Kilmainham Gaol Museum to Christopher E. Duffy, New York, NY.
9 - Easter Week Rising, 1916, SDU Garrison Signatures, Bureau of Military History, Dublin.

Chapter 1: An Introduction:

1 - *A History of St. Mary's National School Blessington: 125th Anniversary 1882-2007*, (Naas Printing Ltd., Naas, Co. Kildare), p. 15.
2 - *Ibid.*, p. 13.
3 - *Leinster Leader*, "Blessington Catholic Schools," 8 July 1882.
4 - www.clanarans.com, "Cullen."
5 - www.census.nationalarchives.ie, "What was Dublin like in 1911?"
6 - *Ibid.*
7 - *Ibid.*
8 - *Ibid.*
9 - Sean O Mahony, *Frongoch: University of Revolution*, (FDR Teoranta, Killiney, Co. Dublin, 1995), p. 168.
10 - Dan Breen, TD, Witness Statement 1739.
11 - Tim Pat Coogan, *Michael Collins*, (Arrow Books Limited, London, 1991), p. 134.

12 - *Ibid.*, p. 135.

13 - O'Connor, op. cit., p. 107-108.

14 - *Ibid.*, p. 108.

15 - Piaras Béaslaí, *Michael Collins and The Making of A New Ireland,* Vol. I, (Edmund Burke Publisher, Blackrock, Co. Dublin, 2008), p. 131.

16 - David Neligan, *The Spy In the Castle,* (Prendeville Publishing Limited, London, 1999), p. 32.

17 - *Ibid.*, p. 99.

18 - *Ibid.*, p. 99-100.

19 - *Ibid.*, p. 100.

20 - T. Ryle Dwyer, *The Squad and the Intelligence Operations of Michael Collins,* (Mercier Press, Douglas Village, Cork, 2005), p. 13.

21 - *Ibid.*, p. 13.

22 - *Ibid.*, p. 13.

23 - Béaslaí, op. cit., Vol. I, p. 212-213.

24 - Coogan, op. cit., p. 83.

25 - Béaslaí, op. cit., Vol. II, p. 24.

26 - *Ibid.*, Vol. I, p. 279.

27 - *Dublin's Fighting Story 1916-21,* (Mercer Press, Cork, 2009), p. 287.

28 - Neligan, op. cit., p. 100.

Chapter 2:

1 - Paul O'Brien, *Uncommon Valour: 1916 & the Battle for the South Dublin Union,* (Mercier Press, Cork, 2010), p. 48.

2 - Larry Nugent, Witness Statement 907.

3 - *Ibid.*

4 - John P. Duggan, *A History of the Irish Army,* (Gill and Macmillan Ltd., Dublin, 1991) p. 2.

5 - Nugent, Witness Statement 907.

6 - Duggan, op. cit., p. 3.

7 - William Henry, *Supreme Sacrifice: The Story of Éamonn Ceannt 1881-1916,* (Mercier Press, Douglas Village, Cork, 2005), p. 30.

8 - James Kenny, Witness Statement 141.

9 - Liam Ó Flaithbheartaigh, Witness Statement 248.

10 - Coogan, op. cit., p. 32-33.

11 - *Dublin Brigade Review,* "The Fourth Battalion," (undated), p. 35.

12 - Henry, op. cit., p. 34.

13 - W. T. Cosgrave, Witness Statement 268.

14 - Henry, op. cit., p. 34.
15 - *Ibid.*, p. 35.
16 - *Ibid.*, p. 35.
17 - Kenny, Witness Statement 141.
18 - Henry, op. cit., p. 43.
19 - Béaslaí, op. cit., Vol. I, p. 52.
20 - Henry, op. cit., p. 53-54.
21 - Desmond Ryan, *The Rising*, (Golden Eagle Books Limited, Dublin, 1966), p. 172.
22 - *Ibid.*, p. 173.
23 - Michael McNally, *Easter Rising 1916: Birth of the Irish Republic*, (Osprey Publishing, Oxford, England, 2007), p. 40.
24 - A Volunteer, *The Capuchin Annual*, p. 201.
25 - O'Brien, op. cit., p. 23.
26 - *Ibid.*, p. 48.

Chapter 3:

1 - O'Brien, op. cit., p. 21.
2 - *Ibid.*, p. 21-22.
3 - *Ibid.*, p. 13.
4 - Cosgrave, Witness Statement 268.
5 - *Ibid.*
6 - O'Brien, op. cit., p. 26.
7 - Desmond Ryan, op. cit., p. 181-182.
8 - A Volunteer, *The Capuchin Annual*, p. 209.
9 - *The Catholic Bulletin*, (M. H. Gill & Son, Ltd., Dublin, March, 1918), p. 360.
10 - Desmond Ryan, op. cit., p. 175.
11 - Robert Holland, Witness Statement 280.
12 - Desmond Ryan, op. cit., p. 179.
13 - *Ibid.*, p. 182; 179-180.
14 - *Ibid.*, p. 185-186.
15 - *Ibid.*, p. 186.
16 - Cosgrave, Witness Statement 268.
17 - Annie Ryan, *Witness: Inside the Easter Rising*, (Liberties Press, Dublin, 2005), p. 134.
18 - Ó Flaithbheartaigh, Witness Statement 248.
19 - O'Brien, op. cit., p. 102.
20 - *Ibid.*, p. 88.
21 - Piaras F. Mac Lochlainn, *Last Words: Letters and Statements of the*

Leaders Executed after the Rising at Easter 1916, (The Office of Pub-lic Works, Dublin, 1990), p. 129.

22 - Personal communiqué between Paul O'Brien & author, 26/7/2010.

23 - Fr. Aloysius, *The Capuchin Annual,* (undated), p. 286.

24 - Annie Ryan, op. cit., p. 135.

25 - Cosgrave, Witness Statement 268.

26 - Mac Lochlainn, op. cit., p. 131.

27 - Annie Ryan, op. cit., p. 135.

28 - O Mahony, op. cit., p. 17.

29 - Cosgrave, Witness Statement 268.

30 - Ó Flaithbheartaigh, Witness Statement 248.

31 - Béaslaí, op. cit., Vol. I, p. 81-82.

32 - *Ibid.,* p. 72.

33 - Coogan, op. cit., p. 46.

34 - *1916 Easter Rebellion Handbook,* (The Mourne River Press, Dub-lin, 1998), p. 49.

35 - Personal communiqué between Niamh O'Sullivan & author, 14/10/09.

36 - *1916 Easter Rebellion Handbook,* op. cit., p. 70.

37 - Béaslaí, op. cit., Vol. I, p. 70.

38 - Personal communiqué between Paul O'Brien & author, 6/5/10.

39 - Desmond Ryan, op. cit., p. 260.

40 - Ruth Dudley Edwards, *Patrick Pearse: The Triumph of Failure,* (Poolbeg Press Ltd., Dublin, 1990), p. 318.

41 - Niamh O'Sullivan, *Every Dark Hour: A History of Kilmainham Jail,* (Liberties Press, Dublin, 2007), p. 115.

42 - Ó Flaithbheartaigh, Witness Statement 248.

43 - O Mahony, op. cit., p. 21.

44 - *Ibid.,* p. 58.

Chapter 4:

1 - Anthony J. Jordan, *W. T. Cosgrave 1880-1965 Founder of Modern Ireland,* (Westport Books, Dublin, 2006), p. 39.

2 - Béaslaí, op. cit., Vol. I, p. 48-49.

3 - O Mahony, op. cit., p. 167-168.

4 - Byrne, Witness Statement 1014.

5 - *Ibid.*

6 - *Ibid.*

7 - Coogan, op. cit., p. 73.

8 - Sean O Mahony, *The First Hunger Striker: Thomas Ashe 1917,*

(1916-1921 Club in association with Elo Publications, Dublin, 2001), p. 25.

9 - Coogan, op. cit., p. 74.

10 - James Mackay, *Michael Collins: A Life,* (Mainstream Publishing, Edinburgh, 1996), p. 86.

11 - *The Wicklow News-Letter,* 20 April 1918.

12 - Petty Sessions (Ireland) Act. 1851, (Form A a.), Information. Britten v. Cullen.

13 - Petty Sessions (Ireland) Act. 1851, (Form C.), Recognizance to Keep the Peace. Britten v. Cullen.

14 - Michael Foy & Brian Barton, *The Easter Rising,* (Sutton Publishing Ltd., Phoenix Mill, Thrupp, Stroud, Gloucestershire, UK, 2000), p. 5.

15 - *The Wicklow News-Letter,* op. cit.

16 - *Ibid.*

17 - *Ibid.*

18 - *Ibid.*

19 - Byrne, Witness Statement 1014.

20 - Mackay, op. cit., p. 89.

21 - Béaslaí, op. cit., Vol. I, p. 122.

22 - *Ibid.,* Vol. I, p. 121.

23 - *Ibid.,* Vol. I, p. 132.

24 - Byrne, Witness Statement 1014.

25 - Béaslaí, op. cit., Vol. I, p. 122.

26 - Letter from Collins to Cullen, 10 April 1918.

27 - Béaslaí, op. cit., Vol. I, p. 122.

28 - Unknown newspaper clipping, William O'Grady obituary, 28 May 1955.

29 - Sheelah O'Grady, *From Under The Stairs: The Story of Sheelah O'Grady,* unpublished & undated remembrances.

30 - *Ibid.*

31 - *Ibid.*

32 - *Ibid.*

33 - *Ibid.*

34 - *Ibid.*

35 - *Ibid.*

36 - *Ibid.*

Chapter 5:

1 - Dave Hennessy, *The Hay Plan & Conscription in Ireland during*

WWI, (Waterford County Museum website, www.waterford countymuseum.org, 2004), p. 4.

2 - Thomas Hennessey, *Dividing Ireland, World War I and Partition, The Irish Convention and Conscription,* (Routledge Press, New York, 1998), p. 221.

3 - Robert F. Foster, *W. B. Yeats: A Life, Volume II: The Arch-Poet 1915-1939,* (Oxford University Press, New York, 2003), p. 132.

4 - Béaslaí, op. cit., Vol. I, p. 48.

5 - Coogan, op. cit., p. 63.

6 - *Ibid.,* p. 64-65.

7 - Batt O'Connor, TD, *With Michael Collins: In the Fight for Irish Independence,* (Aubane Historical Society, Millstreet, Co. Cork, 2004), p. 73-74.

8 - Mac Lochlainn, op. cit., p. 142-143.

9 - Joseph F. Groome (Ed.), *St. James' Church Centenary Record: 1844-1944,* (Metropolitan Publishing Co., LTD., Dublin, 1944), p. 27.

10 - *Ibid.,* p. 27.

11 - *Ibid.,* p. 27.

12 - *Ibid.,* p. 29.

13 - Gerard MacAtasney, *Seán MacDiarmada: The Mind of the Revolution,* (Drumlin Publications, Manorhamilton, Co. Leitrim, 2004), p. 140.

14 - *Ibid.,* p. 141.

15 - *Ibid.,* p. 141.

16 - Michael Foy & Brian Barton, op. cit., p. 234.

17 - Béaslaí, op. cit., Vol. I, p. 145-146.

18 - *Ibid.,* p. 131-132.

19 - *Ibid.,* p. 131.

20 - *Ibid.,* p. 141-142.

21 - *Ibid.,* p. 159.

22 - *Ibid.,* p. 140.

23 - Coogan, op. cit., p. 94.

Chapter 6:

1 - Jordan, op. cit., p. 36.

2 - *Ibid.,* p. 37.

3 - Béaslaí, op. cit., Vol. I, p. 162.

4 - *Ibid.,* p. 206.

5 - *Ibid.,* p. 206-207.

6 - Dwyer, op. cit., p. 23.

7 - *Ibid.*, p. 13.

8 - Neligan, op. cit., p. 71.

9 - *Ibid.*, p. 71-72.

10 - Mackay, op. cit., p. 130.

11 - Michael T. Foy, *Michael Collins's Intelligence War: the Struggle between the British and the IRA, 1919-1921,* (Sutton Publishing Limited, Phoenix Mill, Thrupp, Stroud, Gloucestershire, UK, 2006), p. 42.

12 - *Ibid.*, p. 42.

13 - Peter Hart, *Mick: The Real Michael Collins,* (Penguin Books, New York, 2007), p. 205.

14 - Béaslaí, op. cit., Vol. I, p. 213.

15 - Dwyer, op. cit., p. 13-14.

16 - *Ibid.*, p. 14.

17 - *Ibid.*, p. 17-18.

18 - Frank Saurin, Witness Statement 715.

19 - Charles Dalton, Witness Statement 434.

20 - Daniel McDonnell, Witness Statement 486.

21 - Miss Lily Mernin, Witness Statement 441.

22 - *Ibid.*

23 - Coogan, op. cit., p. 121.

24 - Dwyer, op. cit., p. 18.

25 - *Ibid.*, p. 20-21.

26 - Dan Breen, *My Fight for Irish Freedom,* (Anvil Books, Dublin, 1993), p. 31-32.

27 - Béaslaí, op. cit., Vol. I, p. 179.

28 - *Ibid.*, p. 131.

29 - *Ibid.*, p. 174.

30 - Dwyer, op. cit., p. 28.

31 - *Ibid.*, p. 34.

32 - Béaslaí, op. cit., Vol. I, p. 207-208.

Chapter 7:

1 - Foy, op. cit., p. 36.

2 - *Ibid.*, p. 41.

3 - *Ibid.*, p. 37-38.

4 - Dwyer, op. cit., p. 38-39.

5 - Foy, op. cit., p. 21.

6 - Dwyer, op. cit., 39.

7 - Mackay, op. cit., p. 128.

8 - Foy, op. cit., p. 18.

9 - *Ibid.,* p. 24.

10 - Owen McGee, *The IRB: The IRB from the Land League to Sinn Féin,* (Four Courts Press, Dublin, 2005), p. 15.

11 - Foy, op. cit., p. 20.

12 - *Ibid.,* p. 21-22.

13 - *Ibid.,* p. 25.

14 - *Ibid.,* p. 29.

15 - Coogan, op. cit., p. 116.

16 - Dwyer, op. cit., p. 45-46.

17 - *Ibid.,* p. 52-53.

18 - Béaslaí, op. cit., Vol. I, p. 213.

19 - Foy, op. cit., p. 52.

20 - *Ibid.,* p. 43-44.

21 - Béaslaí, op. cit., Vol. I, p. 213.

22 - Foy, op. cit., p. 54-55.

23 - *Ibid.,* p. 57.

24 - Annie Ryan, *Comrades: Inside the War of Independence,* (Liberties Press, Dublin, 2005), p. 204.

25 - Frank Thornton, Witness Statement 615.

26 - Dwyer, op. cit., p. 46-48.

27 - *Ibid.,* p. 48-49.

28 - Béaslaí, op. cit., Vol. I, p. 243.

29 - Dwyer, op. cit., p. 68.

30 - Béaslaí, op. cit., Vol. I, p. 250-251.

31 - Foy, op. cit., p. 54.

32 - Neligan, op. cit., p. 64.

33 - Dwyer, op. cit., p. 75.

34 - *Ibid.,* p. 75.

35 - Joseph E. A. Cornell, Jnr., *Dublin in Rebellion: A Directory 1913-1923,* (The Lilliput Press, Dublin 2009), p. 147.

36 - Dwyer, op. cit., p. 82.

37 - Paul Gorry, *Baltinglass Chronicles 1851-2001,* (Nonsuch Publishing Limited, Dublin, 2006), p. 176.

38 - *Ibid.,* p. 177.

39 - Dwyer, op. cit., p. 87.

40 - Béaslaí, op. cit., Vol. I, p. 260-261.

41 - Foy, op. cit., p. 74.

42 - Thornton, Witness Statement 615.

43 - Béaslaí, op. cit., Vol. I, p. 262-263.
44 - Thornton, Witness Statement 615.
45 - Dwyer, op. cit., p. 89.
46 - Béaslaí, op. cit., Vol. I, p. 263.
47 - Dwyer, op. cit., p. 107.
48 - Coogan, op. cit., p. 123-124.
49 - Mackay, op. cit., p. 154.
50 - Béaslaí, op. cit., Vol. I, p. 283.
51 - Major General P. [O']Daly, Witness Statement 387.
52 - Joseph Dolan, Witness Statement 663.
53 - Dwyer, op. cit., p. 100-101.
54 - Béaslaí, op. cit., Vol. I, p. 283.
55 - Dwyer, op. cit., p. 101.

Chapter 8:

1 - Béaslaí, op. cit., Vol. I, p. 278.
2 - *Ibid.*, p. 278.
3 - *Ibid.*, p. 278-279.
4 - Foy, op. cit., p. 82.
5 - Dwyer, op. cit., p. 201.
6 - Foy, op. cit., p. 185.
7 - Coogan, op. cit., p. 132.
8 - *Ibid.*, p. 132.
9 - *Ibid.*, p. 132-133.
10 - Béaslaí, op. cit., Vol. I, p. 281-282.
11 - *Ibid.*, p. 282.
12 - Foy, op. cit., p. 83.
13 - *Ibid.*, p. 93.
14 - *Ibid.*, p. 89-90.
15 - Coogan, op. cit., p. 157.
16 - Jim Slattery, Witness Statement 445.
17 - Foy, op. cit., p. 94.
18 - Mac Lochlainn, op. cit., p. 45.
19 - Dwyer, op. cit., p. 112.
20 - P. [O']Daly, Witness Statement 387.
21 - *Ibid.*
22 - Dwyer, op. cit., p. 112.
23 - P. [O'] Daily, Witness Statement 387.
24 - *Ibid.*

25 - Dwyer, op. cit., p. 146-147.

26 - Foy, op. cit., p. 124.

27 - Béaslaí, op. cit., Vol. II, p. 47-48.

28 - Coogan, op. cit., p. 158.

29 - Béaslaí, op. cit., Vol. II, p. 45-46.

30 - Padraic O'Farrell, *Who's Who in the Irish War of Independence and Civil War 1916-1923*, (The Lilliput Press, Dublin, 1997), p. 24.

31 - Breen, op. cit., p. 145.

32 - Dwyer, op. cit., p. 150.

33 - Béaslaí, op. cit., Vol. II, p. 46.

34 - Dwyer, op. cit., p. 150.

35 - Foy, op. cit., p. 136.

36 - Béaslaí, op. cit., Vol. II, p. 46.

37 - Foy, op. cit., p. 145.

38 - Béaslaí, op. cit., Vol. II, p. 55.

39 - *Ibid.*, p. 55.

40 - Foy, op. cit., p. 147.

41 - Connell Jnr, op. cit., p. 74.

42 - Béaslaí, op. cit., Vol. II, p. 55.

43 - Neligan, op. cit., p. 122.

44 - Béaslaí, op. cit., Vol. II, p. 56.

45 - Connell Jnr, op. cit., p. 125.

46 - Dwyer, op. cit., p. 168.

47 - *Ibid.*, p. 159.

48 - Mackay, op. cit., p. 179.

49 - Béaslaí, op. cit., Vol. II, p. 57.

50 - Neligan, op. cit., p. 123.

51 - Coogan, op. cit., p. 161.

52 - Dwyer, op. cit., p. 186.

53 - Foy, op. cit., p. 168.

54 - Breen, op. cit., p. 158.

55 - Coogan, op. cit., p. 161-162.

56 - *Ibid.*, p. 162.

57 - Mackay, op. cit., p. 183.

58 - Foy, op. cit., p. 176-177.

59 - Béaslaí, op. cit., Vol. II, p. 58.

60 - Coogan, op. cit., p. 163.

61 - Dwyer, op. cit., p. 189-190.

62 - Mackay, op. cit., p. 189.

63 - *Ibid.*, p. 189.

64 - *Ibid.*, p. 189.
65 - Coogan, op. cit., p. 166.
66 - *Ibid.*, p. 166.

Chapter 9:

1 - Margery Forester, *Michael Collins: The Lost Leader*, (Gill & Macmillan Ltd., Dublin, 1989), p. 178-179.
2 - Connell Jnr, op. cit., p. 99.
3 - Foy, op. cit., p. 189.
4 - *Ibid.*, p. 188.
5 - Coogan, op. cit., p. 170.
6 - *Ibid.*, p. 171-172.
7 - Forester, op. cit., p. 177-178.
8 - Dwyer, op. cit., p. 206.
9 - Coogan, op. cit., p. 134.
10 - *Ibid.*, p. 134.
11 - Dwyer, op. cit., p. 207-208.
12 - Mackay, op. cit., p. 190.
13 - *Ibid.*, p. 191.
14 - Forester, op. cit., p. 181.
15 - Béaslaí, op. cit., Vol. II, p. 112.
16 - Thornton, Witness Statement, 615.
17 - *Ibid.*
18 - Foy, op. cit., p. 196.
19 - *Ibid.*, p. 197-198.
20 - Dwyer, op. cit., p. 222.
21 - *Ibid.*, p. 225.
22 - Béaslaí, op. cit., Vol. II, p. 139.
23 - Dwyer, op. cit., p. 226-227.
24 - *Ibid.*, p. 227.
25 - Joseph Hyland, Witness Statement 644.
26 - *Ibid.*
27 - *Ibid.*
28 - Dwyer, op. cit., p. 241.
29 - *Ibid.*, p. 241.
30 - Foy, op. cit., p. 215.
31 - Dwyer, op. cit., p. 242.
32 - P. [O']Daly, Witness Statement 387.
33 - Foy, op. cit., p. 217.

34 - Dwyer, op. cit., p. 249-250.

35 - Foy, op. cit., p. 239.

36 - *Ibid.*, p. 220.

37 - Mackay, op. cit., p. 200.

38 - *Ibid.*, p. 204.

39 - Eunan O'Halpin, "Collins and Intelligence 1919-1923: From Brotherhood to Bureaucracy" in *Michael Collins and the Making of the Irish State* edited by Gabriel Doherty and Dermot Keogh, (Mercier Press, Dublin, 1998), p. 74-75.

40 - *Ibid.*, p. 75.

41 - Coogan, op. cit., p. 397.

42 - *Ibid.*, p. 398.

43 - Eunan O'Halpin, *Defending Ireland: the Irish State and its Enemies Since 1922*, (Oxford Press, USA, 2000), p. 11.

44 - Brian O'Higgins, *Wolfe Tone Annual, 1962: Salute to the Soldiers of 1922*, (Brian O'Higgins, Ireland, 1962).

45 - C. S. Andrews, *Dublin Made Me*, The Lilliput Press Ltd., Dublin, 2001), p. 270.

46 - *Ibid.*, p. 214.

47 - Coogan, op. cit., p. 278.

48 - *Ibid.*, p. 287.

49 - Meda Ryan, *Michael Collins and the Women Who Spied for Ireland*, (Mercier Press, Douglas Village, Cork, 2006), p. 57.

50 - *Ibid.*, p. 58.

51 - *Ibid.*, p. 60.

52 - León Ó Broin (Ed.), *In Great Haste: The Letters of Michael Collins and Kitty Kiernan*, (Gill & Macmillan, Dublin, 1996), p. 219.

53 - Béaslaí, op. cit., Vol. II, p. 197.

54 - Mackay, op. cit., p. 225.

55 - Forester, op. cit., p. 230.

56 - Mackay, op. cit., p. 226.

57 - *Ibid.*, p. 227.

58 - Duggan, op. cit., p. 77.

59 - Mackay, op. cit., p. 246.

60 - Duggan, op. cit., p. 84.

61 - Eamonn Cunningham, Unpublished Memoir.

62 - *Ibid.*

63 - Duggan, op. cit., p. 75.

64 - *Ibid.*, p. 84.

65 - Cunningham, op. cit.

66 - *Ibid.*
67 - *Ibid.*
68 - Duggan, op. cit., p. 78.
69 - Cunningham, op. cit.
70 - Duggan, op. cit., p. 83.
71 - *Ibid.*, p. 81.
72 - Coogan, op. cit., p. 386.
73 - Cunningham, op. cit.
74 - Frederic Harvey, "Dublin Guards Lead Free State Attack," *(The New York Times,* 4 July 1922), p. 5.
75 - Coogan, op. cit., p. 400.
76 - Ibid., p. 415.
77 - Risteárd Mulcahy, *My Father, the General: Richard Mulcahy and the Military History of the Revolution,* (Liberties Press, Dublin, 2009), p. 228.
78 - Meda Ryan, op. cit., p. 192.
79 - Béaslaí, op. cit., Vol. II, p. 288-289.
80 - Dwyer, op. cit., p. 259.
81 - Frank Pakenham, *Peace By Ordeal: The negotiation of the Anglo-Irish Treaty 1921,* (Pimlico, London, 1992), p. 288.
82 - Padraic O'Farrell, *Down Ratra Road: Fifty Years of Civil Defence in Ireland,* (The Stationery Office, Dublin, 2000), p. 77-78.
83 - Maryann Gialanella Valiulis, *Portrait of a Revolutionary: General Richard Mulcahy and the Founding of the Irish Free State,* (Irish Academic Press, Blackrock, 1992), p. 199.
84 - *Ibid.*, p. 202.
85 - Uinseann Ó Rathaille Mac Eoin, *The I.R.A. in the Twilight Years 1923-1948,* (Argenta Publications, Dublin, 1997), p. 98-99.
86 - *Ibid.*, p. 99.
87 - *The Wicklow People,* 26 June 1926.
87 - Valiulis, op. cit., p. 219-220.

Chapter 10:

1 - *The Wicklow News-Letter,* 26 June 1926.
2 - *Ibid.*
3 - *Ibid.*
4 - *Evening Herald* [Dublin], 21 June 1926.
5 - *Evening Herald* [Dublin], 23 June 1926.
6 - *The Wicklow News-Letter,* 26 June 1926.

7 - *Ibid.*

8 - *Ibid.*

9 - *Ibid.*

10 - Letter from An Taoiseach Cosgrave to Delia Cullen, 24 June 1926.

11 - *The Wicklow News-Letter*, 10 July 1926.

12 - Letter from Delia Cullen to An Taoiseach Cosgrave, 17 July 1926.

13 - Letter from An Taoiseach Cosgrave to [most likely] Rev. Michael J. Cogan, C.C. Wicklow, 26 January 1927.

14 - Letter from Rev. MJ Cogan to [Minister] K. [Kevin] O'Higgins, 28 March 1927.

15 - Letter from An Taoiseach Cosgrave to Minister for Justice, 14 April 1927.

16 - Letter from An Taoiseach Cosgrave to Diarmuid O'Hegarty, 14 April 1927.

17 - Letter from An Taoiseach Cosgrave to Minister for Posts and Telegraphs, 14 April 1927.

18 - Letter from An Taoiseach Cosgrave to Minister for Local Government and Public Health, 14 April 1927.

19 - Letters from An Taoiseach Cosgrave to Minister for Finance & Minister for Education, 14 April 1927.

20 - Letter from Delia Cullen to An Taoiseach Cosgrave, 20 April 1927.

21 - Letter from Minister for Posts and Telegraphs to An Taoiseach Cosgrave, 20 April 1927.

22 - Letter from Secretary for Local Government and Public Health to An Taoiseach Cosgrave, 20 April 1927.

23 - Letter from Rev. MJ Cogan, CC to An Taoiseach Cosgrave, 13 June 1927.

24 - Letter from An Taoiseach Cosgrave to Rev. MJ Cogan, 19 June 1927.

25 - Letter from An Taoiseach Cosgrave to Rev. MJ Cogan, 23 June 1928

26 - Letter from An Taoiseach Cosgrave to Mr. Commissioner MacLysaght, 23 June 1927.

27 - Letter from Rev., MJ Cogan to An Taoiseach Cosgrave, 25 June 1928.

28 - Letter from Delia Cullen to An Taoiseach Cosgrave, 26 June 1928.

29 - Letter from An Taoiseach Cosgrave to Delia Cullen, 29 June 1928.

30 - Letter from Minister for Local Government and Public Health to An Taoiseach Cosgrave, 2 August 1928.

31 - Letter from Commissioner MacLysaght to An Taoiseach Cosgrave, 15 August 1928.

32 - Letter from MacLysaght to An Taoiseach Cosgrave, 9 August 1928.

33 - Letter from An Taoiseach Cosgrave to Minister for Local Government and Public Health, 22 August 1928.
34 - Letter from Rev. MJ Cogan to An Taoiseach Cosgrave, 20 August 1928.
35 - Letter from An Taoiseach Cosgrave to Rev. MJ Cogan, 22 August 1928.
36 - *The Wicklow News-Letter*, 2 September 1933.
37 - *An Phoblacht*, Winter, 1965.

SELECTED BIBLIOGRAPHY

A History of St. Mary's National School Blessington, 125th Anniversary 1882 – 2007, Naas Printing Ltd., Naas: 2007.

Ambrose, Joe, *Dan Breen and the IRA,* Mercier Press, Douglas Village, Cork: 2006.

—, *Seán Treacy and the Tan War,* Mercier Press, Douglas Village, Cork: 2007.

Andrews, C. S., *Dublin Made Me,* The Lilliput Press, Dublin: 2001.

Barry, Tom, *Guerilla Days in Ireland,* Anvil Books Limited, Dublin: 1993.

Béaslaí, Piaras, *Michael Collins and the Making of a New Ireland,* 2 Volumes, Edmund Burke Publisher, Blackrock: 2008.

Breen, Dan, *My Fight for Irish Freedom,* Anvil Books Limited, Dublin: 1993.

Brennan-Whitmore, W. J., *Dublin Burning: The Easter Rising from Behind the Barricades,* Gill & Macmillan Ltd., Dublin: 1996.

Connell Jnr, Joseph E. A., *Where's Where in Dublin: A Directory of Historic Locations 1913-1923,* Dublin City Council, Dublin City Library & Archive, Dublin: 2006.

Connolly, Colm, *Michael Collins,* Weidenfeld & Nicolson, The Orion Publishing Group, London: 1996.

Coogan, Tim Pat, *1916: The Easter Rising,* The Orion Publishing Group, London: 2001.

—, *Michael Collins: A Biography,* Arrow Books Limited, London: 1991.

Coogan, Tim Pat & Morrison, George, *The Irish Civil War,* Weidenfeld & Nicolson, The Orion Publishing Group, London: 1998.

Cottrell, Peter, *The Anglo-Irish War: The Troubles of 1913-1922,* Osprey Publishing, Oxford: 2006.

De Rosa, Peter, *Rebels: The Irish Rising of 1916,* Ballantine Books, New York: 1992.

Doherty, Gabriel & Keogh, Dermot (Eds.), *Michael Collins and the Making of the Irish State,* Mercier Press, Dublin: 1998.

Doyle, Jennifer, Clarke, Frances, Connaughton, Eibhlis & Sommerville,

Orna, *An Introduction to the Bureau of Military History 1913-1921*, Military Archives, Cathal Brugha Barracks, Dublin: 2002.

Duggan, John P., *A History of the Irish Army*, Gill and Macmillan Ltd., Dublin: 1991.

Dwyer, T. Ryle, *'I Signed My Death Warrant': Michael Collins & the Treaty*, Mercer Press, Douglas Village, Cork: 2007.

—, *Michael Collins: "The Man Who Won the War,"* Mercier Press, Cork: 1990.

—, *The Squad and the Intelligence Operations of Michael Collins*, Mercer Press, Douglas Village, Cork: 2005.

—, *Big Fellow, Long Fellow: A Joint Biography of Collins & de Valera*, St. Martin's Press, New York: 1998.

Ebenezer, Lyn, *Fron-Goch and the Birth of the IRA*, Gwasg Carreg Gwalch, Llanrwst, Wales: 2006.

Edwards, Ruth Dudley, *Patrick Pearse: The Triumph of Failure*, Poolbeg Press Ltd., Dublin: 1990.

Ferriter, Diarmaid (Introduction), *Dublin's Fighting Story 1916-21*, Mercier Press, Cork: 2009.

Forester, Margery, *Michael Collins: The Lost Leader*, Gill and Macmillan Ltd., Dublin: 1989.

Foy, Michael T., *Michael Collins's Intelligence War: The Struggle Between the British and the IRA, 1919-1921*, Sutton Publishing Limited, United Kingdom: 2006.

Foy, Michael & Barton, Brian, *The Easter Rising*, Sutton Publishing Limited, United Kingdom: 2000.

Hart, Peter (Ed.), *British Intelligence in Ireland, 1920-21: The Final Reports*, Cork University Press, Cork: 2002.

—, *Mick: The Real Michael Collins*, The Penguin Group, New York: 2007.

Henry, William, *Supreme Sacrifice: The Story of Éamonn Ceannt 1881-1916*, Mercier Press, Douglas Village, Cork: 2005.

Hopkinson, Michael, *Green Against Green: The Irish Civil War*, Gill and Macmillan Ltd., Dublin: 1988.

—, *The Irish War of Independence*, Gill & Macmillan Ltd., Dublin: 2002.

Jordan, Anthony J., *W. T. Cosgrave 1880-1965: Founder of Modern Ireland*, Westport Books, Dublin: 2006.

Kiberd, Declan (Introduction), *1916: Easter Rebellion Handbook*, The Mourne River Press, Dublin: 1998.

Liam, Cathal, *Blood On The Shamrock: A Novel of Ireland's Civil War*, St. Pádraic Press, Cincinnati: 2008.

—, *Consumed In Freedom's Flame: A Novel of Ireland's Struggle for Free-*

dom 1916-1921, St. Pádraic Press, Cincinnati: 2010.

MacAtasney, Gerard, *Seán MacDiarmada: The Mind of the Revolution*, Drumlin Publications, Ireland: 2004.

Mackay, James, *Michael Collins: A Life*, Mainstream Publishing, Edinburgh: 1996.

Mac Curtain, Fionnuala, *Remember...it's for Ireland: A Family Memoir of Tomás Mac Curtáin*, Mercier Press, Douglas Village, Cork: 2006.

Mac Lochlainn, Piaras F., *Last Words: Letters and Statements of the Leaders Executed After the Rising at Easter 1916*, The Office of Public Works, Dublin: 1990.

McNally, Michael, *Easter Rising 1916: Birth of the Irish Republic*, Osprey Publishing, Oxford: 2007.

Mulcahy, Risteárd, *My Father, the General: Richard Mulcahy and the Military History of the Revolution*, Liberties Press, Blackrock: 2009.

Neligan, David, *The Spy in the Castle*, Prendeville Publishing Limited, London: 1999.

Nelson, Justin, *Michael Collins: The Final Days*, Justin Nelson Productions Ltd., Dublin: 1997.

O'Brien, Paul, *Blood on the Streets: 1916 & The Battle for Mount Street Bridge*, Mercier Press, Douglas Village, Cork: 2008.

—, *Uncommon Valour: 1916 & the Battle for the South Dublin Union*, Mercier Press, Cork: 2010.

Ó Broin, León (Ed.), *In Great Haste: The Letters of Michael Collins and Kitty Kiernan*, Gill & Macmillan Ltd., Dublin: 1984.

O'Connor, Batt, *With Michael Collins In The Fight for Irish Independence*, Aubane Historical Society, Millstreet: 2004.

O'Connor, Frank, *The Big Fellow*, Poolbeg Press Ltd., Dublin: 1991.

O'Connor, Ulick, *The Troubles: The Struggle for Irish Freedom 1912-1922*, Mandarin Paperbacks, London: 1992.

O'Farrell, Padraic, *Down Ratra Road: Fifty Years of Civil Defence in Ireland*, The Stationery Office, Government Publications, Dublin: 2000.

—, *Seán Mac Eoin: The Blacksmith of Ballinalee*, Uisneach Press, Mullingar: 1993.

—, *Who's Who in the Irish War of Independence and Civil War 1916-1923*, The Lilliput Press, Dublin: 1997.

O Mahony, Sean, *Frongoch: University of Revolution*, FDR Teoranta, Killiney, Dublin: 1995.

—, *The First Hunger Striker Thomas Ashe 1917*, The 1916-1921 Club,

Dublin: 2001.

—, *Three Murders in Dublin Castle, 1920,* The 1916-1921 Club, Dublin: 2000.

O'Malley, Ernie, *On Another Man's Wound,* Anvil Books, Dublin: 1990.

O'Sullivan. Niamh, *Every Dark Hour: A History of Kilmainham Jail,* Liberties Press, Dublin: 2007.

—, *Written In Stone: The Graffiti in Kilmainham Jail,* Liberties Press, Dublin: 2009.

Osborne, Chrissy, *Michael Collins: A Life in Pictures,* Mercier Press, Douglas Village, Cork: 2007.

—, *Michael Collins Himself,* Mercier Press, Douglas Village, Cork: 2003.

Pakenham, Frank, *Peace By Ordeal: The Negotiation of the Anglo-Irish Treaty 1921,* Pimlico, London: 1992.

Pinkman, John A., *In the Legion of the Vanguard,* Mercier Press, Dublin: 1998.

Ryan, Annie, *Comrades: Inside the War of Independence,* Liberties Press, Dublin: 2005.

—, *Witnesses: Inside the Easter Rising,* Liberties Press, Dublin: 2005.

Ryan, Desmond, *The Rising,* Golden Eagle Books Limited, Dublin: 1966.

Ryan, Meda, *Michael Collins and the Women Who Spied for Ireland,* Mercier Press, Douglas Village, Cork: 2006.

—, *Tom Barry IRA Freedom Fighter,* Mercier Press, Douglas Village, Cork: 2003.

Taylor, Rex, *Michael Collins,* Four Square Books, London: 1965.

Twohig, Patrick J., *The Dark Secret of Béalnabláth,* Tower Books, Cork: 1991.

Valiulis, Maryann Gialanella, *Portrait of a Revolutionary General Richard Mulcahy and the Founding of the Irish Free State,* Irish Academic Press Ltd., Blackrock, Dublin: 1992.

White, G. & O'Shea, B., *Irish Volunteer Soldier 1913-1923,* Osprey Publishing, Oxford: 2003.

ABOUT THE AUTHOR

Cathal Liam is keenly interested in early twentieth-century Irish history, particularly Ireland's revolutionary years 1914-1924. His first book, *Consumed In Freedom's Flame: A Novel of Ireland's Struggle for Freedom 1916-1921*, chronicles the events surrounding Ireland's 1916 Easter revolt and its ensuing War for Independence, 1919-1921. First published in hardcover (2001), it's been reprinted six times in trade paperback and is fast becoming a "classic." It won ForeWord magazine's 2001 bronze medal for historical fiction.

His next effort, *Forever Green: Ireland Now & Again*, received a 2003 honourable mention for travel essay, also by ForeWord magazine. A collection of imaginative stories, political commentary and original poems, it portrays a changing Ireland in the twentieth century.

In 2006, *Blood On The Shamrock: A Novel of Ireland's Civil War (1921-1924)* was published as a follow-up to *Consumed In Freedom's Flame*. It chronicles the events sparking Ireland's tragic ten-month-long, internecine conflict. Now in its second printing, the story-line follows a handful of imaginary characters as they interact with the real historical figures and the actual events of the time. The book received an honorable mention award in the general fiction category by Midwest Independent Publishers Association.

His newest work is an exciting true-life novel, a gently-fictionalised biography entitled *Fear Not The Storm: The Story of Tom Cullen, An Irish Revolutionary.*

ALSO FROM
ST. PÁDRAIC PRESS

"Historical fiction is a slippery slope, too often fraught with disconnects between the fictional characters and those real figures of history, too often missing the naturalness of behavior and language; too often erring on either the side of pure history or of fictional device. But, Cincinnati author Cathal Liam has trod deftly in his *Consumed in Freedom's Flame.* This is a book full of romance and adventure woven against the heartrending struggle of the Irish people for independence. In every case, the scenarios created by Liam ring as true as if a cache of long-hidden partisan letters has been unearthed."
　　　　–Carole L. Philipps, *The Cincinnati Post* (Cincinnati, Ohio)

"The Irish have always had more history than they knew what to do with. Essayist and poet Cathal Liam has joined such fiction writers as Morgan Llewelyn and Liam O'Flaherty by assembling a comprehensive and intelligent piece of historical fiction for the general reader as well as those who can recite 'The Bold Fenian Men' at a moment's notice. One does not have to read too far into the narrative to know that Liam understands how to capture an era filled with colorful and tragic men and women. As a result, '*Freedom's Flame*' is as compelling as the events it recounts."
　　　　–Rob Stout, *The Patriot Ledger* (Quincy, MA)

"Unabashed support for the men and women who fought for Irish freedom in the early years of the 20th century is a rarity in these politically correct and revisionist times. Cathal Liam…sets himself against the tide in a story that follows the life of Aran Roe O'Neill, a fictional rebel who finds himself in the thick of the 1916 Rising and subsequent events."

—The Irish Echo (New York, NY)

"This meticulously researched and well-written novel, *Consumed in Freedom's Flame*, not only evokes the authenticity of a fascinating period of Irish history, 1916-1921, but sustains constant interest and more than a little suspense. It is a lively and evocative read!"

—T. Ryle Dwyer, historian and author of
Big Fellow, Long Fellow: A Joint Biography of Collins and deValera, and Others (Tralee, Ireland)

"Ireland was never in the mainstream of European history but the story of its fight for freedom can take its place with the legends of all great Rebellions. *Consumed in Freedom's Flame* captures the passion and drama necessary for the breaking of chains."

—Ronnie O'Gorman, *Galway Advertiser* (Galway, Ireland)

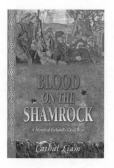

"*Blood On The Shamrock* resumes the chronicle of Aran Roe O'Neill, a fictional Irishman, and his determined comrades, who continue Ireland's ongoing struggle for independence and self-government. This time, however, the foe is not so much England as it is their fellow Irish.

The tragedy of Easter, 1916 lies behind them. Spurred on by the euphoria born of London's willingness to negotiate a settlement ending

the War for Independence (1919-1921), Ireland finally senses it stands on the brink of triumph: autonomy from British rule. But almost overnight, the green hills of Éireann turn red again—blood red—as the bitter dregs of Anglo-Irish politics erupt into unholy Civil War, the repercussions of which are destined to sully the dream of Irish unity for years to come."
…from A Word to the Reader in *Blood On The Shamrock*

"Cathal Liam takes the central character of his War of Independence novel *Consumed In Freedom's Flame* and carries the story onward through the tragic months of the Irish Civil War. In his Foreword, Mr. Liam remarks on the fact that very few serious attempts have been made to take this terrible and convoluted period of Irish history into the realms of fiction. He lists a mere seven writers from Seán O'Casey in 1924 to Morgan Llywelyn in 2001. Approaching his task strictly, he lists his cast of characters in some detail, between the historic personalities who appear and his fictional central characters who carry the story forward. Mr. Liam sticks closely to historic fact in dealing with major events and includes a glossary and a good bibliography. He is one of few novelists who consider footnotes detailing the factual record as necessary to his story. But then, this is a story of which many Irish families have a version…God grant peace to them all."
—Mary O'Sullivan, *Ireland of the Welcomes* (Dublin, Ireland), September/October, 2006

"*Blood On The Shamrock* is the sequel to *Consumed In Freedom's Flame*, Cathal Liam's [new] historical novel about Ireland's Civil War in the 1920's. Fictional hero Aran Roe O'Neill continues in the struggle for Irish self-governance and independence. In this complex network of loyalties and treachery, he faces foes both from within and outside the ranks of Irish patriots. For those who may have missed the first novel, *Blood On The Shamrock* stands very nicely on its own as a great historical novel. Twentieth century Irish political reality evolves through the pages, with many references to its cultural and historical heritage. *Blood On The Shamrock* is immediate and personal; it will serve to enlighten many readers about the later days of the Irish Civil War. Ending in the 1960's, [it] is a complete read in and of itself. But one wonders (and hopes!) if there will be another novel to the present day?"
—*Midwest Book Review* (Oregon, WI), September, 2006